ACCLAIM FOR YVONNE KALMAN'S

GREENSTONE

"LIKE *THE THORN BIRDS, GREENSTONE* HAS ALL THE INGREDIENTS OF A HIT ...GUILT, GRIEF AND LOVE IN A STORY OF REVENGE, MANIPULATION AND FATE."
Richmond Times-Dispatch

SILVER SHORES

"YVONNE KALMAN IS A TRULY GIFTED STORYTELLER...*SILVER SHORES* CERTAINLY DOES NOT CONCLUDE THE STORY OF THESE REMARKABLE FAMILIES. I WANT TO ENJOY MORE OF NEW ZEALAND AS SEEN THROUGH THE EYES OF BOTH WRITER AND STORY CHARACTER."
Southbend Tribune

AND NOW, BOOK THREE...

RIVERSONG

Other Avon Books by
Yvonne Kalman

GREENSTONE
SILVER SHORES

RIVERSONG

YVONNE KALMAN

AVON
PUBLISHERS OF BARD, CAMELOT, DISCUS AND FLARE BOOKS

AVON BOOKS
A division of
The Hearst Corporation
1790 Broadway
New York, New York 10019

Copyright © 1986 by Yvonne Kalman
Published by arrangement with the author
Library of Congress Catalog Card Number: 84-91248
ISBN: 0-380-89618-4

First Avon Printing, May 1986

AVON TRADEMARK REG. U. S. PAT. OFF. AND IN
OTHER COUNTRIES, MARCA REGISTRADA, HECHO EN
U. S. A.

Printed in the U. S. A.

K-R 10 9 8 7 6 5 4 3 2 1

To the men in my life:
Fred, Dean & Dad
Max & Marty
Jimmy & Mr. Jacques

RIVERSONG

Prelude

SYDNEY, AUSTRALIA, 1897

Dorrie didn't like the champagne. It was bitter as medicine, nothing like the syrup-based champagne cup she'd tasted before, but she was anxious to please her husband, so she sipped with pretended pleasure and smiled shyly at him.

Bob Farrell's breath caught in his chest. Every time he looked at her he simply couldn't believe that this exquisite creature had wanted to marry him. Her beauty dazed him. Her skin was as clear as moonlight on water, he thought, searching his practical mind for comparisons. And that dazzling warm gold hair, bright as a beach under the hot sun. He wondered how far down her back it would flow when it was finally unpinned. The picture *that* conjured up made the sweat start out on his brow. He felt as foolish as a ranchhand having his first dancing lesson.

"You like it, then?" he managed to ask in a voice that had been scoured flat by decades of bellowing at lazy dogs and roaring orders at Aboriginal stockmen.

Dorrie nodded. Just above her brow perched a frilly concoction of tulle, artificial violets and satin leaves with a misty hood of net that partially veiled her face. She ducked her head to conceal the lie as she murmured, "It's delicious, thank you. Lovely."

"It should be, at this price," commented McGovern, Farrell's station manager. "These froggy winemakers charge like wounded buffalo." He wore a full crinkly beard damp around the mouth and the peevish expression of one who had had to pay for the champagne.

Farrell ignored him. A strikingly handsome man in the earthy outback way, Bob Farrell was as brown as a saddle. He had a smooth granite chin and springy gray hair parted fashionably in the center.

If you could overlook the difference in their ages they'd make a handsome couple, thought McGovern, studying "the boss" and his bride. Him blunt and strong and her tenderly fragile with those enormous, frightened gray eyes. McGovern had never seen such eyes as hers— shadowy and mysterious as deep moonlit pools.

He caught his own thoughts and laughed aloud. The atmosphere must be getting to him. He signaled to the waitress to fetch more champagne from the bar next door, then leaned back in his bentwood chair, tapping his fingers against the stiff folds of the tablecloth as he surveyed the shabby room.

It was stuffy here in the dining hall; the air smelled used. Though it was early spring, flies scrambled against the high windowpanes in the last of the day's sunshine. The paneled room was almost empty, the only other diners being out-of-town ranchers who, like Bob Farrell, used the hotel from years of habit, and like him also ate early.

"Ah!" said Dorrie's guardian aunt, Miss Dora Bennington, when their four plates of food arrived trundled on a little trolley cart. It was the first sound she had uttered since they had entered half an hour earlier. All that time she had sat staring fixedly at the door, her stout body erect and her hands folded in her gray satin lap. Now she caught McGovern's eye and flushed, embarrassed that she had revealed how hungry she was.

"This looks good," said McGovern to encourage her.

The plates were enormous and generously laden. Bob Farrell had ordered steak and eggs, a meal that he consumed twice a day no matter where he happened to be, while the other three had settled for the alternative meal, a roast chicken.

It was ghastly. The chicken was dry as rope and the vegetables had been stewed to a tasteless watery pulp.

After chewing half a dozen stringy mouthfuls McGovern gave up with a shrug. "This old chook must have been a champion runner, what you reckon, Miss Bennington? I estimate that he avoided the chopper for at least ten years." He gave her a friendly nudge. "Cheer up. All Aussie grub isn't like this. We've a cook out at Nullandor who can work magic with a chicken."

"I'm relieved to hear it." She placed knife and fork primly at the side of her plate and, discovering there were no napkins, poked into her reticule purse for a handkerchief with which to dab her mouth.

Dorrie leaned forward. She breathed through parted lips before she began to speak in a nervous gesture that was innocent yet very sensuous.

"Auntie Dora is a splendid cook, too, you know. She bakes the most delicious—"

"I shall be happy to keep right out of the kitchen," stated the aunt quickly. "It's only when confronted by the prospect of something like this," and she prodded a withered wing with her fork, "I am almost tempted to go forth in search of a skillet."

"So you don't like the food." Pausing halfway through sawing his overdone slab of beef, Bob Farrell banged a fist on the table and shouted, "Service!"

Already coming with the second bottle of champagne, the waitress did not quicken her sauntering pace. She plonked the bottle down with the air of someone who cannot be bothered and stood with eyebrows raised, waiting for his order.

Farrell jabbed his knife in McGovern's direction and continued his steadfast chewing.

"Really, don't make a fuss just because—" began the aunt then stopped, frozen by the impudent expression on the waitress's face. Dora's eyes hardened behind her thick-lensed spectacles, and she said, "This chicken is appalling. It's not even freshly cooked, is it?"

"Nobody else has complained." She turned to Bob Farrell. "Your meal's okay, isn't it, sir?"

Farrell grinned and popped another piece of fried potato into his mouth. He was clearly enjoying Miss Bennington's discomfiture, so clearly that McGovern thought, *So she's the worm in his Garden of Eden apple; he wants the girl but it's rankling that he has to take the old biddy along with her.*

"You're enjoying yours, aren't you, Dorinda," Farrell persisted.

Dorrie ducked her head. Her hands knotted and unknotted in her violet silk lap. She shot a miserable glance at Dora. *He's so kind*, she was thinking. *So generous and kind to me. I do wish he could include Auntie Dora in that kindness.*

McGovern interceded. Snapping his fingers to catch the waitress's attention he said, "This food is unacceptable and you know it. Didn't we make it clear when we came in that this is a wedding party?"

She was obviously startled. "Nobody told me," she protested as her attention hopped from one to the other around the table, inquisitive as a sparrow.

"I'll open the champagne." McGovern took it from her. "Just clear these plates, will you, and bring us something more appropriate. Ice cream. Do you have any ice cream? The ladies would like that, I'm sure." He intercepted a hard look from his employer and shrugged, saying, "Relax, boss. This is your big day. Let me worry about the comfort of the guests. That's my job as best man, isn't it? That's what you've got me for."

Farrell addressed himself to the business of attacking his steak. His dislike of Dora Bennington was almost palpable. It seemed ironical that the main reason he'd proposed to Dorrie when he met her in New Zealand was that she was an orphan. He'd had two mothers-in-law—thank you, quite enough for one lifetime. He had assumed Dorrie would come to the marriage alone, while she had assumed that he'd welcome this old harridan into their home.

The matter had been settled within minutes of her setting foot off the ship. "I couldn't begin a new life without Auntie Dora,'' she had pleaded. ''She'd fret about me being so far out in the back of beyond with not another woman for a hundred miles. . . .''

It was more than he could do to refuse. Dorrie was so sweet and beautiful that anything she asked for seemed the essence of sweetness, too.

Now Bob Farrell reflected that there was nothing like an exchange of vows to alter one's attitudes. That aunt had been a pinprick of annoyance before but she was rapidly developing into a septic ulcer.

Dora Bennington was either unaware of his dislike or brazen in her disregard for his feelings. ''That station manager of yours is a real treasure,'' she confided as she took up her dessert spoon and dug into the fluffy pink mass on her plate. ''Ah, it's not true ice cream. A frozen custard of some sort, I'd say, but it's perfectly delicious just the same. Do try yours, Mr. Farrell. A little extra sweetening never hurt anybody.''

She couldn't give a damn what I think of her, he realized. Raising his whiskey glass, he tossed the liquid off in one swallow.

''It *is* lovely,'' Dorrie said softly. She turned her head, attracted by a sound at the far side of the room. As she did so she licked a tiny dab of cream from her upper lip with a sliding movement of her delicate pink tongue.

Bob Farrell's mouth went dry. The antagonism melted away as he thought, *She's all mine. I can hardly believe it. Two skinny mares of wives and now when I'm almost fifty years old and past hoping for magic, this.*

Dorrie clasped his arm, saying, ''Do look, Mr. Farrell. They're bringing in a piano.''

''It's from the saloon bar,'' said McGovern, who was well acquainted with that part of the hotel. ''I think they might be planning to make a fuss in your honor. That's a nice touch to make amends, don't you think?''

At that moment the lights blazed on in the room with a suddenness that made Dorrie catch her breath in a gasp and let it out in a slow, bubbling laugh. "Oh, how perfect! I love dancing!" she cried.

What an entrancing creature she is, thought McGovern, wistfully aware of the unfairness of fate. He had practically no chance of being dealt a hand like hers, while she'd be crushed out there at Nullandor, ground down by the harshness of station life, soon drained and dried by the climate.

The piano was rattling out a rinky-dink tune and Dorrie's gray eyes flashed as her chin nodded time to the music.

Then I'll ask without delay,
What do folks mean when they say,
"Ta-ra-ra! Ta-ra-ra? Ta-ra-ra! Boom-der-e!"

She giggled at McGovern. "I used to play that on the piano!"

"Instead of practicing your scales!" said Dora.

"Go on, boss! Your bride would like to dance, I'm sure."

Bob Farrell poured himself more whiskey.

"Oh." Dorrie looked from her husband to his station manager and back again, confused. "It doesn't matter . . . It's only the champagne," she added irrelevantly.

"Mr. Farrell may not wish to dance, dear. Mr. Farrell may not know how."

He was on his feet at once, emphatic in his contradiction as he offered his bride his arm.

Watching them move onto the floor, McGovern wanted to congratulate the old aunt for the way she had manipulated that little incident, but he said, "I've been his right-hand man for ten years. He's a kind man. Scrupulously fair. He can't abide being crossed, that'll rile him, but otherwise he's one of the best."

"I'm sure he is." She permitted him to top up her glass and stared at the rolling effervescent beads. "I'm well aware that for the moment Mr. Farrell resents my presence, but he is sure to get over that."

McGovern looked doubtful. It was a shame, really. Miss Bennington was a harmless enough sort, quite motherly in a way with her gray satin dress and her iron gray hair puffed out in a soft onion shape, billowy like her cheeks and bosom.

"Attitudes do change, you know," she insisted.

"Mmmm," he said.

Dorrie danced with careful absorption, the train of her dress looped over her wrist to show a chrysanthemum of lace petticoats. To Bob Farrell she seemed light as mist as she floated beside him. Across the room he could see them both reflected in the uncovered windowpanes, their images pelted with the dabbing shapes of moths attracted to the lights. For a moment he imagined the two of them leading the dancing at Coonanbrooke Hall, twirling around the dusty plank floor while his friends watched, openly envious and secretly coveting his beautiful wife.

As it rattled to a stop the tune marooned them near the piano where a painting of the imperious Queen Victoria haughtily stared at them from her foot-wide gilt frame.

The piano player, a stout man with a slick of moustache winked in a friendly way and said, " 'Aving yer last dance with yer daughter, are yer, Guv?'' Flexing his fingers over the keys, he launched into the next volley.

Dorrie pretended not to have heard, but Farrell was angry. Like most kindly men his anger was the shallow type that exploded only against the major irritations in his life. As they danced away he said, "Miss Bennington won't like it at Nullandor, I'm convinced of it. She's too old to adapt to such a different life. She'll miss everything she's used to."

She's used to me, thought Dorrie, her heart shrinking. *Give her a chance,* she begged silently.

"I could book her a passage on the *Manu Moa*. She sails in a week's time. When I made inquiries yesterday the clerk in the office told me that they had several excellent cabins left."

Dorrie's heart was a tight little knot. She did not trust herself to speak. *He's not going to leave it alone,* she realized. *He'll keep on and on until he drives Auntie Dora away.*

McGovern rescued her again, there at her husband's shoulder, smiling into her frightened eyes. "A best man has to have a dance with the bride, boss. It's the law, didn't ya know?" he told Farrell as he stepped between them.

He danced with the dipping and scraping of a badly hung gate and Dorrie tried not to laugh as she followed his awkward movements.

"That's better," he approved. "You look more cheerful now."

Her chin disappeared into the violet ruffles at her throat and he could see the high color on her cheeks. McGovern heard himself say, "Why in the world did you marry him?"

"I beg your pardon?"

It was none of his business but he'd asked now and he wanted an answer. "Why? You're so delicate, so young . . ."

"I'm eighteen."

"And I'm surprised. Why did you do it? You're not in love with him, I can see that. Have you any idea of what's in front of you?"

Her chin came up. It was a pathetic little gesture of self-defense. "He's kind, and generous . . . and he loves me."

"All excellent reasons for marrying him if you were fifteen years older and he was your last chance. Oh, he's attractive and personable enough, granted, and he's got solid money behind him. In fact I'd recommend him to any mature woman without hesitation, but not to a child like you." He could see that she felt trapped; her gaze was flickering around the room seeking an escape and he knew he should let her go, but the champagne had dissolved his sensitivity so he said, "I've been watching you all day and I've come to the conclusion that something terrible drove you into this marriage. You're running away from something, aren't you?"

She gave him one terrified glance and backed away, then turned and fled back to the table.

Bob Farrell stood up as she rejoined him. "McGovern's partners never last long," he observed laconically. "Would you care to finish our dance now?"

"No, thank you," she said, sitting down. "I'm exhausted. This past couple of days has been so hectic."

Immediately the remark caught up with her and she blushed, hoping he'd not take it as a hint that they retire to bed. She remembered Dora's advice to drink "whatever is offered" and reached for her glass.

After half an hour or so Farrell said, "I think I'll take a walk, sample the air before I turn in. McGovern, you'll come with me, won't you?"

"Have a little more champagne, dear," urged Dora when they had gone.

A few minutes after the women had gone upstairs a man walked into the hotel lobby. Without pausing to look around he strode directly to the reception alcove and picked up the brass bell on the desk.

He shook it three times before the waitress finally bustled out from the direction of the dining hall. She saw a tall, immaculately dressed gentleman standing there and she snapped, "There's no call to keep on and on. It's the clerk's night off, Wednesday is, and we have to make do as best we can." Then she looked up at his face and paused with an involuntary intake of breath. "Gawd," she whispered, and in an entirely different tone said, "What might I be able ter do for you, sir?"

He seemed wearily amused by her reaction. "I was hoping that you might be able to help me."

"I hope so too, an' all." He had an Australian accent. Better and better; so many foreign toffs had peculiar ideas about girls who worked in hotels, thought they were muck. And oh, he *was* handsome! Perhaps not to everybody's taste, but that was what attraction was all about, wasn't it? For her personally there was something about hulking redheaded fellows that made her go all syrupy in the legs, especially fellows like this one, tanned but not freckled with those dark eyes that almost matched his hair—she'd had a frock that color once, rusty velvet, and it made her feel special just to put it on.

She smiled helpfully at him. He glanced away and she noticed the lean planes of his face and the way his russet hair clung in waves to the back of his neck. She couldn't help wondering what it would feel like twined between her fingers.

"I'm looking for someone," he said, glancing about as if he expected to find them concealed behind the brass-potted aspidistras in the corners. "The shipping office told me I should try the hotels in this area. They're two ladies traveling together. A young lady and her aunt. Bennington, their name is."

"Nah. No, sir, sorry. Nothing like that here."

"You're sure? I've tried all the other hotels."

"Just a minute—there's two ladies here, a young and an older one. Could be—nah, I don't think it'll be them. They ain't on their own, you see."

"It won't be them, then. Thank you, for—"

"But it could be. Bennington, you said?" She was sure it was not those two in the wedding party but she wanted to delay him a few seconds more. "I'll check the records," she said, flipping the page. "Nah, nothing there. Mind you, we never worry too much about records when we know the customers, and Mr. Farrell booked the ladies in."

"Mr. Bob Farrell?" The skin over his jaw was suddenly hard and pale as pinewood.

"That's him. He's a regular customer, been coming here once or twice a year since way back—long before my time, of course." She simpered, hinting that she'd been there practically no time at all.

Her flirting was lost on him. "What do they look like? Describe them for me," he demanded.

She was piqued by now. Here she was with hand pertly on hip, beaming him a string of her best smiles but he didn't know she was alive. She said, "The old duck is short, gray hair, eyeglasses thick as saucepan lids, and the young one is

fair and pretty, if you like that style." It *is* them, she realized as she read his expression, so she added spitefully,
"The young one is Mrs. Farrell now, of course. They
bought champagne to celebrate the wedding."

"Wedding?"

"That's right." He looked so stricken that she
regretted the blunt way she'd pushed the news at him.
"A wedding party, they said. Two bottles of champagne."

"But *Farrell,* of all people!"

"Our dark horse, he is. Shall I take a message up for
you, sir?" She scurried after him as he walked across the
lobby toward the street. "It would only take a few seconds for me to pop up there and—"

"No! Thank you, but no."

He seemed dazed. She watched him stride out into the
night, hunching his shoulders under the yellow street-
lights. He hadn't even noticed her.

Dorrie pulled back the edge of the curtain and peeked
down into the street where hats bobbed beneath the gaslights as people conversed in the mild evening air. Bunting crisscrossed the street, remnants of gaiety from the
Queen's Diamond Jubilee Celebrations.

SIXTY GLORIOUS YEARS! proclaimed a banner on
the shopfronts opposite.

Lucky her, thought Dorrie. Shivering, she glanced
across to the harbor where lights bloomed in clusters
along the water's edge and kept step along the length of
the quay, giving it a military air of neatness. Beyond
loomed vague black shapes of hills. Somewhere far away
on that vast rolling continent was Nullandor, a place she
was fast coming to dread.

Why did I do it? she panicked, echoing McGovern's
question. She could hardly have told him the truth—*that I
was so desperately unhappy that I wanted to die. This
was my only escape.*

Now that solution seemed like madness. *This was what*

you wanted, she reminded herself, hoping for some reassurance. *You had to get away from him and this was the only way you could do it. Nullandor might as well be the back of the moon because you'll never see him ever again once you set foot on that sheep station. Not him nor anybody else.*

Letting the curtain drop, she squared her shoulders with a decisiveness she was far from feeling, only to be brought up short by the sight of herself reflected in the tall dressing mirror. She looked pale and unhappy, and the ice green of her cotton nightgown and robe heightened the impression of misery.

Shaking her head, she watched her gold curtain of hair drape over her shoulders as she drew her hairbrush through the shimmering lengths.

He said I was beautiful, she thought, giving in to self-pity. *He* said I was the most beautiful creature in the whole world, that he would die if he couldn't love me. Only . . . I can't have been beautiful enough for him, because he soon stopped thinking so, didn't he? He walked away and left me to die instead.

The tap on the door startled her; she had planned to be in bed feigning sleep.

He came in and took of his hat. It rocked on the bedknob. ''Still out of bed, then.''

''I was just going to open the window. It seems so hot in here.''

''If you think this is hot, wait until you've experienced the outback. You'll know all about it then.''

He was standing there, as uncertain as she was. *We don't know the slightest thing about each other,* she thought.

Embarrassed by the silence, she flipped back one corner of the covers and slid between the sheets, keeping close to the edge. The linen was clammy and warm as sweat.

Farrell whistled behind the cloth screen as he undressed. She could hear his collar and cuff studs pop, then the rattle as they rolled into a china dish. *I hope he doesn't use the chamber pot,* she thought, shutting her eyes.

He padded around in bare feet and sat beside her, grasping her hand and clucking—in approval, she thought—when she shrank away from him.

"Don't be afraid of me, dear," he soothed.

She stared up at him, suddenly noticing again what a pleasant face he had, how kind and gentle his eyes were. *He's such a nice man,* she thought. *I shouldn't have married him. I shouldn't have done it. It was wrong of me, terribly, terribly wrong.*

"Please trust me, Dorinda," he said. "This may frighten you a little but I do have experience in these matters and I promise to be as careful as is humanly possible."

He thinks I'm a virgin, she realized. *He probably wouldn't have married me if he'd known the truth.*

That realization struck her through with guilt. In all her desperation to free herself from the intolerable situation she had left behind, it had never once occurred to her that she was being deliberately deceitful.

"It sometimes hurts a little the first time," he said.

He may be able to tell, she thought in terror. *Suppose he can? He'll reject me then, and there will be shame, disgrace . . . Or else he'll just be forever disappointed in me, and that would be worse. He's a kind man, generous and good. There'll be trouble over Auntie Dora, I know that, but nothing is ever completely uncomplicated, is it?*

She shuddered as he lay down beside her and began to fondle her. His fingers and his breath were warm and sticky. He smelled of tobacco.

Panic blocked her throat. This was all a ghastly mistake. She had rushed into marriage in the blind belief that once she had uttered her wedding vows she'd be able to block *him* forever out of her mind, but instead the reverse was happening. She could think of nothing but *him* now and the memories sickened her.

He had gloried in her and she had gloried in that passion, too, keeping step with him every mounting step of the way. Whenever *he* touched her she seemed to flare into life, new sensations blossomed under his fingertips, and she knew that that was surely what she had been made for.

Now her husband was doing the same things that *he* had done, but instead of responding she was fighting down urges to push him away. As his hands traveled over her, her flesh seemed to shrink and wither, deadening wherever his skin came into contact with hers. He was kissing her neck and shoulders and she thought that she had never minded his kisses before, but until now he had only kissed her gloved hands. This was grimly different.

She could feel the embroidered hem of her nightgown sliding up over her knees and she knew she was trapped—lying in a trap that she had constructed herself. Her heart was thumping hard, struggling, kicking out to attract her paralyzed attention. *Stop this!* it signaled. *Break free! Tell him to stop . . .*

His hands were flat on her smooth warm skin, slipping over the soft curves of her body. She could distinctly feel the calluses, little patches of roughness that traced marks over her.

A shudder rippled through him and he suppressed a gasp of emotion, and immediately Dorrie was swamped with fresh guilt. If he wanted to, he could have grabbed her and taken her without any consideration for her feelings, but he was kind and he was gentle, so considerate that she could no longer endure it.

"No!" she shouted, shoving the heels of her hands into his shoulders. He drew back a little, startled, and she grabbed the opportunity to roll free. She huddled in a bunch of arms and legs at the other side of the bed and listened to him fumbling for the gas lamp controls. When the flame flared up, she found him gazing at her with an expression of grave concern.

"Please, Dorinda, I won't—"

"No!" She shook her head emphatically. "I can't. I'm sorry, Mr. Farrell, truly I am, but I can't and I won't."

"It's normal to be nervous, you know."

The patience in his tone stung her. *I must be firm,* she thought. *Even if it hurts his feelings now, it's better than worse upsets later.* She tightened her lips.

"Trust me, Dorinda."

"It's not that. I . . . . I made a mistake in marrying you. It was wrong of me and I know it won't work out. I don't expect you to understand or to forgive me, but I'm terribly sorry, honestly I am. I just can't go through with it, you see. I *can't,*" she repeated in desperation. "You must believe me. It's all been a ghastly mistake."

"You don't care for me."

There was real dignity in the way he met her eyes and she felt so guilty she could hardly stand the shame of it. For a moment she was tempted to tell him the whole sorry story but stopped herself because he would think she had merely made use of him and that wasn't true at all. He had been someone warm she needed to turn to, only things hadn't quite turned out the way she thought they would.

"I do care for you," she told him honestly and noted with relief that he accepted that. Hurrying on, she explained, "I know it sounds confusing, but I shouldn't have married you. I did want to when I agreed, and during the service I still felt happy about the idea, but ever since them I've been having worse and worse doubts, and now I know absolutely, beyond any doubt at all, that I shouldn't have married you at all."

They sat on opposite sides of the bed. She made herself look at him as frankly as she could. He stared into her face, searching for the answers he sought, his own face expressionless. Then his eyes dropped to her body and slid away to stare at his hands knotted in his lap.

He was a practical man. Though his disappointment was keen, he was already sifting through the rubble to find facts on which he could built an alternate plan of action. Either he could force her to accompany him to Nullandor or he could let her go. If he insisted she go with him, he might have real cause to regret it in the future. Reluctant wives could cause all manner of trouble, not to mention embarrassment for their husbands in the outback where men—many of them starving for feminine companionship—outnumbered women fifty to one. On the other hand, if he let her go graciously he had very little to lose. Only McGovern knew about the wedding, and as long as McGovern worked for him there was no danger he would tell anybody the story. He wouldn't dare.

"All right," he said. "It's as well that you told me now instead of waiting until morning. We'll have the marriage annulled, and that will be a whole heap quicker and easier if we don't spend tonight in the same room."

"Annulled?"

"Divorced, but very quickly." He was behind the screen pulling on his clothes again. "I'll fetch Miss Bennington and she can spend the night with you." As he spoke he was already thinking, *At least I'm shot of her.*

Before he left the room he stood beside the bed for a last moment, looking at her. She shook her head. "I'm really terribly sorry. I know it's inadequate to apologize but I wish I could feel differently and I can't. I'm so sorry."

"I'm sorry, too." He reached out a hand to touch that incomparable, glistening hair, then lowered it before his fingers made contact. It was all just a dream, after all.

Dora came scurrying in, her hair in an untidy plait, her clothes hastily buttoned.

"What happened?" she demanded. "What did he *do* to you?"

"Nothing," said Dorrie. "He was kind and understanding. I'm afraid that I've done something terrible to him."

"Nothing that can't be repaired," said Bob Farrell as he stepped into the room. "Let's do the explaining now, shall we? Then we can go directly to the lawyers in the morning."

"Lawyers?" said Dora. "Oh, dear heavens!"

PART ONE

GRANDMAIRE

1886

One

AUCKLAND, NEW ZEALAND, 1886

"Dorrie! *Haere mai ki te kai!* Lunch time!"

Moana Patene, the Maori cook, stood on the step outside Fintona's kitchen door, arms aggressively akimbo as she glared around the garden. She scanned the shrubberies, squinting against the sunlight, for a glimpse of a frilled bonnet, her ears pitched for the sound of Dorrie's low giggle.

"Dorrie! *Haere mai!* Come here, girl!"

Wiping her hands on her apron, Moana went back into the kitchen, sighing with annoyance. On the scrubbed table was a tray bearing two plates of salad, one as delicately artistic as Moana's limited imagination could contrive, the other a rough mound of chopped chicken, potato and cold vegetables smothered in a blanket of boiled salad cream. Beside the tray was a single place setting with a soup spoon and a steaming bowl of porridge, Dorrie's luncheon. Mrs. Maire Yardley Peridot, widowed matriarch of Fintona, believed that porridge was the most suitable food for little girls and the kitchen was the best place for them to eat it.

Moana shoved the porridge bowl into the oven of the coal range and muttered under her breath as she snatched up the tray and shuffled out onto the wide verandah that embraced Fintona like a girdle. It was not her job to be delivering the luncheon trays. She should be on her way home by now to begin enjoying her afternoon off. Where *was* the child?

As she waddled along the creaking floor, shadows

19

from the flowering vines flipped over her face. The noon-
day was drowsy with warmth, with the whine of bees and
the too sweet odor of honeysuckle. Moana could feel a
headache developing.

"Dorrie!" she called once more, glancing crossly out
over the lawns.

Fintona was a rambling, one-storied mansion that commanded a 180-degree view of Auckland harbor from its
clifftop position. As one of the first substantial structures
to be built in Auckland it had once been regarded as an
architectural masterpiece but now it was decaying faster
than its owner. Ragged paintwork curled back to show
dry-rotting timber beneath. Lichen bloomed in smears
over the cracked roof shingles while in the once immaculate gardens trellises sagged under the weight of
unpruned roses and shrubs from Mrs. Yardley Peridot's
native Ireland tangled with weeds in wild disorder. Today everything seemed limp and dull in the heat.

All along the verandah French doors stood open to
catch whatever relief of breeze they could. From any of
these the old lady could observe her Richmond Line ships
coming into or leaving port. From her office in the old
days she used to train a telescope so powerful that it was
said that if the captain had trimmed his moustache that
morning she could follow, by lip-reading, his conversation with the pilot.

But that was long ago. Now the substance of power in
the shipping line had passed to Captain Stephen Yardley,
the matriarch's only surviving child, while her office was
these days occupied by her stepgrandson Jon Bennington, a dour man who managed the Peridot Emporiums, a
string of retail stores that dealt in lingerie, lace, gunpow-
der and a thousand other items.

Moana glanced into the office as she passed. Jon, a
stubby, pale man with a swirl of gray hair, was sorting
papers at his neatly arranged desk. Sometimes he spoke
to Moana—asked what horse she fancied in Saturday's

race meeting's main event—but today he was coughing into his folded handkerchief and did not notice her. His coughs were dry and scraping like a cat's.

Moana shuffled back a pace and stuck her head around the door. "I'll get you some lemonade, eh? Just the story for a cough like that."

"No, thank you, Moana."

"It's no trouble."

"No, thank you."

He sounded irritable. Moana shrugged and walked on.

At the corner of the verandah on one of the cane chairs was Dorrie's new embroidery sampler, a square of beige linen with the beginnings of the title picked out in bright geometric stitches.

WISDO

The O was jabbed through with a needle trailing a loop of scarlet silk. Moana scanned the garden again. "Dorrie!" she called in a low undertone, but still there was no reply.

From the morning room nearby came the monotonous drone of Dora Bennington's voice as she read the Bible to Matua, the old woman. Moana shuffled through the French doors and placed the trays on the table.

The women of the household spent most of their time in this room, a barnlike space that was pleasantly cool in summer but draughty in winter. It reeked of history for it had been decorated entirely with Maori artifacts by Mrs. Yardley Peridot's second husband, Thomas Peridot. Woven flax mats covered the floor and hung on the walls beside dogskin and *kiwi* feather cloaks and *piu-pius*, the rolled flax skirts that were the early Maoris' main garment. On shelves and tables stood carved gourds and wooden trinket boxes that displayed a delicacy of style while polished spears and skull-splitters bore testament to the Maoris' warlike nature.

In this setting of primitive barbarism the old woman leaned back in her gout chair, her feet on the built-in hassock while Jon's sister intoned Bible verses.

"Your lunch, Matua," interrupted Moana.

The old woman ignored her. She was ninety-six years old, hunched and wrinkled as a tortoise; she screwed her face up in a frown as she focused a large silver ear trumpet on Dora's voice. Her eyes were closed in concentration.

"Your lunch, Matua."

The hooded eyes snapped open like pods. They seemed to jut out from under the rim of her black lace house cap. Desiccated fingers pivoted the ear trumpet around and she complained in a wavering voice, "Not lunch already?"

Dora stopped reading and laid a leather marker in the page before folding the Bible shut and swinging the bookrest to one side. She was forty years old, as gray and stout as her brother, and plain to the point of ugliness. Someone had once unkindly remarked that Dora looked as if she had been carved from a turnip. The observation was as accurate as it was cruel, for she did have a turnip's waxy skin, small lidless eyes and a dotting of sprouting moles that resembled hair roots.

When she stood up, stretching, her bustled dress flattened like an apron over her broad abdomen. As she patted her bouffant hair, dark hoops of perspiration showed under her arms. Winter and summer Dora wore gray serge and her only ornament was a large mourning brooch, a portrait of her long-dead father framed in a wreath of plaited hair.

Her voice was strained, scratchy as dry grass. "Is there any lemonade please, Moana? I'm so thirsty."

The request was unanswered. It was not that Moana disliked Dora but as third in the household's pecking order she rated only scant attention. Moana said, "Come on, Matua. It's a nice chicken salad, your favorite. Just a dainty bit to tempt you, eh?"

The withered face puckered. "You're early! Want to go sneaking off, do you, girl? And where's Dorinda? She's supposed to bring the luncheon trays."

Moana looked righteous. "I growled at her and she ran off. She was naughty this morning."

Dora sighed inwardly. *Must Moana always stir the same brew?*

"That child is incorrigible," declared the old woman. "I've told you a thousand times, Dora, that Fintona is not the right place for a young child. She should have been given to your mother to raise, right at birth when your poor sister died. Miss Abby offered to take her then and she still is willing. If you had the smallest particle of common sense you'd accept her offer."

"Please, Grandmaire," murmured Dora. She pronounced the name *Gran-maree* and she spoke wearily for the mention of a thousand times was no exaggeration. She began, "It was Lena's deathbed wish that I—"

"Fiddlesticks!" Grandmaire rapped her brass-tipped cane on the floor, causing Dora to jerk her ankles back out of reach. "Lena was out of her mind, poor thing, giving her helpless babe to a sour old spinster like you."

"Would you like to sit up at the table or shall I rest the tray across your knees?" said Dora.

"What I would like is a little civil attention," complained Grandmaire. "Oh, very well, luncheon it is if you insist, but first you may help me to my commode."

Which meant another hour, thought Dora. Grandmaire knew how hungry she was so she'd employ every delaying tactic. Today's food looked scrumptious, and for once Moana had been lavish with the chicken and potato, but flies were already circling the plates. Dora took a gauze throw-over from a drawer and covered everything before turning to follow the bent figure as it tap-tapped from the room.

While Grandmaire was indulging in the tirade against her, the little girl was only a dozen yards down the corridor performing a dance outside the old lady's open bedroom door.

Dorinda Bennington was a diminutive child with

sturdy limbs, wispy, warm-gold hair and an elfin face
that tapered suddenly like the bud end of a lemon. "A
stubborn, willful chin," Grandmaire often declared,
though Dorrie was neither of those things, merely
dreamy and secretive. At that moment she was indulging
in a favorite daydream to cheer herself. Moana had bellowed at her—unjustly, she felt—her beloved Auntie
Dora was out of reach, and to compound her dejection
there was the gloomy prospect of porridge for lunch. So
here she was, outside forbidden territory staring at the
rocking horse over near Grandmaire's bedroom window.
As she gazed at him in adoration she scuffled her boots
and jerked her knees up in prancing steps, tossing her
head to the rhythm of odd hiccoughing noises that began
in her throat and exploded in soft snorts of breath through
her distended nostrils. While she danced she, too, was a
horse as magnificent as he.

He had been crafted in Spain and was taller than Dorrie
by two spread hands; he had an arching neck and his legs
at full stretch spanned slender polished rockers. He wore
a red morocco saddle that twinkled with brass studs; an
ornately buckled bridle clasped his nose like an exotic
bracelet.

From Moana Dorrie had learned that the horse belonged to a little boy called Rupert. He was Grandmaire's
great-grandson and had lived here until one day his
mother had run away, taking Rupert and his sister with
her and leaving her husband Jon Bennington behind.

"Poor Matua," Moana had mourned. "Ellen, she
took the sunshine away. Matua, she sent men all over the
world to look for Ellen and the children but nobody can
find them. Poor Matua, she was so sad. There was no
more parties at Fintona, no more smiles. Only the nuns
and the priest come to visit, and that's when Matua, she
had all her room painted black, eh."

Dorrie wished she could rescue the horse from that
dark, depressing room. The walls and ceiling were black.
Black curtains swelled at the open window and black

drapes shrouded Grandmaire's tall bed. Even her sheets were black; on washday they flapped on the line like two gigantic bats with the small black pillowslips soaring beside them like offspring.

Edged in black, too, were the dozens of photographs of Rupert that crammed the walls. Rupert clad in a sailor suit with a toy yacht in his hands, Rupert with a book in a setting of classical ruins, Rupert with apples in an orchard, Rupert with a kite, Rupert with a top and a whip, Rupert astride a rocking horse . . .

"I wish I could take you away," whispered Dorrie to the horse. "This is no place for a horse to live."

Behind him the curtains swelled as they filled with a fresh rush of air and the nudge of heavy fabric set the horse rocking gently. He was nodding—or was it beckoning?—to Dorrie.

She giggled. *He wants me to come and play!* she thought in delight. *He's naughty! He knows I'm not supposed to come in.*

But there it was again, that distinct nod as his rockers squeaked on the floor and that wink as his eyes picked up reflected light from the windows.

He does want me! Before she had time to consider the enormity of what she was doing she had propelled herself forward until she was standing, breathless, at the foot of the bed where a long bench table was arranged with Grandmaire's personal effects—her ebony glove box, silver-backed hairbrushes, pin-tray of hat pins and button-hooks and her leather jewelry cases. There was also a silver dish on which lay a large polished greenstone pendant in the shape of a kneeling woman.

Dorrie was instantly attracted to this. She had never seen it before for Grandmaire wore only jet jewelry. She was going to look at it more closely but the unpleasant atmosphere of the room made her nervous. She hurried to the rocking horse and swiftly embraced his neck.

At once she felt better. Up close he was even more glorious than she had imagined. She fondled his hard nose and traced the glowing trappings of his harness. His mane was coarse and silky as marram grass and when she reached out a tentative fingertip she discovered that the twin sprays of eyelashes were as bristly as the stable broom, while there she was, reflected in one port-wine eye, a pale dot of face like the center of a golden daisy.

Dorrie leaned against him in a moment of perfect happiness. Her weight caused the finely balanced horse to move, his rockers scraping with slow wheezes on the floor as he began to nod, contented, in the circle of her arms.

She closed her eyes. They were galloping under a dizzy blue sky, faster and faster until his hoofbeats matched the pounding of her quickened heartbeat. She gripped the saddle with her knees. The wind snatched at her skirt. Her cheeks stung. With hoofs throbbing across a sloping meadow cobbled with buttercups, he glided up and over a stone wall then clattered down a stony path to the beach while Dorrie urged him on.

Across the sand he pounded. His hoofs punched sharp hollows in the damp tongue of sand that licked up to the high water mark; then they dashed through the ragged edge of water, tearing scraps of lace foam from the ocean's hem while seagulls . . .

Suddenly a familiar noise jolted Dorrie out of her reverie.

She mustn't find me here! thought Dorrie as she heard the crabbed shuffle of Grandmaire's boots and the faint chatter of her walking cane. She stood petrified, gaping at the open door. Hastily she glanced about for an escape.

The door was impassable without her being seen, and though the window was open at the top it overlooked a thicket of rosebushes so there was no prospect of escape. She would have to hide. Under the bed!

When Dorrie lifted the draperies she gasped in dismay. A large cabin trunk and a collection of boxes jammed the entire space.

Where then? Dorrie began to cry. The cane's tap-

tapping was like an echo of doom. She backed away, staring at the door, her nervous fingers clutching at the curtains as tears bubbled in anticipation.

The curtains, of course! If she was very still, and stood pressed flush to the wall . . .

She was only just in time. As Grandmaire entered the room Dorrie edged behind them but in the haste of positioning herself she brushed against one of the horse's projecting rockers, bumping him forward.

His long, asthmatic sigh was followed by an ominous silence.

"Who is there?"

The horse wheezed again, this time kicking her on the shins as he began another swing. Dorrie stifled a squeak of fright.

"*Who* is there?"

"What's the matter, Grandmaire?" Dora's voice from the corridor covered the approaching shuffle of the old woman's footsteps.

Dorrie held her breath, hoping that Grandmaire would think it was just the wind, that she would go away, that—

A blow struck her in the center of the chest and slammed her against the wall. Before she could draw breath to shriek, another whack drove a hammer-blow into her breastbone, then before that had blossomed fully into pain the metal tip of Grandmaire's walking cane thudded against the wall beside her head, narrowly missing her ear.

Terror drove her out of her hiding place. Her own wails scoured her ears as she stumbled to her knees in front of Grandmaire's long black skirts. She slumped there, staring at the twin polished toecaps through a red haze, her head bowed over a bright, unfolding rose of pain that filled her chest.

The old woman was quaking with exertion; she rested until Dorrie raised her head, then she scolded, "How dare you come near this room!" The accusation regenerated her rage and strength as she repeated, "How dare you! How dare you!"

The walking cane swung above her head. It blurred in the edge of Dorrie's vision for in the very center of her attention was clamped that hard-eyed, wrinkled face.

Down came the cane, swung with both hands for maximum force. Dorrie saw it too late.

"No!" she screamed. She flung her hands up over her head, then shrieked again as the cane crashed down, crushing the tips of her fingers and glancing off onto her skull. This time the pain was instant, hot and flaring.

Wailing in terror, Dorrie scrambled for the door while Grandmaire followed, driving at her with two-handed chops, whacking at her as if Dorrie were a rat she was trying to destroy.

"Grandmaire!" Dora's rustling skirts were interposed between child and old woman. Dorrie huddled whimpering in the corridor while her aunt wrested the cane free and sent it slithering across the floor. "Grandmaire, what on earth has gotten into you?"

"That child has been warned to stay away from here," the old woman said.

Dora glared at her, then said to Dorrie, "Are you hurt, pet?"

"Of course she's not hurt."

Dorrie held out trembling hands, and as Dora examined them she bit back a cry of outrage. The fingertips on both hands had been so badly crushed that they were oozing blood from where the skin around the fingernails was split and torn.

The pain must be excruciating, thought Dora. She tried to smile at the little girl, who looked up at her with tearful trusting eyes. Barely able to speak calmly she said, "Run along to the kitchen, pet, and I'll come and fix up the hurt."

"You will attend to me," Grandmaire told her.

She can hear perfectly well when she wants to, thought Dora.

Drawing a deep breath she said, "I shall not attend to you. I shall not attend to you in any way until you change your attitude to Dorrie. You hate Dorrie for only one thing. She is here and your precious Rupert has gone. That's what you can't forgive. You can't bear to see her laughing and playing in the garden like *he* used to. You refuse to let her have all these wasted toys." Dora swept a hand along a shelf, tumbling a row of dolls and stuffed animals onto the floor. "She should have them all."

"Leave Rupert's things alone!"

Dora continued coldly, "This room is a shrine and you're entitled to it if it comforts you, but what I won't stand for is the way you blame Dorrie. It's not her fault that Ellen ran away. She was only a baby then, and we lived with the Yardleys at the time. Grandmaire, I don't know why they went, but if I had the power I'd wish them back here again. I know how much you loved that little lad, but you could be fond of Dorrie, too, if you would give yourself a chance."

Grandmaire turned away, lifting the cover of her commode, pointedly not listening.

"Oh!" expostulated Dora. "I give up!"

"Come back here!" cried Grandmaire as Dora stormed out.

Dora was quivering with anger. "Damn you all," she muttered. "Grandmaire most of all, and Ellen for running away, Rupert for being Grandmaire's darling and Jon—yes, John, too—because he may have been the reason his wife and children fled."

"I warn you, Dora!" cried Grandmaire, but her voice was in the distance now.

Moana was impressed. She was pinning on her hat when Dorrie sidled into the kitchen and now she was examining the wounds with interest.

"Boy, Matua, she can whip hard, eh?"

Dorrie nodded. "She even h-hit my head."

Moana cluck-clucked at that, for heads were sacred to

the Maoris. She glanced at Dorrie's legs where her crocheted socks drooped over the tops of her brown ankle
boots. Distinct red marks crisscrossed the skin all the
way up to her knees. "Boy, you got some beauty bruises
coming there, eh?" she commented, twitching the hem
down. "I told you that Matua, she give you *patu-patu*, a
big smack, if you go in there. That's her own place, eh."

Dorrie shivered, gritting her teeth. Pain now cloaked
her like a fever but through it pierced the realization that
Moana's sympathies were with Grandmaire.

"Hey!" said Moana. "Don't you cry now! You be a
big strong girl, eh?"

"Y-you don't care that I'm hurt," whispered Dorrie.

"Sure I do!" Moana pinched the trembling chin. "Ah,
but you'll be all better soon, eh? Poor Matua, her Rupert
went away and she won't never be happy again."

Dora bustled in and was soon dressing the crushed fingers while Moana stood by dispensing unwanted advice.
She shook her head as Dora opened the old wooden medicine chest and took out a vial from the row of stoppered
bottles of bright liquids.

"That stuff won't do no good," predicted Moana,
leaning both elbows on the table. "Pounded flax roots,
that's the story."

"We'll try arnica and calendula first," said Dora, her
tone softened by the favor she was about to ask.

While Dorrie watched fearfully Dora cut two lint pads,
splashed them with lotion, then bound them quickly
around her fingers, making a soft white mitten on each
hand. "There! You've got paws now, like a little kitty
cat." She planted a kiss of approval on Dorrie's brow.
"You're a good girl, no matter what *she* says. Moana,
I'm afraid that Grandmaire and I are having a battle of
wills and it's important that Dorrie is out of the way.
Could you please take her home with you this afternoon?"

Dorrie brightened at once. She loved going to the Patenes' place. "Could I please?" she said.

Moana sniffed. It was her afternoon off and theoretically she could refuse but a glance at the eager little face beside her blighted that impulse.

"She hasn't had her lunch yet," she contented herself by saying. "It's still in the oven, eh."

"I'm not hungry," said Dorrie quickly.

"I don't suppose you are," said Dora. "Take care now, and don't let her bump her hands, will you, Moana."

"Come on then." She would have preferred to refuse, but it was too late now.

Two

The tide was sliding away from its creased warm bed. Haze above the water shimmered so strongly that distant scows and red-sailed Maori canoes seemed to dance on a silver ribbon. Dorrie hurried along in Moana's wake, determined not to let this rare treat be ruined by the hurt that jarred through her body with every step.

They paused to rest a moment on a knobbly-kneed jetty that looked awkward and ugly without its water skirts. Dorrie gazed back up the harbor. Auckland smoked quietly amid its own clutter, surrounded by a sprawl of red-painted roofs. She turned and stared at the far gulf islands that lay nonchalant as a scarf tossed along the horizon, fold upon fold of gauzy blue.

"What's a volcano?" she asked Moana.

"Huh?" Moana was stuffing a corncob pipe with tobacco.

"A volcano. Auntie Dora said that those islands and these hills"— she waved a bandaged hand at North Head directly opposite on the other shore—"are all extinct volcanoes."

Moana tucked pipe and tobacco pouch back into her flax basket. "Time to go," she said. And, "You talk too much, eh."

Dorrie trotted on, obediently silent. Though Moana was her only real friend apart from Dora, she was timid around her in the same way that she minded her *p*'s and *q*'s around Uncle Jon, for fear of provoking an irate response. Disapproval was the thing Dorrie feared most.

Brusque and domineering at times, Moana did have

her moments when she went out of her way to show kindness to the lonely child. Sometimes she let her sit on a high stool in the kitchen while she prepared Grandmaire's delicious one-portion meals and let her taste the imported treats—a morsel of pink salmon, a sliver of smoked ham, a dab of truffled pâté from an earthenware crock sealed with scarlet wax, or, from another crock, creamy blue cheese that stung the tongue yet tasted so indescribably delicious.

"Go on, eh," Moana would coax. "Say me the names in Maori like I learned you."

"Grape. That's *karepe,* right?" Dorrie would point to a platter where grape scissors rested beside a cluster of opaque muscats. She touched the beaded jug cover and said, "Milk, *miraka.* And this is *tiihi,"* she announced as she pointed to the stilton with a giggle. "Cheese. Tee-ee-hee! What a funny name that is! Who do you think might have invented a name like that?"

"You talk too much, eh," was Moana's predictable reply.

The Patene dwelling was an unpainted shack sheltered in a low-slung lap of land only the merest jump from the beach. Twisted *pohutukawa* trees brushed its roof as they leaned out from the creamy cliffs behind, and at the far side a ragged patch of pumpkins and watermelon spread like an apron around a rickety "long-drop" privy. The place was as colorful as a gyspy camp. Washing was spread on bushes while empty bottles and discarded cans glinted in the straggling shore weeds. The cabin of an old tugboat had been maneuvered up close to the dwelling to make a sleep-out for the younger Patene children.

"Coo-ee!" yelled Moana as they approached.

Alerted by her voice, a quartet of *kuri*s, raw-boned Maori dogs, stirred from the shade and hurled themselves down the beach, their barks bouncing off the cliffs.

"Haere! Haere atu! Go away!" scolded Moana, but Dorrie laughed when they thrust their sandy noses

against her gingham skirt. For all their hugeness they were gentle, friendly creatures.

Moana's call had alerted her family, and by the time she and Dorrie had crunched their way over snowdrifts of sun-bleached *pipi* shells, refuse from countless seafood dinners, the entire Patene contingent was waiting to greet them.

Dorrie liked them all, from the distinguished white-haired Mrs. Patene, who often paid courtesy calls on Grandmaire to the half-dozen girls who sometimes gossiped with Moana in the kitchen, right down to the youngest child and only boy, Albert, who accompanied his mother everywhere. Dorrie smiled shyly as she squinted up at them.

"Why, it's Miss Bennington, how nice," said Mrs. Patene. "Isn't that lovely, Albert? She's come to visit us." To Dorrie she said, "We were just going to have our lunch. We always wait for Moana on her day off. Albert, fetch a chair for Miss Bennington, would you? He's a good boy, my boy Albert. Oh, my, is something wrong with your hands, dear?"

Moana shot her the information in a rapid gabble of Maori and Mrs. Patene looked faintly shocked. The children all looked impressed.

"Matua, she *patu-patu* with her stick," finished Moana in English.

Dorrie hung her head.

It was a strange party, like a Royal occasion in some ways. One of the girls wafted a green flax fan over the table to keep the flies away. The breeze seemed to impart a warm salty flavor to the food. From above their heads the *pohutukawa* trees drizzled a fine confetti of pin-shaped petals. They settled in drifts in the folds of Dorrie's floppy bonnet. Moana and the big girls helped themselves, heaping tin pannikins with slabs of bread and coarse yellow cake, *pipis* and mussels and chunks of doughy brown pudding. They leaned against low branches some distance from the table, chattering like birds as they poked the food into their mouths.

Dorrie was hurting too much to be hungry and her fingers could not grip the knife and fork provided in her honor, but she managed to nibble at a jam sandwich while Albert chewed and talked without pausing.

"See those mussels? I got them from out there on the island. I paddled the canoe by myself."

"*Kea,*" hissed his sister Turei, who had been born on a Tuesday. "Liar! You never did."

"See those potatoes? I dug them out of my own garden."

"*Kea!*" accused Emere.

"That will do, Emily. Albert is not a liar. He does help in the garden." Her approval swung over him like a lighthouse beam. "He's a good boy, my boy Albert."

Albert was only a year older than Dorrie but a full decade more sophisticated and confident. He was much paler complexioned than his sisters but had the same full lips and flattened nose which made him look as if his face were lightly pressed against a pane of glass. He spoke with a new aggressiveness now that his mother had defended his boasting.

"See this chicken, this *moa?* I chopped the head all by myself." He squawked and flapped his elbows like wings. "Paaark! Puk-puk-puk! Boy, you should have seen it."

Dorrie paled.

"*Kea!*" said fourteen-year-old Turei. "You wouldn't even help me when you was supposed to. You ran and hid behind—"

"That will do, Tuesday. Miss Bennington doesn't want to hear about that. If you children have had enough to eat, then you can run off now. How about looking for the orange kitty, eh? Oh," she added, beaming in pleasure as a man in a red and black Salvation Army uniform crunched up the beach. "Here's Major Blackett and his boy. Quick, Emily, run and make more tea. Wednesday, rinse out some of these cups, please.'' She raised her voice again. "Major Blackett, what a lovely surprise. Albert, isn't it nice? He's brought his boy to play with you.''

The boy pulled a face, a grimace of embarrassment. Dorrie stared at him with interest. He was a strong lad of about Turei's age in corduroy breeches and a faded cotton jacket from which his wrists jutted like bleached twigs on a scarecrow. His face was pink with the heat like his father's and like his father he had tightly curled fair hair and the palest blue eyes Dorrie had ever seen. She thought him incredibly handsome and smiled when they were introduced but he did not look at her. Instead he glared at the table, flushing when his father boomed, "This is Arundel.''

"It's *Del*,'' he muttered.

"You were baptized in God's name,'' said the Major, a cold edge to his heartiness. "We'll have no arguments—the subject is closed. Now off you go and play with young Albert.''

"Mama's brat,'' muttered the boy. Albert promptly stuck his tongue out in reciprocal insult. It was clear that no ill will was intended on either side, but the Major viewed the exchange differently.

"Arundel!'' he roared, cuffing his son around the ear. The boy grimaced but did not cry.

"C'mon, Del. *Haere mai*,'' said Albert and the two dashed away.

"Us too, eh?'' suggested Emere. "We'll find kitty-cat.'' Dorrie hurried to keep up with her as the bare brown feet flashed over the crushed-shell path.

"Excuse my lad,'' said the Major, settling himself in a chair beside Mrs. Patene. "He's never had a mother to teach him proper manners.''

"As my Albert has never known a father,'' said Mrs. Patene as she picked up the blue teapot. Tea gushed from the spout. "But the wee Bennington *tamahine* has neither mother nor father.''

"Sad case, that." The Major stirred a spoonful of
sugar into the dark brew. "Mother dying in childbirth
and the father drowning so soon afterwards. Tragic case.
Tragic." He frowned. "Ogstanley, that was the father's
name, wasn't it?"

"Miss Dora adopted her. Her name's Bennington
now."

"Yes, Dora Bennington." His tone indicated that he
thought precious little of Dora. "Poor little wretch," he
observed as he watched the children race towards the
point where surf frothed around wet rocks at the harbor
mouth. "What in the world happened to her hands?"

Mrs. Patene hesitated. "Do have some more tea, Major," she urged. "And what about a piece of this cake,
eh? My Albert helped me make it. He's a good boy is my
boy Albert. Which reminds me, Major. I've been meaning to ask you about music lessons. Piano lessons for my
Albert. Do you think you could fit him in, eh?"

And thus the subject of Dorrie's injuries was deftly
avoided.

Dorrie trudged behind Emere down the shell bank to
where sand heaped in gritty hillocks above the high tide
leavings of seaweed and driftwood. Though it was now
late afternoon the sand still retained midday's heat. Dorrie could feel it scorching through her layers of petticoat,
dress and pinafore as she knelt uncomfortably beside the
Maori girl at the entrance to a low sand cave.

"Orange kitty-cat is in there. Can you see her, eh?"

It hurt Dorrie to bend her neck but, always obliging,
she stooped to peer into the wide tunnel. At first she
could see nothing but blackness beyond the bright sand
that glittered under a web of marram grass shadow.

"Kitty, kitty," cooed Emere.

"She won't come," said Dorrie, disappointed. She
loved Orange Kitty.

"Hey, you found her!" Albert slid from the top of the
dune in a spray of sand and landed with a "Whee!" be-

side his sister. *"Haere mai,* Del!" he ordered as he began shoveling sand from the tunnel mouth, scooping it
out doggy fashion.

"You leave her alone!" shouted Emere.

"What's it to you?" Albert shoved his sister away.

"Because she's having babies in there."

"Kea! She is not." But he stopped his shoveling and
with the others crouched to stare into the widened tunnel.

Babies! thought Dorrie in wonder as she looked for
soft-furred miniatures of the mother. It puzzled her to see
only a tiny ratlike knot of squirming slick skin with indistinct features. Orange Kitty ignored this creature while
she licked something else, something that resembled a
chunk of raw lamb liver.

"What's she eating?"

"Boy, don't you know?" Emere was scornful of Dorrie's ignorance. "That's her baby. She's licking it clean,
eh. So far she's got two babies."

Dorrie did not want to believe this but she could now
see that the lamb liver was squirming, too.

"It came out of her stomach, eh," swaggered Emere.
"Just like people babies do."

This was ridiculous of course, but Dorrie was too polite and too timid to call Emere a liar. She looked away,
feeling ill. A shadow moved across her face and she
glanced up to see Del watching her with those curious
pale eyes.

"Kea!" Albert was shouting at his sister. "You never
seen a people baby being born! What do you know, eh?"

She slapped him and he returned the blow, which she
promptly gave back with a sideswipe for good measure.
He retaliated with a wild swing that missed his sister and
instead struck Dorrie in the middle of the chest, right
where Grandmaire's stick had slammed into her only
hours before. Dorrie gasped and sagged in pain while the
brother and sister continued to buffet each other with
slaps and insults.

"You *moho tamahine!* Stupid girl!"

"Boy, I'll show you stupid all right!"

Albert connected a hefty punch to his sister's shoulder and as Emere struggled to keep her balance he struck her again, pushing her so that she staggered back against Dorrie. One knee came down hard on Dorrie's left hand, crushing it inside its cocoon of soft bandange. The agony was unbelievable.

She shrieked with a sharp insuck of air. Struggling to her feet, she lurched away, wailing.

Del watched her go. "Girls always cry," he said.

Emere rested on her haunches. "Boy, she can yell loud, eh?" she observed admiringly.

Weeping, cradling her hurt hand in front of her, Dorrie leaned against a warm black boulder. Tears soaked into the bandage, turning the fresh red to pink, but she let the pain flow and concentrated on trying not to sob, for each hiccoughing breath cramped her chest with tight agony.

Around her the seagulls swooped and screamed. Their cries bounced from one to the other like a ball. Dorrie listened to them, was lulled by the rhythm of their repeating echoes and by the soft heat in the rock until presently the worst of her pain eased.

Lost as she was in a red haze of hurt she did not sense the approach of a party from around the point until she heard a clear feminine voice say, "It's little Dorinda, isn't it? Are you all right, dear?"

Dorrie glanced up with a start and found herself looking into an unfamiliar face, a milky-white, delicately featured face surrounded by a cloud of mahogany-colored hair and shaded by the brim of a white boater hat. The others in the party wore boaters, too; through her tears they were the only detail Dorrie noticed at first, the semicircle of boaters bobbing towards her.

"It *is* Dorinda, isn't it?" repeated the woman as she stepped closer, holding the hem of her white gown clear of the rocks with a white-gloved hand. To Dorrie she looked like a vision of crystal beauty.

"She's hurt," said a young man with a darkly hand-some face, who had been holding the elbow of the woman in white as he helped her pick her way over the uneven terrain.

Mortified, Dorrie thrust both hands behind her back and stayed fixed against the rock but not before one of the other young men had seen the blood-soaked bandages. "Great heavens!" he exclaimed, striding forward and dropping to one knee in front of her. "Let me see," he demanded, holding out both hands.

Dorrie gaped at him in nervous fright and he smiled to reassure her. He had a pleasant face, strong and still boy-ish with soft brown eyes, thick dark-red hair and the be-ginnings of a downy moustache above a full-lipped mouth. It was a kind face, decided Dorrie, but she shiv-ered and shook her head when he repeated his demand.

"She's afraid of you, Nathaniel," cooed the woman in white, and to Dorrie she said, "We won't hurt you, dear, but what happened to your hands? They do look very sore."

Dorrie swallowed. She wanted to run away but these kindly, concerned faces surrounded her and her only es-cape route would be to push right through them.

"My God!" said the young man suddenly. From where he knelt before her he could see the gap between Dorrie's hem and the tops of her drooping socks. "Look at that," he said, pointing to the crisscross of welts on Dorrie's legs. "This child's been beaten!"

"Surely not," said the others, shocked.

"I'd swear to it," said the young man, standing up. "Though it staggers me to imagine how anybody could be so vicious as to beat a sweet little child like this. Her parents must be—"

"Hush," warned the white lady. She looked about to cry herself and this added to Dorrie's bewilderment. Leaning close she asked, "Who hit you, dear? Did Dora do that to you?"

The question and the attention frankly terrified Dorrie.

Whimpering to herself, she lowered her head and ran blindly off towards the Patenes' cottage. Though the strangers could have closed ranks and halted her with ease they pitied her and let her go. Only May Teipa-Bennington reached out a white-gloved hand in a futile gesture to call her back. With tears in her eyes she appealed to her husband. "Surely there is something we can do?"

Patrick Teipa-Bennington frowned. "Do you really think that Dora . . ." He couldn't finish.

"It couldn't have been Grandmaire; she's so old and feeble that I doubt she could swat a fly."

Nathaniel Rosser ran his fingers through his russet-colored hair, then replaced his boater. "What can the child's parents be thinking of?" he said in disgust.

"They're both dead," May told him. "That little girl is my cousin's child. Remember? I told you about her. They used to live with us." She shook her head in despair. "Surely there is *something* we can do," she said.

At dusk a party of Patene girls and their boyfriends brought Dorrie home to Fintona in a Maori canoe. Moana escorted her up the cliff path. The hedge's thick shadow bled over the lawn and the morning room windows were a checkerboard of light set into the verandah's gloom. Below the house the beach was a slab of gray mottled marble, fast covering by the tide. Dorrie could see their footprints when she looked back.

"Go inside," said Moana when they reached the verandah steps.

Dorrie hesitated. Whirring *huhu* beetles were pelting themselves against the glass, drawn to the lights within the room. Dorrie dreaded *huhu*s. They had long switching feelers, spiny legs, crackly wings with a span of almost four inches *and* they could bite.

"Can't we go around the other way?" she pleaded.

"Ssss!" warned Moana, shushing her. "Listen. They's fighting, eh."

Dorrie looked beyond the horrible insects. Auntie

Dora sat in front of a bright fire that leaped in the grate and Uncle Jon stood behind her. Both looked grim. Grandmaire was leaning on her stick, haranguing them.

"I tell you again, Dora, that I'll not be bullied in my own home!" she raged. "How dare you send that child running to May Teipa-Bennington with tales of ill treatment."

"But I told you, Grandmaire. I know nothing of—"

"Then how did she find out? Answer me that, now. This note has the audacity to demand an explanation of Dorinda's injuries! *Injuries,* it says. The child was given a richly deserved whipping, that's all. Injuries, my eye! You've defied me today, Dora, and don't deny it. I insist that you kneel to me now and apologize."

It's all my fault, Dorrie realized, dismayed. That woman in white must have been the cousin Auntie Dora hates so bitterly.

"Now, Dora." Dorrie could see Uncle John prodding her in the back as if to urge her to comply but Dora sat rigid and defiant.

"Very well," said Grandmaire. She picked up a quilted bag and walked with it to the fireplace, bearing it in both hands as if it were a precious urn. Dorrie recognized it as the knickknack bag Grandmaire used to carry a handkerchief and her jet vinaigrette bottle when she walked in the garden.

"This bag contains something of great value, something that belongs to you, Dora. You have one minute to come to your senses and apologize, otherwise you will watch this burn."

Dora and Jon began to quarrel. The firelight heightened the resemblance between them, showing how alike they were with their pallid brows, square chins and puffs of well-groomed hair of which they were coincidentally proud. Their one vanity was a mutual one. Now both faces wore identical expressions of anger as they hissed at each other in low, fierce voices.

Grandmaire watched in obvious satisfaction. The bickering was like music to her. Suddenly she stepped forward and set the bag in the middle of the fire.

Dorrie felt sick with guilt as the flames ran tiny orange flags up the sides of the bag. Auntie Dora was being punished and it was her fault. She watched with a feeling of doom as the black sateen peeled away and the serge padding hissed as flames flowed over it, melting through in no time to the calico lining, unraveling the bag into curling ribbons of gray and white smoke.

"No!" shouted Jon, starting forward. A cake of banknotes sat clearly visible in the fire.

"Stay where you are," commanded Grandmaire. "That money is Dora's—five hundred pounds she would have received in my will. Only Dora can save it."

"Hoo-lee!" whispered Moana reverently. The cake rose in layers like crisp puff-pastry, charring around the wafery edges. "Five hundred pounds, hoo-lee! Boy, I'd *kihi ia papa* for five hundred pounds! Go on, Dora, you silly thing."

But Dora sat, immobile, and watched the money blaze without any expression whatsoever. Through the hot flush of her guilt Dorrie felt extremely proud of her.

Fintona's bedrooms were ranged in a row along one side of a long, dark corridor. Grandmaire's was at the end, Dora was next to her in a converted dressing room, Jon next to that, and then after two empty rooms was the tiny boxroom that had been assigned to Dorrie. It barely accommodated a small bed and a dresser-cum-washstand; the only window was so high up that Dorrie had never managed to see out of it. Dora had decorated it cheerfully with a pink crocheted bedcover, a handmade rag rug on the scrap of floorspace and curtains cut from an old tablecloth. Racehorse pictures from a discarded book of Jon's adorned the walls, for Dorrie loved all animals and longed for a pet of her own. This was Dorrie's nest, and in it she always felt safe.

Now, as Dora fussed over her sore hands, Dorrie felt

her tensions ease, though the guilt feelings remained. After Dora had scrubbed her teeth with a rag dipped in a salt pot, then brushed and braided her hair, Dorrie ventured timidly, "I met a strange lady today."

"What?" said Dora. "I thought Grandmaire was making up all that nonsense about the note. I didn't see anybody deliver it and—" She shook Dorrie gently. "That lady—what did you say to her?"

"Nothing."

Dora frowned. *"Nothing?"*

"She asked who beat me but I didn't say. They saw my legs—and they asked—but I ran away and—" Huge tears welled in her eyes and her shoulders began to quake.

"There, now," soothed Dora, enfolding her to her soft bosom. "Don't cry, lovey." But when the sobbing stopped she added on a serious note, "That person you saw was my cousin, May Yardley, Captain Yardley's daughter. You know the Captain, don't you pet?"

Dorrie nodded. The Captain occasionally came to visit Grandmaire, and always on those visits verbal battles erupted that could be heard all over Fintona.

Dora said, "May was engaged to marry my brother, your Uncle Hal, but just before the wedding she changed her mind and married another relative—someone we never talk about, someone not fit to associate with."

Dorrie wondered if she was referring to the handsome man who had held cousin May's arm.

"They are wicked people, Dorrie. I want you to promise me that if you ever see them again you will do just as you did today. Run away and don't say anything to them."

Why? Dorrie wanted to ask. They had seemed like lovely people, the woman beautiful in dazzling white with a kind face, that quiet man with the serious, gentle expression, and the young man who was outspoken, the man with the wavy red hair and the merry eyes. It was difficult to reconcile any of them with the image of evil.

"Promise me," insisted Dora.

Dorrie promised.

Three

Dorrie kept out of Grandmaire's way. She retreated to the brick-walled service yard where she sat on the chopping block in the shade and, despite the stiffness in her hands, worked steadily on her sampler. The service yard was a barren place that stank of drains, where there was nothing to look at but lines of tea-cloths drying and hens scratching for woodlice between the flagstones.

Now she lived for the visits to the Patenes' where there was good humor, fun, and Orange Kitty's babies, who were now enchanting.

Dorrie's favorite was the smallest of the litter, a mischievous scrap of soft gray fluff. She loved to pick him up and cuddle him under her chin, for the moment she touched him his tiny body began to vibrate with loud purrs.

"Dear little Misty," she sighed as he curled around her neck like a feather boa. "He sounds like an engine. Will he be so cuddly when he's grown up?"

"Won't get to be grown up, eh," said Emere.

"What do you mean?"

Emere looked away but Albert cheerfully supplied the bad news. "They'll all get drowned pretty soon, eh."

"I'm afraid that's right," admitted Mrs. Patene when Dorrie confronted her at the open-air bench behind the cabin where she was preparing vegetables. She wished there was some way she could deny the ghastly rumor but instead explained gently, "It has to be done, eh. Soon the whole beach would be crowded with cats and kittens if we just let them be."

"But *drown* them—they wouldn't eat much, and you catch your own fish."

"They keep having more and more," said Mrs. Patene uncomfortably.

"All *drowned?*" choked Dorrie, unable to absorb anything but that one indigestible fact. "Even Misty?"

"Misty?"

"The sw-sweet little gr-gray one."

"Hey, don't you be so *pouri*, eh? There's worse things to be sad about than a scrawny cat."

Dorrie shook her head, sobbing. "It's c-cruel! Poor little Misty!"

Mrs. Patene wiped her hands on her calico apron as she watched Dorrie bolt away crying. Her own brood were inured to the practicalities of life and accepted the drowning of kittens without a murmur, but this little *tamahine* was genuinely grief-stricken. Sighing, Mrs. Patene picked up the blackened potato-pot and set it on the charred grate over the fire.

". . . and God bless Mama and Papa and watch over them in heaven. Amen." Scrambling up from her knees, Dorrie climbed into bed. Dora's face shadowed her as she bent to brush a kiss onto her forehead.

"Auntie Dora?" The tremulous voice stopped her in the doorway and she turned with the wavering candlelamp. "Do . . . do kittens go to heaven when they die?"

"Of course not," said Dora, and could immediately have kicked herself. Dorrie was obviously fretting over that wretched creature at the Patenes'. "Perhaps animals have a heaven of their own," she suggested.

"Oh, I do hope so! Only, I thought it might be nice for Mama and Papa to have M-Misty to look after. Oh, Auntie Dora, I can't *endure* to think of him being drowned!"

"If only we could do their suffering for them," Dora remarked to Jon later as she made him a cup of tea in the kitchen.

He flapped the newspaper open and folded it to read the racing news. "If you ask me, we're all doing far too much suffering around here, and it's all your fault. The old girl's been in the foulest mood ever since that ruckus. Did you have to make such an issue over nothing? She was disobedient and Grandmaire whipped her. That's—"

"*Whipped* her? Jon, she beat her like a dog. I'll not—"

"Look here." He lowered the newspaper and stared at her coldly. "It's not for us to call the tune around here. We depend on her and don't you forget it. Unless we antagonize her, when she dies we'll both do very handsomely out of her will. You may not care about money—you may be able to watch your share burn rather than utter a simple 'I'm sorry' but I'm counting on that will."

"Then you're crazy," said Dora flatly. "When it comes to inheritance she'll give everything to her own flesh and blood. She may have been married to our grandfather but *we're* not true kin and—"

Jon grabbed her wrist so hard that she dropped the spoon she was holding. "Don't talk like that," he said. "Don't ever talk like that again."

On Sunday afternoon the Fintona residents sat on the verandah in the shade, refreshed by the cooling gulf breeze. Jon dozed with hands lightly clasped over his paunch; Dora sat on one side of him making quick furtive movements over the crochet work in her lap, and on the other side Grandmaire made great play out of squinting through the telescope. Though she could distinguish few details of the ships at anchor, the exercise gave her an excuse to talk without any necessity of reply. Dora was still treating her with frosty disdain.

From Dora's waist dangled a Singapore cricket cage in which hopped and bobbed a roll of lemon wool, and cross-legged on a cushion, almost touching the cage, sat Dorrie as she quietly embroidered her sampler.

If smoothed out now it would read:

> *WISDOM*
> *OH Happy is the Man who Hears*
> *Instruction's Warning Voice*
> *And Who Celestial Wisdom Makes*
> *His Early, Only Choice*
> *This World is all a Fleeting Show*
> *For Mere Illusion Given*
> *The S*

Though Dorrie could read few of the words and had no understanding of the sentiment, she stitched with enjoyment. The creation of something beautiful was satisfying to her.

Grandmaire interrupted her own monologue as Mrs. Patene and Albert approached through the gate in the hedge. Both wore Sunday black, he in a cut-down suit that used to belong to Jon and she in one of Grandmaire's old jackets over an extravagantly bustled black dress. Streamers of netting trailed from her billy-cock hat.

"*Kia ora* and *haere mai*, Mrs. Patene, and you, too, Aparata," cried Grandmaire.

Jon uttered his dry cough as he blinked awake. "Curious how their names translate," he muttered, fumbling for a handkerchief. "*Turei*, Tuesday. *Emere*, Emily. *Aparata*, Albert. Even *Patene* means 'button', you know. You'd think the dashed missionaries would have given the Maoris a full complement of letters to use instead of sticking to the paltry fourteen they already had. What kind of a language uses only fourteen letters, hey?"

Grandmaire was focusing her ear trumpet with a greedy eagerness. She had not had a proper conversation for days and was starving for company. "What a fine boy he is, Mrs. Patene," she said in her feeble voice. "Named for the Prince Consort and worthy of the name, too. And what brings you here to see me, Aparata?"

Albert was rightly confused by the question and stared

at the wooden box he was carrying. He was bringing something to Fintona, not the other way around.

"Speak up, eh." Mrs. Patene gave him a poke and explained, "He's a good boy is my boy Albert, but a bit shy, eh. Go on, say it like Moana learned you."

"Good afternoon, Matua," intoned Albert. "I brung you a cat. To catch the mouses in your kitchen."

Dorrie's heart jammed in her throat.

Grandmaire's lips pleated. "We don't have any mice. Besides, I can't abide animals."

"Especially cats," agreed Jon quickly. "Yowling creatures. Shedding fur about the house, scratching the furniture."

"No, thank you, Aparata," said Grandmaire. "Now come and sit down, Mrs. Patene. Dora will make us a cup of tea."

"It's a good cat," said Mrs. Patene. "Go on, Albert. Open the box and show Matua."

The breath solidified in Dorrie's chest as Albert slid the lid off the box. Misty's head pushed out at once, his green eyes widening in the wedge of sunlight. He tumbled out onto the verandah looking marshmallowy soft and adorable and sat up yawning, showing a tongue dished at the tip like an unfurling petal. *Oh, Misty!* thought Dorrie.

"No, thank you," said Grandmaire, unmoved. "Put it away at once please, Aparata. I simply cannot abide cats."

He obeyed at once, snapping the lid shut.

Dorrie stood up, quaking, her eyes enormous in a paper-white face. "You could have saved him!" she cried. "He's just a little kitten and now he'll be killed!" Blinded by burning tears, she stumbled away towards the kitchen with Dora hurrying after her.

"Goodness me!" said Grandmaire, whose ear trumpet had missed the essence of the outburst. "I think the child must be sickening for something."

* * *

"I finished my sampler," cried Dorrie, skipping into the scullery where Moana was rinsing cups and saucers in a wooden tub.

"Shush," Moana scolded. "Matua is very sick, eh. We mustn't make any noise."

Dorrie pulled a face. For a month now the house had been dark and hushed as the priests and nuns kept silent vigil at Grandmaire's bedside. Grandmaire was dying; Auntie Dora said so. The only trouble was it was taking so *long*.

Unfolding her fancywork so that Moana could see it, she pleaded, "Will you read it for me please, Moana? Auntie Dora said she would help me learn it all by heart. That will be so thrilling—the lines all sound so stirring even though I don't know what they mean. Do you know what 'Glory's Plume' and the 'Fading Hues of Even' are, for instance?"

"You talk too much, eh," said Moana, flapping a dishcloth at her and bidding her to help dry the cups. Moana had a headache. All day she had been trying to rid herself of a *kitenga,* a premonition of approaching evil, and her skull hurt with the effort of trying to thrust it out of her mind.

Dorrie worked solemnly. "Why do the nuns stay with Grandmaire all night?" she asked after a long silence. "Is Grandmaire afraid of the dark?"

The idea tickled Moana. "She's afraid of the big dark, eh."

"Will the nuns help her go to heaven?"

Moana was cynical about the church. "Maybe *Matua* will ask how she can get to heaven, then they'll say a few thousand pounds for the church might be just the story, eh." She splashed a steaming gush of water into the teapot and rattled the lid shut.

"Do you need to buy a ticket to get to heaven?"

"You talk too much. And hurry with those cups, eh. The nuns are waiting for their tea." She shivered, still burdened with that feeling of impending doom.

* * *

That night Dorrie woke in the early hours of darkness. She was a light sleeper and easily disturbed by the muted chime of *more-pork* calls, the heart-chilling wail of distant cats fighting, by the watery tinkle of Grandmaire's bell and Dora's urgent whispers as she tended her, but most often by Jon's coughing as he returned from evening visits to his Gentlemen's Club.

This time the noise was a harsh, wavering cry that tipped Dorrie from her drowsy cuddle of sleep. She opened her eyes to find that the room was glowing with vivid light and that the square of sky visible through her high window was rippled with a sheet of flaming reds and oranges brighter than any sunset.

The stables! she thought as the cry sounded again. Standing up on her bed, she craned her neck in an effort to see the stable roof.

"Gracious, pet, you'll catch a chill." Dora came hurrying in carrying a candle, though the room was bright as morning. She was wearing a camelhair robe and her hair was scraped back into a long "Chinaman" pigtail. "No, it's not the stables," she said. "Your Uncle Jon thinks that it's a—"

She broke off as a low grumbling thunder came bumping across the land towards them, engulfing the house with a shudder that made the windows clatter and the water jug and slop bowl slither on the dresser.

"An earthquake!" said Dorrie. "But what's that screaming noise?"

"It's Grandmaire," said Dora, who was badly frightened herself. She detested earthquakes and Jon's theory about a volcano lighting up the sky made this one doubly frightening. "Here, drink this," she said, pouring out a thimble-sized cup of dark liquid. "It's laudanum to make you sleep. One quick gulp and there's a pear drop to take the taste away."

Dorrie gagged and rubbed her watering eyes. "Is she really dying now? All this light is like that picture in the dining room Bible where Moses is dying and the angels come down on those light rays to take him straight up to heaven.''

"Perhaps," said Dora, rubbing her aching neck. Her shoulders slumped with exhaustion. As the sleeping draught took effect Dorrie's face melted into an innocent, babyish expression and Dora stared at her wistfully. If only *she* could lie down and sleep. If only Grandmaire would go to sleep, too.

A slow rumble crept across the land again and Dora blocked a sob of panic. She bent to place the water jug and slop bowl safely on the floor as Grandmaire's harsh screams called her back to her duty.

I'll try with the laudanum again, she resolved. If only Jon were here to help prevent her dashing the bottle and cup away. Sister Amy was no help at all. Where was Jon? He was taking forever to fetch the doctor—he'd had to go alone, which was another cause for worry. The Maori groom was cowering behind his bolted door refusing to come out. Not that Dora could blame him really. The fiery sky and ominous noise were terrifying.

Another hoarse cry reached out to her like a plea, and despite her fatigue Dora's heart swelled with pity for the old woman.

This is obscene, thought Dora. What a degrading way to depart this world and what a shameful way to enter the next.

In the dim corridor Dora set the candle down on a table and paused to wipe away her tears. The Yardleys would be gathering soon, and above all they must not see her weakness.

I look like a little nun myself, thought Dorrie, as she regarded herself in the hall mirror, studying with distaste her black bonnet and black-dyed dress that had been lengthened with a pleated hem of crepe.

Dora's mother, Miss Abby, shook the rain from her umbrella as she pushed her way into the hall through the

milling crowd of mourners, most of them strangers to
her. She was an obese, wheezing woman with a faint
odor of sweat about her and a matching expression of distaste on her doughy face. Glancing about impatiently, she
saw little Dorrie apparently admiring herself in the mirror
and immediately forged her way towards the child.

"Have you said good-bye to Grandmaire yet?" she
demanded.

Dorrie glanced up in fright and shook her head dumbly.
Before she could ask what her grandmother meant, her
wrist was shackled in Miss Abby's grip and she was being
hustled down to the east wing corridor under the rows of
somber crepe swags, past buckets of dripping umbrellas.

This wing of the house had been closed after Ellen had
run away with the children and Grandmaire no longer entertained. Here were the long-unused formal parlors, the
ballroom and grand dining room, all rich with antiques
and lined with velvet, silver, and expensive porcelain.
The coffin had been placed in the blue parlor, a freezing
room where knots of people shadowed the dim corners
and black gloves held handkerchiefs to bent faces.

For the first time the extent of people's grief impressed
itself on Dorrie's mind. *Grandmaire must have been a
very important lady,* she realized.

The room smelled of camphor and wet wool. Rain on
the roof muffled the sound of soft weeping. Grandmaire
looked tiny in the polished coffin surrounded by lace and
wax flowers, like a small china doll put away in a drawer.

"She was your benefactress," said Miss Abby. "You
owe her respect and grief." When the girl gaped up at her
blankly she said, "Don't you feel sorry that she's dead?"

Miss Abby was crying; it was an intimidating sight.
Dorrie sought to comfort her. "Grandmaire was very
old," she ventured.

"All the more reason we should grieve for her. Now
go on. Give her a kiss and say good-bye properly."

Dorrie was petrified. She glanced at Miss Abby, afraid
to refuse yet unable to comply. Sensing her reluctance,

Miss Abby scooped her up under one arm and with her free hand shoved the back of her bonnet, forcing her face down towards the dead visage. Dorrie grabbed at the edge of the coffin but the pressure was relentless and her mouth rubbed against Grandmaire's forehead. The skin was cold and faintly furry, scented with dusting powder. It was a common beauty aid—Grandmaire's own brand— but to the end of her life Dorrie would not be able to smell that particular blend of scraped French chalk and cologne without a rush of nausea.

"It's disrespectful not to mourn," Miss Abby instructed her. Her own eyes were floating in swamps of grief as she regarded the pinched white face accusingly.

Bile rushed suddenly up Dorrie's throat. Pulling free from her grandmother's grip, she dashed from the room and rushed out onto the verandah where she huddled over the low balustrade, retching her heart out.

"There, now, you mustn't take this so hard, dear," soothed a gentle voice behind her, and Dorrie jerked around to find herself staring into the tranquil face of May Teipa-Bennington. A handkerchief was extended towards her as May said, "You must have loved Grandmaire very much to be so affected by her death. Here, wipe your face, dear, and you'll feel better soon."

Dorrie could smell May's cologne on the handkerchief. Her senses swam and she shook her head. "Please . . . ." was all she managed to gasp before she turned, retching helplessly again.

Dorrie sat at the rain-smeared window of the funeral train and stared up towards the marble mausoleum that had been waiting for years now to receive Grandmaire's body. White as lilies the fluted columns looked atop the drab, fern-smothered hillside.

Six Maori chiefs carried the coffin, which was closed now and blanketed by the feather cloak from the morning room wall. The chiefs wore feather cloaks, too, over their formal suits. They hefted the coffin up the steep path between black gardens of flowering umbrellas.

Mrs. Patene and the girls waved palm fronds as their voices swelled the Maori lament. Albert neither sang nor waved. Rain dripped on the shoulders of his cut-down suit as he stood at attention, a little soldier at his mother's side.

Now the Yardleys moved into view, tall, stooped Captain Stephen Yardley and his sweet-looking wife Juliette, their daughter May Teipa-Bennington and her husband, the darkly handsome man who had been with her at the beach. Idly Dorrie wondered who the other, younger man had been, the one with the merry brown eyes. There was no sign of him today.

May looked up at the carriage window and smiled. It was such an open, friendly gesture that Dorrie found herself responding. May looked pleased. Placing gloved fingertips to her lips, she blew Dorrie a kiss.

Dora had been crying quietly, dabbing her eyes with a sodden handkerchief. She glanced up and out the window at the very moment May made the light-hearted intimate gesture and was instantly angry.

"Come away from the window, Dorrie," she hissed. "There are some not-very-nice people out there."

Dorrie did not need to ask who she meant. She settled on the other side of Dora and stayed there chafing with boredom as she reflected on the paradoxes of life. Why was it that people she was supposed to love, like Miss Abby and Grandmaire, were so difficult to like, yet others she was supposed to hate seemed so kind and friendly?

Four

It had been a long, trying day. Ever since the four hundred people had disgorged from the ballroom after the hearing of Grandmaire's will a state of weary tension had existed at Fintona. The Maori servants had departed to celebrate, Jon had locked himself in his room and was refusing to answer Dora's knocks, and Dora had repaired to the morning room with Dorrie to take stock of a bleak situation.

As Dora predicted, the bulk of the estate had been divided between Captain Stephen Yardley and Grandmaire's adored great-grandson Rupert. That she had remembered everybody who had ever been kind to her came as a surprise to the city and most were delighted with their unexpected bequests of twenty or fifty pounds, but Dora and Jon had been treated stingily with only a thousand pounds apiece, not enough to sustain them for long. Both would be forced to find work.

Dorrie only dimly understood the reason for her aunt's distress. So much grief had washed around her in these past few weeks that she felt like a little island buffeted by waves. Grandmaire could have saved Misty but she didn't, so it was impossible to be sorry that she was dead, and as for the Patenes, Dorrie had never returned to their home after she learned that Misty was to be drowned. She wanted nothing more to do with Misty's murderers.

Now she sat at the table with a pencil and an old calendar, drawing pictures on the back. "Draw me a kitty-cat," Dora had said, but kitty-cats reminded her of poor Misty so she was sketching a horse and pony-trap instead while Dora pored over a row of figures in a notebook.

Suddenly her aunt stood up and walked to the window. It was almost dusk and a full moon hung low in the sky over the gulf islands, like a white bucket spilling milk over the water. The dainty gazebo at the edge of Fintona's lawn was picked out in silhouette and Jon was there heaping black cloth of some kind into a mound.

"What on earth?" said Dora.

He disappeared and a couple of minutes later came staggering back across the lawn bent double under an enormous billowing bundle.

"That's Grandmaire's bedding!" said Dora, going out to investigate. From the doorway Dorrie could see the glint of a knife as Jon slashed at the mattress. "You're drunk!" came Dora's shocked voice, then she said loudly, "You won't find money in there. Turei unpicks the cover every three months and teases out the entire horsehair filling."

Dorrie sidled out onto the verandah as Jon said, "She's *got* to have a secret hoard somewhere. That five hundred pounds—she was able to put her hands on it right away." He heaved the mattress onto the heap of black draperies and his voice was slurred but excited. "I'm going to find it, Dora, if it means pulling the old vulture's room to bits, and I've got to do it now. The Yardleys will be here in the morning and I'm damned if I'll leave that cache for those bastards to find."

"Your language, Jon!"

He laughed, a mad, exulted sound.

From where she stood in the shadows Dorrie watched him make journey after laden journey, flinging down drawers and boxes and armloads of clothes onto the lawn then ripping and tearing at them before heaping the shreds and broken boards onto the pile. Though Rupert was Jon's son his belongings met a similar fate, the toys disemboweled, his clothes scattered and even the photographs dashed into splinters of glass.

Out came a miniature trunkful of jewelry which he rummaged through, then dashed at Dora's feet so that it splashed around her like shale. "She left you that, so take it. Mind you, you can't give jet away now, but there might be something there worth salvaging."

"Please, Jon, please stop this—" but he was away again to fetch a load of drawers, which he added roughly to the heap. Then out came great armloads of the black wall lining as the stripping of the room neared completion.

"Fetch me a lamp," he ordered as he disappeared for his final trip.

Dora hurried to the verandah. Dorrie noticed that she carried something pressed into the folds of her skirt. Following her inside, Dorrie saw that it was the greenstone pendant in the shape of a kneeling woman. Dora placed it on the table and reached up to unhook the lantern.

"Jon smashed the other greenstone things but this fell onto the grass and I rescued it when he wasn't looking," Dora explained. "Wrap it up carefully, would you, pet, and hide it somewhere. It belongs to your old Uncle Samuel—you know, that funny old man whose whiskers tickle when he kisses you. Grandmaire left him all the greenstone and Maori things, so we can't have Jon destroying those, can we?" She smiled into Dorrie's frightened face. "Don't be afraid of him, pet. I know you've not seen him like this before. Jon never touches drink, never! But . . . oh, my goodness, what's he doing now?"

Panting with strain, Jon was dragging the rocking horse along the gravel path. He pushed Dora away when she ran, protesting that surely the rocking horse could be saved for Dorrie. "Nothing!" he insisted as he heaved and pushed it up onto the heap.

"Now!" cried Jon. He snatched the lantern from his sister and dashed it to the flagstone floor where it exploded in a whoosh of burning oil. Then he stood back, coughing, as the bright cloak of fire wrapped itself swiftly right around the pyre.

Dorrie gasped as she hung over the balustrade. The

rocking horse was cradled in the flames. It was a strong and greedy fire, devouring ravenously and spitting out sparks with sharp cracking noises louder than the Patenes' *kuri*s crunching up bones, and it stank of half-digested cloth and breathed out foul clouds of black curdled smoke.

With an ache of sadness Dorrie watched the horse burn. One rocker was a glowing red stump, his hide was charring and peeling away from the metal body, and his tail fizzed with a white flame like fireworks. Still, though he sagged on the collapsing fire there was something proud and noble in the way he held his head above the flames.

"Poor fellow," whispered Dorrie.

Suddenly there was a terrific bang and a second later a missile thudded into the verandah steps close to where Dorrie stood.

"Bloody hell!" shouted Jon. "Someone tried to shoot me."

"Something flew out of the fire." Hitching her skirts clear of the damp grass, Dora skimmed across the lawn and picked up a round plug some three inches in diameter. From its top tufted the remains of a plume of pale horsehair now burned down and ragged.

"Hey on there!" said Jon. "There's money there—a roll of notes!" Using a piece of broken picture frame he flicked it onto the path and unfurled it, smoothing the banknotes between his fingers. "These are five-pound notes! Where in the blazes did they come from?"

"From inside the horse. Look," and she pointed out the hole that the plug had filled. "The rocking horse is hollow, and—"

"Bloody hell. No wonder the old vulture had apoplexy when Dorrie played with the horse. Look, there's more in there, too. Fancy that! When the air inside heated up it expanded and *boom!*" He shook his fists at the sky. "I hope you can see this, Mrs. Yardley Peridot wherever you are. I beat you this time!"

"Don't touch it, you'll burn yourself," warned Dora, so Jon wrapped one of Grandmaire's jackets around his hand and pulled the smoking carcass onto the lawn. He was slicked with sweat and jumpy with excitement. The horse bucked over, suddenly spilling more rolls of money as compact as droppings.

"You crafty old thing!" shouted Jon. "Leading me by the nose all these years, promising me a fortune in your will, then giving me bloody nothing. Well, *I've beaten you!*" Shoveling the rescued notes into Dora's hands, he said, "Take these inside, will you, and bring me out a poker or a toasting fork—something to winkle out the rest—and a bag or something to put it in. We have to hurry before—"

"Hush!" hissed Dora abruptly. She thrust the handfuls of money inside her jacket and pulled the edges tightly around her as she jerked her head towards the gate in the hedge. "Look over there. Behind you."

At the far side of the lawn stood Mrs. Patene and Albert. He carried a wooden box and she, a kerosene lamp, which was now superfluous for the fire was stabbing through the shingles on the gazebo roof and washing the garden with gilt light.

"What a time to come calling," muttered Jon.

Mrs. Patene took a few steps, then stopped when she read the clearly unwelcoming faces. "We saw the fire, eh," she explained. "And since we had to come anyway to bring Miss Bennington her little cat . . . How sad to see this burn, eh. I remember when Matua had this pretty little shed built. She told me it had a special name. A gazelle, is that so?"

"A gazebo."

"Thank you," she said with such dignity that Dora wished she had held her tongue. "It was built for the celebration of your mother's wedding. Flowers were tied all around and ribbons, eh, and a band played music inside there. We all danced on the lawn. Ah, what memories this little shed brings back."

Dora felt terrible. All her life she had respected and admired Mrs. Patene, and now it seemed too awful that she, of all people, should be witness to this vandalism of Grandmaire's property. Jon had wandered away inside, to fetch the poker no doubt, and she felt helpless as she groped for an explanation of this scene of destruction.

"It was an accident," she began. "The lamp broke . . ." Then with relief she seized on the other reason for the Patenes' visit. "Dorrie!" she called. "Come here quickly, would you, pet? Mrs. Patene and Albert have brought you a present."

Misty! Dorrie sat at the table too excited to eat as Misty curled in a soft purring ball in her lap. All this time Dorrie had believed him to be drowned and all the while he was a special secret between Auntie Dora and the Patenes.

"I'd have seen him there if only I'd gone home with Moana like you asked me to. But all the time I was so sad because—" She stopped her musings as Dora laid warning fingers on her arm, then glanced in quick fright at Uncle Jon, and resumed dreamily stroking Misty's velvety fur. *Darling Misty,* she thought, her heart swelling with joy.

Jon was sitting at the far end of the table, morosely slurping soup and coughing dryly between mouthfuls of bread. His face was stained red from the heat and his clothes were sprinkled with ash and cinder burns. The elation had faded; inside the horse they had found a total of nine hundred and sixty pounds, far less than the fortune he had hoped for. The notes were spread on the table where he had counted them. In the hour or so since, he had not once glanced at them.

When Dora got up to refresh the teapot she glanced out of the kitchen window. In the darkness the fire glowed like an orange eye surrounded by spiky iron lashes. She fretted, "What shall we tell the Yardleys tomorrow?"

"Do shut up about the fire," snapped Jon. "This isn't

the first time there's been a bonfire on that cliff. Remember what Grandmaire did when Ellen took the children away? She had all of Ellen's and Roseanne's things tossed out into the garden and—'' He broke off, coughing, then continued in spasms. ''All their things were destroyed—I thought at the time—she'd like to—torch me, too, and listening to the will today I know I was right.''

''Oh, Jon.'' She was instantly contrite, sorry she had railed at him earlier. ''What are you going to do? You're not going to take up Captain Yardley's offer that you continue running the Peridot Emporiums, are you?''

Jon shook his head. His eyes were smoke reddened and he looked unutterably weary.

''Good,'' said Dora briskly. ''We may need the money but there are some principles that cannot be sacrificed.''

''I have to go away.''

''What?'' She paused with the teacup to her lips, astounded.

''You heard what the Captain said. He's ordering a full audit of all the Emporium books. I can't possibly stay here now. I'll go abroad. England, America . . .''

Cup rattled against saucer. Dora was too shocked to comment. Today she had learned that all these years Jon had been drawing a salary five times larger than hers, yet while she managed to save some of hers he had always cried poor and often tried to borrow from her. Now it seemed he was an embezzler as well. She leaned back in her chair. ''Why, Jon? Why did you need to do it?''

''For heaven's sakes, Dora, don't look at me like that. It was only trifling amounts—a few hundred now and again—and only when the slate at the club ran too high.''

''Gambling. Of course,'' said Dora. ''Pity help us all.''

Dorrie took no notice of the quarrel. Her uncle and aunt often disagreed, so arguments were too commonplace to be interesting; besides, all her attention was ab-

sorbed by the precious purring bundle she held in her lap.
With one fingertip she traced the sprays of whiskers
fanning out from either side of his nose. He arched his
neck so that she could stroke the underside of his chin and
his purrs vibrated through her fingers. It tickled; she giggled in delight. "Darling Misty," she whispered.

She was playing with him in the garden when Captain
Yardley's carriage arrived. He had been stalking a long
frond of flax when the crunch of iron wheels on the driveway and the whinny of horses sent him scampering for
the shrubbery, his ears flattened and his tail flung sideways as he fled. Dorrie called to him but it was futile.
She sat on her haunches blinking in the sun as Captain
Yardley and his daughter May walked along the path towards her.

"Dorinda!" said May, pausing as Misty emerged
from his hiding place and arched his back as he
smooched around her hem. She stooped to pick him up
and scratched his tummy with her kid-gloved hands.
"She's a darling, isn't she? What's her name?"

"*His* name's Misty. I couldn't have him before because Grandmaire hates animals. You don't, do you?"

"I adore them," said May, nuzzling Misty, who was
enjoying the attention so much that Dorrie began to feel
jealous. "We have cats and puppies, ponies, rabbits, and
even an Australian opossum. Would you like to come out
one day and—"

"Dorrie!" shouted Dora from the verandah.

She glanced up, guiltily. The anger in Dora's voice
was unmistakable and Dorrie knew why she was so
cross.

May placed Misty in Dorrie's arms. Her smile was
tinged with pity as she drifted after her father.

Dora glared at them both defiantly. "I suppose you've
come to dismantle this very house over our heads," she
accused.

Captain Yardley sighed. In all his dealings with Dora

he had never found a way to melt the icy dislike she wore so determinedly. He said, "I've come to offer you a home with us, if you'll accept it."

"Will you, Dora?" added May eagerly. "Oh, please say yes. We've such a lot of room and I'm sure that with goodwill on both sides—"

"You threw us out before," sniffed Dora. She glanced over to where Dorrie still squatted in the path, the kitten squirming in her arms. She had obviously heard the invitation and her face was alight with hope. Dora's throat tightened with a rush of fresh anger. "How dare you come here talking of goodwill?" she said. "And how dare you offer us charity as if we were poor relations?"

Captain Yardley was too disgusted to reply but May said gently, "We're offering you a *home*. Somewhere comfortable for you and young Dorinda."

"Grandmaire has left us the gatehouse and that will do us perfectly well."

"But it's so—" May broke off when the Captain touched her sleeve, though she had already realized that Dora was intractable in her attitude. With an expression of pained regret she followed her father into the house.

Dora was still fuming over the imagined insults two weeks later when old Uncle Samuel came to visit. Samuel Bennington was a rough old widower with no table manners and very little tact, but most people excused him his failings because he spent his life in logging camps far in the bush and could not be expected to bother about details like keeping his mouth closed when he ate.

He was scarred and wrinkled, toothless as a battered tomcat and he smelled like the stables as he sat in front of the gatehouse coal range with his cracked old boots steaming on the hearth. Dorrie gaped at him, fascinated as he stuffed his pipe with tobacco shreds and sucked noisily on the stem.

"Got this place lookin' right cozy," he observed, staring around the cramped, bleak room. "I wondered how you'd manage alone since Jon rushed off so quickly, but I can see you two will be as happy as pigs in a swamp.''

"Thank you," said Dora doubtfully, then with indignation sharpening her voice she told him how the Yardleys had had the ''impudence'' to invite her back there after the way they'd pitched her out years ago.

"That was only a misunderstanding, lass," said Samuel in reasonable tones. "Besides, Grandmaire needed you at the time. And as for this business, I think May's only worried about young Dorrie having proper care.''

''What!''

Samuel realized immediately that once again he had opened his mouth and put his foot right in it. Dora pounced on the comment and did not let up until she had extracted the information that May had fretted about those injuries of Dorrie's and had suspected that Dora may have been the one who had beaten her.

"It were a reasonable assumption," pleaded Samuel.

"Reasonable!" choked Dora. "She wants to take Dorrie away from me, just like Mama did." She began to pour the tea. The flow of liquid wavered; Dora's whole body was shaking with indignation so that she could not hold the pot steady. "How *dare* she think I'd hurt Dorrie like that! Well, Uncle Samuel, you can tell her from me that the only thing I ever hit Dorrie with is my hand, so if I have to hurt her, I hurt myself just as much. Will you tell her that?''

"Of course, lass, of course.''

The brew was very weak; now that she had to conserve every penny, Dora could not afford to feed herself and Dorrie anything but the barest rations.

Samuel looked into his cup and at the plate of bread thin-spread with dripping that was offered with it. He tried to joke. "Irish tea, eh? Only three leaves! Heh, heh.''

Dora bridled. "Mama can afford to make you stronger tea if that's what you're wanting," she snapped. *"And* she'd be glad of your company, too. She'll be getting no more of mine, I can tell you.''

"Fighting with her, too, are you, lass?" Samuel dunked his bread into the tea and sucked at it with relish while Dorrie watched agape. She would be cuffed if she dared do that.

Dora sighed. As she subsided into her chair all the ginger seemed to leave her and she said, "I suppose Mama's right. She blames me for the fact that she was cut out of Grandmaire's will.''

"Five hundred pounds isn't being cut out," retorted Samuel. "I'd say it was more than she deserved. And she managed to get a bit more, too." He laughed, showing bare pink gums. "I inherited all the Maori things from Fintona, so Abby came to me and asked for a little keepsake of our father's. 'Course I agreed and she settled on a greenstone-tipped spear and a set of paintings of Maori chiefs. Surprised me no end—I never knew she liked Maori art. Next day I found out she'd got eight hundred guineas for the spear and the paintings fetched five hundred more. That's our Abby. Always was hopelessly sentimental when it came to money. I was a little irate about it, actually. That stuff all belongs to the museum by rights. It was collected by our father and that's what he'd have wanted done with it.''

"That reminds me," said Dora. "Put that cat down, pet, and fetch the greenstone we rescued, will you?"

Dorrie placed the silk-wrapped bundle in front of the old man and watched him open it. His eyes glistened.

"Awa Waiata," he whispered reverently. "I thought this was lost long ago.''

Dorrie fed Misty a scrap of bread and dripping under cover of the hand-crocheted tablecloth. "Grandmaire had it in her room.''

"That explains it. I always assumed it were stolen." He held it up in front of Dorrie's eyes. "Look at it, lass. This thing here is worth more money that you'll ever see in one heap. Unless one day you get to feast your eyes on the crown jewels.''

"You're exaggerating," said Dora.

"Maybe a little. But it's a very valuable piece. Our Abby would have snapped it up if she'd seen it.''

"Jon was going to break it," she told him. "I rescued it because it belongs to you.''

Dorrie was gazing at the pendant with awe. She had never really examined it before, but now that Uncle Samuel was holding it up so that it glowed in the light the richness of detail was revealed. The graceful young woman was posed like a mermaid with legs tucked up underneath her; long hair flowed over her shoulders and everything about her was meticulously depicted, from the texture of her feathered hair decoration to the curling moko or tattoo whorls below her lower lip. She was so realistic that the rolled flax threads of her *piu-piu* skirt looked about to sway when she moved.

Samuel smiled at Dorrie's enraptured face. "Her name is *Awa Waiata* and that means *Riversong,*" he told her. "There's a legend about her, too. The Maoris who made her called her Riversong in memory of the mountain stream where the chunk of raw greenstone was found. There's even a little poem about it.'' He cleared his throat and quoted:

> In the stillness of eternity
> I hear the river song.
> The spirit of my ancestors
> Sings a lament for me.

"Oh!" exclaimed Dorrie in delight, clasping her hands up under her chin. "How beautiful that is!"

Dora was moved but hurried to hide it with a brusque comment. "I didn't realize you were so poetical.''

"I'm lots of things if the occasion demands," he told her. "And before I change my mind, I'm giving this to you, lass. The museum's got all the other stuff, and though this is the pick of my father's collection I think you should sell it and put the money to good use—towards Dorrie's education, for instance.''

Dora bit her lip. Her narrow eyes moistened. "I can't take that. *I* couldn't sell it—no more than you could—and it's too valuable a piece to leave lying about here. Anyone could walk off with it.''

"I want to help you, lass, and there's no other way. You've got a struggle ahead of you.''

Dora shook her head. "Give it to the museum. It belongs there like you said. And don't worry about us. We'll manage.''

"We're poor, Uncle Samuel, but we don't mind,'' chirped Dorrie. "Auntie Dora and Misty and me, we're all happy together.''

But Dora walked him out to the roadway when he left. He took both her hands in his and stared shrewdly into her face. "Just how *do* you propose to manage?'' he asked.

She shrugged. The worry showed in strain on her face but she replied as frankly as she could. "We've all Fintona's hens, and there's no rent to pay. The Patene girls will sell us cheap fish and shellfish, I'm hiring young Emere to do the washing, and Albert has promised to come and do the heavy work in the vegetable garden—there's an extensive garden behind the stables. We'll have extra eggs and produce to sell and I'll take in sewing . . .''

"Sell the pendant. Go on, take it.''

"No, I couldn't.'' She tucked the silken bundle back into his pack. "I'm grateful to you, truly I am, and if I knew it would be safe here I'd grab it with both hands. But I could never sell something as lovely as that.''

He flashed her his toothless grin. "Amazing, truly amazing. I don't think you've got a single drop of your mother's blood in you. I thought you'd pounce on this, you know.''

Dora laughed. She had a hollow, booming laugh that

rolled along the ground like a rattle of stones. "You've cheered me up no end," she said.

Dorrie was hunched at the table, weeping quietly as she carefully drew a picture of a beautiful Maori girl with feathers in her hair. Dora looked over her shoulder, astounded that such a young child could have already developed such an eye for design. The likeness was remarkable.

Dora tipped up Dorrie's chin. Seeing the tears, she understood at once. "We can go and visit *Riversong* whenever you want to see her," she said. "She'll be ours on special occasions. All right?"

"All right," agreed Dorrie.

But already Dora was regretting her rash impulse. After supper she stood at the window and stared across the drive at the boarded-up doors and windows of Fintona. Nobody knew when Ellen and the children might return, but Dora hoped it would be soon. Ellen would give her work, feed her and Dorrie, and make sure they wanted for nothing. When Ellen returned they would be secure again.

Dorrie's hand crept into hers. "Why did Uncle Jon go away?"

Dora shrugged. She could not blame Jon. He was weak, but it was a man's weakness. She said, "Grandmaire should have given the Peridot Emporiums to him and Rupert. Instead she gave them to Rupert and Captain Yardley."

"But that's not fair."

"Grandmaire wasn't known for her evenhandedness."

Dorrie shivered. It was cold even this short distance away from the stove; though the gate house was a tiny two rooms it was draughty and damp. "I thought that when Grandmaire died you and Uncle Jon and I would all live in Fintona, and we could open up those grand living rooms and take our meals at that beautiful polished table under the crystal chandelier, and that we'd never, never *never* have to eat porridge again!"

With a smile Dora said, "I'm afraid that we will have to eat our way through a great many more porridge meals, pet. Porridge is nourishing, filling, and it's cheap. Never mind, perhaps Ellen and the children will come home soon. All our problems will be over then."

PART TWO

DORA

1886-1896

Five

Samuel was not exaggerating when he warned that Dora had a struggle ahead of her. New Zealand in the 1880s was in the grip of a depression that scoured the land, impoverished the Colony and decimated the population as tens of thousands fled overseas seeking better conditions. In Auckland poverty raged. Whole streets of houses stood empty, knots of jobless men clogged the corners downtown, and ragged women and children clutching battered containers scavenged the rubbish dumps or hovered near the soup kitchen while they waited sullenly for the shutters to go up.

Dorrie was used to the sight of the poor; they seemed a separate tribe of people, like the Maoris, but to Dora they were a constant reminder of what could happen to them if ever they slipped from their places in the ranks of the genteel impoverished.

For them both, this life meant hard work for very little money. Dora had managed to secure a home job sewing racing silks. At first she had been delighted but soon realized that the patterns were so complicated and the material so difficult to sew that by the time each set was finished she had been working for only one or two pence an hour, and worse still, she found after a time that the close work was taking a serious toll on her eyesight.

For Dorrie, however, this life seemed a game. She didn't mind the chores—emptying the chamber pots, sweeping the path, scrubbing carrots or drying dishes—it was all fun to her, all until the day she turned seven. Then Dora presented her with a new print polonaise-style dress, secondhand copper-toed boots, pinned a black

75

mourning sash around her (for Grandmaire), then thrust into her hand two slices of bread with dripping tied in a cloth with the curt instruction that she was to be good and mind everything the Dominie said. With that Dorrie was bundled off to school.

She loathed it. Each day seemed longer than the one before. It might have been better if she had joined in with the playground games at lunchtime, but because in the evenings she always helped Dora, Dorrie spent her school breaks huddled in the shelter-shed painstakingly learning spelling words and scribing lines of copperplate script that had been set for homework. She was no scholar. Though the Dominie was a kindly man who liked the timid little girl and always spoke encouragingly to her, Dorrie found every lesson grinding labor. She looked forward only to three o'clock when delicious relief was granted by the head monitor who stalked the corridor dashing a bronze hand-bell in a flourish from shoulder to knee.

"Home time!" he'd cry, parodying the towncriers who advertised variety shows outside the Queen Street theaters. "Three o'clock and it's home time!"

And home she would dash along the dusty road so fast that the ferns and gorse on the verges whizzed past in a gold-streaked blur of brown. When she plumped herself down on the chair by the window she would be panting emphatically, her black bonnet askew, her cheeks scarlet and eyes as shiny as new-minted shillings. Misty would leap purring into her lap. Smiling, Dora would fold the arms of the thick-lensed spectacles she had taken to wearing.

"Thank you, Auntie," Dorrie would say as she accepted a glass of water with a slice of lemon floating in it to take away the musty "tank-stand" taste. "Yes, I had a lovely day," she'd lie before asking what sewing there was to be done today.

Once when Uncle Samuel was there he happened to witness this little scene and he marveled at how the dry spinster and the orphaned child seemed to blossom in each other's company. He admired the racing club monograms Dorrie was embroidering, and when she had gone out to feed the hens he said, "She's like a ray of sunshine, isn't she?"

"She's a good girl," replied practical Dora.

"Has she any friends? She doesn't ever have anything to say about her classmates."

"I should hope not! Dirty, grubby lot they are. Sores on their feet and lice in their hair, too, I wouldn't be surprised. I've told Dorrie she's to have nothing to do with any of them."

Samuel was faintly shocked. "She should have friends," he ventured, and when Dora tightened her thin lips he added, "Why don't you take up that offer I made you two years ago? Sell *Riversong* and use the money to send Dorrie to a first-class girls' academy. One of those posh places."

Dora shook her head. "We'll manage," she told him.

Loneliness was a condition Dorrie had known all her life so it never occurred to her to complain about it. Sometimes, on the endless Sunday afternoons after chapel when both work and play were forbidden and Dora habitually took a nap, Dorrie would wander around the overgrown grounds of Fintona, gazing at the broken guttering and the vine-choked gingerbread trim on the verandah. Always she paused outside her old room with the single, high window. She shivered to picture it now, stripped and dim, inhabited only by spiders and mice. And across the neglected lawn she sometimes searched for the pitted flagstone square that was all that remained of the dainty gazebo. After the fire the wrought iron had been ripped out like rotten teeth and all of the charred rubbish had been pushed down the bank behind a screen of *toe-toe* bushes. Until the blackberry and columbine grew over it Rupert's horse was visible there, two blackened legs stretching out of the rubble and the top of a hollow-eyed skull. It saddened her to recall how magnificent he had once been.

"You'll experience that sadness many times," said Dora when Dorrie tried to explain it to her. "Most of our lives are filled with sorrow and regret."

Dorrie was silent, watching Dora stir a pot of soup at the stove. Then she said, "Do you regret keeping me?"

"What?"

"Miss Abby said that it's my fault we are poor. She said that Mrs. Ainley would have taken you as a lady's companion if it wasn't for me."

"Dorinda, that will do!" She rattled the ladle as she dished potato soup into two bowls. "How many times have I told you to take no notice of what Miss Abby says? She is old and sick and you must be polite when we visit her but do *not* believe what she says. Now, is that clear?"

"But—"

"Oh, hush, Dorinda, please. I have a terrible headache."

The sharp note in her voice frightened Dorrie as did the headache—Dora had so many lately—but the subject lay fresh on her mind for a long time.

"I'll make it up to her," she vowed aloud a few evenings later as she sat hunched on Fintona's sagging verandah and watched the Brahma Pootra fowls scratching in the long grass.

A hen paused to look at her, first with one eye, then the other. She was a pretty creature, blue toned, silvery and etched in darker gray with profusely feathered legs that flared like lacy pantaloons and a neat red comb divided lengthwise into thirds, perky as a Robin Hood cap.

"We *are* poor because of me," Dorrie told the hen. "And I *will* make it up to Auntie Dora one day. I'll earn lots of money or marry someone rich so we can have a fine house and a carriage painted white with gold trimmings with two white horses wearing gold harnesses to pull it. And we'll have real, proper food to eat. No more bread and soup and porridge day after day. *Especially* no more porridge!''

"Puk-puk-puk?" clucked the hen.

"Yes, I know you like porridge," Dorrie interrupted herself. "But I detest it. And she'll have beautiful gowns to wear, stylish ones with ruffles and ribbons and those swishing waterfall bustles, and real jewels, too, not that nasty old jet stuff of Grandmaire's that looks like bees' eyes . . .''

Losing interest, the hen walked away.

"I'll manage it, I will!" Dorrie called after her. "Just as soon as I'm grown up."

"When will that be?" she asked Dora that evening after she had washed and dried the supper dishes, rinsed the dishtowel and hung it out on the line.

Dora looked up tiredly from her sewing. "You'll grow up soon enough, pet, but don't go wishing your life away. Here, come and sit under the lamp and read me some poetry while I finish this off." As Dorrie settled herself her aunt glanced surreptitiously at her figure. No, she was as sturdy and flat chested as ever. There was no need to bring up the ugly, the indelicate and "tainted" subject of Eve's curse. Not yet, anyway, she decided thankfully.

Like most Victorian spinsters who had led sheltered lives, Dora knew absolutely nothing about human procreation and only those facts about menstruation that had been unavoidable. She planned to "instruct" Dorrie on her fourteenth birthday but in the meantime did not realize that she was already acquiring a sketchy education.

From observation of her classmates she had decided that the difference between boys and girls was no more significant than that between black and white hens or large and small dogs. Sometimes as she huddled over her slate in the shelter-shed she heard the girls shriek and giggle and gathered that the bravest of the boys had unbuttoned his bib-front overall to flash his little "willie." She also gathered that such wickedness was acceptable from boys because when they grew up they would be called upon to soldier for Queen and Empire, facing danger and death in far-flung dominions. These were facts of life, like the fact that babies were found under gooseberry bushes. Dorrie embraced that belief willingly; it was far more pleasant to picture a plump baby cradled on a bed of fragrant summer grass than to recall what Emere had told her as she stared at Orange Kitty's newborn kittens, all slimy and slicked with blood.

One Saturday afternoon when she was twelve and a half years old Dorrie was beset by a fearful itching in the very place her aunt had instructed her never to think about or to touch except when absolutely necessary. At first she tried to ignore it but as the afternoon wore on her torment increased.

It was raining outside and stiflingly hot inside because Dora was roasting the joint of mutton and baking a flour and egg pudding for Sunday's cold meals. Dorrie felt wretched. Twice she managed to slip away into the bedroom for a few seconds' scratching and blessed relief, but the rest of the time no matter what position she adopted in her chair beside the window her agony only worsened.

"What is the matter with you?" asked Dora. "You're wriggling and fidgeting—I wonder if you need a good dosing?"

"No—no, it's not that," she replied too quickly, for it had already occurred to her that she might be ill. Lately she had suffered itching in her armpits, too, and a tenderness in breasts that were beginning to swell and harden, but she shrank away from the thought of illness because that, inescapably, meant a gulping dose from Dora's blue bottle or—even worse—a purge from the purple one.

"Trouble with your school work, then?"

"Yes, that's it. Auntie, I can't get the hang of these problems." Flushing with guilt, she hurriedly read, "A, B and C went into partnership. A's capital was six hundred and thirty-four pounds, three shillings and ninepence for four years, two months and ten days. B put in

eight hundred and seventy-eight pounds two shillings and
a penny ha'penny for five years nine months and five
days, while C contributed two hundred—''

"Stop!" interrupted Dora. "You've lost me already."

"The problem tells you their gross profit and their expenses, and we have to work out how much profit each
partner receives. The book is full of problems like this."
She sighed. "I'd ask Albert to help me, but I only ever
see him these days when he comes by on his way to music lessons."

"You'd ask *Albert* to help you? Albert Patene?"

"He's very clever. Hasn't Mrs. Patene told you?"

"Many times, but I assumed that she was overpraising
him in that fond way she has."

Dorrie said, "He really is clever. The Dominie said he
solved every question in this book before he went on to
Grammar School. Nobody has ever done that before."

Dora tucked the steel arms of the spectacles over her
ears and scanned the page. No wonder the child was fidgeting! Chains and fathoms and bushels and acres indeed!
What were these schoolteachers thinking of, filling
young heads with this useless nonsense.

"Pop out and feed the fowls," she suggested. "A dash
of fresh air might blow away those cobwebs."

Holding an oiled calico cape over her head with one
hand and clutching a pail of boiled kitchen scraps in the
other, Dorrie pelted out into the downpour, skipping
around puddles and dodging the muddiest patches to
reach the shed behind the stables. Breathing in the odor
of wheat and dry sacks, she measured grain and mixed it
into the scraps with a wooden pestle, all the while hopping in discomfort from one foot to the other, her soggy
hem flapping about her ankles.

The fowls heard her pounding the mush and immediately set up an excited racket, clucking and crowing as
they dashed out into their muddy pen. Dorrie scraped the
mess of food into two shallow troughs and retreated as
the dozen hens and two cock birds jockeyed with

flapping squawks for the best positions. Shutting the gate behind her, she opened the hatches behind the nest boxes. Today there were ten eggs, warm and dusted with tiny curling feathers. Wiping them clean, she placed them on a tray in the egg safe, and as she fastened the door she noticed that the itch was renewing its attack on her, more scalding and insistent than before.

What is wrong with me? she fretted. Deciding to investigate this nuisance while she had the privacy in which to do so she hitched her skirts up around her hips and parted the open crotch of her cream muslin, frilly legged drawers.

To her horror she saw dark blood on the seam facings that passed between her legs and a smear of blood on the inside of one thigh. The discovery gave her such a shock that she dropped her skirts immediately thinking, *I've hurt myself somehow.*

After a moment's giddy panic a sensible attitude prevailed; if she was slightly injured then she would soon be better again, and in the meantime to ease the itching she could wring her handkerchief out in rainwater and press it carefully against the place to soothe the irritation.

At dinner she sat perfectly still and this seemed to help, too. When Dora shook out the dice and the tiny mother-of-pearl fish for a game of Royal Parcheesi Dorrie felt better still—the fun distracted her and by bedtime she was completely better.

Next morning the nasty little problem of the day before swamped her mind again with sickening suddenness when she rose to discover an ominous stickiness in the pit of her lap and dark, damp stains on the nightgown and on the bottom sheet. She now knew it could not be an injury because there was no pain but she was ashamed and terrified.

When Emere arrived first thing on Monday morning to do the washing and went out to the shed behind the stables to light the copper fire, she found Dorrie skulking there at the tub, furtively scrubbing something soapy against the ridged glass washboard.

"Hey, why ain't you at school?" She was a handsome young woman now with a solid, smoothly planed face with the placidness of a *kauri* carving and licorice-black hair that was plaited into a laurel wreath of braids around her head.

"I'm going in a minute," said Dorrie, unplugging the tub to run off the pink-tinged water. "Don't tell Auntie Dora, will you?"

"The Dominie will growl you if you're late," she said practically, then, leaning over the tub said, "Hooo-lee! You got the *pakeke,* the bleeding already, eh? Boy, you growing up fast."

"What? What do you mean?"

"*Pakeke.* Just a bleeding; every woman gets it. Hey, don't worry, eh? Don't you be *tumeke.* It's only the moon casting his spell on you. Every four weeks on the full moon the *pakeke* will come again to you."

Dorrie mutely allowed herself to be elbowed out of the way and Emere took over scouring the sheet. "Maori legend says that the moon, he is the husband of all the women in the world and when you grow up he brings you under his *makutu,* his magic."

"But why? I don't believe you." The moon was an exquisite thing, serene and remote, and if it *could* influence anything surely it would choose dreams or beautiful visions, not something as shameful, as sordid, as *this.*

"It's true." Emere pursed her thick lips, enjoying the gratifying experience of passing on her wisdom. "You shouldn't wash this *pakeke* away. It's a *tapu* thing, a holy thing, eh. A kind of a person, the start of a new life, and everything to do with life is *tapu* to the Maori. You must put rags on yourself and afterwards bury them in a secret place so when a real baby comes it will be strong and healthy."

"What on earth is going on out here?" Dora's bulky frame filled the doorway. She swung her gaze from

Emere's smug expression to Dorrie's frightened face. "What in the world is the matter with you?"

"I—I—" and Dorrie lapsed into tears.

"I suppose you were frightened," said Dora when she had fixed Dorrie up with a box of soft cloth strips from the depths of the wardrobe and curtly instructed her what to do with them. "But if you haven't got a stomachache, then that's a blessing." She recalled her own first time, when she had been doubled over in pain and terror. A Maori servant had helped her, too, old Tawa, Grandmaire's housekeeper. She'd told her the same fables about the moon and embryonic babies that had to be buried in the dead of night.

"That's all nonsense," she assured her niece. "What you're suffering is Eve's curse, given by God to punish Eve for her wickedness. It's our shame, pet. We endure it without complaint and try not to think of it at all."

Dorrie did try to put it out of her mind, but Emere's words haunted her. Every time she burned one of the used cloths she was troubled by the feeling that she was breaking some mysterious faith, a conviction that was to last throughout her life.

But from all the distress and confusion one positive thing emerged. Dora declared that Dorrie was "grown up" now and need no longer attend school. She was to stay at home and help with the sewing.

Six

The next three years were the bleakest the two in the gatehouse had ever known. Well-paid work was impossible to come by so they filled their long hours laboring over poorly paid sewing jobs. "Sweating," Uncle Samuel called it, though he had to admit both Dora and Dorrie looked fit and healthy.

"We eat nothing but vegetables and an occasional egg," Dora told him, "And no, thank you, my answer is the same. I couldn't be responsible for selling that beautiful piece of greenstone, no matter what the price."

"I agree with Auntie Dora," Dorrie chimed in. "We often go to visit her at the museum—sometimes to cheer ourselves up when we've been to see poor Miss Abby at the hospital." She drew a tremulous breath, and with eyes glowing, recited,

> In the stillness of eternity
> I hear the river song.
> The spirit of my ancestors
> Sings a lament for me.

"Well done, lass," said Samuel, touched. Later he watched from the doorway as she chopped kindling and observed, "She's growing into a real beauty, isn't she?"

"I'll thank you not to tell her so," retorted Dora. "You'll only turn her head. She's a sensible girl and that's all that matters."

"She's even more beautiful than your mother was as a child, and I can tell you, lass, she was one of the loveliest young women that's ever been seen in this town." His voice was sad and he bent to pick up Misty, who was purring round his legs. Misty had grown into a large sleek cat, thriving on the plentiful diet of mice that inhabited the still-empty mansion next door. Samuel scratched him under the chin but his thoughts were with his once-beautiful sister who was now very close to death. "I never thought I was in the least fond of Abby, but it's strange how close the bonds are when a strain like this tightens them. I realize that all this time I really have loved the poor foolish woman."

"Hmph," said Dora, who suffered fresh agonies herself on each visit to her mother's bedside, but would rather die herself than admit to a trace of emotion. To change the subject she said, "I don't hold with the 'blood's thicker than water' theory. Never did. Nothing, but nothing, could endear me to the Yardleys, for instance, especially May. Do you know that she is *still* trying to interfere with the way I raise Dorrie? She had the impudence to offer to pay for her to go to the Bradford sisters' school. Said she thought that twelve was too young for Dorrie to cease her education. What nerve that woman has! I told her to look after her own passel of brats. The way she keeps adding another every year you'd think she had enough to do managing her own business, wouldn't you?"

"May means well," said Samuel blandly. He often stayed at the Yardleys' estate farther along the coast. "She's always been concerned for Dorrie's welfare." Seeing Dora's expression, he added hastily, "Everybody likes Dorrie."

"And she belongs to me," said Dora, putting an end to it.

It seemed that Miss Abby found a special place for Dorrie in her heart, too, for though she left a sheaf of debts that neatly cleaned out every penny from her estate there was a special bequest for her granddaughter, the old rosewood piano that had stood unused in her parlor for as long as Dora could remember.

"Auntie Dora, I'm in ecstasies!" cried Dorrie, clasping her hands under her chin as she watched the delivery men place the piano in one corner of the already cramped room.

"Perhaps it should go in the bedroom," wondered Dora.

"Oh, no, please, Auntie Dora!" Dorrie brushed her fingers along the pink-gold veneer and touched the dolphin-shaped candle holders that folded back against the front when not needed to illuminate pages of music. "We couldn't hide this away. It's so elegant that we must show it off. Just imagine how grand it will look with one of your crocheted shawls draped over it, and I could make a whole vase full of those silk roses I do for the millinery store. Wouldn't pink and red ones look splendid arranged on top?"

"Three *shillings?*" Dora said to the delivery men. "That's robbery. Do you know how many hours we have to work to earn three shillings?" Grudgingly she opened her purse.

Dorrie flipped up the lid and trilled her thumb along the keyboard, up and back, then up again. She stabbed at a few notes. "Some of these don't play!"

"I'm not surprised. It hasn't been used for years." She closed the lid to quiet Dorrie's plunking. "Not that it would make a shred of difference if none of them worked."

"What do you mean?"

Dora's head was throbbing. "I mean that I can't play and neither can you, so pretty though that piano may be, it's only going to stand there taking up room, isn't it? Now wash your—"

"You mean I—I won't be able to take lessons?"

"Lessons? Of course not. Piano lessons cost money, pet."

"But—but I thought—" Her chin trembled and the

large gray eyes filled quickly with tears that were just as
quickly dashed away.

Dora frowned. "Wash your hands, pet, and set the
table. It's time for lunch."

Dorrie ducked her head. "I'm not hungry," she
blurted in muffled tones. Before the astonished Dora
could say anything further, the girl dashed from the room
and was running toward Fintona.

"It's not like her to be so naughty," Dora fretted to Samuel when he called in that afternoon. "Two hours she's
been away and she won't answer when I call."

Samuel knocked his pipe bowl on the fender, deciding
as he so often did that this was definitely a time for blunt
speaking. Stuffing shreds of tobacco into the bowl, he
spoke around the stem. "Have you done anything to prepare the lass for growing up, Dora? Have you given any
thought at all to her future?"

"Well," flustered Dora, unprepared. "We're happy
the way we are. I don't see why things can't go on—"

"She's fifteen, damn it all!" He threw his match into
the grate. "There'll be young men soon, and she'll be invited out to social evenings—"

"Surely not!"

"Why not? She's a beautiful girl and she comes from a
fine old family. That'll count in her favor, you know,
when some young man is looking for a wife."

"Uncle Samuel, stop it! I was talking about music lessons and you're about to have her married off."

"It's not too soon to think about it, and I mean that,
lass. If she's going to marry, you want her to marry well.
Someone prosperous, who can look after the both of
you," he added with a sly wink but was exasperated
when Dora merely frowned at him. It was plain she'd
never given the future a moment's real thought. Well,
that was Dora, no imagination whatsoever. What had the
other children called her when she was young? Dull
Dora, that was it, cruel but apt. Once she was settled in

her rut in life she just dug herself in deeper and deeper until she could no longer look over the sides.

"Don't you ever give a thought for tomorrow, lass?" he asked in kindly tones. "Don't you ever make plans?"

"Plans?" sniffed Dora. "Plans are nothing but idle dreaming and there's no place for idle dreaming in this house."

No, nor for magic, either, thought Samuel, drawing on his pipe until the embers glowed. Now that he considered the matter, there was a pinched, starved look about Dorrie. Oh, she was sturdy and healthy enough, no denying that, but at the same time there was a hollowness in her eyes. A loneliness. That was it, loneliness.

Dora capitulated. Uncle Samuel was right; musical accomplishments were important to a young lady in the Colonies in these days of after-dinner recitals, glee evenings, and home entertainment, and a young lady was never presented to better advantage than when performing before an appreciative audience. Even Dora had to admit that.

"The lessons are two shillings and sixpence each, so listen to everything Major Blackett says, and don't fidget," she warned. "Now let me see your fingernails."

Dorrie sighed as she obediently stripped off her gloves and presented her hands for inspection. "I can't wait to learn how to play!" she confided. "A piano sounds so . . . *pixilated,* don't you think? Like a flock of birds singing in tune, or a lacy waterfall cascading over a mountainside."

"Don't dawdle on the way," warned Dora. "Major Blackett is very particular about punctuality."

Dorrie ran all the way along the muddy road, deftly avoiding the worst of the puddles and not even pausing to stare at a wagon that was bogged up to its axles in the mire. Her spirit soared free. It was a glorious spring afternoon and the landscape was a feast of color. Tender green grass shoots thrust through the tangle of bronze fern fronds and the roadsides were starred with white blackberry flowers and scarlet and gold flax blossoms. With a rustle of taffeta wings a glossy *tui* swooped close to Dorrie. It clutched a sagging flax branch while it dipped its scimitar beak into a blossom's throat. Its feathers gleamed like jet and the dab of white bib at its throat was fresh as a puff of whipped cream. Dorrie felt like singing.

She hesitated at the Blacketts' gate, wishing for a moment that Albert Patene had offered to accompany her instead of simply giving her directions. This *was* the place—a long, curving drive lined on either side with row upon row of wire-netting chicken runs, but now that she was actually here she was suddenly overawed.

Dorrie tried the latch on the four-barred gate but all the timber's weight was leaning on it and she could not force the bolt undone. So, after checking to see that nobody in the roadway would see her she hitched her skirt to her knees, climbed over the gate, and sprang lightly to the gravel on the other side. Brushing the crumbs of lichen from her hem, she began to walk along the edge of the puddled wheel ruts.

The hens watched her pass by. Some of the breeds she recognized—Japanese bantams, Leghorns, and the red and white Dorkings. She was looking to see if there were any Brahma Pootras when her attention was snagged by a strange-looking set of fowls. Snowy powder puffs they were, with fluffy cushions for tails and blobs of fluff for heads and feet. Their beak tips pointed from the soft down and there was an occasional gleam of an eye. "Puk-puk-puk?" they said.

Dorrie hugged herself in delight and was smiling at these extraordinary creatures when suddenly the silence around her was broken by a male voice raised in anger. Dorrie realized that someone was standing only a few feet away, beyond the fowl shed.

"Please, Del," said a soft feminine voice with a distinct Irish lilt. "You can't do this—not after all we've—"

The male voice cut in harshly. "How many times must I tell you? I've told you politely, I've told you kindly, and now I'll tell you in the plainest terms. It's over, Maureen. Finished. Over." And there came the sound of sobbing.

Dorrie was alarmed. She was about to hurry away when a young woman came dashing around the side of the fowl run and almost collided with her. Dorrie stepped quickly to one side. Hampered by her long dark skirts, the young woman tried to swerve, too, half tripped, then recovered and went lurching away towards the road, one bare hand jerking outwards as she ran and the other gripping the brim of her shabby gray hat. Her face had been twisted in anguish but Dorrie had recognized her as Maureen O'Reilly, the egg-man's freckle-faced daughter, who had once accompanied her father when he came to buy Dora's eggs.

Terrified that the man might appear next, Dorrie ran swiftly toward the house.

There, in the sun-flooded courtyard between the house and stables another young woman was stooping to pat an extremely hairy black dog. She straightened with a friendly "hello" as Dorrie approached. After her unsettling experience of a moment before Dorrie smiled back in relief.

"This is Bowser," said the stranger in the sweetest voice that had the hint of a French accent. "And I am Marguerite Dupton. But you, I confess, look nothing like *cher* Albert." (She pronounced it Al-*bear* and Dorrie did not realize whom she meant at first.) "This is his lesson time, no?"

"Oh, *Albert!* He changed his time so that I could have this one. He said Saturday mornings suited him better. I'm Dorinda Bennington." She blushed shyly as she spoke, thinking at the same time what an interesting person this was who stood before her.

Marguerite was no taller than Dorrie but seemed a year or two older and was very elegantly dressed in a brown cape and hat trimmed with orange bows. She had a tiny face to match her stature, crimped hair shiny as coal, and dark almond-shaped eyes set in an oval, olive-skinned face. Her nose was slightly hooked and too prominent for beauty, and her front teeth protruded from a full-lipped, perpetually open mouth, but because of the frankness of her expression and the sparkle in her eyes she exuded a vivacious attractiveness that Dorrie warmed to immediately.

She obviously liked Dorrie, too, for she said, "It is a great pleasure to meet you, *n'est-ce pas?* I think we can be friends."

Dorrie blushed, delighted. "Are—have you had your lesson yet?"

It transpired that Marguerite had finished her lesson almost half an hour before but had to wait while her younger sister had her spell of tuition. "Aimee, she is . . ." began Marguerite, then paused, frowning as she groped for the right words to describe her. "Ah, 'ere she comes now."

Major Blackett appeared in the doorway. At the same time Dorrie noticed that two planks had been laid up the low flight of steps to make a gently sloping ramp. Major Blackett was dressed in his scarlet uniform and he was talking in a loud, jolly voice. He pushed a wicker wheelchair in which hunched a dark-haired girl, slightly withered and wearing a scour scowl.

"Come now, Aimee," cooed Marguerite, taking control of the handles from the Major. *"Allons-y."*

Marguerite shrugged apologetically at the Major, who said, "She does love her piano lessons."

"All the time at home, she practices," said Marguerite. "Every day, all the time."

"We could do with more like her," said the Major. "Miss Bennington? Follow me."

Bemused by everything that had happened, Dorrie

trotted behind him into the house and up the hallway, the untidiest hallway imaginable. Rickety stacks of books toppled against stained walls, chairs sank under overflowing loads of papers and magazines called *The New Zealand Farmer, Bee and Poultry Journal,* and dusty cobwebs draped from the ceiling. The Major marched ahead of her into a large, paneled, bay-windowed room that contained even more clutter, more toppling stacks of *Farmer, Bee and Poultry* magazines, and more rickety furniture. Tambourines and drums were stacked in one corner and Salvation Army banners blazoned the dark walls. "BLOOD AND FIRE!" they proclaimed. Dorrie shivered; it sounded like a threat.

Near the window in the only clear space stood the piano. Light from the smeared windowpanes illuminated its dusty surface. Major Blackett sat on the piano bench and thumped out a row of chords, heavy as fenceposts. With jaws working briskly, setting clouds of fair beard trembling, he bellowed:

> We'll storm the forts of Darkness,
> Bring them down, bring them down!

At first Dorrie wanted to laugh, but as the hymn roared on she felt progressively more uncomfortable. It was unpleasant being an audience of one while those pale blue eyes pierced her like pins. She recalled Uncle Samuel's teasing advice—"Don't let him convert you!"—and wondered uneasily if this was what he was trying to do.

"Halleluia!" he shouted at the end. Then swinging his legs around from the bench, he beamed at her with satisfaction.

"That's the Auckland Aggressives' battlecry, Miss Bennington. Our platoon anthem. Reckon we might win the National Brass Band contest in Wellington with that, if we're lucky."

Dorrie smiled back nervously. "Is Mr.—is your son in the band, too?"

"Arundel?" His pale paintbrush eyebrows swept together in an expression of distaste. "Arundel is not. My son, Miss Bennington, is little better than a heathen. Now if you would be so good as to sit here, our lesson shall begin."

"Has he got you playing Chopin yet?" said a voice by the stables when Dorrie emerged from the house half an hour later.

Pausing, she blinked in the sunlight. The Major's son was standing in the shadows, a scoop full of grain in his hands. "Come and look at this," he said.

Dorrie obeyed reluctantly, staring at him curiously as she slowly walked towards him. He was a strongly built young man of perhaps twenty with heavy shoulders and thick forearms that jutted from the rolled-up sleeves. Blue suspenders held up tight-fitting trousers that were jammed into tall leather boots. He gave the impression that he was about to burst out of his clothes. There was a rawness about him that made Dorrie feel apprehensive.

When she was close to him he suddenly took a step towards her and looked right into her face, so close that she could see individual specks of stubble on his jaw. His eyes were that clear blue that she remembered, bright as the sky and he smelled of clean sweat and warm wheat sacks.

"Hey, don't be frightened of me!" he chided, smiling to show teeth as squared and close-set as piano keys. "I only eat young ladies on Mondays, didn't you know?"

He sounded so kind, so reassuring that Dorrie was shocked to hear herself say, "Did *you* make Maureen cry?"

At that he started as if she had slapped him, and the blue of his eyes turned gray and cold. Dorrie wished she could snatch back the words but in a second he had recovered and was smiling again, though less warmly than before.

"Maureen made herself cry," he said firmly. "Now

come and look at this. He's the pride of my whole collection."

In a long run built against the stable wall strutted a magnificent bird with golden feathers edged with black and a fluttering cockaded head and tail of burnished copper.

"Do you like him?"

Dorrie nodded, confused because she thought he looked faintly ridiculous, the way his wickedly spurred legs high-stepped six steps one way, then six precise steps the other. "He's very military looking, isn't he?" she ventured.

This time she had said the right thing. "I think so, too," agreed Del. "He's a Golden-spangled Polish and I call him Hans, even though he hasn't got any!"

Dorrie laughed. She had heard so few jokes in the time since her schooldays that this one came as a breath of delight.

Del watched her, chuckling, too, for her innocent mirth was infectious. "Let me show him to you properly," he offered. Before Dorrie could protest he unlocked the gate with a key from the string on his belt. Hans demonstrated how tame he was by jumping at once into Del's outstretched arms and in the next moment Dorrie was cradling him against her.

He was light and soft, like a down-filled cushion. He stared at her with one round, stony eye while she gingerly stroked his feathers.

"He likes you!" declared Del, approving. "His perception of character is as keen as mine." He paused, then with his strong, work-roughened fingers tipped her chin up so he could gaze into her face. "I know you, don't I?" he challenged her. "You're the little girl with the sore hands. You were playing with those Maori children on the beach."

Dorrie nodded. He was staring as closely as the Major had done while he sang his hymn, but Del's scrutiny was infinitely more pleasant. The afternoon was dying around

them; there was a dusty golden sweetness in the air, crisp
as a dessert apple. She shivered. He continued to stare at
her.

"What are you thinking?" she asked.

"Trade thoughts?" he said and, when she nodded
agreement, added, "I was thinking how beautiful you
are. Now, what were *you* thinking?"

"Are you really a heathen?"

"What?" He looked astounded. "Who said that?"

"Your father."

She wondered if she had angered him again, but he
laughed, genuinely amused, and to the astonishment of
both of them bent suddenly and brushed a kiss onto her
temple, below the bonnet brim. When he straightened up
he said, "If the Major said I'm a heathen, perhaps he's
right. Will you pray for my soul?"

"Do you want me to?" Dorrie whispered. Her heart
was racing; she was overcome by the strangeness of this
unkempt young man. He had *kissed* her!

He placed one hand against her cheek. It was rough
and hot, not like anybody else's hand. His voice was
low; the intensity of it thrilled her.

"Oh, yes. I want you to," he said.

When Dorrie came waltzing home in the coppery twilight
with flowers fluttering around the band of her bonnet and
a dreamy smile on her face Dora met her at the gate, her
voice sharp with worry.

"Where on earth have you been? Dawdling, I suppose! Your lesson finished over an hour ago."

"I had to wait for ages," said Dorrie vaguely. She
scooped to pick Misty up and rested him against her
shoulder while she buried her face in his dense fur. Her
cheek still burned where Del's hand had rested against it.

Dora was regarding her suspiciously. There was something different about Dorrie and she could not make her
mind up what it was. "And while you waited for your
lesson?" she demanded. "What did you do then?"

"I made a friend," Dorrie told her. "Isn't it wonderful, Auntie Dora? I have a real, true friend!"

"It's anything but wonderful if you ask me," sniffed Dora as she dipped a beheaded hen into a pail of boiling water and began plucking off the loosened feathers. "And don't you go taking her side either, Uncle Samuel. Perhaps Dorrie was lonely, but did she have to choose someone like Marguerite Dupton? The girl's full of artificial airs, which, Lord forbid, Dorrie has begun to imitate, and as for her family—" Dora paused as if mere words could not describe her opinions.

Samuel looked uncomfortable. Dora had seized on his arrival as the chance to dispatch a hen that was now too old to lay. He didn't mind chopping the head off but he was reluctant to be used as a weapon in a tussle between Dorrie and her aunt. "I don't know much about them," he said at last. "He's manager of the Empire Theater, isn't he? Seems a nice chap. Quiet and well spoken. Interested in trout fishing I believe."

"No better than a showground roustabout," declared Dora, wresting feathers with determined tugs. "And she's French or something equally foreign. Then on top of it all there's that wretched mad child—"

"Aimee! She's not *mad*, Dora. She was injured in a fall when she was just a baby, so she can't walk. And they say she's a gifted musician—"

"So her parents claim," retorted Dora. "But people can say what they please, can't they? I've seen her being pushed up Quay Street in that bathchair contraption with her head lolling, shouting demands at her mother." She dunked the carcass again. "Why couldn't Dorrie have made friends with some nice, *normal* people?"

Like the Yardleys or the Teipa-Benningtons? Samuel was tempted to say, but for once he held his tongue.

Because Dora was so plainly dismayed about her friendship with Marguerite, Dorrie decided it would not be pru-

dent to mention Del. It was easy to imagine what
scathing remarks Dora might make about him; worse,
she might forbid her to speak to him or even stop her music lessons. Dorrie felt guilty about keeping something of
this magnitude back from her aunt and the secret was
gnawing to be told.

"Has the Major tried to convert you yet?" asked Marguerite one Saturday afternoon. She was giggling over
scales at the rosewood piano while Dorrie sat with a
heaped basket of silk scraps making piecework roses for
the millinery store. Dora had walked up the road to measure Mrs. Edelburt for a blue Louis velveteen blouse.

Dorrie was biting her tongue while she threaded a
needle and did not reply immediately, so Marguerite
rushed on herself. It was one of her mannerisms Dora
most disliked, the way she had of asking a question and
never waiting for an answer. "He's *always* singing
hymns to me," she complained. "I used to tease *Maman*
that I was going to join the Sallie Army, but Papa said
that if I did he would put me to work outside the Empire
with my tambourine and I could sing songs about the latest show he had playing! Tell me, do you ever see Del
when you go for lessons?"

"Sometimes," confessed Dorrie, though in truth he
managed to catch her on the way home nearly every
Thursday afternoon. He gave her a bunch of daffodils
once and often talked to her in the soft twilight, stroking
her face and gazing into her eyes. She was jittery though,
so nervous in his company that she always made an excuse to hurry away after only a few minutes. His intensity
unsettled her.

Marguerite swung around and said, "Does he flirt
with you? He often comes along and—"

"He kissed me once," said Dorrie abruptly.

Marguerite gasped. In the following silence Dorrie
looked up to find her friend staring at her with a strange
expression in those dark, almond eyes. Jealousy—or dis-

belief perhaps. Dorrie smiled at her timidly, but she frowned in reply.

"Well!" she said at length. "Well, this is a surprise! He's kissed me, too, of course. Many times," and she laughed to show how unimportant such an occurrence was. "In fact, he's quite a flirt, our Del, *n'est-ce pas?* He's so earthy—so *primitif,* but one must make allowances, considering his mother died when he was born. Just the same, one could never take him seriously, not a flirt like him, *non?*"

"I suppose not," said Dorrie. As she tugged on the thread her heart seemed to give little tugs, too. She kept her eyes fixed on the rose she was making.

"Besides, I have a secret admirer," prattled Marguerite, tossing her head. "It's so secret that I wasn't even going to tell you about it." She laughed. "But since you'll be meeting him anyway next Saturday I might as well unburden my heart to you, *non?*"

"I don't know about Saturday."

"You must come to see the hot-air balloons! Surely your *tante* will permit you? Oh, you must! My secret admirer will be there. His name is Mr. Nathaniel Rosser and he is so so handsome, and he's a gentleman, too, not like Del. *And* he's rich. You know how rich Mr. Teipa-Bennington is?"

Dorrie shook her head. "May Yardley's husband?"

"Don't you know *anything?* Mr. Teipa-Bennington owns the breweries and he's the richest man in all of Auckland, but my Mr. Rosser is even wealthier. He's an Australian, from Sydney, and he owns a whole string of theaters and other things besides, and the Empire Theater, too, so *Papa* works for him, which is so lovely because I get to see him often. He's coming to dine on Friday after his ship arrives. Oh, Dorrie, I wish that he would stay at our house, too, but he's been staying with the Teipa-Benningtons for years, so though he'd really prefer to stay with us, I know, he wouldn't want to hurt their feelings by—"

"Hush!" warned Dorrie urgently. Dora's wooden-soled shoes could be heard crunching along the path. If she came in and heard the Teipa-Benningtons being discussed, that would really ruin things.

Marguerite, who had been informed about the feud, obediently hushed.

To reach the Domain where the hot-air balloon demonstration was taking place they had to cross Grafton Cemetery Bridge, a quivering sling of wire and timber that spanned a fern-shaded gully so deep that from autumn to spring it lay in perpetual shade.

Dorrie, Marguerite, Mrs. Dupton, and Aimee paused at a wooden arch under the sign that read "No Running. No Loitering. Penalty Five Pounds." While Mrs. Dupton bullied the duty policeman into helping her with the wheelchair Dorrie peeked through the railings. All down the gully slopes terraces had been carved out for gravesites. It was now overgrown. Dorrie thought the crumbling tombstones looked like neglected teeth.

"Go first, girls," said the policeman.

Dorrie looked at the shuddering bridge and at the spidery shadow it flung down to meet the blackness below. She snatched at the handrail and trotted as quickly as she could while the boards stuttered under the soles of her old boots.

"Hoi! No running there!" shouted the policeman, but his voice only panicked Dorrie into hurrying faster.

By the time she reached the far side she was white faced and gasping to draw breath. Her arms shook loosely in their sockets while her legs felt as insubstantial as a puppet's, but Marguerite skipped off the bridge a few seconds later gurgling with laughter and declaring she had enjoyed the experience.

"What fun, c'est épatant," she cried. "I'd go across again if we had time. Oh, Maman—"

"Come along," said Mrs. Dupton. She was a short, pudgy woman with a dark complexion and such a pronounced moustache on her upper lip that Dorrie had to force herself not to stare at it. "Come along," she repeated in her low, harsh voice.

"But it's such *fun*," insisted Marguerite. "Don't you think so, Aimee? Tell me, Dorrie, do I look pretty enough for Mr. Rosser?"

"Marguerite!" snapped Mrs. Dupton, then fired a rapid volley of French in which the words *Monsieur Rosser* featured several times. Marguerite seemed unabashed by the scolding, but Aimee covered both eyes with her hands and shrieked with what could have been either mirth or rage.

"Do I look pretty?" repeated Marguerite while Mrs. Dupton tried to quiet Aimee by shaking the chair and clucking at her.

"You always look pretty," said Dorrie, trying to smother the wistful note in her voice. Dora had scoffed that Mrs. Dupton put "every penny on that child's back," but Dorrie still yearned with an envy she could not suppress. Today Marguerite wore a long red-and-gray-striped gown with matching jacket and smart little gray hat ringed with scarlet daisies. As always, Dorrie wore her secondhand navy serge coat—now an embarrassing two inches above her ankles—and an unfashionable navy bonnet. Despite her adornment of some homemade blue silk roses, Dorrie thought she looked as drab as an old tea-cosy.

While Mrs. Dupton trundled the wheelchair along, Marguerite and Dorrie hurried with the crowds that swept down the slope towards the Domain basin. They rounded a hillock and there, in the center of a great flood of people, were two blossoming silken globes.

"That one's Mr. Rosser's!" Marguerite pointed to the gigantic red and yellow puffball which, like the blue one beside it, was enclosed in a coarse net and anchored all around with guy ropes. Both swelled under the restraints, flexing their hot-air muscles.

From the band rotunda at the edge of the rose garden

the Salvation Army band scraped out a lively marching tune. Major Blackett conducted with jerks of wrists and elbows, flinging himself into the music like someone struggling against the blasts of a gale. There was no sign of Del.

"Where's Mr. Rosser?" breathed Marguerite, frowning.

Men formed the mass of the crowd. In colonial New Zealand the poorer women stayed at home to mind the children while the husbands attended the entertainments. Everybody wore hats and many of the men wore uniforms.

"I can't see him *anywhere,*" complained Marguerite. "All these men look so alike. I can't even find *Papa!*"

The Patenes walked by along the slope above, a whole troop of them loaded with rolled flax mats to sit on and baskets of food. Mrs. Patene leaned on Albert's arm. He was a head taller than she now, and very handsome; his skin was pale as milk fudge and he had dark, slumbrous eyes. Turei waved to Dorrie. She and Emere looked very smart in their Salvation Army uniforms.

"Where *is* he?" muttered Marguerite. "Oh, there he is. Look! Over there, by *Papa.*" Marguerite grasped Dorrie's wrist and tugged her along faster to where people clustered around a giant wicker basket. *"Papa!"* she piped, and a portly middle-aged man turned to greet them, a smile lighting his tired face. A frill of fuzzy gray hair rimmed his bowler hat.

"Angel," he said. And then, "Good afternoon, Miss Bennington."

Marguerite joggled his elbow. "Where did Mr. Rosser go? I want to introduce him to Dorrie."

"Mr. Rosser is a very busy man," Mr. Dupton said patiently.

"So you keep telling me," pouted Marguerite.

He chucked her under the chin and she pulled away, so he spoke to Dorrie, explaining that today's hot-air balloon demonstration had originally been organized by one

Captain Dare, who had printed posters and handbills and now was threatening to sue because Mr. Rosser and his hot-air balloon were "cribbing the limelight."

"He can't make Mr. Rosser leave!" cried Marguerite, hot patches scalding her cheeks as she listened to her father explain again in French. "This is a public park, *non?* Mr. Rosser has just as much right . . ."

While she ranted on a young gentleman walked up close behind her and by placing a finger to his lips indicated that they must not warn Marguerite that he was there. He was obviously Mr. Rosser, and every inch as attractive as her friend had described—a dandy gentleman in his dark suit, white shirt with stiff, scalloped collar over a silk tie, and plum-colored velvet waistcoat strung with a heavy silver watch chain.

He winked at Dorrie, and in that second she decided he was gorgeous. His wide-jawed face was framed by wavy russet hair, merry brown eyes danced, and a soft moustache set off a decidedly impish smile. Dorrie smiled back at him; she felt as if she already knew him.

"I'm flattered, Miss Dupton," he whispered in an Australian twang. "All this indignation being lavished in my defense."

Marguerite colored, mortified.

He realized at once that he had humiliated her. To make amends he took her hand and placed it against his lapel, saying, "On my heart I assure you I'm grateful."

Marguerite looked as if she could expire with happiness.

"Did you settle it?" asked Mr. Dupton.

Nathaniel Rosser's attention slipped away from Marguerite as soon as he let go of her hand. He was explaining earnestly that Captain Dare did have a valid point, but Marguerite kept interrupting as she tugged at his arm, telling him not to back down. He seemed not to notice her.

"Oi! Mr. Ross!" The aeronaut thrust through a surge of people and landed squarely before them. He was dressed as if for a day's yachting in a silver-buttoned blazer and a peaked cap that proclaimed CAPTAIN DARE on an embroidered band. He rocked on his toes as if something sticky were holding him in place.

He waved a fistful of programs at them and shrugged his shoulders like a boxer swaggering into the ring.

Marguerite shrank back. "His real name's Archie Flett and he's a cabbie," she hissed to Dorrie. "Sylvia Prescott—you know, the judge's daughter—told me that he's been in *jail*. For violence," she added significantly.

"My," said Dorrie, impressed. It seemed strange that Nathaniel Rosser was laughing out loud.

"What, Archie? An exhibition bout?" he mocked, and before the angry man could protest he snatched the programs and flourished them aloft.

"Oi! Gimme them back!" Captain Dare squeaked and the crowd pressed closer—but not too close.

"You might as well all go home!" called Nathaniel as Captain Dare gaped at him, astonished. "We have decided to call a postponement. Yes, you heard me. A postponement!"

The Captain's jaw sagged. Dorrie thought he looked like a small terrier who had lost his bone to a Great Dane and was uncertain whether he should put up a fight or slink away.

A ripple of murmurs hummed through the crowd and someone near the band rotunda bade the Salvationists to stop the music.

Nathaniel continued, "We realize that you will all be disappointed because you came expecting a rousing good show—aye, and a free one, too! Then imagine Captain Dare's disappointment if you will! *He* came today expecting to earn a few miserable coppers with which to sustain his wife and family. That's what he was expecting, ladies and gentlemen. A living!"

He's reveling in this, thought Dorrie, *and he so obviously likes everybody around him that they're obliged to give him their attention.*

"Did you honestly think that a man of such skill and daring can exist without funds? That he can conjure up food for his family out of thin air? That he can *command* a roof to appear for their shelter? Of course not! And furthermore, ladies and gentlemen, some of you may think that all the hot air these balloons swallow comes free. Then think again! Hot air costs money these days, as anyone in politics will tell you! Good, you can appreciate a joke, so perhaps you'll also appreciate this man's plight. Unless Captain Dare sells all these programs he won't be able to afford to launch his balloon, and until he does I'm obliged to stay grounded, too. So dig in your pockets, folks, and buy one to help me out." He muttered in an aside to the Captain, "How much are these accursed things?"

"Ask fourpence each. They cost me—"

"Only sixpence each, folks, and a bargain at half the price. Every one an artistic masterpiece and a valuable memento of this forgettable day. Look, they've an etching of the aeronaut himself so you won't forget his face and a pretty ribbon trim to tickle the ladies. Take one! Take two! Take them all!"

With that he thrust the sheaf at Captain Dare and without waiting to gauge the effects of his oratory he disappeared into the crowd as people surged forward in a rush. Chattering in alarm, Mrs. Dupton shepherded the girls closer to the basket. Aimee shrilled with laughter and her father gave her a look of despair.

"Isn't he wonderful?" sighed Marguerite. "But why didn't he stay?"

"Mr. Rosser is a busy man, angel."

"Look, there he is!" she cried, pointing to the crest of the nearby slope where groups of youths stood near their own homemade balloons. Eight or ten feet high, they were constructed of paper plastered over wicker skeletons with oil lamps burning in brackets beneath. Some were moored in place with hand-held ropes. Others wobbled on anchors.

"We made one of those at Sylvia Prescott's birthday party," Marguerite told her. "There they go! Wheee!"

Up rose the balloons, swaying at first, then leaping away higher and higher, their pinks and reds and oranges bright against the sky. Dorrie squinted after them until her eyes watered.

"Ices!" squealed Marguerite. "Look, *Maman!* Mr. Rosser is bringing us ices!"

They were cupped in his large hands—six paper tubs of shaved ice, each with a cherry, a thin slice of orange, and a tiny wooden paddle jabbed in at the side.

"Take one, go on," Nathaniel urged Dorrie, who stood gaping at them shyly. She had never tasted ices before.

With a whispered "Thank you," Dorrie lifted one from the group only to have Aimee lean forward and snatch it from her hand. *"C'est à moi!"* she shouted in triumph. Nathaniel shrugged and gave Dorrie another.

Awed, Dorrie dug into the confection. The first few mouthfuls tasted of wood as much as anything else, but after that the sweetness seeped through and it was a pure delight.

Nathaniel was laughing. "Look at them!" he marveled, for people were still crushing around the Captain to buy his programs. "He must have sold fifty pounds' worth by now. It never ceases to amaze me, Mr. Dupton, how people love to throw their money away. All you have to do is put a smile on a man's face and he'll put his hand in his pocket. That's what makes our business magic, don't you think? Ah, here comes the photographer to record our moment of glory!"

While the photographer set up his tripod and adjusted the focus his assistants cleared the crowd back so that Nathaniel and Captain Dare could pose in front of the balloons. Dorrie took no notice of what was happening. She was concentrating on the novelty of this exquisite taste, a little like flower scent and a little like the banana old Uncle Samuel had given her as a treat one Christmas. It was

very, very good. Dorrie tried to make each mouthful lin-
ger, holding it in her mouth until her teeth ached with the
chill and forced her to swallow.

Suddenly, as the people moved back to clear the space
someone jostled Dorrie from behind and flung her forward. Because she was cupping the paper container in
one gloved hand and clutching the tiny paddle with the
other, she had no time to protect herself. Her ankle
caught on one of the guy pegs and she sprawled in the
mud at Nathaniel's feet.

At once he was helping her up, so solicitous that her
embarrassment threatened to overwhelm her. Her ankle
hurt ferociously. She looked at the smear of mud down
the front of her coat, at her filthy gloves, and at the spat-
ter of pink ice in the dirt, and she tried her utmost not to
cry.

"Your flowers!" cried Marguerite just as Dorrie saw
the posy from her coat being carelessly trodden into the
mud by a passerby's boot.

"Oh . . ." said Dorrie.

A roar erupted around them and Captain Dare's balloon was straining at the ropes, but Nathaniel was more
concerned with Dorrie's feelings. How old was she—
sixteen? seventeen? Her face was too classically perfect
to interest him at first glance, but when he looked closely
he noticed that her forehead was a little too broad, she
had an oddly shaped chin that gave her face character,
and her eyes shone with a clear innocence that he found
utterly refreshing.

"No, please leave them," she said as he stooped to
pick up the ruined posy. "I made them last night—
they're nothing."

"All the more reason to rescue them." He searched
for something clever to say. "They represent a portion of
you for the time you gave to make them. What are we but
the sum of all the hours we spend on earth?"

The crowd was roaring and hats waved. Those large
gray eyes were fixed on his face but he did not know

whether she had heard him in the din. Suddenly the sky was full of balloon; for a fraction of a second the entire sky was blocked out by the gigantic blue globe and its shadow covered all the Domain basin like a picnic basket. For that split second it seemed to pause, gathering its strength, then in one bound it leaped away upwards at an astonishing speed.

Tingling with fright Dorrie watched it go. Already it was as small as the moon but was slowing now. Captain Dare, a tiny, toy Captain Dare, was just visible, fragile as a little spider clinging to a web.

"Well," said Nathaniel Rosser. "My turn next." He brushed the worst of the mud off Dorrie's blue posy with his white handkerchief and to her amazement tucked it, grime and all, into his buttonhole. "That's for luck," he said.

"All that mud!" said Marguerite, shocked. "It will make you land in a cow yard." Which made them all laugh. She fumbled with her hat pin as she added, "I'll take one on *my* flowers off for you instead."

"No!" He stopped her firmly. "No, thank you, these will be fine."

Marguerite looked hurt but was prevented from speaking by the arrival of another couple, he, a dark fellow with a fine-featured face, and she, very white skinned with rich mahogany hair swirled into a chignon below the brim of an elegant dark green hat. She was very pregnant, a fact which her dark green cape failed to disguise.

"I'm so glad we're in time, darling," said May to Nathaniel. She had a slightly nervous, fluttery manner which Dorrie thought very appealing. "It took forever to set the cameras up and the children are being so naughty. Of course they all wanted to come and watch their special Mr. Rosser set off on his adventure. We're over there on the hill, babies, nursemaids and baggage, so don't forget to wave as you leap into the sky, will you? I'll be the one with my head under the black cloth!" She turned to seize her husband's arm and in that instant saw Dorrie standing shyly at the edge of the crush.

Dorrie wished she could run and hide. Acutely conscious of her muddy clothes, she felt her cheeks flushing with embarrassment. With both hands she held her sodden gloves in front of her as she tried to hide the worst of the damage.

But May seemed not to notice. She said gently, "Dorinda? It is Dorinda, isn't it? I'm your cousin May. Your second cousin, or your great cousin, I can never work out these details. I haven't seen you since . . . since you were at school, remember? I gave you a ride home in my carriage when you were caught in that dreadful thunderstorm."

Dorrie remembered. There was a worse thunderstorm when Auntie Dora looked out the window and saw the Yardleys' carriage rolling away through the sheets of hail.

"You're a young woman now, and a beautiful one, too, isn't she, Patrick? Dorinda, has anybody ever asked you to pose for a camera, to have your portrait taken?"

"May," warned Patrick. "You know what Dora—"

"Of course." May smiled at Dorrie. "Perhaps I'll write her a note. It's all such a pity, dear, isn't it? But it was lovely seeing you again anyway." Impulsively she leaned forward and kissed Dorrie's cheek. She smelled of roses.

They spoke to Nathaniel again, wishing him luck, then disappeared into the crowd. It was only then that Dorrie realized she had not uttered one word throughout the encounter.

Nathaniel pulled on leather gloves, then exchanged his dark jacket for a heavy tweed coat. Mr. Dupton took his top hat and folded it into a round flat box while he donned a peaked hunting cap and pulled the flaps over his ears. He looked very funny but Dorrie could not laugh at him. She kept looking at the balloon, at the frail ropes and the ridiculously small wicker basket. She wanted to beg him not to do it.

"I suppose I should say a few last words," Nathaniel

joked as he smiled around at them all—Marguerite, Mr.
and Mrs. Dupton, Aimee, who hunched in her chair,
chewing her wooden paddle, and finally at Dorrie. He
was about to move away but the stillness and terror in her
face stopped him. He thought, *She's as pure as spring
water, and she's afraid for me.* He was flattered and, in
an odd way, enchanted.

"It's just a lark, truly. I'll come to no harm," he said,
but when she continued to gaze at him with those wide
gray eyes he bent and with enormous gentleness kissed
her on the lips.

Marguerite gasped. "Kisses!" she cried, recovering
swiftly and using the same tone with which she had her-
alded the arrival of the ices. "Kisses! We're having
kisses!"

Nathaniel was shaken but he laughed to show it was all
great fun. Swinging Marguerite off her feet, he declared,
"One must always kiss the ladies for good luck. Here's a
kiss for my favorite little sister." Giving her a brief peck
on the cheek, he disengaged her hands from around his
neck, adding as he planted another on Mrs. Dupton's
brow, "And here's a kiss for the most important lady of
them all." Without so much as glancing at Dorrie he
climbed into the basket.

Moving back obediently, Dorrie kept her eyes fixed on
the basket as the balloon leaped into the sky in one enormous bound. Nathaniel smiled and waved and she saw
that he had her muddy posy clutched in one leather-
gloved hand. Within seconds the wind was whipping the
balloon like a spinning top, driving it across the sky.
Dorrie thought that if she kept it in view Nathaniel would
be all right so she stared at it doggedly, not daring to
blink.

May had called him "darling," she was thinking. That
struck chords of memory in her mind. "Of course," she
said, half to herself as the balloon disappeared beyond
the rim of hills. "That's where I've seen Mr. Rosser be-

fore. On the beach with May Teipa-Bennington and her husband.''

She glanced at Marguerite, eager to share this piece of information with her but recoiled in dismay when she was met by the resentment in her friend's eyes.

"How *dare* you make such a fool of me!" she hissed, tugging Dorrie a pace away so that her father couldn't hear. Mrs. Dupton was cooing over Aimee and the crowd was jostling noisily all around as people began to leave.

"What's the matter?" pleaded Dorrie.

"What's the matter?" mimicked Marguerite nastily. *"You* are the matter. To think I actually hoped that Mr. Rosser would like you! How could I have dreamed that you would throw yourself at him! You flirted with him and—''

"Marguerite, stop this please! It's not true."

"You encouraged him to kiss you, and right after that he called me 'little sister'.'' She was sobbing with rage. *"Little sister!"*

"Oh, please—I—''

Marguerite dashed her hand away. "Leave me alone. Your hands are filthy and you are, too. I hate you, do you understand that? I *hate* you!''

Seven

Worse was to come.

On Monday Dora went out to deliver the Louis velveteen blouse and returned with the angriest face Dorrie had ever seen. Banging the door shut behind her and without stopping to take off her hat or hang up her coat, she confronted her niece.

"Hobnobbing with the Teipa-Benningtons, were you?" she demanded as Dorrie looked up from her sewing, her face flushed with guilty fright. "Don't try to deny it either, young lady. Mr. Edelburt saw you there on Saturday chatting away to *him* and *her* as if you were old chums."

But I never said a word! Dorrie wanted to protest but she dared not argue.

Dora's eyes were furious sparks in an ash-white face. "He said you kissed her. *Kissed* her! Really, Dorinda, if you wanted to stab me in the back—" She walked over to the fireplace and rattled the grate as if she had to be doing something violent with her hands. Turning to Dorrie she said, "There'll be no more associating with that Dupton girl, and no more music lessons once this term is over. I've paid until Christmas and that will be an end to it."

It was not, however, the end of Dorrie's punishment. The following Thursday Dorrie hurried to music early, her mind throbbing with apologies and conciliatory phrases she planned to offer her friend. Surely Marguerite would understand that Dorrie was not flirting with her Mr. Rosser, that she was only frightened for his safety. Surely Marguerite hadn't meant that outburst of hers. She and Dorrie had been friends for over a year now. *Surely* their friendship was strong enough to over-come this little quarrel.

To Dorrie's dismay she found a stranger in Marguer-ite's place, a gawky grammar school boy who filled in time while he waited for his lesson by flinging sticks for Bowser to fetch.

"Nah," he said in response to Dorrie's question. "Those Dupton girls are having private tuition now. The Major gives them their lessons at home, that's how come he let me have this time. Private tuition—all right for some, don't you think?"

Dorrie couldn't speak. *She really does hate me,* she thought. *I'll never see her again.* She turned away quickly so that the boy would not see her tears.

An air of deep sadness surrounded Dorrie. Once her own anger faded, Dora began to regret the severity of her pun-ishment, especially when she saw Dorrie's desolation. She endured the gloomy silence for several weeks, then said, "I've decided to allow your lessons to continue." To her astonishment Dorrie burst into tears and declared that music no longer meant anything to her, nothing could make up for the loss of her friend.

Perhaps it's all for the best, decided Dora when the full story came gushing out. Dorrie was a sensible lass; she could see for herself that an emotionally unstable girl like Marguerite was worthless as a friend. She would re-cover from this blow and things would be as they were before Miss Dupton came into their lives with her high-pitched giggling and her silly, theatrical mannerisms.

Besides, there was something exciting to distract her now. After all these years, Jon had finally written to say that he would be home for Christmas, and shortly after that letter arrived, Major Blackett came to see Dora on a "delicate matter" connected also with Jon.

It seemed that the Prohibitionists, of which Major Blackett was a member, were looking for someone to contest the local seat in the next General Election, due to be held in a few months' time. Their own candidate had been forced to withdraw because of ill health and Jon's name had come up.

Everybody agreed that Jon would be the perfect choice for the Prohibitionist platform. He had the experience of several terms of Parliamentary life before he gave up a career in politics to manage Grandmaire's affairs and he was well known as a teetotaler with a stainless reputation.

It was a marvelous opportunity, the Major told Dora. With women now receiving the vote, any Prohibitionist candidate was virtually guaranteed success.

"After all," boomed the Major, "it is the womenfolk who suffer all the insidious evils of the liquor traffic." He cleared his throat. "But there is just one thing—the delicate matter to which I referred. Miss Bennington, your brother will be required not only to denounce the traffic itself, but also those who promote the vile trade, namely innkeepers, brewers, and so on, and it could be awkward because the main profiteer in Auckland is Mr. Teipa-Bennington, who, I understand, is your half brother. How will Jon feel about denouncing a close relative? You can see I must have this point cleared up before we can—"

Dorrie thought her aunt was about to choke. She drew herself in, then seemed to swell about the neck like a frog as she said, "There is *no* family connection between this household and *those people*. My father, God rest him, was misguided—grievously misguided—in one aspect of his life, but we never dwell on that. *Never!*" And for emphasis she touched the faded mourning brooch she always wore.

"Good," said the Major, clapping his hands to his knees and standing up. "Then it's settled."

"He's going to be so thrilled," Dora said as she surveyed the table with satisfaction and rearranged one of the blue rosettes—Prohibition's color—that had been heaped in the center as decoration for the festive dinner. "I tell you, Dorrie, this will be a turning point in Jon's life."

Though she did not say so to Dorrie, Jon's letter had disturbed and frightened her. Though it was a long letter, it told her nothing of these past years since he had left New Zealand nor did he mention Ellen or the children (who were, Dora suspected, the object of his restless searching). Instead, page after page had been filled with the meandering reminiscences of a weary and heartsick man dwelling on incidents of his youth, trivial happenings that Dora had long since forgotten. He sounded old and beaten, unlike the Jon she remembered.

"A seat in Parliament," Dora said as she glanced into the mirror and adjusted a strand of her bouffant hairstyle. She wondered if Jon would find her aged. *"Parliament!* He'll be so surprised! He used to talk about going back into politics, so imagine how pleased he'll be to have all his expenses paid—*and* for supporting a cause he believes in! Prohibition is a noble cause. You know that, don't you, Dorrie?"

"Yes, Auntie"—though Dorrie was unable to summon up any enthusiasm for either the prospect of having Jon bed down in the living room of their cramped quarters or for a cause that seemed increasingly to smack of personal vindictiveness on Dora's part. It had been explained how, if Jon won the election, all the public houses and liquor stores in the entire area would be immediately shut down at a considerable personal loss to Patrick Teipa-Bennington. He would not receive a single penny of compensation. If Dorrie could have been stirred she would have felt indignation but the loss of Marguerite still numbed her soul.

"I wonder if he's changed," fretted Dora. "He may have put on weight, or grown a beard. I can't imagine Jon with a beard, can you?"

"I can't remember him at all," said Dorrie listlessly.

Dora lifted one edge of the curtains and gazed through

a veil of rain into the blackness. "This could be him now. Oh, it might be him!"

Lights wavered in the driveway. Dorrie and Dora stood shoulder to shoulder at the open door. The scent of Dora's lavender water mingled with fragrant smells from the stove where the roast pork dinner kept warm in the oven. Dora smoothed her apron with nervous hands.

One light splashed towards them. Rain was coming more heavily now, running a comb over the porch roof and dashing along the path like shot.

"Miss Bennington?" called the cabby who was swathed to the neck in a rubber raincoat.

Dora stepped forward, peering through the night.

"I've a passenger for you," he said. "He's a bit non compos, you might say, but he reckons he's your brother." With that he turned back to the cab and a few moments later came treading back towards them half-supporting, half-dragging Jon.

"He's ill!" cried Dora, wringing her hands as she followed them into the living room. "Oh, do be careful with him. Set him down carefully please. He might be injured."

"Nothing a few hours' sleep won't cure," the cabby told her bluntly, his wet face shining in the lamplight. "He's got Irish poisoning, Miss. Scotch Rheumatics, as they say." When Dora gaped at him he explained, "He's drunk, Miss Bennington. As a lord."

"But he can't be. He's only ever—"

The cabby tossed Jon a scornful glance. He was a clean-living man himself, with scant sympathy for a baggage the likes of which he'd just dumped on the sofa. *What was the fellow thinking of?* he wondered as his gaze took in the prim yet welcoming room, the festive table invitingly set, and the two anxious women all spruced up in their best clothes.

"Sorry it's spoiled your evening, but you might as well know. One of his fellow passengers put him in the cab. Told me that he'd been like this ever since the ship left Singapore. That'll be one and ninepence now please, and sixpence for his trunk. I'll fetch it if you like.''

''Please,'' whispered Dora. When the cabby had gone she slumped into a chair and gazed at her brother in helpless despair. He looked so much older that her heart contracted with pity. He was shabby and unshaven, his overcoat had no buttons and his once-beautiful crest of hair was yellowish and disheveled. His head lolled back against the crocheted antimacassar and his eyes were open, unfocused, though he was snoring hoarsely.

''Major Blackett will be here first thing in the morning to offer him that candidacy,'' Dora said. ''We can't let him see Jon—not like this.''

''The driver said he'd be all right in the morning.'' Dorrie was studying her uncle with interest. She had often seen men similarly inebriated sprawled on the steps outside public houses or sitting mournfully in the gutters.

''It'll take more than a night's sleep to cure him, I'm afraid,'' diagnosed Dora. ''He's sick right through with it. He's an *alcoholic*, Dorrie, and the Major is going to ask him to campaign for Prohibition. Oh, my stars, what are we going to do?''

Dorrie soon hated her uncle. At night she would lie awake listening to him cough. On and on he would until there was a scrape of the hob cover and a hacking sound as he spat into the embers of the fire. Dorrie would bury her face in her pillow as she fought back tears. *He's loathsome*, she thought. *Loathsome!*

It astonished her that Dora doted on him so fondly, coddling him and scraping together extra pennies so that she could buy him crisp paper collars or a feathered hatband to smarten his billycock hat. When she had finished work for the day she spent hours toiling to freshen his clothes, brushing, pressing, darning and patching, yet for all her efforts he gave only complaints in return.

He sits about like some country squire, thought Dorrie

resentfully as she peeked through the window to where he dozed under the oak tree in the summer sunshine.

"The poor love," remarked Dora, looking over her shoulder. "Take him his tea now, pet, and don't forget to tell him he looks smart."

Dorrie pulled a face. Taking a large black tin from its hiding place behind the flour crock, she levered off the lid and stirred a large spoonful of the contents into her uncle's tea. The label on the tin read:

BLUE LILY SECRET LIQUOR CURE
Guaranteed to save your loved one from a life of disease, poverty and degradation.
Can be safely given to any sufferer young or old
WITHOUT HIS KNOWLEDGE OR SUSPICION.
Abolishes all craving and desire for liquor.
The flush of his complexion subsides, the step becomes steady and a higher moral tone will be upheld.

Jon blinked and yawned when she stood beside him with a tray of tea and sultana cakes. "Hmph!" he said, patting his paunch to find the watch fob. "A quarter to four! I'd better gulp this and go. Promised Mr. Harrison I'd meet him in town at five. Some business to discuss before the meeting."

"Auntie Dora and I are coming with you."

"What, again?" He glared at her as if it was her idea. "Wants to keep an eye on me still. Both eyes." He gulped the tea and thrust the cup and saucer at Dorrie. "Fetch me another cup of tea, girl, and tell Dora we'll need to leave at six."

"What about Mr. Harrison?" Dorrie inquired sweetly.

Jon just glared at her.

They arrived at the Quay Street hall at dusk. A train was hissing and thumping into the station next door and flocks of people hurried through the floury clouds of steam on the spidery wooden overbridge.

Dorrie dawdled reading the billboards. *Crowther's Stables, Sun Gloss Starch, ST. JACOB'S OIL CONQUERS PAIN.* The air was rich with a tang of fish and the thick odor of hops and malt from the brewery—Patrick Teipa-Bennington's brewery—across the road.

Dorrie read the beginnings of a new billboard that was right now being pasted up in long bright strips: *Grand Magic Lantern and Talk . . . Amplifying Horn . . .*

"Dorinda!" said Nathaniel Rosser, who was watching the workmen erect his poster. He appraised her admiringly. She was wearing the dress Dora had made for her seventeenth birthday, a lemon and gray checked gown with braid-trimmed ruffles around the hips and smaller ruffles cascading down the puffed-to-the-elbow sleeves. A white boater wreathed in artificial jonquils sat forward on her brow while her hair, glossy as butter, was folded into a netted chignon at the back of her head. As she smiled at him she blushed and lowered her eyes. Nathaniel Rosser, who had playfully courted some of the most beautiful young women on both sides of the Tasman, suddenly found himself without a thing to say.

"You look well," he managed. "I was hoping to see you on my last visit to Auckland, but Marguerite says she hasn't seen you for quite some time."

"Not for nine weeks," she replied in a strange voice, without looking at him.

"Dorinda!" called Dora, turning. Dorrie hurried to catch up with her.

The Sallie Army meetings were boring, decided Dorrie after the novelty of the first one. All Hallelujahs and Amens and much shouting and thumping of drums, yet to Dorrie it seemed as dull as the nuns and priests and the long faces they wore around Grandmaire. She wished she could throw herself into the service the way Turei and Emere did, belting out hymns to the tunes of Variety comic songs and rattling their tambourines as they solicited pennies and threepences for the collection, ''priming the guns for the attack on Beelzebub.''

When the last hymn sheet had been rolled away Major Blackett stood at center stage. ''Now, friends,'' he boomed, his voice echoing against the bare hall's corrugated iron roof, ''we shall enjoy a short interval and, if the wind is not still blowing across from the brewery, a breath of fresh air!'' He beamed at his own joke and Dorrie saw suddenly a strong likeness to Del. ''I urge you all to stay for the rally afterwards and support Mr. Jon Bennington, *your* candidate in the forthcoming elections. As you all know . . .''

His next words were squashed by a dull explosion, the shattering of glass, and a thud as a brown cabbage rolled to a halt near the Major's feet. Almost immediately there was a second explosion and another cabbage, then the hall was in an uproar as rotten fruit and vegetables flew through the windows pelting the stage and exploding over the congregation. A dead cat skidded to where Jon stood on stage. Jon looked dazed.

''It's because of 'im, yer know.'' The Salvationist woman beside Dorrie nodded significantly at Jon. ''That Bonnington's chap.''

''*Ben*nington,'' said Dorrie automatically.

''It's Bonnington's on account of 'is cough. Bonnington's Irish Moss, the cough syrup.''

This is insane, thought Dorrie. *Here we are talking about nicknames while missiles bombard us from all sides*.

''It's the Prohibition business, yer see.'' The woman nodded her Salvation Army bonnet. ''The businessmen don't like it. Lots of money tied up in liquor, yer know.''

''It's *those people* behind this,'' said Dora suddenly. ''Well, I'm not going to let them do it. They're not going to disrupt Jon's campaign!'' And before Dorrie realized her aunt's intentions Dora had heaved herself up and was forging her way through to the door at the back of the hall. By the time Dorrie had pushed through the crush be-

hind her Dora had already been swallowed up by the
darkness. From the wedge of light flung out by the open
door Dorrie saw a handcart trundling away; then as her
eyes became accustomed to the dark she saw Dora
sprawled at the foot of the steps.

"He hit me," she groaned as Dorrie rushed to help
her. "Just a young whelp, too, but he knocked me
down!" She rose to a sitting position and the light fell
over her head, illuminating her pulled-askew hat and disheveled hair. She was gasping in long, shallow breaths.

"Dorinda, are you all right?" came Nathaniel's voice
and she glanced up to see him emerging from the night
with two Maori policemen.

Jon thumped down the steps behind them in time to
hear Dora say, "I've seen you in town hobnobbing with
the Teipa-Benningtons. You're behind all this, I
shouldn't wonder." Without waiting to hear what Nathaniel said Jon danced up to him, fists raised, and
punched him right in the center of the chest. It was a foolish, useless punch. Dorrie looked away, disgusted.

"What?" Jon was saying to the policemen. "Our hall
is attacked, our meeting disrupted, and you're threatening to arrest *me!*"

Dorrie lowered her head in shame, wishing that she
were anywhere else. Nathaniel was smoothing things out
with the policemen and she was grateful for his concern,
but she wished that he, too, had not been here this evening. It was because of him that her friendship with Marguerite had shattered and just seeing him reminded her of
everything she had lost. She knew it wasn't fair but she
couldn't help blaming him for her unhappiness.

Summer was gaspingly dry and hot, Dora said, as purga-
tory. Dorrie was perspiring when she got out of bed in the
morning and limp with fatigue when she sagged into bed
at night.

Flies and dust plagued the little family in the gatehouse. Nothing stayed clean. Washing browned on the

line, Dora's pictures of Queen Victoria bloomed a film of
dust, and each mealtime became a pantomime of waving
hands as they tried to keep the flies away from the table.
Crickets sang in the closet as they chewed on the Benningtons' winter clothes, mites infected the hens so that
Dorrie had to give them dust baths with tobacco powder
and sulphur, and for one whole day a bee swarm hung under the porch eaves driving Dorrie jittery with nerves.

Jon frittered every day away lounging in the shade under the oak tree while Misty, who had developed an "al-
lergy to boot-leather" since Jon's arrival, now lived
under the closed-up mansion next door and skulked over
for a meal and a smooch only if he was sure Jon was out
of the way.

Dorrie had no time to worry about her pet. Because
Jon's weight had flung an intolerable burden on the
household budget, she was now forced to take an outside
job and, for twelve shillings a week, began work at Mr.
and Mrs. Hopkins' millinery shop on Parnell Road.

Exclusive Hats
for
Ladies of Discernment

was less than a mile from Fintona, a pleasant walk
through back lanes that led her along a stream bank that
edged the Blackett property. Dorrie loved the walk and
appreciated being away from Jon, all the more now that
she could stay home alone in the evenings to continue the
piece sewing and flowermaking that had previously taken
up her days.

The work fascinated Dorrie. That the corrugated iron
workshop was broiling hot did not matter to her; she
could cheerfully put up with heat rash and prickly perspiration for the pleasure of what she was learning. Unlike
the Queen Street milliners who bought her flowers to
decorate their cheap, mass-produced bonnets and
boaters, Mr. and Mrs. Hopkins created exclusive de-

signs, each lovingly crafted from the frame up, each impeccably stitched so that not a glimpse of thread showed, each exquisitely trimmed and every one outrageously expensive.

"Nine guineas," Mr. Hopkins would say as he peered over his semicircular spectacles on his nose to box a hat Dorrie knew contained at the most five shillings and sixpence worth of materials, but later he would reiterate to her that price was very important.

"If I charged too little I'd lose my best customers," he was fond of explaining. "Folks love to toss their money away and if you help them do it in a pleasurable way they'll be grateful to you."

"Mr. Rosser once said much the same thing," said Dorrie.

At once Mrs. Hopkins fixed sharp eyes on her. Her beaky face and liver-spotted skin put Dorrie in mind of a thrush. "Well, I never," she said tartly. "Fancy you being a friend of *his*"—as if Dorrie had no right to associate with someone so grand. Ignoring her protests that he wasn't exactly a *friend,* Mrs. Hopkins went on to gossip about how wealthy Mr. Rosser was, how his father had built up a business empire that young Mr. Rosser had no respect for. "Do you know how he chooses to spend his time?" she finished indignantly. "By playing about with projectors and phonographic machines and other such nonsense."

"A good many young ladies have set their caps at him," added Mr. Hopkins. "No doubt we've made bonnets for that very purpose."

He and his wife chirped with mirth. Dorrie was silent.

A few days later she was crouching on a jutting rock shelf, her stripped-off gloves beside her as she bathed her fingers in the tingling cold water. She was on the stream path that bordered the Blacketts' place, a cool, quiet place away from the dust and traffic of the main road with its roof of leafy branches that filtered the sunlight. Fantails darted around her as she bent over the water.

"Ah, that's better," she said, flexing her fingers, then reimmersing them in the refreshing ripples. "That's much better."

"Better than what?" drawled an impudent voice.

Dorrie turned so suddenly that she almost lost her balance. Del was sitting on the opposite bank, wrists resting on drawn-up knees.

"You look like a deer, do you know that? What are you doing there?"

Dorrie scrabbled for her gloves and stood up hastily. Before she had hurried half a dozen paces, Del had crunched from one rock to another in huge strides and was barring her path.

"I've missed you," he said. "I've missed you and that's a fact."

She kept her gaze fixed on a point beyond his shoulder. That familiar nervousness was rising in her throat and she could feel her heart skittering.

"I used to look forward to seeing you. It's not the same old week without Thursdays to brighten it up."

She ducked her head. He was so close that he could see the faint peach down on her cheeks, the fine wisps of straying hair at her temples. He'd forgotten how beautiful she was.

"Look at me," he said.

When she obeyed, her boater rim almost brushed his face. Her eyes were candid yet shy; he remembered now how she always used to seem poised, ready to run. He recalled how that irritated him.

"Why were you bathing your fingers?"

She flustered. "Oh, I was stitching some obstinate material . . . I took off my thimble, and I didn't realize . . . when I looked, there were the blisters . . ."

"Let me see." He imprisoned one wrist and made a play of tugging her glove off by plucking gently at the seams. When he glanced from the abraded skin to her face, he saw that she was crimson with embarrassment and he tipped back his head and laughed.

She stiffened and tried to pull her hand free.

His eyes narrowed as he tightened his grip. He was still laughing at her when he lifted her hand up to his lips and deliberately kissed the hurt fingertips, but the moment that happened his expression altered and the strangest look, a hurt, hungry look, came into his eyes.

Dorrie was unable to move. She had suffered almost three months of desolation over her broken friendship and that loneliness had been intensified since Uncle Jon had pulled the focus of Auntie Dora's attention onto himself. The young woman who now gazed helplessly into Del's face was lonely to the point of starvation and totally unable to make judgments about what would be good for her. She knew Del, and though she felt uneasy in his company, she could see that he was offering the one thing her soul craved, warmth. Accepting, she leaned towards him.

The silence of the trees enfolded them, a blanket torn in a few frayed places by the trill of fantails. His arm slid around her and his face moved closer until all she could see was his mouth with her fingers still pressed against the cushioning softness of his lips.

And then he took her fingers away.

The gentleness of the kiss astonished her. He embraced her as lightly as if she were a soap bubble, likely to vanish under the slightest pressure. She stood perfectly still—the *outside* of her perfectly still—while his hands slid over her shoulders and up her throat until he was cupping her chin like the steam of a goblet as his mouth moved tenderly, enjoying her mouth.

When he let go of her, she was suddenly dizzy. He saw the gasping helplessness on her face and drew her against his shoulder, stroking her back like a baby's as she recovered, trembling, against him.

His voice was unsteady. "There. That wasn't so bad,

was it?'' He brushed a quick kiss against the side of her
cheek and set her away from him. ''Was it so bad?''

''No. It was . . . nice.''

''Good. Then you won't be afraid of me anymore.
You won't run away, will you?''

''No.''

''Fine.''

She may have been mistaken. It may just have been a
trick of the light, but for a moment she thought she saw
triumph in his eyes.

''Have you said anything to your aunt about me?''

It was a casual remark, a pebble dropped into the pool
of amiable silence on which most of their conversations
floated. Neither of them ever said much to the other;
being together seemed to be all that was needed and both
were satisfied.

They were sitting on a large square of clean sacking
that Del had spread in an open glade on his side of the
bank. From nearby came the comforting murmur of
water over rocks. Low shafts of sunlight illuminated the
upper branches of some of the trees so that the two
seemed to be resting at the bottom of a tilted pool of
shade.

Dorrie squinted sideways at him. ''What if I had told
her all about you?''

She was not surprised to see a swift coolness slide into
his eyes. It was always like that; his mouth would smile,
showing a little tip of tongue sometimes, but his eyes indicated displeasure.

Dorrie giggled. ''I was joking. Of course I've not told
her. I've not mentioned you to anybody.''

''Why not? Would she disapprove?''

''Uncle Jon would, and he would scold her. I hate
that.'' *He disapproves of almost everything I do,* she
thought, *the way I talk, the dishes I cook when I'm helping Auntie Dora, the way I iron his shirts when he wants
one in a hurry, the time I waste playing with Misty. I*

*can't even practice the piano when he's there, now, but
it's always* her *that he growls at, not me.*

"So I'm a secret, am I?"

"Yes, if you like. I always wanted a secret and now I
have one."

He put his head in her lap, his eyes mirrored the sky.
She twined her fingers in his fair, woolly hair, then said,
"I do have to go now."

"Already?"

Her excuses were always prepared in advance. "I
have to finish a Leghorn hat for one of the customers.
It will take most of the evening as it is." She had freed
herself and was brushing out the creases in the gray
and lemon gingham, shaking her head, then settling
her boater, tying the chin ribbons and carefully avoiding
his eyes.

"Dorrie." He snatched her hand and tugged gently,
trying to pull her down beside him.

"I do have to go. Truly. I'm late as it is—"

"I love you."

She could feel her heart stop. The way his voice
dropped for sincerity when he said those words. The glorious feeling that overcame her. Her eyes closed for a
second as a quick rush of happiness gushed through her.
This made it all worthwhile—the loneliness, the years of
not quite fitting in, the lifetime of feeling as though she
were a burden, now she was truly loved and she felt like a
just-emerging butterfly, bright and unblemished, serene.

"Oh, Del . . ." she said, her heart blocking her
throat, her feelings jammed up behind it. "If I could only
tell you— If I could only show you—"

"All in good time," he said.

He helped her down the bank and across the stream,
playing their little game where he pretended to let her fall
in while she gurgled and cried and clung more tightly to
his arms. At the other side he enfolded her in a rough hug
that jolted all the breath out of her.

"Tomorrow," he said. "I'll be waiting."

* * *

It was cold and poorly lit in the bedroom. Dorrie hunched on the bed, stockinged feet tucked under her, one of Dora's crocheted shawls about her shoulders, and a conglomeration of spools, scissors, and snippets of thread cluttering her spread skirts. She frowned and held needle and cotton close to the wavering lamplight as she made her third attempt to thread up.

Next door in the warm, well-lit living room Uncle Jon was burping in after-dinner contentment while Dora fussed around him, pressing him to take another cup of tea, offering him sugar biscuits.

She could hear her through the thin walls. "I bought them specially because I know how partial you are to them. An extravagance, really, but I know how you like your little treats after dinner."

Dorrie pulled a face. It was worth putting up with this discomfort to get away from *him*. Trying not to listen, she turned the half-finished hat over in her hands. It was one of the latest styles, dark blue with pale blue silk under the brim, more pale silk swathing the crown in an elaborate turban effect. She had brought it home on the pretext of doing extra work on it so that she could measure and cut patterns for the pieces that composed it. Her templates had now been made, labeled and stored in a large flat box on top of the wardrobe. As she worked now Dorrie was jotting down details in an old notebook. She listed each material used, its official description, quality and quantity, what trimmings had been incorporated in the design, and how much each of these things cost. Then, if she was fortunate enough to be present when Mrs. Clement came to collect her green and white floral hatbox, she would also learn what outrageous price was being charged for the finished article.

Gradually she was building up a dossier on the millinery business, learning the tools and the tricks of the trade. She already had a few precious scissors, awls, hooks, and special needles put away for when she would begin her own business.

One day, she resolved. *One day soon!* She had calculated that it was not until she had her own shop that she would be able to make any real profit. With her own place all her dreams could be realized and she would be able to set Auntie Dora up in comfort.

"When *he's* gone," she decided. "When *he's* away in Parliament—then we'll be able to afford to set up shop."

Through the wall Jon was carping in that way she detested, "It's good to know you've got money to throw around." He began to cough harshly and she guessed he had swallowed a crumb of biscuit the wrong way. There was a thumping sound then, "Leave me alone, dammit! Sometimes you give me the devil and his doings, I swear you do."

He's been drinking again, she thought.

Despite Dora's careful supervision and the lavish doses of Blue Lily Secret Liquor Cure, they were unable to prevent Jon's lapses, and he managed to sneak away regularly to the nearest saloon bar.

"I'm sorry, Jon," Dora was saying. "I only want to help."

"Then help me, dammit!" snapped Jon. "The campaign has only four weeks to run and I can't possibly complete it without money. After those damned Sallie Army types let me down so badly, I'm snookered. I've got to get funds from somewhere."

You let us down, thought Dorrie fiercely, stabbing her needle into the pillow. *Getting sozzled and missing meetings, standing up and being too drunk to make your speech on Prohibition. The whole town's laughing at you.*

But Dora wouldn't see it that way, of course. She was busy apologizing to him, saying that if she had any money he'd be more than welcome to it, but the gatehouse couldn't be sold and there were no savings left in the bank. . . .

There was such a long silence that Dorrie held her breath and turned her head to press her ear to the wall, wondering if she'd missed something. At last Jon spoke.

"Don't playact with me, Dora. You've got something you could sell." His voice chilled like a rising wind. "Don't pretend you don't know what I'm talking about. You know, all right. I met someone who works at the museum. You must have seen the museum, Dora. It's the place where they keep items of value, historical artifacts, *greenstone,* and so on." He was hacking again, harsh, ugly coughs that turned Dorrie's stomach. When he recovered he gasped, "It's in your name, Dora, so you could sell it at any time. Know what the curator reckons it's worth? Eight thousand pounds at least. Eight thousand pounds!"

Dorrie's heart shriveled. *Don't give in to him,* she begged silently as her needle punctured the pillow with staccato jabs. She could have cheered when Dora said, "I don't regard *Riversong* as mine, Jon. I could never sell her and have her shut away in somebody's safe. I'm—fond of her, and Dorrie loves her, too. Besides, it gives me a good feeling to know she's there. Security, that's what it is. I always had that feeling while Grandmaire was alive, and in the strangest way *Riversong* gives me that feeling now." She twisted a pleading note in her voice as she said, "I do hate to deny you anything, dear, but I hope you understand."

He laughed. "I can't believe I'm hearing this. Dora, I need the money!"

"You'll manage, dear. Your campaign has been going so well, I'm sure they'll all vote for you on the day. . . ."

There was silence. Dorrie could picture him glaring at her.

"Who is the head of this household?" he demanded.

"You—you are."

She's crying, thought Dorrie. Sweeping the paraphernalia off her skirts, she scrambled from the bed and eased the door open.

Dora was standing beyond the hoop of light cast by the lamp above the table. Dorrie could not see her face.

Jon was planted on the sofa, hands grasping his thighs like a wrestler braced for action. There was something odd in his whole posture as if he were in pain.

"Dora, I'm ordering you," he gasped, but she did not reply with so much as a movement of her head. After an interval he stood up. His face was gray and set. As he reached to unpeg his coat and hat from the rack a fit of coughing seized him and shook him like an old doormat. Dora reached out a tentative hand to him, but he looked neither at her nor at Dorrie as he opened the door and stepped out into the night.

Dora sagged onto a chair and rested her face in her hands. Her shoulders quivered. "He's not a well man," she said. "Oh, Dorrie, pet, he's not a well man. It didn't do any good, did it? Nine shillings the tin and all for nothing."

"You tried. You gave him his chance."

"Yes, his chance. And now he wants a different sort of chance, but I can't do it. If I did sell *Riversong,* he would run through the money faster than a dose of salts and not a penny of it would be to his betterment, either."

She sounded so depressed that Dorrie was alarmed for her. "I'll tell you what," she coaxed. "You put your feet up while I fetch you another cup of tea, then I'll brush your hair for you. That always makes you feel better."

Standing behind her, Dorrie plucked out the hairpins and dropped them into the pearl cup of a scallop shell. Lifting out the gray, crescent-shaped chignon she put it away in a bedroom drawer before beginning to brush Dora's hair with long, firm strokes. The fine strands flew out in a moth-wing cloud around her head. Dora sighed and closed her eyes. She felt so old, beyond caring.

With ineffable sadness she said, "We're a family of bachelors and old maids, us Benningtons. All lonely, all

unwanted. Look at us. Hal jilted by May Yardley on the
eve of their marriage, Jon deserted by his wife, me, well,
nobody's ever given me a first glance let alone a second,
and as for poor, poor Lena, she had the most
wretched—'' She stopped, suddenly realizing what she
was saying.

"What about my mother? What were you going to
say?"

"Never mind."

"But—"

"I said never mind." Dora's tone softened as she
added, "Jon has us—even if he doesn't appreciate us—
and we do have *Riversong*. Quote me the poem, Dorrie,
there's a love."

She would rather have heard what Dora had to say
about her mother, but obediently she recited,

> In the stillness of eternity
> I hear the river song.
> The spirit of my ancestors
> Sings a lament for me.

"Yes," sighed Dora. "That's what we need. A lament."

I don't, thought Dorrie. *I need songs of joy. I'm not
unloved. Del loves me, doesn't he?*

PART THREE

DEL

1896-1897

Eight

One day a customer brought Dorrie a gift, a packet of large round seeds. At the lady's urging Dorrie filled a glass with water, dropped one seed in, then almost dropped the glass in astonishment as a beautiful scarlet poppy unfolded, full blown in the water. All afternoon she sat with the glass beside her, glancing at it from time to time as she worked, and as soon as five o'clock came she packed up swiftly and hurried away down the path.

Her face was alight with excitement as she picked her way along the river bank. Del was not in the usual place so she crossed the stream and hurried through the trees towards the house, calling to him.

He called in reply to let her know where he was, and when she approached he was wiping his hands on a rag and grinning with delight. In the sunshine he seemed even bulkier and more vital than ever, but she no longer felt that shiver of apprehension at first sight of him. He was hers now, and he loved her.

"I brought something to show you," she said. "But I need a glass of water first, and—"

"Then come on into the house. It's all right. The Major is at band practice. The Auckland Aggressives are off to Dunedin for the National Championships in a week or so. Great excitement." His voice was flat. "Come in. I have to go and wash up and change anyway. I want to kiss you, don't I, and I can't come near with these grubby clothes."

She hesitated. He laughed and seized her hand. "Come in. It's all right, I do assure you."

Bowser came leaping around them as they crossed the yard. Sunlight shimmered over the spread of netting and smacked hot bursts of light off the corrugated iron roofs. There was a warm drone of bees in the honeysuckle and the clip-clip of sparrows as they jostled around some spilt birdseed near the stable door.

The hall was as chaotically untidy as before, but when Del showed her into the kitchen she was surprised that it was a comparatively tidy room with cheerful red and white curtains at the windows and red rugs on the timber floor.

"I hate mess," said Del. "We have lots of fights over this room. When Mama died he vowed he'd never let another woman past the door, but whenever he goes away with his band I bring someone in to clean this room out. It's the kitchen, after all. We have to eat in here. The rest of the time I try to keep it reasonably clean. Wait here, I won't be long. The glasses are on that shelf."

She filled a glass, placed it on the table with one seed beside it, then sat on a sofa under the window. She was flicking through an old copy of *War Cry* that she had found behind a cushion when he came in and sat down beside her, slipping one arm about her shoulders and with the other hand snatching the paper out of her grasp.

"Don't read that. You could contaminate your mind. Do you know what religion is? An attempt by a minority to gain control over the masses."

"Auntie Dora says it's a kind of comfort, to give people something to look forward to, to compensate for the misery of their lives."

"What do you think? Is your life a misery?" And he stroked the side of her neck with his fingers.

"It used to be," she whispered. "But not now."

Seeing her expression, he smiled, running the tip of his tongue around the flat cutting edge of his upper teeth, a gesture he made to tease her sometimes if she became suddenly bashful in his presence. "Fox's teeth," it meant.

"I don't think you're ever going to get used to the fact that I'm a man," he said, taking her hand and pretending to nibble her fingertips.

"No," she said, "But in the evenings when I'm sitting on the verandah at Fintona—I go there after I've taken care of the hens and stay there until Auntie Dora calls me, it gets me away from you-know-who. Sometimes then, when I think about you . . ."

"Only sometimes?" he inquired, nibbling her wrist.

"Only very rarely. Then I think about you and I'm glad you're a man. I mean, you're my friend like Marguerite was, so that I can tell you all sorts of things, but you're more than that."

There was a silence. Dorrie knew that he was willing her to look into his face, so she kept her eyes carefully down, fixed on the edges of his shirtfront where they not quite came together.

"Who mends your clothes?"

"Hey, what's all this? I thought we were talking about us? In what way am I more than just a friend to you?"

Dorrie flicked the front of his shirt and stepped her fingertips up in marching strides from one torn hole to another. "All your buttons are ripped off. They need to be sewn back on. If you like—"

He captured the hand and slid it inside his shirt, against the bare, hot skin of his chest.

"Oh," she said.

He leaned closer towards her. Her instinct was to take her hand away from that burning skin, yet she knew she wanted to keep it there, to let her fingers glide over those smooth planes and to feel the heat of him flow through her palm. His breath was tickling her forehead and she could smell the lemony laundry-soap smell of his shirt.

"Dorrie," he whispered and she turned her face towards him. She loved this feeling of closeness. When she was alone and thinking private thoughts about him, it was this sensation that she hungered for. She felt safe when he held her, murmuring that he loved her, safe and cherished, and here in this cozy domestic setting those feelings blossomed fully so that she was more relaxed and at ease than she had ever been in the glade.

"I love you," he breathed lazily as he kissed his way along her jawline and then made the quick, brushing hop to her mouth.

She sighed and a shudder rippled through her. Always when he first kissed her, she thought she would swoon with a surfeit of joy. As she moved her hand the throb of his heart jumped under her palm like the kicking of a small animal. Del grasped her other hand and placed it on his shoulder, covering it with his for a second. As soon as he let go she slid it up his neck and twined her fingers in the crisp, damp curls.

"Dorrie, you're beautiful, you're so beautiful."

"You are, too," she whispered shyly. "Your skin is warm and lovely and I can feel your heart beating."

He lifted his head for a moment and looked into her eyes. She was smiling at him with a drowsy, gloriously happy expression.

"My beautiful love," he said. This time, when he resumed kissing her his right hand briefly cupped her chin before his fingers stroked the curve of her throat down as far as her collar.

Like all colonial women who had no servants to help them dress, Dorrie's gown fastened at the front with a strip of buttons running from her prim high collar to well below her fitted waistline. When she felt Del popping the first few yellow-covered buttons undone, she stirred, but as he progressed downwards her unease increased and she pulled away from his embrace. Though he put an arm around her and tried to scoop her close again, she struggled to stay free.

"What are you trying to do?" she asked.

She looked frightened. One hand clutched the open edges together but not before he glimpsed milky skin and the curve of one softly rounded breast.

Dorrie, he thought. *Oh, Dorrie, don't run away this*

time. His voice reassured her. "You liked feeling my heart beating so I wanted to feel yours. Surely you don't mind that?"

"Well . . ."

"If it was a good feeling, wouldn't you want me to share it, too? After all, I want to share all my good feelings with you."

"Do you?"

"Of course. All of them. That's what love is all about, isn't it?"

"I suppose so."

"That's my lovely girl." Del nudged her towards him again and placed a hand lightly on her throat. "You feel my heartbeat and I'll feel yours. When you want me to stop just say so and I will."

Though she was full of misgivings, she said, "All right then, just for a moment."

She gasped when his hand glided under the bodice of her gown and under her lacy undergarment straps, so he swiftly bent his head to kiss her again, keeping his hand perfectly still until he was sure he had lulled her back into a state of relaxation. Only then did he permit his eager hand to steal down to that warm, silky roundness.

She pulled away, trembling. Deliberately he left his hand where it was. His thumb brushed over her nipple.

"Please, Del—please don't."

"You're beautiful and I love you." His palm circled, gently caressing.

"Please stop, *please!* You promised."

"Very well, don't get agitated." He sat up and moved away to lean back against the far arm of the sofa, staring at her through narrowed, speculative eyes. An uncomfortable silence dropped between them, a silence that cooled as it stretched. She was huddled half over, gazing miserably at the floor. Del noticed that though she was bunching the front of her dress in one hand she had made no move to rebutton it. This he found encouraging.

"Are you very angry?" she asked timidly.

She glanced around, then dropped her eyes in dismay. He was staring at her with that cold expression she hated so much. She always got the feeling that he didn't like her in the least when he looked at her like that.

"Please talk to me," she begged.

"What's the point?" She could tell by his voice that he was shrugging her off, dismissing her. A well of panic burst in her throat as she heard him say, "I thought we loved each other but I was mistaken."

"I do love you, Del. I—"

"There's no need to pretend just to make me feel better," he said. "People change their minds. It happens all the time. There's no hard feelings, truly. You can just go home and we'll forget all about each other."

"No!" He was proposing to end *everything*. It was unthinkable. No more meetings in the glade on her way home from work, no more kisses, no more glorious feelings of closeness. She couldn't bear that.

"It's all for the best, Dorrie. I don't want to make you feel bad. After all, *I* love *you* very much. If my embraces are so distasteful to you, then let's just say good-bye right now and part as friends."

Dorrie was struggling not to cry. He was the calm, logical one while she seethed with a jumble of conflicting emotions. The craziest part of all this was that she liked the feeling of his hand on her breast. When she pushed him away she had been obeying an instinct, the same instinct that would make her flinch if someone was trying to hit her. But Del was not intent upon hurting her, quite the opposite, so why did she react so strongly to him?

"I don't understand any of this," she pleaded. "I do love you, though, and I don't want us to stop—" She hesitated.

"To stop being lovers?"

She nodded.

He held out his arms. "Come here. Put your arms around me. Here, under my shirt." He tugged it loose from his waistband. "There's my girl."

When they lay down again together all the buttons had been undone and all the ribbons untied so that warm bare skin was against warm bare skin, and Del was intent upon the next step toward his conquest.

Now he moved with care, caressing her breasts and her shoulders and the smooth pulsing throat and all the while whispering loving things to her, kissing her until he felt that he was being drawn down, down into a whirling pool and that she was his only hope of salvation. He would drown if he didn't have her. He would die. Over and over again he told her so, and she murmured something in reply but he could not hear because of the dull roaring in his head. Handful by handful he hitched her skirt and petticoat up until they were bunched at her waist. She stirred when he first touched her thigh between the lace of her drawers and the garters that held her stockings above the knee, but he soothed her with more loving words, more kisses until she lay still again.

Dorrie was trying just as strenuously to calm her own undefined fears. It seemed wrong, all wrong, to be lying half-naked in a man's arms while he stroked and caressed all the places which were normally properly hidden under her clothes. What Del was doing was an assault on her sense of modesty, yet undeniably she was enjoying it— more than that, reveling in it. Until now Dorrie had never given much thought to her body, and now, all of a sudden Del was revealing it to her as a source of wonder and delight. She loved the feeling of her bare breasts against his chest, for it was that cherished feeling of closeness intensified to an unimaginable degree. She was happy in his arms, gloriously happy and brimming, too, with that marvelous feeling of giving, of making Del feel happy, too.

His hand glided over the warm skin of her stomach. She caught her breath when his fingers touched that most secret place of all. His intrusion there was a shock both physical and mental. Why would he *want* to put his hand down there? What on earth could be attractive about that part of her? She was puzzled and embarrassed for the first few moments, then as his fingertips gently stroked and fondled her she was overwhelmed by a torrent of sensations that made her moan against his lips while her body moved subtly and involuntarily against his hand.

I never suspected, she thought wildly. All this time these feelings have been here and I never suspected. I was waiting for Del and waiting for this moment and all along I never knew . . .

He raised himself up on his elbows and looked down into her face with that odd triumphant expression. She was spread below him, so beautiful and sweet that he was aching all over with anticipation. Her head was thrown back, the curve of her neck pale in the filtered sunlight, her partly disarranged hair like a cushion of crumpled silk under her head. Her lips were parted and she was breathing in soft little gasps. He could see her eyelids quivering, bluish and delicate with the dark fringe of lashes, and he realized how young and vulnerable she was.

"I love you, Dorrie. I won't hurt you," he told her hoarsely as he fitted himself between her thighs.

Her eyes flew open in surprise as the full weight of him forced down on her chest. He smiled at her, an absent, preoccupied smile and she smiled back and arched her neck so that her lips fitted against his again.

The rubbing continued and Dorrie sighed, relaxing and parting her thighs a little more. It felt tingly and moist and very, very good, and she was greeting each new sensation with the confidence of a delighted explorer in a strange land, until suddenly the nudging and rubbing became forceful pushing and delight was replaced by a stretching, burning feeling.

"Del, you're hurting me!"

"Hush," he said, pressing harder.

"Del, stop! You're *hurting!*"

"I won't hurt you," he repeated in the same, hoarse voice. "Keep still, I won't hurt you."

"Del! Stop it—"

He covered her mouth with his so abruptly and so hard that she felt her lips grinding against her teeth. She could not move her legs and her chest was pinned down, so with her fists she beat on his shoulders as hard as she could.

"Ah!" he cried suddenly. At the same instant she twisted her face away from his and screamed as the pain tore into her. Clumsily he pushed her head around again but when she twisted away from his kiss he covered her mouth with his hand. His breath was coming fast, panting in her ear like a dog after an exhausting run and all the while he was slamming against her. It no longer hurt quite as much—the first thrust had been the worst— but Dorrie was sobbing now, buffeted and sore and miserable, but above all totally bewildered.

At length he stopped with a long exhalation of breath and a shudder that rippled through him as if he were a ship and she a sandbank. For a full minute or two he lay very still, his face cradled in her neck while she snuffled and cried with tears etching paths across her cheeks. She could hear his breathing winding down now and the clicking of the pendulum clock above the mantelpiece, and she felt dead inside, dead and confused and still utterly bewildered.

He said into the silence, "I'm sorry. I'm so sorry. I didn't mean to hurt you."

She was still in the circle of his arms but she might have been a million miles away from him, so distant did she feel.

"Please, Dorrie. I honestly didn't think it would hurt. At least, not very much. I wouldn't hurt you for anything. Please believe that."

There was nothing she could say. She stared, unseeing, at a blotch of mildew on the ceiling.

"Dorrie. Sweet Dorrie." He joggled her elbow and she moved floppily, like a doll. "Please listen. I thought that you were enjoying what I was doing so I kept on with it. Once I got so far I couldn't stop. I didn't mean to hurt you, please believe me.''

"I want to go home." The blotch was right above her head and she kept her eyes on it as if she were afraid it would move if she glanced away. She did not want to look at Del, not with his face sick with guilt.

Resignedly he moved away from her, pulling her skirt down as he did so. Then he went around and leaned on the sofa arm with his back to her. She permitted herself to look at the back of him while he tucked his shirt in and fidgeted with the front of his clothing, but when he combed his fingers through his curly hair and turned to look at her again she was gazing back at the ceiling.

After studying her for a second or two he said, "I'll make you a cup of tea."

"No," she said quietly. "Please just go. Leave me alone to tidy myself up. I'm late and Auntie Dora will be starting to worry.''

"I can't let you go like this."

"You have to."

"I love you, Dorrie."

Those words had always meant such a lot to her; they hung in the air after he had gone. As she stood up and re-fastened her bodice the other things he had said kept running through her mind the way a tune did sometimes, and no matter what she did, she could not get rid of it.

Perhaps Del was right. She *had* been enjoying what he was doing and perhaps he couldn't stop himself. It was easy to accept that he hadn't meant to hurt her—look at how distressed and guilty he was directly afterwards. Anyway, the hurt was fading already because now that she was moving around she felt immeasurably better; she realized now that it was the unexpected shock of it that had struck her more forcefully than the actual physical pain.

She wound her hair up in a bun, stabbed it through with pins, and fastened her hat on, aware that her hands were shaking. At the sink she splashed some cold water on her face, then patted her opened handkerchief over her eyes. As she did she remembered what she had originally come into the kitchen for.

Her surprise. The mysterious seed that would burst into bloom when it was dropped into water. She had planned to slip it in unobtrusively and hand the glass to Del so that she could laugh over his surprise as the petals unfolded right before his eyes.

Hesitating by the table, she looked at the seed and the glass, then, on impulse she held the seed above the water's surface and let it roll and tumble into the depths.

Del was standing in the shade of the porch looking wretched. His eyes searched her face as she came out. She hesitated again, then swept past him and did not stop until she was beyond the stables. Only then did she turn back towards him.

"There's something for you on the table," she called.

"What was that?"

"Inside, on the table."

By the time he had dashed in, seen it, and dashed outside again she had disappeared.

Nine

With the Salvation Army support withdrawn and without funds to hire himself a hall, Jon finished his campaign with a series of open-air meetings. His final speech was to be delivered from a balcony on the south side of the Town Hall.

Dorrie and Dora walked the two miles into town along roads still deeply rutted and iron-hard although the summer drought was easing. Rain was threatening and by the time the two women reached Queen Street the evening had thickened and chilled. As the lamp-lighter prodded the gas lamps into life with his long pole, each flared yellow behind a veil of fine drizzle. The damp air smelled sour.

Del was leaning against a hawker's barrow outside the Empire Theater where the horse-drawn buses were backed in ready for customers. When Dorrie walked by, he fell into step behind her. Dora was too busy fretting to notice.

"I hope he succeeds, pet," she kept repeating. "If he doesn't get elected he'll blame me for refusing to sell *Riversong*. I wonder if I should have given in to him?"

"You did the right thing," Dorrie assured her. She, too, hoped Jon would succeed, for if he were elected he would be off to Wellington, some four hundred miles away, whereas if he failed he would be there, forever in their tiny cottage. That thought was too ghastly to contemplate. She glanced around; Del was still following her.

The streets were crowded and it became increasingly difficult to progress quickly. Outside the Civic Theater

146

Dora was intercepted by Mr. O'Reilly, who was selling hard-boiled eggs from a basket slung around his neck. Del touched Dorrie's arm and moved closer to talk to her.

"Are you all right?" His eyes searched her face; he had not seen her since that afternoon in the kitchen. She looked away, obviously ill at ease. He said, "I've waited by the stream for you every afternoon. You're avoiding me, aren't you?"

She said nothing.

"Please, Dorrie, don't be like this." He could see Dora nodding good-bye to Mr. O'Reilly so he said quickly, "Here. Here's something to say I'm sorry." And he slipped a card into her sleeve so that Dora would not see it. With that he disappeared into the throng.

He was there again, waiting for them when they pushed into the crowd that packed the space below the balcony. A banner stretched across the balustrades. It read JON BENNINGTON, THE PEOPLE'S CHOICE in a wreath of blue rosettes that Dora had spent countless hours sewing. There was no sign of Jon.

Del was laughing as he leaned back against a lamppost, arms folded and hat tipped back to show a frizzy ruff of yellow curls. "Evening, Miss Bennington," he said boldly to Dora. "Your brother's putting on quite a show tonight."

"I can't see him at all."

"He's there, on the steps, giving those hecklers what-for. See him now?"

"Oh, my stars!" cried Dora. "He's *brawling.*"

From the window of the Sunset Ballroom across the street Nathaniel Rosser was watching the drama unfold. He had just signed a purchasing order acquiring the ballroom as a venue for his latest venture, a Cinematograph show, and was feeling pleased with the deal he had made. The ballroom had everything—a stage deep enough for the live acts that would perform between projections, a narrow orchestra pit, and plenty of room for the customers who would queue to see such an exciting new development in entertainment. His head was buzzing with plans as he stood at the window slapping his notebook against his thigh and gazing absently out across at the political rally.

Why, that's Bennington! he thought as Jon began to address the crowd. Anything that drew any audience was of interest to Nathaniel. Sallie Army, Suffragettes, dancing bears, or snake-charmers, all appealed to him, but·because Patrick Teipa-Bennington had spoken of Jon as an object first of nervous fear and now of pity, Nathaniel was particularly fascinated by him. It was hard to believe that only weeks ago he was promoting the image of a prim, dour teetotaler. Now he was flushed, his jacket off and waistcoat rumpled, stringy gray hair flopping over his brow as he jabbed at the air to emphasize his phrases and the crowd laughed and applauded in appreciation of his jokes.

They're laughing but they'll never vote for him, thought Nathaniel as he appraised the situation. *He's a pathetic figure of fun.*

He was about to turn away when his attention was taken by a couple of rowdies who were capering on the lower steps, mocking Jon as he leaned over the bannered balcony. The crowd clapped and hooted as they made a great show of climbing up to where Jon stood, indicating that they intended to pummel him.

Nathaniel felt a surge of anticipation as he watched. The rowdies were hired by Jon himself, no doubt. There was nothing like a scrap of rough stuff to attract sympathy and make Jon look like a winner, for it would take a real man to beat off two husky young thugs.

The stage management was well done. Both rowdies swung at the same time and Jon pretended to sag under the dual blow. Shouts from the crowd called for more, but as the punches kept slamming into him and he made only the feeblest efforts to retaliate Nathaniel stepped closer to the window in alarm, as he realized the attack was real.

Hurrying for the stairs, Nathaniel took them three at a time and was running out into the street at about the same time that Dorrie and Dora arrived at the square. By now the brawl had descended halfway down the steps as Jon struggled to escape his attackers. Nathaniel forced his way through the crush and stood gasping at the foot of the steps.

"Bennington!" he shouted.

Jon grabbed at the stair-rail and clutched at the coat of one of his attackers just as he was lunging toward him again. The coat dragged upward, momentarily pinning the thug's arms, and he and Jon rocked together for what seemed several seconds. Then Jon slumped over sideways and the thug, propelled by his own violently kicking legs, lunged out of balance and toppled over the railing, amid screams, to the pavement below.

The other youth bolted, pushing past Nathaniel and rushing around to help his friend up. At that moment a police whistle blasted close by and a Maori constable appeared to sort out the troublemakers.

"They've gone, officer," Nathaniel told him. "Paid thugs, I'd say, but who paid them and why we'll not find out unless they're caught."

"We know who paid them," declared Dora, brushing past Nathaniel and up the steps to where Jon was sprawled, retching and wretched amid the ruins of his banner. As soon as she had satisfied herself that he was alive she jolted back a few steps and glared, bosom heaving, at the policeman. "Ask him," she demanded, jerking her head at Nathaniel. *"He* knows all about this. There's only one man in Auckland who hates Jon enough to attack him in this cowardly way. That's the man who stands to lose most when Jon gets elected tomorrow."

Dorrie stood very still in the shadows, hoping that Mr. Rosser would not see her there. The constable looked expectantly at him; his eyes gleamed like wet pebbles and there were faint ridges of tattooing on his nose and forehead. He smelled of the same sweet oil that the Patene girls used on their hair.

Nathaniel had his back to Dorrie. He said, "Please make allowances for Miss Bennington. She's understandably upset."

"Upset? *Upset?* Sir, I'm furious! Jon's not a well man, I'll have you know. A beating like this—" She turned away.

"Miss Bennington, please," said Nathaniel with great gentleness. "Please let me help you."

They rode in Nathaniel's carriage all the way home. Dora stared stonily out the window into the black and yellow night. Dorrie sat beside her, silent with embarrassment as Jon lolled against Nathaniel. Her uncle was obviously drunk; the carriage reeked of whiskey fumes, and between his coughs and groans Jon belched in a way that made Dorrie wince with shame.

Nathaniel could not keep his eyes off her. She tilted her head proudly but he could see by the dim carriage lamps that she was suffering keen humiliation. He wished that he might be able to speak to her but knew that this was not the right time to try to make a favorable impression.

The two opposite reminded him of a fairy tale—maiden and her dragon—an idea that made him smile inwardly. And he had no illusions of what might happen if he tried to rescue that maiden, either. She'd be as swift to defend her aunt as her aunt would be to protect her.

When they were almost at Fintona, Nathaniel broke the silence by saying, "I know you think badly of the Teipa-Benningtons, but please believe me when I assure you that Patrick would never have instigated an attack like this. I know him well and I'm positive that—"

"You may save your insults, thank you," retorted Dora.

"Insults? Miss Bennington, I—"

"You insult me by denying what I know to be the truth. I know *those people* and what they are capable of." The carriage squeaked to a halt in the driveway. "Come, Dorinda. Help me with your uncle."

Iron-faced, Dora watched Nathaniel settle Jon on the sofa, and cold-voiced she thanked him. Dorrie rattled around, poking up the embers and checking the water level in the kettle. Dora hung up her coat and went into the bedroom. Her sobs were faint but audible.

Hurrying in, Dorrie sat beside her on the bed, arms about her aunt's thick waist while Dora wept with a weariness beyond endurance.

I'll make all of this up to you one day, vowed Dorrie. *All the sacrifices you make, the toil, the ruined hopes and crushed dreams.*

"Auntie, please don't cry," she whispered, rubbing her knobbly-corseted back.

"It's my fault," said Dora unexpectedly. "I've been so selfish. If I'd done what Jon asked and sold *Riversong,* he would have had the money to hire a hall and finish his campaign properly. This has ruined things for him, I know it has, and it's all my fault." She stood up and moved dispiritedly through to the other room. When Dorrie followed, it was to see Dora trying to coax Jon to sip some of the tea she had just poured. "Do have just a little," she begged. "A wee drop just for my sake, mmmm?"

A "wee drop" is half his trouble, thought Dorrie with a flash of rebellion.

Dora said, "He's not well. I'm worried about him. Perhaps we should send someone for the doctor."

"I'll go if you want me to," said Dorrie, drinking her tea quickly and hoping that Jon would not start coughing until she had finished it. There was nothing more disgusting and off-putting during a meal or a snack than the raw, scraping sound of him hacking up his lungs.

"He's so pale," said Dora. "So terribly pale."

Dorrie glanced across at him as she was pouring another cup of tea. At that moment his head jerked back, then forward in a sudden, violent movement as if he had been whacked between the shoulder blades, and as his head flung forward a great dash of blood came with it. There must have been a cupful or more of blood in his mouth and nose, all held there loose and waiting, for it came out in an abrupt splatter down his front and over his waistcoat, his trousers and his shirtsleeves where his arms rested in his lap.

Dorrie witnessed it in utter disbelief. Things did not happen like this. She wondered, dimly, if he had been shot.

"What—what—" Jon tried to say. He slumped back, gasping, with more dark viscous blood dripping from his mouth and his nose. His astonishment was as great as theirs.

"Keep still, dear." Dora's voice was tight and sharp. "Dorrie is going for the doctor. I'll stay right here with you." She glanced up at Dorrie and her face was blank with fright. "Do hurry," she whispered. "Tell him Jon's had a hemorrhage. But do *hurry.*"

"She's fast asleep now and I don't think she'll stir before morning," said Dorrie as she shut the bedroom door behind her. It was still faintly light with a watercolor sky just beginning to curdle and darken.

"Good thing you sent for the doctor," Uncle Samuel said. "I never thought she'd stop crying. Funny she should take on so. Dora's always so . . . strong."

"She blames herself for what happened."

"That's ridiculous." Samuel shook his head. "Nasty business that. 'Course he'd had consumption for years, but that beating finished him off properly. Mercy in some ways. He'd never have won the election, not after the way he was ridiculed in the newspapers."

Dorrie shivered. She was plagued with guilt, too; all day she had been trying unsuccessfully to feel sorry that Jon was dead. She said, "If there was no chance of him winning, why did those liquor dealers have him beaten up?''

"Is that what you think? That May and Patrick had a hand in this?''

Shrugging unhappily under his gaze, Dorrie said, "Auntie Dora is adamant that it must have been them.''

"She's wrong. Dead wrong. Somebody put those two up to it, but it certainly wasn't the Teipa-Benningtons.''

"Then who?''

He placed a finger alongside his nose. "Just a hunch. But don't be surprised if Ellen and the children come home very soon. Rupert's twenty now, and it's time he started learning the business.'' He laughed at her startled face. "Hey, lass, don't read too much into what I say. I'm just a meandering old man. Well, think I'll mosey on out to see Captain Yardley. Said he'd just opened a barrel of porter and he'd like my opinion.''

"Good for you.''

"Funerals are a nasty business. Your Uncle Hal always said the only funeral he ever intended going to was his own. Can't say as I blame him.'' At the doorway he turned and stared into her face. "Oh, another sad piece of news came our way today. Major Blackett died. Down in the South Island.''

"Major *Blackett?*''

"Sorry to rock you like that. Forgot he was your music teacher. Drowned, poor blighter. The ship ran aground and somehow in the turmoil your Major fell out of the lifeboat, and when he tried to climb into the one following he was dragged underneath it. Nasty business and bad luck, too. He was the only one lost. Gone down for that band championship, they said.''

"Poor Del.''

"What's that?''

"Never mind.'' When he had gone she opened her workbasket and from under the heap of carded silks withdrew the small, scalloped-edged card Del had tucked into her sleeve. In the fading light she could barely distinguish the picture of a violet and the copperplate words. *"You are my own true love,"* she whispered as she traced them with her finger. "Oh, poor Del."

Half an hour later she was walking up the driveway towards the Blackett house. The air smelled of ripe fruit, and as she walked by the rows of yards she could hear the fowls stirring on their perches, reminding her that her own Brahma Pootras had gone to roost hungry tonight, because in the confusion after the funeral, Dora's hysterics, and the doctor's visit, she had forgotten to feed them.

One light illuminated the dark blankness of the house. It was an upstairs window—probably Del's bedroom. She had not expected him to go to bed so early and paused to reconsider, but in that moment, alerted by the crunching of her shoes on the gravel, the dog set up a flurry of angry barking that made her start with fright. The chain jangled as he thrashed about on it, but because the night had closed down so tightly she could not see him or his kennel.

"Hush, Bowser," she soothed. "It's only me."

The curtain scraped away from the window and Del's silhouette appeared, his hair haloed with lamplight. He opened the window and called, "Look, I'm sick of telling you. Go home and stay there."

Dorrie hesitated, Bowser had stopped barking; now his tail was drumming against the wall of his kennel. Del reached to close the window so she quickly made up her mind. "Del? It's me, Dorrie. I've come to— I heard about—"

"Wait there." It was an urgent command. Within a minute he was with her, his hands grasping hers as if he were afraid she would run away. There was a faint smell of ale about him and his body was warm against hers, pleasantly so as he put one arm around her and led her inside to the kitchen. "You came to me!" he said, his voice mingling triumph and wonder. "I never imagined

you would. I thought—'' and he choked off a burst of
laughter.

She wished she could see his face. She stood shivering
beside him, though not from the coolness of the room.
He thought I was someone else, she thought, and was
about to ask him who he had called out to, when instead
of lighting a lamp he groped for her face and cupped it in
his hands while he kissed her lingeringly, his mouth loving hers while his fingertips traced her eyebrows and the
feathery strands of hair on her temples. *It's going to happen again,* she thought, but instead of panic she felt a
strange calm.

In his room she was quietly docile, gazing impassively
at the glowing oil paintings of farmyard scenes—hens
and hunting dogs—and at the polished dresser with water
jug and slop bowl standing beside silver-backed hairbrushes. She walked over and picked one up. It was very
heavy and embossed with a design of peacocks and lilies.
In the mirror she could see Del standing by the high brass
bed, standing and waiting for her. The expression on his
face made her heart race.

''It's beautiful,'' she said, of nothing in particular.

''The brush? It belonged to my mother. Most of the
things in here were hers. That china bowl, and that pin-
tray—'' He pointed them out without moving. ''Those
books were hers and even the dresser itself. The moment
his ship pulled away from the wharf I came home and
moved her things into my room.'' He paused, one hand
on the bed rail. ''Everything was in *their* room before.
Now I won't have to put it all back again.''

''No, you won't. Del, I'm so sorry about your—''

''Hush. Please, no. Not now. Just come here.''

She was still gazing at the reflection of his face, of that
sad and hungry, almost hurt, look in his eyes. She understood it perfectly for her emotions were pitched exactly to
his. Without taking her eyes off him she stripped off her
gloves and placed them beside the silver hairbrush, then
untied the chin-ribbons on her black bonnet and lifted it

off her head. Raising both hands, she drew the hairpins from her coiled hair one at a time, placing them on the silver pin-tray. Each made a tiny pinging sound, clear in the complete silence that had fallen in the room, and all the time Del watched her in an agony of hunger, half-holding his breath and half-afraid that she might change her mind. It was not until she suddenly shook her head and that silvery gush of hair flowed over her shoulders to stop like a foam-edged wave halfway down her back, not until then did the breath rush out of him in a sigh and he strode over to her.

When she saw him coming, she closed her eyes, trembling. She felt him pick her up and swing her around, not lowering her until she was buoyed up by the yielding puffiness of the mattress.

His face was suspended like a lamp above her face, suffused by conflicting emotions. He was frowning, uncertain.

"Dorrie, you're not afraid?"

"A little," she said as she reached up to undo the buttons at her collar.

"Let me do that."

She watched his face, heavy with concentration as he fiddled with the tight buttonholes. His lashes curved, making a screen over those clear eyes, but she could see the faint down on his cheeks that stopped in a clear line where the shaving began. She adored these little masculine things about him, the squareness of his hands, his strong neck, and the firm set of his mouth, and watching him now, she felt as if her heart could burst any moment from love of him.

"I want to be close to you," she explained. "I want to be close to you so much that I hurt inside."

"I know," he said in that hoarse voice, lifting her shoulders so that he could peel the dress away. "No," he urged as she held her hands modestly over her lace-trimmed corset top. "Please don't be shy, please. You're so beautiful, you really are."

"Am I?" Even with his reassurances she suspected that he was just being polite, for Dorrie had a deeply rooted belief that everything under her clothes was ugly and not for display.

Del guessed that her natural reticence was inhibiting her. "Dorrie," he said gently. "I want this to be beautiful for you. I want it to be the most beautiful experience you have ever had. I want to make it perfect for you. Darling girl, if you feel shy then take off the other things by yourself—I'll turn my back if you like—then slip under the covers." He dropped a kiss on the corner of her mouth and whispered, "I'll meet you under the covers, shall I?"

He turned away to lower the lamp flame, and when he flicked a glance back she was sitting on the far side of the bed, unrolling her stockings with her head bent and a curtain of hair screening her face. *Oh, God*, he thought. *Oh, God but she's the loveliest ever.*

As she slid under the sheet she held her discarded petticoat up in front of her until the last possible moment. Del was already there, looking harmless and innocent with his hair a smudgy fuzz against the pillow and his eyes seemingly closed, though she thought she saw a glint of reflected light there. She giggled with nervousness as her body sank between the cool sheets.

"What's funny?" asked Del.

"Why, every—" she began, then stopped with a gasp as he rolled towards her and there, quite suddenly, was the entire length of his body pressed against hers, all that warm, smooth skin indescribably delicious, sliding against her skin from her shoulders right down to her feet.

"Does that feel good?" he said, his breath thick in his throat. When she nodded, her face drowsy and helpless, he smiled with satisfaction and said, "What about this? And what about this? Does this feel good, too?"

His hand stroked her with a luxurious unhurried rhythm following the curves and hollows of her body, trailing a hot, tingly sensation that focused and expanded on that aching need inside her. His caresses lingered over her breasts and fondled the smooth indentation of her waist and the soft hollows at her hip bones and navel. His palm and spread fingers glided across the flat plane of her belly, but then, when she was so sure that he was going to touch her *there,* his hand veered away to draw rippling patterns of sensation over her thighs. It was not until she thought she would cry out with the hunger of wanting more, more, that his hand drifted at last to the waiting downy hollow place and she parted her legs immediately at his touch and moaned a little, deep in her throat because it was so incredibly, wonderfully good.

"Dorrie," he cried, his own urgency gripping and shaking him until he could hold back no longer. As he slid across to fit himself to her body she tensed in apprehension and he murmured reassuringly to her. It would be all right this time. This time everything would be beautiful for them both.

And it was. He managed to wait, nudging moistly until he felt her relax, then with a shuddering intake of breath he plunged into her as silkily and easily as if they had been sculpted from matching molds. This time she clung to him, her hands tight around the small of his back; this time her cries were of pure deep pleasure and this time instead of feeling that he had killed some part of her she felt that he was giving her a precious new dimension to life itself.

"Move with me," he whispered, tucking his hands under her buttocks and cradling her, lifting her to show her how. Not quite understanding, she followed his directions and gloried in the intensified delight their mutual movement brought her. Then, unexpectedly a series of spasms rippled through her body, devastating her with an avalanche of shattering sensations. Only distantly was she aware that Del was also panting, gasping, clinging to her with the same desperation that she was experiencing.

The full onslaught of their passion smothered them both, leaving them struggling to draw breath.

It was over. A few seconds when the world crashed around them, then empty silence. Del pulled away and lay close to her but not touching.

Dorrie idly stared at the shadows cast by the ornate picture frames, curling patterns looping across the wall in waves. Her fingers were still twined in Del's hair. Close to his scalp it was damp; his whole body was faintly slicked with moisture, and when she reached over to kiss his shoulder it tasted of salt. She wished he would put his arm around her but he lay perfectly still, his eyes closed as if he were asleep.

"I'm glad I didn't run away," she confided. "I nearly did, you know, when Bowser started up that racket and you shouted at me to go away."

"I'm glad you didn't," he murmured.

She wanted to ask whom he had mistaken her for, but instead said, "I'm sorry about your father, Del."

"Don't be."

"I liked him a lot. I got such a shock when I heard—"

"Leave it be!" He sat up and punched the pillow. "Oh, damn it all. I was so angry when the police brought the news. So damned angry." He certainly looked angry now, his face thrown into golden furrows by the lamplight and his eyes cold and hard. Dorrie was frightened into silence. "To cheat me by slinking away and dying like that. I thought he'd grow old and sick, that I'd have plenty of time to have it out with him. He always blamed me, you see. Reckon I killed my mother."

"*Killed* her? But how?"

"By being born. Same way you killed yours." She gaped at him, too stunned to reply as he continued, "All my life he's blamed me for it. I reckoned that one day I'd really have it out with him, throw it right in his face, and make him see how wrong he was, but I left it too long, didn't I? Now I'm so angry—" He stopped and tried to smile at Dorrie. "Look, please don't bring the subject up again, all right? I'm sorry, but I can't help this . . ."

She nodded.

"And—and maybe you'd better go now. It's late and—"

"Of course." She reached over to kiss him; he still seemed angry and tense as though there were a tight metal spring coiled up inside him. Because she hungered for a little of that warmth and closeness they had shared earlier, Dorrie was disappointed.

The moon had risen, coating everything with a satiny frost. Dorrie quickened her pace as she tried to calculate how long she had been gone. Two hours? Three? Dora might have awakened in her absence and would be worried.

She was scrambling over the gate when, without warning, someone said, "I *thought* he was expectin' a visitor."

Dorrie's heart stalled. She turned her head quickly, still clinging to the gate rails.

Maureen O'Reilly stood behind her. Her face was unreadable under the rim of her bonnet, just as her voice, swollen and harsh, was unrecognizable. "Lattle Dorrie Bannington," she said, "So it be you he's taken up with now, is it than?"

Dorrie decided not to answer her. She was shuddering all over with aftereffects from her fright.

"I thought he would," she said, barring Dorrie's way. "Last tame whan his father ware away it ware me he coaxed into visitin'. He said he loved me, that he did. Come tame for his father to come back, he didn't want me anymore." She leaned into Dorrie's face, her eyes glinting. Her breath smelled sour and damp like rain as she said, "He did it to me an' he'll do it to you, mark my words, lattle Miss Bannington. When he marries, he'll marry money, that one. He wants to gat on in the world, does our Dal."

"I don't believe you." Dorrie tried to sound confident but her voice wavered.

Maureen snorted. "I'll prove it to you than. Ask him what he does the minute his father leaves than. I'll tell you, shall I?"

"No, thank you. Please let me by."

Maureen called after her, "He takes all his mother's things and he puts them in his badroom, that he does. And come tame for his father to come home, he takes them all and puts them back again. I tell you, lattle Miss Bannington—"

Clapping her hands over her ears, Dorrie fled. She did not stop running until the Fintona driveway, where she paused, clutching her sides, heaving for breath. Misty slunk out of the shadows and smooched round her skirts, giving her already frayed nerves such a jolt that she almost screamed.

"Misty!" She picked him up and nuzzled him. "Misty, please tell me it's not true!"

Misty purred.

Ten

Ellen and her children were coming home. To prepare for them Fintona underwent a transformation so rapid that every day when she arrived home from work there was some new improvement for Dorrie to admire. The roof was scoured of moss and the house repainted, the lawns trimmed, garden beds stripped and restocked with flowering plants while inside the house everything was so efficiently varnished and wallpapered and refurnished that it was obvious Ellen had been planning this move for a long time.

Dorrie mourned the loss of her private domain. There would be no more secret dreams on Fintona's verandah; vanished were the soft shadows, the spiders' webs, and the air of gentle solitude. At the same time Dorrie was grateful that this interest was winching Dora out of her depression. To Dora, Ellen's return was a long-awaited miracle that would transform their lives.

"She's very wealthy, Dorrie, and she'll share with us. Fintona will be alive again. I know she's planning a full social life—why else would she send a dozen servants, enlarge the kitchen, and refurbish the ballroom? All the best people in Auckland will come. You'll be shown off, Dorrie. Oh, I'm so glad that you've kept up your piano practice!"

At which Dorrie laughed tolerantly. She cared nothing about being shown off; she had Del and he was all she needed.

Though Del was clearly thrown by the questions she asked about Maureen O'Reilly, he had rallied at once and given her full, frank replies. Yes, he had flirted with

Maureen once, long ago, he may have even kissed her
once or twice, but she had certainly never been inside the
house. How did she know about his mother's things?
That was easy. Mr. O'Reilly himself had helped Del shift
the bed and the dresser once, when Del had hurt his back
and couldn't manage the weight.

"He collected sacks of grain for me from the feed merchants' and did all sorts of odd jobs around the place until
the Major returned," Del explained smoothly. "Look,
I'm sorry if Maureen upset you, but there was nothing to
it. Nothing."

Dorrie was eager to believe him.

One afternoon Dorrie arrived home to find Dora gone
and a note on the table. *Come and meet your cousins,* it
said.

Crystal, the parlor maid, met her at the door. She wore
a long blue dress with a ruffled cap and apron and a
haughty expression. She sniffed at Dorrie and led the
way down a corridor lined with fresh Regency striped
wallpaper and scented with lemon wax. Somewhere in
the house a piano was being played extremely badly but
with enthusiasm.

"Is Mrs. Bennington taking music lessons already?"
asked Dorrie. Uncle Samuel had told them that Ellen had
lived quietly in Sydney and had supported herself as a
music teacher until Grandmaire's will freed them from financial worry.

Crystal replied with another sniff. "That's Miss Roseanne," she said, leaving Dorrie at the door of the morning room, telling her to show herself in. Dorrie entered
timidly, marveling at the change that had been wrought
in this room where Dora used to read the Bible to Grandmaire surrounded by a lifetime collection of Maori artifacts. Now the woven flax mats had been replaced by a
fitted oriental carpet on which stood tightly upholstered
and buttoned green plush furniture that echoed the pale
willow green of the walls. The feather and dogskin

cloaks had gone, and in their stead huge paintings gave the impression of windows opening onto the English countryside they depicted. The French doors that took up one wall had been hung with soft lace curtains, and it was near them, in the best light, that the piano stood, its surfaces like black mirrors. A young woman was seated at the keyboard playing with exaggerated theatrical flourishes while her audience, their backs to Dorrie, leaned forward in an attitude of polite appreciation.

Nobody heard her come in, but as the young woman bent and swayed to ripple her fingers along the higher octaves she saw Dorrie standing shyly inside the door and stopped playing immediately. Resting her hands in her lap, she stared at Dorrie with a challenging directness that further unsettled her.

All heads turned, and Dora stood up at once, saying, "Here you are, then! I was telling your aunt how well you play so she had Roseanne demonstrate her own musical talents for us." Her voice had an excited, gloating note and Dorrie inferred that she was delighted that Dorrie was already proving to be superior to Roseanne in something. "Come over here, dear. Come and meet everybody."

Why, they're just ordinary, thought Dorrie, disappointed when faced with this mysterious family that so many people had tried so hard to find. Aunt Ellen she had pictured as being something between a vamp and a vampire, guessing that she would be lushly beautiful with a magnetic charm, so she was bemused now to be shaking hands with a spare, prim woman of about forty with a severe hair style the color of a dusty stove and a tiny mouth that clicked open and snapped shut—like a miser's purse, thought Dorrie—when she talked.

Ellen looked Dorrie up and down with unfathomable eyes and with a tight smile that pushed her mouth into a neat V. "Too pretty by half, but she looks sensible—not in the least like her mother," she said with an implied "thank goodness" in her tone. Then with a nod to Dora

and a brief excuse about something needing to be seen to
she left the room.

Rupert, the darling of Grandmaire's heart, looked as if
he wanted to follow his mother out of the room, but Dora
said, "Don't run off, Rupert. Dorinda has been so looking forward to meeting you, haven't you, Dorrie love?"
So he sat down again with a reluctance that blighted any
chances they might have had for an amiable conversation. He was a shorter than average young man with dull
brown hair and badly spotted skin that he was trying to
disguise with a scrubby growth of beard. Because he
slouched on the sofa avoiding her eye in order to examine
the toes of his boots stretched out in front of him, Dorrie
turned her hesitant smile in Roseanne's direction instead.

"You interrupted my playing," her cousin informed
her loftily. "Didn't you know that you should wait outside the door until the piece is finished?"

"No, I didn't know," said Dorrie, taken aback.

Rupert flicked a glance in her direction and said, "I
say, Roz. Leave off the Duchess stuff."

Roseanne lifted her chin and stood up in one fluid
motion. She seemed taller than her brother, with jet black
hair, a narrow, rather "horsey" face, and a pale complexion marred by excessively pink cheeks. Dorrie suspected rouge and was intrigued; nobody except trollops
and very old ladies dared appear in Auckland wearing
paint.

"Play something else for us, dear," said Dora.

"Pity help us all," murmured Rupert.

Crystal appeared in the doorway. "Miss Bennington,
the mistress said she needs someone to write out some invitations for her. She said you'd offered—"

"Of course. At once," said Dora.

Roseanne laughed. Her laughter was like medicine,
sweetness masking an astringent taste. "Beware, Aunt
Dora. Dear Mama will treat you like an unpaid servant if
you don't watch out."

Shocked, Dora said, "Roseanne, I'm sure you don't mean that."

"Perhaps I do," was the airy reply. "Anyway, meanings are dull. The perfect conversation is one where every sentence is scintillating but where nothing has any real meaning. Don't you agree, Dorinda?"

"I don't know," said Dorrie.

Roseanne laughed again. "I don't imagine you do," she said.

"It seems to me that you take a mighty long time just to walk a few yards home," accused Roseanne. "I've been waiting ages."

She was perched sidesaddle on Silk, her chestnut mare. Today Roseanne was elegant in yet another riding costume, pale blue slashed with inserts of navy with a navy blue boater clouded with veiling, but she wore her usual sour face as she demanded that Dorrie hurry up and join her. None of the Fintona Benningtons (as Auckland was already calling them) had worn so much as a scrap of crepe mourning for Jon, and Dorrie resented the fact that she had to perspire through summer's late swelter wearing black for a man she disliked while his own wife and children ignored his death.

She tried to smother her irritation. She was still feeling tingly and warm from Del's embrace and when she moved her mouth she could easily feel his lips bruising hers. "I'm sorry but I promised to help Auntie Dora make those flowers for your dress for tomorrow night."

She wheeled her horse around. "I already checked with her. *She* says that you finish work early tomorrow so you can make them then."

"But I—" began Dorrie, then stopped, cursing inwardly. She had just promised Del that they would be able to enjoy a full hour together tomorrow, a lingering, tender interlude much more satisfying than today's hurried kisses. Because Dora would be at Fintona helping with the dinner preparations there was no danger of Dorrie being missed.

"Aunt Dora said you'd come right now," insisted Roseanne. "So don't dawdle. Jones has Sateen saddled and ready for you."

Sighing in exasperation, Dorrie went into the gatehouse and dumped her lunch basket on the table. Dora glanced up through thick lenses and paused, needle hovering over a blouse she was altering for Ellen. Seeing that, fresh irritation coursed through Dorrie. Every time she came home these days it was to find Dora either working for Ellen at Fintona or toiling over her wardrobe, doing unpaid work.

Lowering her voice because Emere was beyond the open window folding sheets and towels, Dorrie said, "Couldn't you *please* help me to avoid Roseanne? I don't want to go riding. That horse is so frighteningly large and I never feel safe perched on his back. Besides, I don't really like Roseanne. She's so clinging and demanding, and she never says anything nice about anybody."

Dora chose to pretend that this was a new complaint. "Ellen is being very generous to us, including us in her social life the way she does."

She treats us like servants! Dorrie wanted to protest. *Ordering us about in front of the other guests, acting as if we were charity projects or as if we didn't smell very nice.*

"You're getting to meet all the eligible young men in Auckland," Dora pointed out. "And don't forget that as soon as we come out of mourning you have a whole trunkful of Roseanne's clothes to wear."

Dorrie had examined those clothes, her heart shrinking in dismay. Stale food spilled down the fronts, mud dried into the hems, lace trimmings torn and stained, all were in such a neglected state that no amount of cleaning and mending could make them fresh again.

"You should be grateful," continued Dora, making

Dorrie heartily sorry she had complained. "You wanted a friend and now you've got one. You should be pleased."

"I'll try to be," said Dorrie. It was the only thing she could say.

Today Roseanne decided to ride inland and made Dorrie show her where she worked. She gazed at the bare tin shed in sour contempt. "What a horrid, dreary place."

"It's not really. I'm happy in my work, you see, and that makes the surroundings pleasant. Happiness makes all the difference."

After a long pause, Roseanne said, "Mother says that only very stupid people are happy when they have no reason to be."

"Did she?" Dorrie's lips twitched.

She wheeled her chestnut mare around. "And poor people and *working class* people have no reason to be happy at all!"

This time Dorrie was unable to restrain her amusement. "I'm so very glad that you told me that," she said, laughing out loud.

Roseanne was angry and offended. "You might show a little *respect,*" she retorted, strumming the riding crop and galloping away in straight-backed indignation.

Dorrie's laughter was cut off at once as she struggled to rein her mount in. It was always the same: When Roseanne's horse Silk broke into a gallop, then Sateen wanted to do the same and Dorrie was not yet confident enough to try anything faster than a sedate walk.

"It's time you were more daring," Roseanne told her when Dorrie finally caught up on the bridge near the Blacketts' gate. "Sateen would love a good hard canter, wouldn't you, pet?" And half-playfully, half-spitefully she reached over and thwacked his hindquarters with her crop.

Dorrie saw it coming, and swiftly freed her heels from the stirrups. As Sateen reared up she was able to slide deftly from the saddle to land safely on her feet, shaken but unhurt.

"Well done!" applauded a familiar voice, and she turned to see Del leaning over the gate. "You're going to make a competent little horsewoman, Miss Bennington."

She led Sateen over to the gate. This was the first time she had been with Del in the presence of a third person since they had become lovers and she enjoyed the new sensation of a shared, intimate secret. As she walked towards Del she was aware of another new experience, that of seeing him through Roseanne's eyes and therefore noticing afresh that rugged, almost threatening masculinity, that handsome square-cut face with its softening halo of fair curls and those breathtakingly beautiful sky-blue eyes.

And he loves me, she thought with a great rush of joy to her heart.

"Are you all right?" he said.

"Perfectly, thanks. But if you could please help me up into the saddle again? I can't manage alone."

"How fortunate," he murmured. "I think I might be able to enjoy that."

A shadow fell across them as Roseanne maneuvered Silk up close. "Well," she said pertly. "Are you going to introduce me to your friend?" She watched, waiting while Del assisted her up again. One hand was firm around her thigh while the other grasped her ankle and Dorrie blushed, knowing that Roseanne was missing nothing.

"Mr. Blackett, Miss Bennington," she said as she recovered her composure.

Roseanne's eyebrows were raised but she was smiling. "A pleasure, Mr. Blackett. A real pleasure," she said.

She's flirting with him, thought Dorrie with mild indignation mixed with amusement. *Why, she's positively simpering and coy. I haven't seen her like this before.*

Del gave her a wicked grin. "Any friend of Dorrie's is a friend of mine—I hope," he said.

"I don't like the way you said that to her," protested Dorrie, giving Del a playful pat on the chin with her fingertip. "She was ever so impressed with you, too. Wanted to know all about you on the way home. She must have asked me a hundred questions."

"I hope you didn't tell her *all* about me."

"Brute!" She laughed and nudged him lovingly, glad that she had risen at five this morning to finish Roseanne's gown decoration before she left for work—just so that she and Del could still have this time together.

"So that's your cousin, is it?" he mused. "She seems an attractive enough young lady. Not exactly like your description of her, I must say. She's quite pretty in her own way, and she certainly can ride."

"You're only talking like this to get a rise out of me," said Dorrie as she snuggled down into his arms. "Anyway, you'd best keep well away from Roseanne. She only wants one thing and that's a husband." She laughed. "And she'll find one soon enough, I shouldn't wonder. Aunt Ellen has settled a ten-thousand-pound dowry on her plus a two-thousand-pound-a-year allowance as her share of Grandmaire's estate."

Del whistled.

"I know. It makes me ill to think of what we could do with that. Auntie Dora could have servants to do all the housework—Emere does the washing, but that isn't really enough—and as for me, I'd never have to eat porridge again. But that's the way life is. Roseanne had the right mother and the right brother so she will never have to work for her living. Not that I envy her, though, despite her wealth. Money isn't everything."

He made no reply.

"I said, 'I don't envy her, though.' "

"Mmmm?" he said absently, stroking her hair. "Why not?"

She was suddenly shy but very, very happy. "Because I have you, that's why," she whispered.

"Mmmm? Oh, of course," said Del.

Because the Blacketts had never been part of Auckland society Del was not invited to any of Ellen's gala social evenings, nor were the Duptons (being also low down on the scale of importance) until one night when they attended a Fintona ball with Nathaniel Rosser. Dorrie crunched across the driveway to the front door just as the Duptons' carriage arrived.

Nathaniel alighted first. His eyes sparkled with warmth when he saw Dorrie lingering in the shadows of the pillared porchway and he held both hands out to her as he said, "Dorrie, how marvelous! Come here and let me see you properly." She stepped forward shyly, feeling drab in her black poplin mourning dress, the only concession to festivity being a confection of lace and black satin ribbon in her piled-up hair. Nathaniel did not seem to share her views for he said with undisguised admiration, "You look . . . so elegant. Black becomes you, don't you think so, Marguerite?" He turned as she alighted beside him.

For a second Marguerite's eyes widened in the faintest echo of that expression she had worn last time Dorrie had seen her, but it was only for a moment. Then her eyes filled with tears and she rushed to embrace Dorrie. "I have missed you!" she declared. "I really have. It seems like ten years instead of just one. Please say we're friends again."

"Of course," said Dorrie. She smiled back at her regained friend and realized that things would never be quite the same again. Nor would she want them to be. Before, she was always slightly in awe of Marguerite but now she knew that it was she, Dorrie, who was the strong one. She could even feel traces of pity as she watched Marguerite hug Nathaniel's arm and smile up at him possessively.

"You look lovely," said Dorrie, for she did, in her ruffled emerald taffeta gown with a flock of tiny bows like butterflies in her cloud of crimped black hair.

Mrs. Dupton was watching the wheelchair being unstrapped from its bracket behind the carriage while Mr. Dupton lifted Aimee out. The child was thinner and more withered looking than ever and just as undisciplined. When she was introduced to Ellen she darted a hand out suddenly and plucked at the bracelets on Ellen's pale arm, scratching the skin.

"Really," said Ellen, her mouth making a V shape of disapproval. "Is this young lady quite *ready* for the excitement of a ball, do you think?"

"I'll let her stay only a few minutes," apologized Mr. Dupton, so embarrassed that even the top of his tonsured head looked pink. "She tires very quickly."

"I'm delighted to hear that," said Ellen. "Dorinda, look after *your friends* while I take Mr. Rosser to renew his acquaintance with Roseanne. We were *great* friends in Sydney, weren't we, Mr. Rosser?"

Marguerite gaped after them in dismay. "Does she always use that tone of voice to you?" she asked Dorrie. *"Mon Dieu!* I've been snubbed before, but this—"

"Don't let her spoil your evening," advised Dorrie, adding unconvincingly, "she's quite charming when you get to know her."

While she danced with one young man after another Roseanne watched Dorrie jealously. Dorrie was sitting in one corner of the gold ballroom under a canopy of ferns and flowers with Marguerite, Nathaniel, and Rupert, and they were talking and laughing in such an animated way that Roseanne began to feel excluded. Because she was obviously in mourning, men didn't ask Dorrie to dance. Instead they drifted over, attracted by her vivacious beauty, and joined the group around her until it seemed to Roseanne that half the eligible men in the room were clogging that corner.

"Your cousin is very much admired," Roseanne's partner commented as he steered her through the steps of the reel. Roseanne glared at him; Bob Farrell was a twice-widowed rancher they had known from their days in Australia, handsome and wealthy, but in Roseanne's opinion, deadly dull.

"Perhaps you'd like to be introduced to her?" suggested Roseanne.

Bob Farrell's face brightened. "Very much," he said and was astonished when Roseanne stopped dancing, pulled away, and walked over to her mother, leaving him standing in the center of the floor.

"Are you having a good time, dear?" asked Dora, who had just handed Ellen a glass of lemonade.

Roseanne snapped open the fan that hung over her wrist. "It's too hot," she said.

"Dora will fetch you some lemonade, won't you, Dora?" Ellen patted the chair next to hers. "Sit down, Roseanne. I want to talk to you. And don't pull faces either. This is for your own good."

"Isn't this exciting?" said Dorrie to Marguerite. "Remember how we used to sit out on the verandah and I'd describe this wing of the house to you, and we'd pretend that we were attending a grand ball here? It's almost unbelievable that here we are now and in a few minutes I'm going to be playing for you. Isn't that thrilling?"

"I hope your playing's improved," giggled Marguerite. "Do you remember how we used to play 'Ta-rara-boom-de-re' as a duet, getting more and more boisterous until we bumped each other off the piano stool? Your poor aunt used to go out into the garden just to escape from the noise."

"Actually, my playing is terrible," said Dorrie.

"It's very good," Rupert corrected her. He colored as he spoke to Dorrie and there was a slight stammer of nervous excitement in his voice. "It's m-miles better than Roseanne's." He glanced up, then whispered, "Here comes trouble. This fellow has been staring at you all evening, Dorrie. I'd watch out for him if I were you."

Bob Farrell arrived at their corner with Dora, who was fluttering beside him like a weak moth. "May I present my niece?" she said.

The rancher bent over Dorrie's gloved fingers, an action that startled her. She looked at Nathaniel, who winked at her so wickedly that she struggled to suppress a giggle.

"What do you think of him?" whispered Dora later.

"Who?" asked Dorrie. They were making their way over to the low stage for the duet she was to play with Roseanne.

"Mr. Farrell, of course."

"He held my hand much too long."

"He's very rich," Dora told her comfortably, as if being rich gave him the right to hold her hand as long as he pleased. "At one time Ellen hoped to attract him as a suitor for Roseanne but now that she has Mr. Rosser in her sights she says she doesn't mind if—"

"I see. I'm to have Roseanne's cast-off suitors, too."

"Dorrie!"

She sighed. "I'm sorry, Auntie."

"I should think so. It's for your own good, you know."

She's beginning to sound like Aunt Ellen, thought Dorrie. *I don't blame Roseanne for being rebellious.* She hoped that what Auntie Dora said about Nathaniel Rosser wasn't true. He was a warm, gorgeous, and thoroughly nice man, far too good for someone as sour and haughty as Roseanne.

Ellen stood on the stage as the drummer played a roll for silence. In a confident voice that made it easy to picture her as a music teacher she said, "Ladies and gentlemen, friends. My daughter Roseanne has graciously agreed to entertain you now. The piece she has chosen is called "In Evening's Tranquility," and I'm sure you will all enjoy it. Oh, I mustn't forget, Miss Dorinda Bennington will accompany her.''

The two girls could not have made more of a contrast, Dorrie modest in black and Roseanne overblown as a tea rose in sateen brighter than her cheeks, the trails of flowers down her skirts matched by so many artificial flowers and ''wings'' of feathers in her piled-up hair that she appeared at first glance to be wearing a hat.

It was almost entirely her show, a fact that became apparent as soon as the girls settled themselves on the long piano seat. Ellen had selected a piece of music that would artfully enable Dorrie's playing to mask Roseanne's clumsy stumblings, and she had arranged the floral display for the piano top with equal care. When Dorrie sat down she was completely hidden behind an enormous cascading display of ferns and lilies. If any of the gentlemen present wished to gaze upon feminine loveliness while they listened to the music, then they would have to be content with looking at Roseanne.

''I'm sorry to bother you, Miss Bennington, but I never did imagine such a thing would happen, not here at Fintona.'' Mrs. Patene stood outside the front door, her face tight with shock under the loose veil of her hat.

Dora escorted her into the gatehouse where she sat on an offered chair, stiffly dignified. There was silence.

''And how is Albert?'' asked Dora, though she had seen him only the day before as he cut through the property on his way to the university. She thought Albert would be the safest topic with which to break the ice. ''Every time I see him I think what a fine lad he is. He chopped some wood for me last winter and wouldn't take a penny for it. There's not many—''

''Unfortunately there's peoples who don't see it your way. I was just insulted, Miss Bennington, and by your sister-in-law, too. I've known Miss Ellen since she was a child, eh, and I never did think I'd hear her talk the way she just spoked to me. I stopped by there just now to say

'*Kia orana*' to her, to pay my respects, and she said, 'Is that your boy I see walking down my path sometimes?' and I say, 'Yes, Mrs. Bennington, that's my boy Albert,' and do you know what she said to that?''

"What did she say?" asked Dora with a nasty prickle of premonition. Most of Ellen's servants had been sent ahead by her from Australia and all were of good, British stock. "No Maoris for us," she had once explained to Dora.

"She said, 'Then you can tell him to go to town another way—I have a daughter here and I don't want no Maori fellows hanging around.' Can you imagine that, Miss Bennington? Can you imagine my Albert causing trouble with her daughter?''

"Indeed I cannot," said Dora. There was another long silence during which she wondered if she should say something else. A sympathetic "cluck-cluck" was hardly substantial enough to soothe the magnitude of this insult, but, Dora reasoned, what could she say? It was easy to see Ellen's side. She didn't want Roseanne to be like May Teipa-Bennington, producing a milk-chocolate baby every year.

Aware that she had failed Mrs. Patene, Dora watched her go, wondering if the set of the older woman's shoulders was an implied accusation. She felt as guilty as she had the night Jon burned the contents of Grandmaire's bedroom, and, like that time, this really had nothing to do with her.

It was not until Dorrie wandered in from work that she was to realize what her silence had cost her.

"What in the world has happened at the Patenes'?" asked Dorrie, scooping Misty up to cuddle him under her chin.

"Nothing. Nothing to do with us. Now mind out what you're doing. That cat is shedding everywhere. It will take you ages to brush the fur out of your dress."

"Poor Misty, he's getting old, that's all," she said, setting him down again. "Something *has* happened at the

Patenes', though. I saw Emere up the road and she was acting as if the sky had fallen on her head. Have you quarreled with her?''

"I haven't even spoken to her.''

"That's odd.'' Dorrie picked up the hat Dora was retrimming for Ellen and examined it critically. "Emere just told me that she's not coming back here to work anymore. She said it was on account of the trouble. What trouble is that?''

"Not trouble of our causing,'' said Dora. "But trouble I might have prevented, I'm very sorry to say.''

Eleven

"I do hope that your aunt is better soon," said Marguerite as the two girls strolled across Fintona's lawn towards the croquet green. "It seems a pity that she worked so hard to help make today a success and then missed out on the fun. And this has been fun, hasn't it?"

Dorrie nodded. It was a glorious winter's afternoon, mellow and warm, with the glittering harbor and its floating emerald necklace of islands doing its utmost to give an illusion of a clear summer day. Dorrie squinted out at a puff of sail on the horizon as she said, "Auntie Dora is so exhausted that she is making herself sick. I'm going to have to give up work."

"Really? But how will you get by then?"

Dorrie's thin shoulders shrugged unhappily under her black poplin. "I'm going to start making hats at home. For private customers. So if you know of anybody who wants anything really special created—"

"Send them to you! Oh, I will, I will!" She hugged Dorrie's arm. "But you don't seem very excited about it."

It was a decision Dorrie had reached with the greatest reluctance. Since Ellen had arrived at Fintona, Dora's financial contribution to the household had dwindled away to nothing, for if Dora wasn't with Ellen in her study writing letters or invitations for her, she was helping make placecards, arrange flowers, or, much more often, laboring until all hours over Ellen's or Roseanne's wardrobe. Their vegetable garden had been taken over by Fintona again as had the hen-house, and though half the fowls still belonged to Dora, the Fintona servants were not fussy about leaving a few eggs for her, nor did they bother which hens they beheaded when some were needed for the pot. Of course there were no surplus vegetables to sell; Dorrie and Dora were lucky if a few carrots or a cabbage were tossed their way by the gardeners. All of the Fintona servants treated them in the same way— with scant respect and generous scorn.

All this was iron in Dorrie's soul. She longed to get away from Fintona and not spend all her time here. It was fun at work and there was the added benefit of those occasional stolen hours with Del. It would be difficult to see him if she were at home all the time.

"I have to do it," Dorrie told Marguerite. "The time I spend walking back and forth to work each day could be spent doing the laundry." She laughed offhandedly. "Auntie Dora asked Aunt Ellen if the Fintona laundress could do ours with theirs. It would have been fair enough really, because it's only Aunt Ellen's attitude that's prevented us from hiring another Maori girl and we simply can't afford a European one—and oh, you should have been there to see it. The laundress is a big woman, fatter even than Auntie Dora, with red arms like boiled legs of mutton. She snorted when she was asked and said, 'If you want me to quit, Mrs. Bennington, just ask me straight out and don't force me into it like this!' So you see, there's nothing for it. I'll have to stay home and help out.' "

"I wish you good luck," said Marguerite sincerely.

"I'm going to need luck, and plenty of it," Dorrie sighed. "At least Auntie Dora is happy. She loves running about after Aunt Ellen, you know. Grandmaire used to have her at her beck and call all day and I think Auntie Dora really missed having someone to wait on."

"Rather her than me," said Marguerite. "If someone ordered me about the way *they* order you two, why, I'd turn right around and tell them to do it themselves. Wouldn't that make their breath suck in!" They were approaching the croquet lawn now, walking slowly over the damp, spongy ground. Nathaniel was clearly visible, half a head taller than any of the others with the sunlight burnishing his coppery hair. "I'm beginning to despair," said Marquerite frankly. "I've adored him for—for so long it feels like forever, but he simply doesn't notice me. *Maman* says it's the way he's been brought up, in a wealthy home with a nanny to teach him perfect manners and self-sufficiency. Apparently people raised like that are able to hold themselves aloof no matter how deep their feelings run, and that I must be patient."

Dorrie hesitated, then said cautiously, "Half of Auckland is after him, you know."

Marquerite's face darkened. "Then I'll thank you not to tell me about it!" She stalked ahead, then turned abruptly, the ribbons on her bonnet and parasol fluttering. "Do let's tell Mr. Rosser all about your millinery venture! *C'est épatant!*" And before Dorrie could protest, she was dashing ahead again, breathlessly eager to divulge Dorrie's plans.

"I was hoping to speak privately to your aunt," said Bob Farrell. He had drawn Dorrie away from the group into the rose garden and was now looking deep into her eyes in a way that always made her feel dissected. Her conversations with him felt more like job interviews than friendly chats.

"They told me she was ill, so I wrote a letter to her instead." He slipped his hand inside his jacket and brought out a paper which had been folded small and sealed with dabs of green wax. As he handed it to her he watched her closely. "I hope that she, and that you particularly, will look on it with favor."

It's a proposal, thought Dorrie, her skin prickling with a sudden chill. *Mr. Farrell wants to marry me!*

His hands were still grasping hers with the folded paper between. She could feel the heat of him through her cotton gloves.

"I'd prefer a reply before my ship leaves tomorrow on

the afternoon tide, but if that's not possible then my address is included in the letter. There's no cause for haste. I'm not an impatient young man.'' He paused; she was blushing and her dark gold lashes screened her eyes. "A word, if I might, about this millinery business. Commercial industry, in my opinion, does not become a young lady. *Domestic* industry is what women were created for. A young lady like you would do well to bear that in mind.''

Dorrie would have gasped at these words but the gentle tone in which they were uttered removed all the sting. He was saying that she was worthy of a much better life.

"A proposal?'' sniffed Marguerite a few minutes later. "I've had at least a dozen, so far. None that I'd take seriously, of course.''

"A dozen?''

"Mostly from widowers, but one or two were at least as attractive as your Mr. Farrell. You should regard it as a compliment.''

"He's not my Mr. Farrell, and I'm not flattered. I feel guilty, as if I've been encouraging him unfairly. . . .''

Marguerite was not listening. She and Dorrie were walking back towards the house and now Marguerite stopped and placed a hand on Dorrie's arm. "Look, there's your cousin on the porch swing with a young man! I say, I wonder if that's the mystery guest she's been making such a drama about. You heard her before, didn't you? Giggling and dropping artful hints—''

Roseanne saw them and waved. She and the young man were lounging together cozily on the low-backed wicker swing. His arm was draped along behind her shoulders. Her face was flushed and she was laughing.

Dorrie followed Marguerite up the verandah steps. The young man stood up at once and Marguerite said, "Del, you are naughty, closeting yourself away here when Dorrie and I would like to share your company, too. Wouldn't we Dorrie?''

Dorrie was so shocked to see who it was that she could not reply. No wonder she had not recognized him at first, he was smartened up so much he looked nothing like his everyday self, in a smart dark suit with a red tie loosely knotted. Above the knot his collar jutted out in sharp little points like teeth biting into a red apple. His hair had been dressed with something that made the center-parted curls resemble wet macaroni and he had a gloss about him, a prosperous, self-satisfied air that did not suit him.

"Good afternoon, ladies," he said, but it was Dorrie he directed his special smile to.

Her dismay faded as quickly as it had come and with it went that instinctive prickle of jealousy. Del was "in society" after all! He would be invited to other gatherings, she would be able to introduce him to Auntie Dora, the official path of their romance would be smoothed and so it would go. The future unrolled before Dorrie like a bolt of bright carpet.

"Del arrived late so I made him stay here and keep me company as a penance," said Roseanne, watching everything with narrow, unblinking eyes. "I hope it hasn't been too much of an ordeal for him."

"An ordeal? It's been a pleasure."

What else could he say? Dorrie told herself.

"How sweet of you." Roseanne smiled at him, looking up from under her lashes.

She's flirting with him again, thought Dorrie, amused. *She's flirting with him and the wicked fellow doesn't mind a scrap.*

Marguerite seemed equally amused to see Roseanne making a fool of herself. "Del is sweet to all the ladies, isn't he, Dorrie?"

"Oh, definitely," she said, and they all laughed, Roseanne the loudest of all. For once her laughter did not have that tinny, mechanical ring. She sounded prosperous and self-satisfied, too.

* * *

"I've had a formal proposal," Dorrie told Del next day.

She had given in her notice and left work an hour early. Brimming with news to share, she had hurried along the path beside the stream, crossed on the stepping stones and followed the clapping sounds of an axe until she found Del cutting wood behind the grain shed.

"Come on in," he said. "I was about to light the fire again. Some customers called for a set of Black Javas and took an eternity to make up their minds. Meanwhile the fire went out, so—anyway, come in."

It was not until now, when she sat on the sofa watching him busy himself with wood chips, paper, and matches that she began to wonder if something were amiss. He didn't seem as pleased to see her as he usually was, nor did he seem to be listening to what she said.

"I've had a proposal," she repeated.

He blew into the grate and rattled the damper knob. "What kind of a proposal?"

"A marriage proposal, of course." She added after a pause, "I suppose it's rather fun really. A joke."

"Why a joke?"

"Because I won't take it seriously. Auntie Dora is in a flap about it, though. She wants me to consider it. He's very wealthy." She sighed. "Del, you don't seem in the least put out. Another man has *proposed.*"

"You said yourself it was a joke. Anyway, what brings you here so early in the day?"

A chill began to settle over Dorrie. She had arrived glowing from her brisk walk through this blustery day, but now she began to shiver. *He's not even interested,* she thought, dismay seeping through her. *He must realize that it's someone he met yesterday but he isn't even bothering to ask the fellow's name.*

He was waiting, eyebrow raised, but she decided not to confide her other news about the gigantic leap she was taking. If he was in this kind of a mood she'd be better to postpone telling him anything important.

Instead she said, hesitantly, "Del, is something wrong?"

"Lots of things are wrong."

"Well," she shrugged unhappily, "can you tell me?"

He studied her for a few seconds, then dragged a bentwood chair across from the table and placed it close to the sofa with the back towards Dorrie. He sat down straddling it so that the back made a kind of barrier between them.

"You guessed accurately. There's something rather serious the matter. Are you sure you want to know about it?"

She nodded mutely, still shivering.

He glanced at her face, then away again. She was unable to read his expression; he was tense, choosing his words as carefully as if he were composing a letter.

"My father's will was probated today. It's all been delayed until now because there were some complications with Mother's estate. Well, today they gave me the news. Both barrels, as it were. I tell you, the contents of his will came as quite a shock. There was only me and a couple of officers from the Salvation Army there at the lawyer's, and I don't know who was more staggered, me or them."

"Oh? What's wrong?"

He was looking at her now but his eyes were narrowed and all she could see was a hint of blue and no expression whatsoever.

"The Major left everything he owned to the Salvation Army. Everything." When she continued to gaze at him expectantly he thumped the back of the chair in exasperation. "For heaven's sake, Dorrie, don't you understand what I mean? Father left this house, this ground, *everything* to the Sallies. He cut me out of his will. I'm destitute, for heaven's sake."

"You can't be."

He bristled, plainly annoyed that she questioned his veracity.

"But your business, the fowl breeding—he can't de-

stroy all that, surely. You're doing so well. All the prizes
your birds won, at last summer's agricultural fairs—''

"You can't eat prizes nor buy land with them. That's
what I want. This land. Mine.''

"Oh, Del. They won't take it, surely. They can't evict
you.''

"They're going to decide soon what to do. This house
is in a valuable location and the place is big enough to be
ideal as a home for alcoholics or rescued women.'' He
shrugged bitterly. "It's ironic that in the process they'll
make me equally destitute, though.''

"Oh, Del.'' Her hand stole out to cup his where it
gripped the chair frame. "How terrible.''

He did not seem to notice her hesitant caress. "Pretty
bad news, huh? I knew the old man despised me, but I
didn't know how much. Since I came home I've been
alternating between wanting to burst out laughing and
wanting to smash things up.''

She stroked his fingers, torn by an agony of remorse.
To think that she had been small-minded enough to worry
that his remoteness meant a cooling of his feelings towards her. Contrite, she said, "I'm so sorry.''

"No point in being sorry.''

"I suppose not. What are you going to do?''

"I can fight it out. But I'll lose for sure. The courts
will decide in favor of a religious, charitable organization
every time. Or I can buy my property back. If I can find
the money. You don't happen to know where there are a
few stray thousand pounds lying around, do you?''

Riversong, thought Dorrie at once. If it was hers she'd
give it to Del without a second's hesitation, just as she
would cut out her heart and sell it if that would help him.
But she had to be practical, and if her business got off to a
good start she might be able to tuck away a few shillings
here and there . . .

"Perhaps I might be able to help a little,'' she ventured.

His hand jerked from under her caress as he con-

vulsed with a dry, snorting sound. There was no
warmth in the laugh or in his eyes. If anything, he
seemed embarrassed and Dorrie sensed that she had
made an inappropriate suggestion. "You? How could
you help with your ten-shillings-a-week wages?" It was
said not unkindly, but he got up as he spoke and walked
back to the fire, crouching before it to prod at the flames
with the poker. The reflected light slicked his face with
wet gold.

"Please don't be cross with me, Del," whispered Dorrie.

"I'm not cross with you. Of course I'm not cross."

"Promise?"

"I said I'm not cross."

She bit her lip, waiting for him to say something else.
He was poking at the fire, humming to himself as if he
were alone in the room. *This is insane,* she thought. *Here
we are, Del and me and we* love *each other. Then why
am I afraid to talk to him, to go over and put my arms
around him? Why am I so certain that he would rebuff
me? This doesn't make any sense at all.*

Del continued to hum and stare into the maw of the
stove while Dorrie waited dumbly for him to speak. She
felt so bewildered by his attitude that she was terrified
she was going to cry. What in the world was the matter
with them?

Finally he broke the silence. "I'm sorry I'm being so
rough on you, but—"

"I only want to help," she said eagerly.

"I don't *want* your help. Look, I know you mean well
and I'm grateful, but truly, Dorrie, I'm at a low point
right now. I'm not myself."

"I understand. It's natural when you've had a shock as
bad as this."

"Yes." He glanced at her, then away again.

"Would it help—would you feel better if we went upstairs?"

He was silent.

She had never offered herself to him before, and now as she waited and waited for some response she wished she could retrieve those hasty words. Treacherous tears prickled behind her lids and she could feel her throat burning with tension.

"Dorrie," he said awkwardly. "I don't quite know how to say this—"

"You want me to go." Flinging it out eased the pain in her throat. It was a relief to have something to throw at him in return for the anguish he was making her suffer.

At once he said, "No! No, of course not, but—"

"*Good,*" she said before he could say anything more. "Good, because I don't want to go. Not while you're so unhappy." As she spoke she stood up and half-ran, half-propelled herself across the floor until she stopped abruptly against him with such force that he had already wrapped his arms around her and received her kisses before realizing what was happening.

"Dorrie, please—" he managed to protest. Then, "You're crying."

She nodded, shuddering.

"Oh, my darling girl. I don't want to hurt you. I don't want to make you unhappy, you must understand that."

"I do, I do."

His face was so sad that it frightened her. He said, "You deserve the very best, Dorrie. If only there was some way—I don't want to hurt you. I never wanted to cause you pain. Believe me, please."

A sob turned to a tiny explosion of laughter. "Don't keep saying that! You sound like Uncle Samuel's 'Sorry old girl, but this is nothing personal,' when he chops the head off one of the hens. Of course you're not hurting me. I was a wee bit shaken there, but I'm fine now. Del, we're here together and we love each other. What could be more important than that?"

Del groaned. His face was buried in the curve of her

neck and she could sense the anguish in him. Her heart swelled with protective love. "There, now," she soothed. "Everything will work out for the best."

He did not reply.

Twelve

Though she had been nudged into it against her inclination, Dorrie could not have chosen a more propitious time to go into business. All of Auckland was caught up with plans for the celebration of Queen Victoria's Diamond Jubilee.

Everyone would participate. From the Patenes, who had a faded Coronation picture in pride of place, to Dora, who cut out every picture of the Royal Family she could find and pressed them in a giant scrapbook, to Ellen, with her collection of Royal Doulton cups and plates commemorating every event in the Queen's life—everybody loved her.

In many ways Victoria was the age she represented, the Victorian paterfamilias, fixing her subjects with a cold eye, her bearing more regal than the most authoritarian head of any household. She *was* the Empire on which the sun never set, and when women "shut their eyes and thought of England" they saw her, for had she not suffered in the same way to bear so many princes and princesses for her own dear Albert?

New Zealand may have been the farthest-flung outpost of the Empire but it was not going to be outdone by the celebrations brewing in India and Africa. In Auckland there would be parties of every kind, fireworks displays, regattas, parades, horseraces, fetes, and public holidays. Every lady in Auckland would be going to at least a dozen separate festivities and for most of those they would need showy new hats.

Her first project was a hat for Marguerite to wear on Regatta day, a rolled brim creation swathed with a cloud of bronze-spotted veil and adorned with a spray of Japanese silk poppies in autumn tones with deep gold throats. To show it off she covered one of Dora's old hatboxes with silver-and-white-striped paper and topped the lid with an extravagant silver chrysanthemum bow. While she worked she could hear Roseanne over in the old boxroom thumping away on Fintona's practice piano, rattling out a jaunty tune.

"She seems much more cheerful lately, what I've seen of her," commented Dorrie. "Oh, I do hope Marguerite likes this hat."

"Certainly should, since you're practically giving it to her," said Dora acidly.

Dorrie said, "I did explain to you, Auntie, that Marguerite's mother is giving a luncheon for a dozen lady friends and the idea is that Marguerite will show this hat off to them. She'll do it discreetly, of course, showing just one at a time as if they were privileged to be in on a special secret, and *then* she is going to allow them to pry my name out of her. I do hope her strategy works."

Dora pursed her lips. "They'll be a lot of nobodies, I suppose. Bakers' and butchers' wives and the like. You'd have been better to look around at some of the ladies who come to parties at Fintona."

"Perhaps so," said Dorrie, nestling the hat into its tissue paper bed. "But when I told Roseanne what we were doing she said all this was gross and vulgar and she hoped I wouldn't ask *them* to do anything like that. I must say, Auntie Dora, I thought her attitude was ungrateful. After all the things we've done for them I'd—"

"That's different, pet," interrupted Dora firmly.

Is it? thought Dorrie, but she said, "I suppose so. It doesn't matter, anyway. From what I've learned at the Hopkins' place, bakers' wives and butchers' wives are the ones with money in their purses, and they don't mind spending it, either!"

"I'm pleased to hear it. Now you'd best be on your way if you want to get that hat to the Duptons and then do your shopping in time for Samuel to meet you outside the Post Office at three. Though I don't imagine he'll mind waiting if you're held up anywhere. He always finds someone to yarn to—one of the advantages of getting old, I expect.''

"It was lucky, him coming by this morning, wasn't it? Mind you, I suppose all these things could have come on the delivery wagon, but that could mean waiting until Friday or even Saturday, and I'm so anxious to get started!'' Taking the list from behind the tea caddy, she perused it, frowning. "Wire, crown shapes, silk taffeta, buckle shapes, hat pins, trimmings with a question mark. Mmmm. I think I'll just get a little of straw braid and horsehair braid in three or four colors, some aigrettes—or could we make those plumes?

"Just a very little of everything,'' said Dora beside her. "There's one thing ladies can't stand, and that's the feeling that someone else is wearing an identical hat. Look, wait a second and I'll pop on my hat and coat and come with you.''

"*Would* you? But what about your cold? You still sound very froggy and there is a sharp wind about.''

"I'm not missing out on this,'' said Dora, taking off her spectacles, rubbing them on her skirt and fitting them back into the dents on the bridge of her nose again. "Cold or no cold, I'm coming, too. That way we can decide on the spot what we can make and what we have to buy. And we can go to all the Queen Street hat shops and try on their most expensive models.''

"See what the competition is and resolve to do better.'' Dorrie hugged her aunt, her enthusiasm bubbling up in her. "I'm glad you're coming. I wouldn't have the courage to breeze in and ask to try on the 'select creations'. I'd sidle in and if a saleslady so much as glared in my direction I'd run out. Oh, isn't this going to be fun? Wouldn't it be marvelous if every one of Mrs. Dupton's guests came by to order one of our creations? Just think of it, a dozen orders to begin with!''

"Just think of this: He who expects nothing is seldom disappointed," warned Dora, but she smiled as she spoke.

Dorrie was under the oak tree working with pliers and wirecutters measuring lengths of flexible wire for basic hat frames when the first prospective customer arrived early next afternoon.

Dorrie knew Mrs. Edelburt by sight, a tall fussily dressed woman that Dora had sometimes made clothes for. "Hard to please and slow to pay," Dora had complained on more than one occasion.

She introduced herself and added that her husband was "high up in officialdom," as if the bureaucracy were a separate country. Dorrie knew he worked in the town clerk's office. She stared down her flinty face at Dorrie and said, "But you're Miss Bennington's niece! I must say when Miss Dupton told me about you I hardly pictured a chit of a girl toiling away in a *backyard.*"

Dorrie explained that she had brought this work outside so that flying snips of wire could cause no damage. Mrs. Edelburt made no comment, merely stared at Dorrie, at the wire, and, with much greater interest at Fintona, where the groom could be seen outside the stables as he currycombed the chestnut horses in the sunshine.

Finally Dorrie blurted out, "Have you come to see me about a hat, Mrs. Edelburt?"

"Well, of course I have. What did you think my errand was—dog chains?" and she glanced at the litter of metal scraps. "But there's no need to be impertinent, child. If you are in business for yourself you should try to keep a civil tongue in your head. Well, where are these hats of yours?"

Dorrie glanced around in the direction of the Fintona side door where Dora had disappeared with some of Ellen's mending a few minutes earlier. Between them they had agreed that Dora would talk to the customers, but Mrs. Edelburt had caught them totally unprepared. Marguerite said that the luncheon would not be over until at least three.

"Well, child? I don't expect to be kept waiting, you know. My time is valuable."

"You'd better come inside," said Dorrie reluctantly, adding, "I mean, please Mrs. Edelburt, if you would care to step this way?"

In a flurry of embarrassment and wishing that Dora would come and rescue her, Dorrie, in a fair imitation of the way Mr. Hopkins greeted his customers, seated Mrs. Edelburt by the window and brought out two of the hats she had made recently, a cream lace creation with pink satin ribbons and a gray Gainsborough plumed with sweeping ostrich "Amazon feathers" that she had made for Dora.

"I make everything to order, you understand," she murmured, placing a Paris millinery catalogue close to the hats.

"And I like to see what I'm getting," sniffed Mrs. Edelburt, examining the satin-covered buckles and parting the rows of lace to look for flaws in the stitching before turning her critical eye on the Gainsborough. She peered closely at the flat velvet bow which neatly covered the place where the plumes were anchored to the brim.

"Is this all you have?" she asked, and when Dorrie admitted meekly that it was, she said, "Well, your quality of work is passable enough, I suppose, though whether or not the *value* is there depends on the price, doesn't it?"

Dorrie nodded, biting her lip.

"Can I assume that your prices will be approximately half of what the Hopkins would charge?" She smiled, knowing that Dorrie was so utterly cowed that she could now afford to be pleasant.

"Well—I don't know if—"

"Speak up, child. That is a reasonable assumption,

isn't it? Everybody in town knows that the Hopkins'
prices are absolute highway robbery, but then they can
get away with it because they are an established business
with an exclusive clientele. Now let us say, shall we, two
pounds for this model of hat and two pounds five shillings for this. That sounds eminently fair.''

Dorrie was flabbergasted. Last night after comparing
prices of the select models they had tried on in the shops,
she and Dora had decided that they would ask seven
guineas for hats similar to the lace one and eight and a
half guineas for the Gainsborough. This kept their prices
just below both the shops and the Hopkins' tags, but still
high enough to be in the exclusive bracket.

With her head tilted on one side, Mrs. Edelburt considered the hats again, first one, then the other. ''Perhaps
black lace with pale blue trim—that new ice blue color—
and a jet cabouchon or two to set it off. Yes, write that
down, girl—you may call that a definite order.''

''But Auntie Dora—''

''She knows where I live. You may deliver when it's
ready. Shall we say Tuesday?'' And with a curt nod she
moved briskly from the room in a rustle of silk skirts
leaving the door—and Dorrie's mouth—wide open behind her.

''The other ladies were much nicer, thank goodness, *and*
thank you!'' said Dorrie to Marguerite. ''Mrs.
Wrightsman ordered the most expensive creation, but
Mrs. Harry wants eight dear little matching bonnets for
her daughters, so we've miles of work to be going on
with.''

The girls were at the City Public Baths enjoying the
first break Dorrie had permitted herself since she started
in business three weeks earlier. She was beginning to
miss Del terribly and had promised herself that on the
way home she would stop by and spend an hour or two
with him.

In Roseanne's cast-off costume, a loose tunic with

wrist-length sleeves, stockings and ballet slippers, she shivered at the pool's edge. Marguerite was more skimpily dressed in the latest "Parisienne" style with puffed sleeves, a sailor collar, and bloomers to the knee. As she tucked her hair under the matching lemon wrap-around turban she said, "The first swim of the season! How I look forward to this!"

From her vantage point on the high stool surrounded by the paraphernalia of her office, life rings, rescue pole, and danger signs, Mrs. Weak, the bathkeeper's wife, eyed Marguerite's exposed arms and calves with disapproval. Marguerite noticed and giggled. "Aaaah!" she cried, leaping in. "Oh! It's *freezing!*"

Dorrie stepped back from the splash, then huddled on the edge dangling her legs in the water, deciding at once that it was too cold for her and she would leave total immersion until next time. A chill breeze swooped over the corrugated iron fence and tugged at her old black bonnet. She tightened the chin ribbons, shivering.

Both girls were strong swimmers. Now Marguerite carved out five steady lengths using the popular sidestroke style with scissor leg movements and her turbanned head clear of the surface, then she glided back to Dorrie where she paused, treading water while her lemon skirt bulged up like floating seaweed around her.

"You look so *miserable*. Won't you come in?"

Dorrie shook her head, trying to smile. Her legs were numb with cold.

"Did I tell you? *Papa* got a message from Mr. Rosser and he's coming to Auckland for the entire Jubilee month! Did I tell you that?"

"You told me."

"I'm so excited about that! Usually he stays only five or six days, so think of it, a whole month! Did I tell you that he is making more New Zealand films to show the Queen herself, that she liked the other ones so much that—"

"You told me. Many times." She managed a smile

this time. "I'm going to have to get changed, Marguerite. This is much too cold for me."

"It's that old-fashioned costume," Marguerite told her frankly. "It soaks up the cold and doesn't allow your limbs to move freely." She swum a few strokes back and forth, her legs flashing like silver fishes. "Perhaps when your business is a success you'll be able to afford to buy yourself something more stylish, *non?*"

They swung home in the slanting evening light, Marguerite carrying her bathing costume and towel in a smart European satchel of blue leather and Dorrie with hers in an open-weave Maori flax kit with string handles. They separated near the Dupton house, Dorrie declining the invitation of a glass of lemonade.

"I'd love to," she said, "but there's work at home."

"Somehow I get the feeling that I'm going to hear that song again," said Marguerite. "Never mind. I'll stop by after tennis tomorrow and if your aunt agrees perhaps we can go for a walk together to deliver Mrs. Wrightsman's hat."

"I'll finish it tonight then," promised Dorrie. I should tell her about Del, she thought with a pang of guilt for her deception as she watched Marguerite until she had disappeared up her driveway between the tall hedgerows.

When she was sure she had gone, Dorrie picked up her skirts and dashed along the opposite road from the one she should have taken for the most direct way home. Her boots flew over the dirt and gravel and it was not until she had rounded the next corner that she slowed her pace to a sedate walk. All the time she ran, her heart had been thumping for fear that Marguerite, having thought of one last thing to say, would come back out of her gateway as she so often did.

I must see Del, I must, she thought. They had not been together since the day he gave her his terrible news, and though she had later relented and told him about her hats she knew that he would be interested to hear how well she was doing, just as she was eager to learn whether he had taken any practical steps towards securing his property. She was confident that there was some way Del would be able to buy it back. The Salvationists were practical people but humane and they would surely permit him to keep the place and use it while he bought it back gradually.

As she stepped up the drive her heart was brimming with cheerful phrases and loving things to say, and her mind hummed as she sorted out the snippets of news she had been saving like coins to spend with him. She warmed in anticipation as she visualized telling him about her early success and how he would say how very proud he was of her. Perhaps they would even make love as a special celebration—*that* hadn't happened the last time nor the time before that. She missed him and ached to be close to him again.

The house seemed deserted. Bowser greeted her with frantic barks and the jangling of his chain so she paused to rumple his coat. As she was patting him she took the opportunity to peek into the shed. The farm cart stood there in the gloom.

Dorrie gazed all around. "Where's your master, eh, boy?" she said, glancing up at the house. Just then she saw a shadow move across one of the upstairs windows— Del's. It was a quick pass of darkness, like someone moving away from the curtains.

Smiling to herself, Dorrie climbed the back steps and turned the door handle. The door was locked.

That's very odd, she thought, because she had never known Del to lock the door unless he was closing it on the outside world for the two of them, and the first time he had done so he had to scrabble around before he found the key.

She knocked on the door, then waited, hearing faint sounds that may have been merely echoes of her knocking resounding further back in the hollows of the building.

There was no response. She knocked several more

times in case Del was asleep or ill and needed more time
to get down to open the door, then she reluctantly picked
up her kit of damp clothing and walked slowly away. At
the head of the drive she turned to look back at the upstairs windows and again she thought she saw that flash
of shadow at Del's window. It must have been a trick of
the evening light, she thought, just the twilight flickering
over the pane of glass. As she returned to the road she
walked slowly in case she might meet him returning from
wherever he had gone.

She was approaching the bridge when a faint nickering
attracted her attention. Thinking it was a bird—the
multisonged *tui* perhaps—she turned her head to catch a
glimpse of it and heard the sound again, this time unmis-
takably a horse and coming from the corner of the Blackett property. Dorrie immediately wondered whether
Del's horse Chester had broken loose from her enclosure
behind the stable, and crossing the road, she stood on tip-
toes and craned her neck to see over the low bank of
shrubs and ferns. There, behind a great clump of feathery
toe-toe bushes was Roseanne's mare Silk. With bridle
tethering her to the fence she was cropping the grass that
grew around the shrubs, the shiny black sidesaddle swaying slightly as she raised and lowered her head.

Dorrie stood staring at the horse for several minutes,
then slowly continued on her way, but when she was a
dozen paces past the bridge she abruptly changed her
mind, hurried back and pushed her way through to where
Silk was tethered.

She had wiped the dishes and was replacing them in the
wooden rack that evening when Roseanne tapped at the
door. There was nothing unusual in her visit; she often
wandered in complaining that Rupert was reading a book
and Ellen was writing letters and she was *utterly bored*,
though this was her first evening call for several weeks.
Tonight she was flushed and seemed agitated.

"You may watch me sort these sequins," said Dora,

pushing out a chair for her. "I was putting them away and Misty got underfoot—I think he's getting deaf in his old age—and next thing I knew these were skidding all over the floor."

Roseanne wrinkled her nose. "Cats are detestable," she said.

Dora glanced over her spectacle rims. "Strange that you should have such an aversion to them," she mused. "You must have inherited that from your father."

Roseanne clamped her mouth shut. This was her standard response whenever Jon was mentioned, a fact that did not faze Dora.

Dorrie was filling the warming pigs, tipping boiling water into the holes in their backs, counting to three to let the steam escape, then replacing the bungs, thumping them in firmly. As she carried them off into the bedroom she said casually, "I found your horse wandering out today. Did the groom tell you I brought her home?"

She paused in the doorway and glanced across at her cousin. Roseanne flushed with such an expression of furtive guilt that Dorrie was surprised. She had already considered explanations for the fact that Silk was tethered inside the Blackett property, and finally decided that she must have wandered off on her own and been found by Del, who intended to return her later. To suspect anything else was unworthy. *That's the trouble with leading a secretive life,* she told herself. *One begins to suspect others of doing the same thing.* As she tucked the warming pigs into the beds Dorrie began to wonder all over again.

"You didn't tell me about that," said Dora.

"No, because you were busy with Mrs. Wrightsman's hat. How did you come to lose Silk, Roseanne?"

Roseanne said quickly, "Is the hat finished, Aunt Dora? I'd really like to see it if I may."

Gratified, Dora lumbered over to the piano and lifted down the hatbox. Out came a blue box turban hat which was swathed in a cloud of gray veiling that was covered all over with tiny blue birds.

"The birds were Dorrie's idea," said Dora proudly. She cut them out of velvet, fronts and backs, then glued them with the veil between. Mrs. Wrightsman wanted something completely unique to match her blue and gray Regatta costume and she agreed to pay the highest price if we could come up with something magnificent to surprise her."

"It's—it's beautiful," breathed Róseanne, picking it up.

"I can't wait to see Mrs. Wrightsman's face when she opens the box," said Dorrie. "Auntie, could Marguerite and I please deliver it tomorrow afternoon? It's such a pretty walk along the shore path, and I love the Wrightsmans' place."

"Perhaps you'd like to go, too, Roseanne?" offered Dora. "You'd like to see the gardens, I'm sure. Mrs. Wrightsman had cliff terraces cut out all the way down to the beach and she planted them with every kind of flower and shrub you could imagine. The path up to the house is a blaze of color all year around."

Roseanne held the hat reverently between her hands. "It's absolutely *beautiful*," she said.

Dorrie wanted to snatch it off her. "Mrs. Wrightsman will love it, too," she said.

Roseanne smiled at Dora. "Do you know, this hat would exactly match the peacock blue costume I'm wearing to the Governor General's garden party. I came over here this evening with the intention of asking your advice about a hat to wear with it. And this, Auntie Dora, this would be *perfect!*"

"But we can't—"

"If you like it so much, then you must have it," Dora interrupted Dorrie firmly. "I promised Ellen that if there was anything that ever took your fancy—"

"That's what she told me," said Roseanne, delighted.

* * *

Dorrie found that, provided all the materials were at hand, it was possible to complete one very complicated design or two simpler models in one day, though in order to do that she had to rise at daylight, pause during the day only long enough to gulp down a cup of tea, then interrupt herself briefly at dinnertime before working until late in the evening. Dora had to work hard, too, but if customers called it was the older woman who set her work aside to chat to them while Dorrie kept her fingers deftly moving.

"How's it going?" asked Rupert one day when Dorrie begged a ride to town with him when the millinery supplies needed restocking. He was a curiously expressionless young man, neither friendly nor unfriendly, but passive to the point of indolence. He was supposed to be learning how to manage the Peridot Emporiums but from what Dorrie could see he spent most days lounging on Fintona's verandah engrossed in light romantic novels about European princes and nights of passion, just the kind of thing she and Marguerite used to giggle over in the first year of their friendship.

"The hat farm," said Rupert, rubbing at his beard where the spots were itching. "How's it coming along?"

"Fine, thank you," she said.

"Thought so," he said. "Between them Mama and Roz must be giving you trade worth a fortune. Every time one of them goes over to the gatehouse they come back wearing a new bonnet. I've lost count! You must be pleased to have such good customers right next door."

"It's not quite like that," said Dorrie evenly. In truth, Ellen and Roseanne were costing the business a substantial slice of its profits. Not only did they swoop on the best hats (unless Dorrie was quick enough to hide them) but if their gaze happened to fall on some particularly fashionable or expensive piece of trimming, then without fail a gown or jacket or coat would be produced and Dora asked to sew that trimming on it.

"You mean they get all those hats for nothing?"

Dorrie swallowed. "Auntie Dora says it's good for our business in the long run. That Aunt Ellen will tell people about us and in that way more customers will come by."

"They won't, you know." He stared at her, rubbing his cheek. "I heard Mama tell the Governor General's wife that the blue hat Roz was wearing—that fancy thing with the tiny birds flying round it—was specially imported from Paris. You made that, didn't you?"

Dorrie nodded. *I'll think this is funny one day,* she told herself. At the moment she felt like crying.

"That's Mama, all right," said Rupert uncritically. "She always arranges things to her advantage. Right now she's breaking her neck to marry Roz off. She's set her hopes on that entrepreneur fellow Rosser, but if someone equally wealthy came along, I suppose she'd fasten onto him, too."

Then she won't want Del, thought Dorrie, heartened by this news.

"Mind you," continued Rupert, "Roz is so rebellious these days I wouldn't put it past her to up and marry the coal man."

Dorrie smothered a flicker of unease. "What about you, Rupert?" she teased. "Have you some news you'll be sharing with us soon?"

"Not me."

"Nor me," said Dorrie. "Not yet."

"At last!" Dorrie said, her voice alight with joy. "I can remember how once you accused me of trying to avoid you. Now I am beginning to wonder if the boot is on the other foot."

"What do you mean?" Del paused, a sack of grain bowing his shoulders under its weight. Dorrie had arrived at the house to find him in the process of unloading the wagon after his fortnightly visit to the feed merchants in town.

"I mean that it's almost impossible to find you these days. I mean that you're never here. I mean that this is the third time I've called in without being able to see you.''

"Well, you're seeing me now.'' He hefted another sack onto his back, grunting slightly as he took the full weight. Bowser leaped from the wagon and raced ahead of him into the shed.

"Yes, and you're looking well, too. I'm so glad I called in on the off-chance—I'm on my way to deliver this hat to a lady up the road. Do you like the way Auntie Dora decorates the hatboxes? She's clever, isn't she?''

"Very. Watch out there. I wouldn't like to drop one of these on you.''

Dorrie tagged after him. He would be at least a half an hour with the wagon and she had only a few minutes to spare with a million things she wanted to say.

"Del, have you made any progress about the property? Have the Salvation Army come to terms with you about it?''

He paused on the way back, dusting off his hands, his face strained with effort. "Look here,'' he said. "I want you to forget I told you that stuff about the will. I shouldn't have said it and I want to take it back. All right?''

"But I'm glad you confided in me! That's what I'm here for, to share things with—''

"Forget it. All right?'' His eyes were cold as the sea on a winter's day.

"If you say so,'' whispered Dorrie. "But I was going to offer to help you. Our business is attracting lots of customers and—''

"I said forget it.'' He turned to wrestle another huge sack onto his shoulders, cutting her off before she could elaborate.

Crushed, she watched him stagger into the shed. The plan she had hoped to outline for him was a simple one. They could marry sooner than expected, sell the gatehouse, and she and Dora could move in here away from their avaricious relatives so that the business could prosper and grow. In no time the property would be paid off and everybody would be happy.

When he came back he saw her standing downcast beside the wagon and regretted his curt manner. It was not her fault.

"Look here," he said. "I'm sorry about just now. You've caught me at a very busy time. There's so much on my plate these days."

"I know the feeling."

He gave her a tight grin. "The fact is, Dorrie, that this situation between us can't continue. I've been thinking about it a lot lately—oh, blast it."

Bowser dashed away along the drive, barking, towards the sound of trap wheels and raised voices.

"There's a customer coming."

Dorrie put her hand on his arm. She felt ridiculously breathless with happiness. "I'm so *glad* that you feel that way, too—about us, I mean."

"Eh?"

"I've been thinking about it, too. It was different when I could see you so easily, after work most days, but now when we're both so busy the situation has changed, hasn't it?" She talked fast, aware that their privacy could now be measured in seconds. "Before, this business between you and I was a lovely secret, wasn't it? But now that I seem to be having to make up excuses and tell lies every time I go out of my way to come here, it's spoiling everything. Oh, I'm so glad that you're sick of all the deception, too." She reached up impulsively to kiss him. "This is going to be wonderful. This is going to be marvelous! Oh, Del, I'm so *happy!*"

"I say, Dorrie—" he began in alarm but was interrupted by the arrival of a transport wagon at the curve of the drive. It was a "celestial chariot" in which sat three men in Salvation Army uniforms.

"They don't waste any time, do they?" said Dorrie.

"Look, forget what I said about them, *please*. And

come back very soon, will you? We need to have 〔 ous talk and the sooner the better. All right?''

"I'll look forward to it." She squeezed his a ⅃ quickly and walked away, swinging the hatbox. ''Good morning, gentlemen!'' she piped sweetly as she passed by.

"I don't think I'll go to Roseanne's poetry evening," said Dorrie. "I'll try to finish off those shepherdess hats since there's no chance of being interrupted while she and Aunt Ellen are socializing. Auntie," she continued as Dora shot her a swift, reproving glance, "do you think we might get *Riversong* out of the museum for the Jubilee month? You could wear her with your gray costume, and I could retrim your gray hat with some aigrettes of emerald green beads and add a spray of emerald coque feathers to really set it off. What do you think?''

Dora sighed. "My head aches too much to think," she said. "Besides, I never wear any jewelery other than this brooch. Are you sure you don't want *Riversong* to wear for yourself?''

"*Could* I? Greenstone is all the rage just now, and—''

"No, dear. Perhaps in a year or two." She took off her spectacles and massaged the red dents at the bridge of her nose.

I'll be married then, thought Dorrie, letting her mind drift to the reverie that had sustained her on many evenings when her eyes burned from the close work and her mind thirsted for sleep. In her dream they were all living in the Blackett house with servants to do the heavy work and a flourishing but very exclusive little hat *salon* in the old music room. There were mirrors everywhere and soft golden lighting as their most exclusive creations were displayed for customers to try on. One seamstress helped in the workshop, a parlormaid brewed and poured tea for customers, and all Auntie Dora had to do was chat graciously to elegant ladies and assist them in their selection.

"Goodness, child! Whatever has gotten into you?"

"I'm sorry, I was miles away."

"Perhaps you should come this evening," said Dora. "I have to go, anyway, so I can't stay and help you. The Dupton lass will be there, I hear, and I've noticed that Rupert is beginning to take quite an interest in her. Really, Dorrie, you shouldn't let the grass grow under your feet there. If you're really not at all interested in that nice Australian rancher—"

"Oh, Auntie!" Dorrie sat down opposite Dora, picked up a scrap of silk, matched it with another, and began automatically fashioning a Japan poppy. The bubbly mood of this morning lingered in her veins with a faint effervescence and she was thinking, *Why not tell her now? She'll know soon, anyway.*

"What would you say if I told you that I had a young man interested in me, seriously interested, I mean?"

Knotting a thread Dora said, "It's not Rupert? No, well, in that case I'd ask you his name and the size of his fortune, just as any caring guardian would."

"He's not rich." Seeing her aunt's forehead bunch like a cauliflower, Dorrie added quickly, "But he will be one day. He works hard and has a good business. It's Del Blackett. Arundel Blackett, the Major's son." Before she quite realized what she was doing she had poured out a gush of assorted details, how she'd first met Del when she began piano lessons, how they'd become friends, and how they'd often chanced to meet when Dorrie was on her way home from work.

Dora listened indulgently, seeing nothing to be alarmed about. Dorrie was a sensible girl, and she'd read Dora's own copy of *Everyday Etiquette for Young Ladies.* It was not until Dorrie said, "He loves me, Auntie. He's said so lots of times," that she felt a shadow of apprehension.

"Then why hasn't he been to speak to me?" she asked.

"He intends to soon, truly he does, but he's been busy and he has so many worries lately."

"He shouldn't have any worries. His father left a substantial amount of property. The Major was a comfortably wealthy man."

Bitterness seeped into Dorrie's voice as she said, "Yes, and he left the whole shooting-box to the Sallie Army. Del was completely disinherited."

Dora rested her sewing. "Whatever gave you that idea?"

"Del did, of course."

"Did he now?"

"Is something wrong?" asked Dorrie after a silence.

"No, pet," said Dora wearily. "My head has a sledgehammer trapped inside it, that's all. I think I'll lie down for an hour. And as for you, young lady, you'd better come to the musical evening. I really think you should."

"Why? Isn't it more important that these shepherdess hats—"

"Because your young man will be there, that's why," said Dora as she pushed herself up from the table. "And I think I'd better introduce myself to him. Properly."

Dorrie was pleased to see Nathaniel Rosser at the Fintona that evening. His presence put Marguerite at her sparkling, vivacious best, and Nathaniel always had such interesting stories to tell. His work seemed to absorb him and when he was describing a special variety act he had hired or a new Cinematograph film he was making his eyes glowed with an enthusiasm that warmed everyone around him. Tonight he entertained them with an account of his most successful venture, the Phantasmagoria show, which was advertised as being "not for the faint-hearted."

"It's not so terrifying," Marguerite said encouragingly. "People may shriek and scream but they come out laughing. Do tell Dorrie about it, Mr. Rosser. She's never been to one.''

He turned to Dorrie with that familiar mischievous expression. ''You must promise not to swoon with terror,'' he said.

''I'll try.''

''Then imagine this. A theater about the size of the ballroom here, but lit so dimly that people beside you appear only as the vaguest shadows. All about hang thin silk curtains, tattered as cobwebs, and these waft billows of smoke. Suddenly the room darkens even more and you are sitting alone in the middle of an overgrown, decaying graveyard. Headstones waver on the silk screens. Ghosts rise with eerie moans. Lightning flashes, thunder rumbles, and—''

''Ladies and gentlemen!'' interrupted Ellen from the platform. ''We'll begin our program now if you'll be so kind.''

''A specter!'' whispered Rupert wickedly, and when they all laughed he said, ''Will you sit by me, Miss Dupton?''

Dorrie looked around hopefully but there was as yet no sign of Del, so she took her place on Rupert's other side.

The program began with a selection even more dreary than the usual soiree fare. Dorrie fidgeted as a violinist cawed and scratched for what seemed like an hour, then Judge Prescott's daughter read some of her recent poetry. In a high, clipped voice she recited verses crammed with references to Callicrates, Athena Nike, and the Saronic Gulf. A wave of relieved applause swept her back to her seat, and as she stepped from the platform Dorrie noticed Roseanne move from her place and hurry to the door. Del had arrived.

Dorrie stood up, removing her wrap from the seat she had saved beside her, and waved to Del so that he would see her waiting for him. To her astonishment he did not so much as glance in the direction of the guests but strolled to the piano, helped Roseanne take her place at the keyboard and nonchalantly placed one hand on the polished piano top. As Roseanne struck the first chord he burst into song.

And what a song it was! Dorrie was stunned, and a collective ripple of appreciation traveled the room as Del's rich voice swelled to the ceiling.

Marguerite gasped and leaned across Rupert to whisper to Dorrie. "I had no idea," she said. "No idea at all!"

Dorrie glowed with silent pride. *What a marvelous life we shall have,* she dreamed. *Our home will overflow with music.*

Marguerite leaned over again. "Have they a flirtation going?"

It was an innocent, gossipy inquiry but Dorrie reacted with unusual sharpness. "What a silly idea!" she said.

When their encore died away the guests drifted forward to congratulate Del. Roseanne was clinging to his arm but as soon as her mother intercepted them and made an excuse to distract Roseanne, Del came straight over to Dorrie.

"That was magnificent, Del," she said.

"It was all impromptu," he told her, but it was so obvious a lie that she was dismayed. Dorrie was not a jealous person, and it would not have mattered to her if Del and Roseanne had spent hours practicing, but his lie made her feel betrayed.

Dora was speaking to Del now, inviting him to come to dinner one evening. "That will give you a chance to tell me all about yourself and about your plans," she said. "It will be just Dorrie and me at our cottage—simple surroundings and plain food, I'm afraid—but you'll be more than welcome."

He looked bewildered, made flustered excuses, and drew Dorrie away from the group. "What did you tell her?" he demanded.

"Just a little about us. Why? What does it matter?" His obvious anger puzzled her.

"I must talk to you, Dorrie. It's urgent, it really is."

Roseanne appeared at his elbow. Her cheeks were very bright on her flour-white face as she said chidingly, "You mustn't talk that way, Mr. Blackett. Hasn't anybody ever told you that words like *urgent, important,* or *critical* don't belong at a party? Look, there's Sylvia. We must tell her that her poetry was like a leisurely cruise through the Greek Isles. That will console her for the fact that you missed it, don't you think? Oh, Sylvia . . ."

Dorrie turned abruptly away and almost bumped up against Nathaniel's shirtfront. He and Marguerite were standing so close behind her that she wondered how much they'd heard.

"Poor Del!" exclaimed Marguerite. *"Look* at how your cousin is throwing herself at him. He looks like a puppy with a tin tied to his tail."

"He looks like a man well satisfied with life," said Nathaniel, accepting a sandwich from a tray that Crystal was offering around. "Mind you, I'd be pleased with myself if I could sing half as well."

Dorrie glanced after them. Roseanne was heaping Sylvia with extravagant compliments while Del watched on benignly, a cool smile twitching at the corners of his mouth. He *does* look well satisfied, thought Dorrie.

Nathaniel said, "I was looking forward to hearing you play again, Dorrie."

"I've been so busy—Roseanne had to make the program up without me," said Dorrie, though in truth Roseanne had not even invited her to be on it. Only now was she beginning to wonder why not.

"It was a disappointment." He smiled into her eyes. *How* nice *he is,* she thought.

"I'm sure that Del made up for any twinge of disappointment. Wasn't he splendid?"

"Outstandingly good. Is he that music teacher's son? The Salvation Army fellow who was lost in that ghastly accident?"

"Yes," said Dorrie. "He's an orphan now, just like me."

Something in her voice made Nathaniel look at her more sharply. It was a wistful, plaintive air like a straying wisp of melody. As she spoke she was gazing at Del, her eyes drowsy with softness.

For heaven's sake! he thought in exasperation. *Surely he hasn't won her over with a song!*

"I say, Dorrie," cut in Marguerite. "Did I hear your aunt inviting Del to dinner? That sounds very mysterious. Is it?"

Dorrie bit her lip. She didn't want to risk any more of those cold blue looks from Del. Placing a finger to her lips, she said, "I'll tell you later."

"A secret? Oh, what *fun!*" She looked up into Nathaniel's face. "Don't you love secrets, too?"

He shook his head. "Not a bit, I regret to say." *For heaven's sake,* he thought. *I'm concerned about her, genuinely concerned for her happiness.*

Though he didn't admit it to himself, he was also jealous.

Thirteen

Now that Regatta Day was only three weeks away the gatehouse was in a constant turmoil of activity as Dorrie and Dora worked longer, more intensely busy hours to fill incoming orders. Though Dorrie reveled in the work and experienced a warm gush of pleasure each time another delighted customer received her hat, she was beginning to grow seriously worried about her aunt. Every morning Dora complained of a headache, and by midafternoon her hands developed a tremor that worsened as the evening closed in. Dorrie had to thread needles for her now, snip threads, and tidy up the rough edges on every piece of work Dora did.

It seemed like Providence when, at around this time, Dorrie heard about a young married woman who wanted to resume work as a milliner's assistant. Iris Pine was a cheerful lass of about twenty, dumpy and round faced with straight mousy hair twisted into a bun at the nape of her neck and a gauzy frizz of fringe. Dorrie found that with the slightest encouragement she would talk nonstop, but if left alone she was a deft, skilled worker well worth her three shillings a day.

She worked in the bedroom where a bench for daytime use was fitted over Dorrie's bed. The room smelled of musk and sweat after Iris had spent the day there, so before she retired each night Dorrie aired the room and cleared away the clutter of tools, scraps, and hatboxes.

"It's only until Regatta Day, the twenty-first of June, thank goodness" sighed Dorrie, resigning herself to the fact that she would probably not see Del until then.

She no longer had time to make deliveries. Fintona's

twelve-year-old stable-boy had been pressed into service as a delivery agent to take hats to customers Dora was sure would pay, and to deliver notes that advised, "Your order is ready, please collect" to those ladies about whom there was some doubt.

As Regatta Day approached Dora's tiredness and snappishness grew so much worse that now Dorrie tried to intercept customers in order to deal with them herself. She was grateful, however, that nature had called her away when Mrs. Edelburt finally arrived to collect her order. A fierce quarrel erupted when Mrs. Edelburt questioned first the price and then the color of the trim. Dorrie returned from the privy to find Dora showing lace samples to prove that ice-blue and eggshell-blue *were* subtly different and the hat, therefore, was as ordered.

"I'll take it, but I assure you that I'll never come back again," she said.

"That's kind of you to say so," said Dora in a voice that could freeze cream. Dorrie ducked into the bedroom, giggling.

"That's not the proper way to speak to a customer, and I know she'll say nasty things about us at the next Daughters of the Empire meeting, but for once that really was called for," she said to Iris.

"She is a one, i'n't she?" clucked Iris. "Oh, Miss, a boy brought this note for yer while yer aunt were busy with 'er. There it be, on the dresser."

Back in the other room Dorrie smoothed it out in her lap and read, *Dear Dorrie, I must speak to you without further delay, about an urgent matter. A. Blackett.*

When Iris had gone home that evening Dorrie showed it to her aunt. "I think he might be going to propose!"

"If he is, then this is not the proper way to go about it. Mr. Farrell did the right thing, approaching me first. What I say is, if he's so hell-bent on seeing you, why doesn't he present himself here? That note sounds as if he expects you to take yourself to him."

"I suppose he does, but please don't be put off by that.

It's only Del's manner—I suppose he's busy, in a hurry or something. Do you think I could go and see him after dinner?''

"What? But it will be pitch dark then. If somebody sees you wandering about, your reputation will be in shreds before you can say 'Mesopotamia.' '' She looked over her spectacles thoughtfully, watching Dorrie scrub carrots for their dinner. "Do you ever suspect, even slightly, that this young man may be trifling with your affections? There's something about him and about this whole business that frankly disturbs me.''

"Auntie, no!'' Dorrie dropped the scrubbing brush and turned to face her aunt, but a flame of color had burst into her cheeks. "Of course he isn't trifling with me! Auntie, he says he *loves* me! I mean to say, why should he tell me a thing like that if it wasn't true?''

"Why indeed?'' murmured Dora.

"I know he's been a bit offhand lately, but that's because he has so many worries on his mind. What with being disinherited and being so busy with the struggle to build up his business it's only natural that he should have his time full. Look how busy we are, and *we* have help.''

"Mmmm,'' said Dora, not quite convinced. "But don't get agitated over this. If the young man needs desperately to talk to you then you must go tomorrow. The only way to sort the matter out is to hear what he says.''

"I'll pop around there first thing in the morning,'' she decided, scrubbing brush poised but still. "And I'll try to persuade him to come around one evening soon to talk to you. Would that be all right?''

"Not just yet, please!'' groaned Dora. "All I ask is that you leave it until—''

"The twenty-first of June,'' Dorrie finished for her, laughing. "All right then. We can wait a bit longer. After all, we have the rest of our lives to look forward to, haven't we?''

"Dorrie,'' said Dora, frowning. "Don't you think that

perhaps you should—'' She stopped, wondering whether to finish expressing her doubts.

''What's wrong?''

Dora shook her head. ''Never you mind what I was going to say. After all, I'm an old lady and I've never had a young man courting me, so I'm in no position to offer advice.''

''You're *not* an old lady, and I'd value your advice. So what were you going to say?''

''Nothing. Look, pet, perhaps you'd better leave those carrots. If we wait for them to cook we'll be dining at midnight, and I'm famished now. Let's have bread and butter with the stew instead. Butter and beef, goodness! One good thing about being so busy is at least we're well fed.''

''I don't care what we have,'' said Dorrie blissfully. ''I'm far too happy to eat anything.''

Still frowning, Dora set out the knives and forks, the bread and butter plates, the condiments and the dish of plum jam. Though she could seldom share Dorrie's jubilant soarings of mood, she was usually amused by them, but not this time. She couldn't put her finger on it but there was something about this affair that made her feel gravely uneasy.

It was a little before seven-thirty when Dorrie marched up the drive the next morning, humming to herself and enjoying the bracing freshness of the air, the crisp whiteness of an early frost crunching under the soles of her boots. The sky was clear and hard as a pane of glass. In the bare *kowhai* trees a flock of sparrows grouped and regrouped in shivery flutters, waiting for the time when the fowls would be fed so that they could swoop down on the remnants of spilled grain.

Bowser was asleep in his kennel. When she reached in to pat him he licked her hand but did not come out. ''Softie!'' she chided. ''It's not so cold as all that!''

At the door she hesitated, knuckles raised, then swiftly

opened the door and stepped quietly inside. The kitchen was cold and silent, with the remains of a meal cluttering the table and a drift of ash from the open grate lying on the hearth. Dorrie walked over to the table, curious to see what kind of meals Del cooked for himself. On the plate was a congealed mess of chicken stew and beside the plate three crumpled envelopes rested on top of an account from *Messrs. Attenborough & Sons, Feed & Grain Merchants*. Two envelopes were compacted into balls but the third had partially unfolded and she could see that it was one of the large square type that Ellen used to convey invitations. Smoothing it out, she read Del's name and address written there in an upright firm hand.

That's Roseanne's writing, she thought, glancing towards the mantelpiece where upward of a dozen cards were propped all along the polished shelf. Picking them up one at a time, she glanced at each before she replaced it, thinking *How marvelous!* We're going to the Fells' party, too, and to the Blackinstones' patriotic dinner, and to the Wilsons' Empire Ball. How absolutely splendid!

All the Fintona invitations were embossed with a circlet of roses and separately they invited Mr. Arundel Blackett to two dinners, three concerts, a masquerade ball, and a black and white ball. All were filled out in Roseanne's handwriting and in every case the words "and partner" had been struck through with a single heavy dash. By the time she had examined the last of these Dorrie was giggling with repressed delight. She and Del would be seeing each other almost every evening.

There was no sound from upstairs. Treading carefully, Dorrie climbed the stairs and tiptoed along to Del's room. When she stood in the doorway, holding her breath, she could hear the slow, even sounds of his breathing and could see him lying with his face pressed into the pillow, the bedclothes wildly disarranged as if he had been thrashing about in his sleep. Smiling to herself Dorrie walked softly to the bed, paused and then swiftly undressed and slid in beside him.

"What the—" He raised his head, gasping to free himself from the wrappings of sleep.

"It's only me," she whispered from the pillow beside him. Her fingers trailed over his skin. "You feel hot," she said, snuggling closer.

"Dorrie! My God! What are you doing here?"

"Hush," she whispered, reaching up to kiss him and feeling him stir as the contact of her cool body brushed full length against his sleep-warmed skin. She stroked her hands up his back and across his shoulders, then combed her fingers through his fair curly hair, gently pressing his head towards hers. "I've missed you," she murmured as their lips met. "Haven't you missed me, too?"

He groaned, feeling the powerful hunger as his senses stirred. "Please Dorrie." It was a half-hearted protest and even as he sank he scorned the feebleness of his efforts to pull away. She had surprised him at his most vulnerable and now he was submitting to the pull between them with only the briefest and faintest of struggles. All it took was one kiss and one lingering caress, then he was insane for her, starving for her, frantic to have her.

Less than a minute later he was gasping like a beached fish and loathing himself more than he had ever hated anything. He had seized her like a starving creature and in a few swift spasms it was all over.

Dorrie was bewildered, too. "That was very strange," she said after a long, still silence. "So rough and quick." She strummed her fingers over his rib cage. "You're a funny old thing. Don't you wear a nightshirt?"

He was still panting. "They tangle around my neck. I'm a restless sleeper."

She had never heard him sound so gloomy. "Del, you're not sick, are you? I mean—to be lying in until this hour—"

"I was at the deBretts' until three."

"Well, no wonder you were still asleep. Roseanne and Rupert and Aunt Ellen were there, too, weren't they?"

She wound a lock of his hair between her fingers. "Was it fun? Did they serve a gigantic roast of wild pork? They're famous for their roasts of pork, you know."

"They served pork," he said miserably.

"Del, what's worrying you?"

"It's you." And when she looked at him, startled, he burst out, "Haven't you a single jealous thought in your head? Don't you mind that I was at the deBretts with your cousins?"

"Why should I mind? I'm pleased for you. Of course I'd have liked to be there, too, but even if we'd been invited Auntie Dora and I are too busy to go anywhere. Once June twenty-first comes, things will be so different, but—"

"Dorrie, please!"

Abruptly she was silent, gazing up at his face with hurt puzzlement in those clear gray eyes, her hair loose around her shoulders and her lips trembling with the words she had been prevented from uttering. Though she looked beautiful all flushed and rumpled from the violence of his passion, at that moment he hated her, hated her simply for being there, and hated himself even worse.

He pulled the sheet up to cover her decently to the shoulders, then realized that it was no use. He could never tell her like this.

"I must get dressed," he said as he rolled over and sat on the bed, pulling his trousers on hastily, furtively, aware of her questioning eyes on his back. "Dorrie, please get dressed, too," he said without turning around.

"I just wish you'd tell me what's the matter," she said, though she moved to obey him, rolling her stockings up her legs and slipping the garters on over them, fastening them tight above the knee. As she reached to the bed end for the petticoat that hung there she noticed a narrow black box on the dressing table beside his mother's silver pin-tray.

"What's this?" She picked it up and opened the delicate metal clasp.

He turned in time to see her lifting the lid.

"What a beautiful bracelet," she gasped, examining the silver and gold scrolls that formed an interlocking pattern. The central scroll had slipped a little to one side. Dorrie pushed it with her finger and it swung away revealing a tiny oval clockface.

"Don't," she said to Del, who snatched it out of her grasp. "That's one of those new wristwatches, isn't it?"

"It belonged to my mother," he said, shoving it in a drawer.

"How could it have?" Dorrie said as she buttoned her petticoat. "Marguerite said they're the very latest thing. She's been pestering her poor father for one."

Del did not reply. He was dressed now in his working clothes, corduroy trousers and a thick warm shirt with a cravat at the neck and a tweed jacket, socks and soft leather slippers. As he stooped to lace the puttees around his calves he said, "I must talk to you seriously now. Let's go downstairs, shall we?"

Picking up his mother's silver-backed hairbrush, she stood at the mirror and began to groom her hair. Early morning sunshine slanted through the window, turning the flying threads into spun silver. To his reflection she said, "Could you talk to me now, while I get tidy? I'd better not stay away too long or Auntie Dora will be wondering if something has happened to me."

So while she brushed her hair with his mother's hairbrush and wound it into a series of neat petals on the back of her head, he told her with much stumbling and awkwardness that they were not going to see each other alone, ever again.

"Why?" she said when he had finished.

"Because my feelings have changed," he told her.

She turned to face him, baffled. "Are you sure you're not sick, Del? I mean, none of this makes the slightest bit of sense. Only a few minutes ago we were in that bed together, loving each other in the way you told me that means we shall care for each other forever and ever, and now you try to say that it's all over. How can it be? People's feelings don't change so quickly, do they?''

"It's true, Dorrie. I'm sorry but I do mean it.''

A shadow of pain crossed her face but passed away quickly. "You've been under a lot of strain. Worries about your father, worries about money—''

"Dorrie, do you remember me saying that I never wanted to hurt you?''

She nodded, frightened by the white, sick look on his face and the grim tone in his voice.

"I know I'm going to hurt you, and I really don't want to, but I have to somehow find the courage to say it.''

Dorrie watched his face, her eyes enormous. After a brief silence she said, "I have to go now.'' She wanted to get away.

"I mean it. It is all over between us,'' he said.

She gazed into his face. He was the same dear Del that she loved so much. True, his eyes were cold, but that was Del's way and soon he would be smiling again. True, he hadn't said today that he loved her, but he wasn't quite himself today, was he? There had been times before when he'd been unloving and cold but he'd always come round in the end.

"I mean it, Dorrie.''

"I don't believe you,'' she said simply. "We love each other. You proved that to me, just a few minutes ago.'' She raised her chin with dignity but she was shaking so much as she left the room that the door handle slipped twice out of her trembling fingers before she could grasp it firmly enough to open the door.

"Dorrie! Listen to me!'' he shouted down the stairwell.

She leaned, quivering, against the passage wall, assailed by a dark flood of panic that swept over her, weakening her still further. He couldn't mean it! He couldn't!

This was a passing whim, a black mood, nothing for her to worry about, nothing . . .

"Dorrie, I'm serious! Stay and listen to me!"

Gathering her pitiful reserves of strength, she fled down the drive, tottering on legs that threatened to give under every step she took. Staggering to the gate, she leaned on it gratefully, closing her eyes and resting there, the sun warming her face and glowing orange on her eyelids.

When she opened her eyes she marveled that the world looked exactly the same as it had an hour earlier, when she had swung up the drive buoyed by that gloriously happy mood.

The sky was still a flat plane of crystal decorated by cloud bunting, the grass lay like rough-textured powdered sugar in the shadow of the hedge, and the birds still shivered in their stark *kowhai* tree. It was as if the events of the past hour had never happened.

Dorrie allowed herself to be reassured by that thought. He is sick, she told herself firmly. He didn't mean what he said. By the time Regatta Day comes round everything will be all right again. Of course it will.

Swinging along the road she hummed determinedly to herself. She had reached the main highway and had half a mile still to cover when a carriage and pair rattled up from the direction of town, drew level, and then stopped.

"Dorrie!" exclaimed May Teipa-Bennington. "What a delightful surprise. We've just been down to the wharf to bid my mother and father farewell. They're off to San Francisco to visit my brother Daniel and his family."

"They'll miss the Jubilee celebrations," said Dorrie stupidly. She felt slightly disoriented. May was leaning out of the open carriage, her face looked white and vulnerable in the center of a crumpled fur traveling rug that was heaped all around her. On the front seat were Patrick Teipa-Bennington and Nathaniel, who was driving. All were smiling, all in a holiday mood. Dorrie felt as if she had awakened from a drugged sleep to find all three staring at her. She wondered why they had stopped, what they expected of her.

"Go on," said Patrick. "If you're going to ask, ask." He clapped his arms about his body, fighting off the cold.

"In good time," said May, wrinkling her nose at him. "I haven't seen Dorrie for such a long time. Mind you, we seldom use this way to town." Her smile faded and she looked earnestly into Dorrie's face. "I believe that you and Dora are in business together? Mrs. Wrightsman showed me the hat you made for her to wear to the Regatta, that beautiful blue one with the tiny gray bird made out of real feathers with that long swooping tail. Dorrie, I don't think I've ever seen such a gorgeous creation."

You should have seen the real one, thought Dorrie.

"Dorrie, what I wanted to know, is, would you please make a hat for me, too? I'd really appreciate—"

"Oh," said Dorrie in dismay, stepping back a pace. She and May read each other's expressions and both stopped speaking at once.

"You won't," said May.

"It's not that I *won't,*" Dorrie said hastily. "I can't, truly I can't. We have so many orders that I don't know how—"

"It's all right. You don't have to explain."

In the periphery of her vision she could see the men's faces. Patrick wore a resigned expression, Nathaniel looked disappointed—that hurt her for she had a high opinion of Nathaniel and hated to think he might believe ill of her—while May looked crushed.

I've insulted them all, thought Dorrie miserably. She said, "It's not that I don't *want* to—" She felt like crying.

"You don't have to explain," repeated May.

"What kept you?" asked Dora as Dorrie slipped inside and hung up her bonnet.

"I met someone on the road, someone who wanted me to make another hat for them."

"I hope you refused. Nicely, of course, unless it was Mrs. Edelburt."

"I refused." She stood with her hands still grasping the shoulders of her coat; her whole body was trembling with fatigue.

"Tell me what your Master Blackett had to say for himself," demanded Dora. She had glimpsed Dorrie's face as she entered and knew at once that the interview had not gone well. "Here, sit down and tell me everything."

She listened in silence as Dorrie blurted out a tangle of sentences, then halted her with an upraised hand. "Let me get this straight. When you arrived he was as usual, friendly and warm."

Dorrie nodded, her eyes bleak. "Loving," she said.

"And then quite suddenly he informed you that his feelings had changed and he wasn't going to see you again."

"He changed into a complete stranger, Auntie. I don't—"

"He's trifling with you, sure as eggs are eggs."

"No!" The denial gave her something positive to cling to. "He's not himself. He has worries. That business over his father's will—" She paused as Dora took down her coat and wrapped a scarf around her neck. "Where are you going?"

Dora jammed her hat on and skewered it with a six-inch-long hat pin. "I'm going to find out about this will of the Major's. I know we haven't time to turn around right now, but I think we'd better make time to look into this. When Iris comes, set her working, will you, and don't stand about chatting."

The Patenes were at breakfast. A loaf the size of a football, crumbed on top with gray ash from the fire in which it was baked, was being carved on a rutted wooden board. Turei was smearing a slice for herself with plum jam.

Mrs. Patene was scrupulously polite. Too polite, thought Dora. She hasn't forgiven me for Ellen's rudeness, she decided as she accepted a cup of tea and a portion of plain bread.

Leaving that matter to sort itself out, she went directly to the point.

"Major Blackett's will?" said Mrs. Patene, ruffling her brow to indicate that it was all a mystery to her. "My boy Albert will tell you about that, eh. You know how it is when you get old, eh Miss Bennington? Your mind gets hazy and little details muddle up together. That's why I'm so grateful to have Albert to do all the thinking." She shuffled to the doorway, cupped one lean hand to her mouth, and called, "Hey, Albert! Miss Bennington wants to talk to you."

She saw him through the window, blocking the doorway of the old tugboat that still crazily rode the groundswell a short distance from the main cottage. He was a tall, almost femininely graceful youth with long hands and feet and sleepy eyes. His slender neck held his head aloft like a flower on its stalk. When he came inside he looked momentarily disappointed that "Miss Bennington" was Dora, but he put his book on the window ledge and sat down opposite her at the crumb-dusted table.

"How are your studies going, Albert?"

"Fine, thank you." He was extremely polite, too.

"He's doing better than fine, Miss Bennington. Best marks in his group, best by a mile. He's a very clever boy, is my boy Albert. The teacher, Professor Agney, he said—"

"Never mind what he said," interrupted Albert, but the half-expressed praise pleased him and the ice was broken. Attentively he listened to what Dora wanted to know.

"The contents aren't public knowledge yet, so you

don't need to apologize for not being cognizant of them," he assured her. "I imagine that the newspapers will print the details when they are released, which in turn will be when the wrangling is settled. The Salvation Army don't want to be seen wrangling over money, you understand."

"The will is in dispute, then?"

"Only the manner in which it is to be settled," said Albert.

"So you see, pet," said Dora that evening. "Major Blackett left a large estate. His wife had private means, apparently. She owned a long string of houses in Carnaevon Street, all rented out to dockside workers, and because she was very religious she left the income to her church, some little sect that was eventually absorbed by the Salvation Army. Major Blackett could see that when he died Del would not continue to give the church that support, and because the string of houses had been left in trust to Del by his mother, the Major countered by leaving his own house and grounds to the Salvationists."

"So it was true," whispered Dorrie.

"Well, only technically. Major Blackett's house was worth far less than the Carnaevon Street houses, but in order to keep it Del has found that he is forced to do some horsetrading. Albert said he's obliged to sell three houses and then pay out another hundred and fifty pounds to retain that property of his. But as for money worries, I'm afraid, pet, that he hasn't any. On the contrary, he's worth a very tidy sum indeed."

Dorrie said nothing. Her face was white.

Dora decided to tell her everything. She was angry—angry that Del had deceived her niece, angry that Dorrie was going to be hurt, but above all furious with the girl for allowing herself to be maneuvered into such a situation. Dorrie should have had more pride, more dignity than to give her affection to someone so patently unworthy.

"Turei chimed in at that stage—she couldn't wait to tell me all the gory details," she continued. "She said that 'young master Blackett' caused a terrible scene. He called the Salvationists blood-suckers and announced that he wasn't going to sell anything to satisfy them. They could try and tip him out of his home if they dared, he said. Apparently he was terribly rude about their church, too. The lawyer called a swift end to the proceedings and the Salvation Army officers walked out without anything being resolved."

Dorrie sat very still. Her lips were trembling and her eyes flicked from one object to another on the table.

Dora said, "Of course, we have only their word. They may have their facts wrong, but—"

Dorrie was silent.

Above their heads the lamp began to gutter, throwing heaving shadows about the room. Dora stood up and unhooked it, then lifted off the glass chimney and fetched some scissors to trim the wick. Tending the lamps was yet another job that neither of them had time for.

Dorrie felt as though it would hurt to move any part of her body; even her brain cramped in pain as she drew back from accepting what was being put before her. "Perhaps he did mislead me," she pleaded. "But he *was* sorry about it. He told me to forget what he'd said about the will. I know he wasn't deliberately trying to hurt me."

The words had an empty, pathetic ring to them, like the useless begging of a condemned person. Dora realized that if she pretended to believe, her pretense would strengthen Dorrie's own shaky convictions, but instead of pity rage rose like bile in her throat.

"For heaven's sake," she said, exasperated. "Do I have to take you by the shoulders and shake it into you? A proper, respectable gentleman comes courting openly, and he doesn't go wallowing in details of his financial hardships real *or* invented. This young man is a ratbag, Dorrie. It's as simple as that."

"But he said he loves me, Auntie Dora," whispered Dorrie. "Why would he say that if it wasn't true?"

"Why indeed?" said Dora. She shook her head, unable to think of a reason either. "Come on, pet, let's go to bed," she said finally. "All this mess will sort itself out, you'll see."

Fourteen

Uncle Samuel was at the gatehouse when Dora and Dorrie came in from their first shared outing in weeks. Windblown and buffeted, they hurried inside to hang up their coats and found him toasting his boots on the hearth, with an expression of contentment spread over his face.

"You might have warned us you were coming," snapped Dora, brushing up a scattering of dry tea leaves where he had carelessly spooned tea into the pot.

"And you might have known to expect me, lass. There's very few folks around now who can remember the time when our bonny Queen came to the throne, but I'm one of them. Ah, I remember the day well. We was all on the lawn of Governor Hobson's house. The men went inside to sip porter while the ladies drank tea outside. They had a picture of the young Queen Victoria propped up with necklaces of flowers hung all around it. Real flowers, all wilting in the sun like seaweed. Aye, she was a pretty lass." He gave Dorrie one of his toothless grins. "Not much older than you, she were."

"Well, she's a sour old widow now," observed Dora, looking sour and widowy herself. "And she's not going to have much of a Regatta if this wind doesn't die down. Are you coming out on the ferry with us, then?"

"Not me, lass. I came down from the Bay of Islands by ship forty-six years ago, and I've not set foot on a deck since. I'll watch from the shore, but it will be all the same to me. I couldn't miss her Diamond Jubilee, could I now?"

"I suppose not," said Dora. "Though we've just

come from a memorial service where the immediate *family* didn't show his face—that's right. Major Blackett's service. They waited until now to hold it so that all the out-of-towners who were coming to the Jubilee Regatta could attend."

"Major Blackett, eh? I'd have gone to that if I'd known. You know how it is, living alone out in the wop-wops, and my eyes givin' me the devil and his doings so I can't read the paper."

Dora laughed shortly. Uncle Samuel had never learned to read; it was an open secret but everybody pretended to believe his excuses. "You weren't missed," she told him, "but his son was. Think of it. Over a thousand people there praying for his soul and not hide nor hair of that ungrateful lad of his."

"Auntie, please!" whispered Dorrie.

"I'll tell it like it is."

Samuel looked from one to the other. Dora's pudgy face was reddened by the wind but around her eyes and mouth was a bluish stain, the tinge of extreme exhaustion. There was a heavy slump to her shoulders and her eyes were dull with fatigue.

Hunched by the window, Dorrie looked no better, a sick, ruffled blackbird in her mourning clothes. Her drawn, gray face was impassive as she stared from the oak tree being blown.

He knocked his pipe bowl on the grate, making up his mind. "I'll be on my way," he said. "You two look like dregs from a workhouse, and you don't want me in the way. It's plain as the nose on me face that you need rest."

"Don't be silly, Uncle Samuel. I can put the bed up for you in a trice. Only, you'll have to excuse us if we go off to bed early. We were up late last night finishing the last of the orders, and that walk today was the final straw. My feet have never been so sore."

"Then if you're sure it's all right, I'll mosey on out to Captain Yardley's and see if he's opened any interesting

barrels recently. They're always kind to me out there, but
frankly, that grand house of theirs overwhelms me—all
those servants unpacking me swag and fussing around
me, counting the holes in me socks. I like a simpler life,
even if it means getting up in the morning and having to
empty me own—''

"Yes, yes," said Dora, and when he had gone she
pulled a face, half-wryly. "I suppose it is nice to be
wanted, even if it is because we're poor and humble. I
felt like snapping at him properly when he said that."

Dorrie said, "Can we have a bath now, do you think?
It will be impossible in the morning if he's here." *And I
want to look my best,* she added silently. *I must look my
best. Tomorrow at the Regatta when Del sets eyes on me
he must be made to realize that he's made a terrible mistake.*

Every day, while she toiled over the millinery work,
Dorrie had thought of little else but their next encounter,
planning what she would wear, how she would look,
what she would say. Those last words of his still gave her
cold chills whenever they came unbidden to her mind.
Dorrie, I'm serious! Stay and listen to me! She tried to
bury the memory of the raw urgency in his voice, but the
recollection kept bobbing to the surface, piercing her
complacency.

She refused to permit her spirits to sink for long.
*Everything will be resolved the moment we see each
other again,* she promised herself. *He'll confess how
wrong he was, he'll beg my forgiveness . . .*

Stubbornly she set her back against the cold and unpleasant facts for which there could be neither excuse nor
forgiveness. He had allowed her to leave his house in a
state of extreme distress without offering her comfort,
nor had he sent a note of apology, nor had he made inquiries to see if she were all right.

It's just his way, she soothed herself later as she ran a
ribbon of boiling water from the tap beside the stove into
the portable tin bath, and carried a pail of cold water from

the outside tap to mix in with it. Del is just a bit thought-
less at times, but that comes of having no mother. He's
not used to sharing love.

As she drew the curtains she noticed a light on in
Fintona's music room. Roseanne's distinctive trills
floated across the lawn cushioned by a deeper, softer
laughter.

Roseanne has a suitor, she thought. No wonder we've
seen nothing of her lately.

Dorrie undressed in the gloom and slipped into the
soft warm water, sighing as she felt the doubts and tensions begin to leach out of her bones. Of course every
thing would be happily resolved tomorrow. Of course it
would . . .

She was standing beside the tub briskly toweling herself down when a plaintive cry and a rasping on the door
reminded her that Misty hadn't yet been in for his supper.

Hastily donning her nightgown, Dorrie unlatched the
door, whispering, "You'll wake Auntie Dora, you silly
old thing. I almost forgot you."

He forced his head through as soon as the door began
to swing open, and Dorrie saw that the evening had
closed in. A hundred yards away Fintona's porch was a
fuzzy glow of gaslight. Roseanne stood on the step
waving to someone who was walking away quickly down
the drive.

Why, that's Del! she thought with a stab of shock. As
she watched he glanced toward the gatehouse and tugged
his coat collar up around his face. Roseanne went inside;
the click of the front door was clearly audible, then nothing disturbed the evening calm except a faraway crisp
crunch of boots on gravel and the purring of Misty
around her ankles.

Regatta Day unrolled to dancing sunshine, a glossy
spread of harbor and skies so warm and blue they could
have been torn from a page of midsummer. Dorrie was
up early putting the last stitches to her "costume" before

sunrise. By the time the world was stirring and the first
traffic rumbled along the road she had lit the fire, fed the
fowls, and was mixing the breakfast porridge.

Her mood was sunny, bright enough to match the day.
Long before she fell asleep she had decided that Del must
have come to see *her* last night, seeking her out to plead
forgiveness for the cruel way he had treated her. When he
had seen the gatehouse was in darkness, he had gone to
Fintona instead. Perhaps she should not be too eager to
forgive him either, she resolved, smiling to herself as she
rehearsed their reconciliation.

At breakfast she swallowed the detested porridge in as
few gulps as she could, then began clearing away around
Uncle Samuel, who was always maddenly slow with his
food.

"Leave it to me, I'll tidy up," he said. "You go and
make yourself beautiful for your cruise. I've all day to
putter around and wander down to the wharf. Might even
watch the show from the lawn here. We always used to in
the old days, you know. Lived on an' off here when I
were a lad. Did I ever tell you about that?"

"You may have mentioned it in passing," teased Dorrie.

"My dad was married to Grandmaire. Never could
stand the woman myself," he said, sucking at a piece of
tea-sodden bread, but Dorrie was gone, having kissed the
top of his head and skipped out quickly before he could
launch into another of his meandering reminiscences.

When she emerged from the bedroom she posed in the
doorway and said tentatively, "Do I look all right?"

He looked up from buttering another slice of bread and
said, "You look a treat, that you do. But come over into
the light, eh, so I can see you better."

Twirling for his inspection, she gave a graceful dipping bow, acknowledging his compliments.

Her ensemble was a masterpiece of ingenuity. With
Dora's help she had dismantled two of Roseanne's cast-
off gowns, a caramel velvet and one in much darker

brown, and from the two had fashioned a single "costume" of skirt and jacket, under which she wore a new apricot blouse pin-spotted in dark brown, with an extravagant bow at the throat and cascades of ruffles down the front to her nipped-in waist and at the buttoned wrists of her jacket. The hat was a simple picture style in cream designed to complement the elegant chignon into which her hair was folded. She had dressed the hat with a froth of curling apricot-colored plumes whose tips darkened to brown, like fur, and had added a further accent of brown with a twist of braid.

"You look like a duchess, or a princess, or some such," tried Samuel, whose vocabulary was seldom used to compliment beautiful women.

Dora, coming in from pegging out the dishtowels, thought Dorrie looked frail and hopeful. *She's setting herself up to be hurt again,* she thought helplessly. *She's going to all this trouble hoping that he'll notice her again.*

"Very nice," she said curtly, masking her worry with a show of impatience. "But there's no time for pirouetting and preening. Rupert will be here any second to take us down to the ferry. Pop out and wait for him, will you, pet?"

"There's a madhouse over there," Samuel said as he wiped his lips with his shirtsleeve. "Something's in the wind. When I was over there earlier, Ellen was rushing about and the servants were all babbling. There's going to be an announcement today, Crystal told me, but she wouldn't say exactly what. If you ask me, Ellen's getting remarried."

"Surely not! Jon's only been dead—"

"That doesn't matter, Dora. She never once clapped eyes on him all those years they lived apart, and though I often wonder if she had a hand—" He stopped himself, then continued at a tangent, saying, "I'll hand it to them, they weren't hypocritical enough to wear black for him as if they were sorry he'd gone."

"An armband or a sash wouldn't have gone amiss," sniffed Dora. "Though I suppose you're right. It would have been a mockery."

"Nothing standing in her way, then."

"I think she'd have told me," mused Dora, glancing out towards Fintona. "Or perhaps she wouldn't, if she thought I might disapprove. Here comes Rupert now. He'll solve the mystery."

"I'll be glad when today's over," said Rupert as they approached the wharf. "All this fuss and frolic makes me dizzy. Why Mother had to have the party on a boat I'll never know. Rotten things, boats."

"But it's going to be such fun," insisted Dorrie. *"C'est épatant,* as Marguerite would say. Champagne and punch, and sailors' tots of rum to be traditional, and a cold collation if anyone feels peckish. They're having three bands on board, a juggler, a musician, and even a gypsy fortune-teller for the ladies' saloon. I think I'll have my fortune told today, I'm in such a lucky mood." She broke off and waved so wildly that Dora placed a warning hand on her arm to subdue her. "Look, there's Marguerite walking along! Doesn't she look gorgeous, Rupert!"

"Gorgeous," he repeated gloomily. "Enough to make me wish I was six feet tall with wavy auburn hair and a life so filled with interest that it fascinated everybody."

"Why, Rupert!" She realized he had described Nathaniel Rosser. Before she could say more he stopped so that she could alight and join her friend, who, with Mr. and Mrs. Dupton and Aimee in her wheelchair, were strolling towards the thickening crowd beside the ferry.

Dora remained in the buggy. As soon as Dorrie was out of earshot she asked Rupert about the rumored "announcement."

"It's supposed to be a secret," he said, "but I'll tell you anyway. Roseanne's decided to get engaged to that poultry breeder fellow. Don't think anything of the idea myself. I think she's only doing it to spite Mother, and I rather suspect she thought Dorrie was sweet on the fellow—made it a challenge to snare him for herself."

"How did she get that idea?" asked Dora faintly.

"I don't know. It's just a suspicion, really. I can see by the look on your face that you don't give tuppence for the fellow either." He helped her down, then vaulted into the driver's seat and flapped the reins. "I'd better go fetch the happy couple," he said. "See you on board. *Bon voyage*, Auntie!"

Perhaps we should make our excuses and stay behind with Samuel, thought Dora as she walked slowly to join the others. She knew that if she feigned illness Dorrie would return to Fintona with her. There she was now, chattering with the Dupton girl, each talking and neither listening. The fact that Dorrie interrupted herself every few seconds to glance around expectantly exasperated Dora. She was searching for *him* with a look of hopeless infatuation.

As Dora drew closer she noticed that young men in groups nearby were turning their heads to admire Dorrie. Voices were raised, laughter exaggerated, just to catch her attention. Young men nodded or flicked the rims of their boaters as her gaze swept over them, but Dorrie was oblivious to them all.

And she's squandered herself on that worthless Mr. Blackett, thought Dora grimly. *Well, the sooner she's disillusioned, the better.*

The jetty was becoming uncomfortably crowded as more and more guests arrived, gentlemen in smart suits and bell-toppers with pointed shoes and matching points on their embroidered waistcoats, their ladies attired in every scent and color of a flower garden, all with parasols in case the sun grew tiresomely hot and sealskin wraps in case it did not.

Rupert's buggy trundled back, this time with Ellen, Roseanne, and Del. As they stepped down Roseanne smiled into Del's pink face with an expression of gloating

ownership that turned Dora's stomach. She glanced
across at Dorrie. Nathaniel had joined the group. The
girls were laughing; Dorrie's head was thrown back and
her mouth was slightly open, showing her neat mother-
of-pearl teeth and pink, healthy tongue. She looked radiant.

Dora felt genuine pity for her but did not waver in her
determination that Dorrie meet the truth of the situation
face to face.

"Let's board, shall we?" she suggested to Mr. and
Mrs. Dupton. "I see my sister-in-law going up the gangplank now. If the hostess has arrived, I suppose it's
timely for us to board."

They were expecting Ellen to greet guests at the top of
the gangplank, but none of the Fintona Benningtons were
immediately in sight, so Nathaniel guided the party to a
sheltered spot on the middle deck as he helped maneuver
the wheelchair. Aimee was asleep; Dora thought she
looked drugged.

"Here we are, ladies," said Nathaniel, dusting a chair
with his hand. "Shady and not too close to the band-
stand. Now can I fetch you something, Miss Bennington?
Mrs. Dupton?"

"You *are* a gentleman," said Dora. "Pity about the
company you keep."

He looked startled, then realized she referred to the
Teipa-Benningtons. "A pity altogether," he said, repeating their sentiments. "If only we all could get on together, how pleasant the world would be."

"And how dull," she retorted.

"Don't mind Auntie Dora," laughed Dorrie. "I'd like
some champagne, if I may."

Del had evidently been making the other ladies a similar offer, for as Nathaniel disappeared into the saloon bar
Del emerged, two glasses of champagne balanced in each
hand. Dorrie saw him threading his way through the
crowd and before Dora could stop her she had hurried
away in his direction.

She intercepted him at a corner of the deck between the stairs and the lifeboat. "Hello, Del," she said breathlessly.

He looked up from the slopping champagne glasses into her bright, eager face. For a second joy shone in his eyes. Then his eyes went cold and he wore the same face she had looked into when he said he no longer loved her.

"Excuse me, Dorrie," he said.

"Del!" This was not the way it was supposed to happen. There should be apologies, pleas for forgiveness, love in his eyes. Tears burned her lids and his image swam vaguely in front of her.

She said, "I was hoping—"

"Dorrie, please." His voice was hoarse and low. He reminded her of someone shaking off a beggar in a public place, anxious that no one would see how uncharitable he was. "Look, I said I didn't want to hurt you, and I meant it. You'll have to take my word for that. *Please.*"

His eyes had slid away from her as he spoke and he moved quickly away, too, leaving her clinging to the railing. People brushed past but she did not notice them. Marguerite called out but she did not hear. She was there several minutes before Nathaniel came to fetch her. When he touched her arm it was stiff and cold. He saw that the narrow band of skin between her frilled wrist and the cuff of her glove was pale.

"Dorrie, what's wrong?" he said. Her gaze swung up to him; he looked into her dilated pupils and realized she had received a shock. "Dorrie, what's happened?" he said.

The warmth in his tone revived her. *How stupid I am,* she thought. "It's silly of me," she said slowly. "I've done something terrible to offend someone, and for the life of me I can't think what it was. I mean, people don't go all cold and hateful for no reason at all, do they?"

"No, but I can't believe you would offend anyone so terribly," he said, steering her back to her place. She did not appear to be listening.

Marguerite was fluttering with excitement. "You've missed something wonderful, *magnifique!*" she said, clutching Dorrie's hands. "Roseanne came by a minute ago, and do you know what? She and Del are engaged! *Que c'est romantique!* He's given her a darling *petite* bracelet watch, all silver and gold, with the inscription, *Time has no meaning when I am with you.* Who would have thought that Del would be so romantic? Oh, there he is! Looking so handsome but sheepish, too, *non?* Let's go and congratulate him."

Dorrie sat down.

"Fancy our Del being a secret lover!" chirped Marguerite. *"C'est épatant,* it's all great fun, *non?* He's going to be your cousin now, just imagine that!"

Nathaniel said, "Dorrie, drink this." To Marguerite he explained, "I think she's a trifle queasy."

Dorrie took the proffered glass and gulped a large mouthful. It tasted like metal polish when it mingled with the bitterness in her mouth, but she swallowed it resolutely and took another long gulp.

"Can I get you anything else?" he said.

She looked up into his kind dark eyes and felt ashamed. She had been taught that personal feelings should never be displayed in public and now she understood why. All she hoped now was that Mr. Rosser could not guess the cause of her distress.

He said, "Here comes your aunt. Shall I tell her that you don't feel well?"

She made a brave attempt at a smile and for some reason he felt proud of her when she said, "Of course not, but thank you just the same. This is going to be a simply delightful day, isn't it? It would be a pity if anything spoiled the fun."

That's typical of her, he thought. *Everybody else first, herself last.* This time he felt angry with her.

For almost fifty years Auckland had marked every occurrence worth celebrating with a splendid regatta and today's festive display was suitably spectacular. It was a feast for the eyes and excitement for the senses which interspersed sailboat races with whaleboat sprints and immaculate displays of clipped precision rowing to contrast with the magnificently unruly exhibitions of fully manned Maori war canoes dashing through the paddle-churned water to the rhythm of ferocious battle chants.

Dorrie watched the entire program without seeing any of it. She had been drained of the ability to move. *Del and Roseanne!* she thought over and over. *Del and Roseanne!*

Understandably, Marguerite was elated to hear about the engagement. Ever since the Benningtons had moved to Fintona she had been uneasily aware that Ellen was trying to engineer a betrothal between Nathaniel and Roseanne, so she was giddy with relief. She chattered endlessly about the news, one minute speculating that Del was probably marrying her for her money—"he's known to be shrewd and hard, is our Del"—then using the next breath to sigh over the romance of it all.

Nathaniel watched Dorrie with concern. It did not escape his notice that whenever Del was mentioned, Dora shot a glance in her niece's direction as if trying to gauge her reaction. Dorrie, meanwhile, showed no more emotion than did poor Aimee, who slouched listlessly in her chair, subdued, he guessed, with laudanum.

When Nathaniel discovered that Rupert had made two trips to the wharf to bring everybody, he insisted on escorting Dora and Dorrie back to the gatehouse in his large hired carriage.

Samuel shuffled over to meet them when they arrived. A real character this, thought Nathaniel, wishing he could capture the old man's essence with his Cinematograph camera. He noted the baggy suit and the shiny-gummed grin that was oddly babyish in the walnut-wrinkled face.

He put one foot on the swing-down step and peered

into the carriage. Nodding a greeting to the Duptons and Nathaniel, he said without preamble, " 'Fraid we've had a bit of bother here this afternoon, Dora. I was trundling into the drive and that gray cat of yours ran straight under the trap wheels."

"Misty?" cried Dorrie, jolted into awareness by this piece of news. "Was he hurt?"

"Not hurt as like. Just killed outright, he were. I couldn't avoid—"

Dorrie screamed. Her shrieks reverberated inside the carriage as she thrust forward, pushing past the others, scrabbling with the door catch and almost tumbling into Uncle Samuel's arms in her frantic dash to run inside. In the carriage Aimee was disturbed by her screams and began to wail, too; her loud, unearthly cries seemed as though they were being unrolled from some reel deep within her.

Nathaniel hurried after Dorrie. She was standing at the table, white-knuckled hands squeezing the back of a chair as she cried with long, rasping sobs. Without a word he loosened her grip on the chair rail and slipped his arms around her. As she felt his touch she slumped against him.

"Was he old?" he said, thinking it might be therapeutic for her to talk about Misty.

For a moment she did not answer, then, "He was born the first day I saw you—along the beach."

"Great heavens, you remembered that," he mused.

Her sobs were harsh and raw, like a cloth tearing. "It's not Misty," she managed to say. "It's—it's—"

Cradling her in his arms, he whispered soothingly to her. The brim of her hat was digging a furrow into his neck. It hurt but he was reluctant to pull away.

Dora came puffing in and said, "That is quite enough, young man. I would be much obliged if you would leave any comforting to me."

"So would I," added Marguerite under her breath. She had witnessed some of the scene and was prickling with jealousy. Aloud she said, "She'll be all right, Mr. Rosser. It was only a cat, after all."

"I don't think you understand," he told her.

At first Dora paid scant attention to the depth of Dorrie's distress. She was familiar enough with exhaustion to know how easily little things can take on an inflated significance when one is overtired, but as the days wore on and Dorrie's condition failed to improve she grew worried and finally sought medical advice.

"Hysteria," came the prompt diagnosis. For the next week the doctor called every day to check her progress. Dorrie could hear him through the wall, prescribing cold compresses, small doses of laudanum, and complete quiet. In the most delicate terms he explained to Dora that hysteria was an affliction exclusive to unmarried ladies, and if all else failed Dora must be prepared to make a serious effort to find a husband for her, if they were to avoid "more drastic remedies." Listening to that wisdom, Dorrie twisted her head into the pillow and shed the bitterest tears of her life.

Her hours alone were a hell in which she relived every scene she had ever played with Del. In vain she searched for some clue as to why he had abandoned her. She must have some hideous flaw that had, that fateful morning, been made suddenly apparent to him. But what could it be?

Like mocking taunts his words of love came back to her as again she heard him whisper that he could not live without her, that he would die, surely so, if he could not love her in the sweetest, most intimate way.

As these words echoed around her she found herself gradually altering perspective. Once she would have leaped to Del's defense no matter what trivial criticisms might be leveled against him, but as she lay there in the dark she realized that she herself was beginning to form silent accusations against him. The love in her heart began to curdle.

One evening toward the end of the second week Ellen came over to spend an hour with Dora. Knowing that Dorrie could hear what was said, her aunt futilely attempted to keep the conversation on neutral topics.

"He seems an extremely *sincere* young man," said Ellen after having been interrupted three times while Dora tried to coax her down a different path. "Unfortunately Rupert cares nothing for him, but that I put down to brotherly jealousy. He always has been particularly fond of Roseanne, and I wondered what would happen when the time came for her to marry."

"Tell me, what was your opinion of the Empire Ball?" Dora broke in. "I have heard such conflicting reports. Do you think the music was too 'military' in tone for dancing?"

"Not at all. Rupert and I managed perfectly the one dance we had together. I like to have one dance. Such a waste of time getting gussied up, otherwise." She shut her mouth with a snap and opened it again. "As I was trying to say, Mr. Blackett is utterly devoted to Roseanne. He's never been in love before, of course, but never had the slightest *hint* of a special young lady either. I think that's rather touching, don't—"

"Look at the time!"

"Don't you? Love at first sight and both of them innocent as babes on a spring morning—"

"Just *look* at the time! I should have given Dorrie her laudanum an hour ago and it quite slipped my mind. Please excuse me, Ellen."

"You might like to cheer the girl up by telling her that Roseanne has selected her to be one of her bridal attendants. As soon as she's *properly* well she can come on over to Fintona for her first dress fitting. Roseanne chose pink sateen with deep lace borders for her. Very tasteful, even if I do say so myself, and reasonably priced. Fourteen guineas should cover the entire outfit, the dressmaker said."

When she had gone Dora took a deep breath, walked

into the bedroom, and jerked the curtains wide. "Now, pet," she said firmly. "Don't you think it's time you stopped—"

Dorrie was sitting up in bed fiercely pummeling her pillow with a bunched fist. She stared wildly at her aunt, tears battling with rage.

"How *dare* he say he's never been in love before!" she choked. "How dare he act as if I hadn't even existed, as if I'm so unimportant that I don't rate mention as a special young lady—not even as a *hint* of one! To think that I've been lying here dreading that he's whispering to Roseanne about me—making fun of me—but this is far, far worse. I actually *hate* him, Auntie, I really do."

"Thank goodness."

"What?"

"I said, thank goodness. I came in here all set to demand that you take a hard look at this selfish young man and see what he is truly like. But it seems that I don't need to demand anything."

"No. I'm sorry about being such a fool. I can't believe that I couldn't see all this before."

"I'm thankful that it's come at all. You've recovered your senses at last."

"Not quite." In response to Dora's questioning look she said, "I hate him, and that's not really lucid either, is it? But I can't face the thought of ever seeing him again. And as for being one of the bridal attendants—"

"I don't fancy that thought either." Dora patted her hand. "We'll think of something, pet."

The problem, once examined, was larger than either woman had realized. Avoiding Del would be impossible if they stayed in Auckland. Living in the gatehouse, Dorrie would be forced to witness a virtual parade of happenings in Del's and Roseanne's lives, and Dora's attitude towards the Fintona Benningtons had cooled, too. Running errands and being at Ellen's beck and call was no longer the attractive pastime it had seemed before.

Because Dora was so restricted in her thinking and Dorrie still too wounded to function properly, their prospects seemed limited. Dora decided to sell the gatehouse, but found that it would only fetch a couple of hundred pounds if she were lucky. Neither of them was keen to sell *Riversong*.

"We should put her up for sale," said Dora. "We really don't have any choice."

The two were shivering in the draughty museum hall, staring through the plate glass cabinet that shielded *Riversong* from the world. She had been moved since their last visit and was now placed near one of the museum's barred windows so that light from the milky pane could shine through her thinnest edges, heightening her contours and adding a velvety richness to the deep emerald.

"We can't sell her," said Dorrie in a colorless voice. The young woman seemed to smile; she held that mermaid's pose, knees bent and ankles lightly together, hair and *piu-piu* flowing in fluid lines over her supple body.

Closing her eyes, Dorrie murmured, soft as a stream.

> In the stillness of eternity
> I hear the river song.
> The spirit of my ancestors
> Sings a lament for me.

She opened her eyes and sighed. "No, Auntie Dora, we couldn't ever sell her. Everybody needs to own one beautiful object, a talisman against the specter of hard times. I've decided what to do. I'm going to accept Mr. Bob Farrell's proposal." When Dora gaped at her and opened her mouth to argue, Dorrie shook her head. Something that might have been the beginning of a smile twisted the corners of her mouth.

"He's rich, and he has a large home with room enough for you—I'm sure he has. No, please, Auntie. I got us into this mess and I've decided that this is the only way out. It *is* the only way, you must realize that."

The deadness of her tone stunned Dora. "Oh, my dear," she said. "Pet, you don't need to—"

"Yes, I do." The idea had been growing since she overheard the doctor's bizarre advice that a husband would cure her hysteria. Bob Farrell would do nothing for this ache, but Dorrie knew time would cure that. In the meantime she had to be practical.

"It will be an adventure," she said. "Think of it, Auntie. If we tire of living like rich ladies in the outback we can always amuse ourselves by making hats for the Aborigine women!"

Outside it was threatening to rain, a weak, strained threat as curds and whey darkened the sky. Fumbling to open her umbrella and taking hopping steps so as not to drag her hem through the puddles, Dorrie scurried ahead of Dora to the tram stop. Fatigue and tears were attacking her again. She plonked herself down on the slatted wooden tram seat, stared at her muddy shoes that rested on the sawdust-covered floor, and began to cry quietly, turning her head so that Dora wouldn't notice.

PART FOUR

NATHANIEL

1898-1899

Fifteen

The pounding on the door intensified. Dora woke with a jump and for a few seconds was convinced that she was back on that ghastly ship with the infernally thumping engines. Her stomach heaved and she sat up; she reached automatically for the bowl in which to be sick again.

"Miss Bennington!" called the man outside her door, and Dora realized that she was not on a ship at all but in the shabby bedroom of some second-rate hotel near the Sydney docksides. Last night she had sipped champagne while she watched Dorrie waltz around the floor with her new husband.

Far too much champagne, she thought ruefully, and with an impatient, "All right, I'm coming!" she belted her camelhair robe tightly around her, flipped her pigtail over her shoulder, and padded to the moonlit dressing table to light the lamp.

"What on earth—?" she said as the door swung open and Bob Farrell stood there, his face blank as an unpainted wall.

"I'm sorry to disturb you, but there's a problem we'll need your help with." He stepped forward into the light and Dora saw that he was fully dressed in the dark suit and brocade waistcoat he had worn yesterday.

"Oh, dear, the poor lass," muttered Dora as she followed him along the corridoor. "It's all my fault. I should have asked Ellen far more questions—I should have forced myself to find out more." She glared at Bob Farrell's solid back. Unless it was all *his* fault.

Dorrie was hunched under the covers at the very far

side of the bed. When Dora came in alone she looked up and said, "I'm so sorry, Auntie. The marriage is all over."

"What in the world—?" said Dora. "That's ridiculous!"

"I'll let her explain," said Bob Farrell, coming into the room so that he could listen to her explanation, too.

There was little else she could add, apart from apologies and the assertion that it had all been a ghastly mistake, that she'd only realized it since the wedding, and that she was so terribly sorry.

"It can be annulled if we haven't spent the night together," Bob Farrell told Dora. "She can even marry again, quite legally and within any church, too. It will be as if this never happened. Only next time, out of fairness to everybody, make sure the girl knows what she's doing, will you?"

It is my fault, thought Dora. She showed him to the door.

Turning to face Dorrie, she said, "Pet, I don't know what to say. I should have had a married lady talk to you, explain a wife's duties, and the things a husband has a right to expect— Oh, Dorrie, don't cry."

Dorrie shook her head. "Don't blame yourself," she said. "I couldn't go through with it because—because I've been with someone else. Mr. Farrell was being kind and considerate to me, but he thought I was an innocent young girl, and when I realized that I was playing a monstrous deception on him, I just couldn't go through with it. I couldn't bear to have him touch me either, after—"

"Do you mean to sit there brass faced and tell me that worthless Del Blackett's had his way with you?"

Dorrie nodded. She stared at the frayed edging on the downturned bedcover.

"Oh, my *God,*" said Dora after a silence. "Well, missy, you know what this means, don't you? You can never marry anybody now. Never, not anyone unless you can pass yourself off as a widow and you can hardly do that when everybody in Auckland knows you.''

Her eyes flew up, startled. "You mean we're going back there?''

"We most certainly are. And for the rest of our lives it's just you and me, so we'd better make the best of it. Back to Auckland and the millinery business and pity help us both if word of this fiasco ever gets out.''

"Auntie, I'm so dreadfully sorry—''

"Apologies won't change things.'' She seemed very angry, yet at the same time Dorrie sensed a strong note of acceptance in her voice. She seemed resigned but in an odd way pleased. She said, "I never did warm to Mr. Farrell anyway. Miserly fellow, that.''

Unlike the threadbare accommodations they had shared on the voyage over, their cabin on the *Manu Moa* was positively luxurious. At short notice this was the only space available and Dora grumbled that she hoped the superior cabin—and fare—would buffer her against seasickness.

"You couldn't be ill in surroundings like this,'' said Dorrie, admiring the sycamore-paneled walls, the Swan electric lamps, tasseled velvet bolsters, and twin button-backed gilt chairs. "This table is real marble, and we have hot water right here in the cabin. And look, here's a bell-pull in case we need to summon the stewardess. Shall we order tea?''

"No, thank you, Dorinda.''

Dorrie stood with her face framed in the circlet of brass-bound porthole and watched the clutter of the docks, the flocks of scows and sailboats and the broken city skyline recede and then dissolve in the bright midday haze. Insulated from the bracing salt fish smells of the harbor, she wrinkled her nose against the hot, oily odor of the ship's engines. It was throbbing under her feet like the heartbeat of a gigantic mechanical beast. Despite her depressed state she felt her senses quicken.

Behind her Dora lay on the lower bunk, spectacles folded on the shelf near her shoulder, a scarlet rug pulled over her stockinged feet, her eyes closed. *She looks utterly exhausted,* thought Dorrie with a rush of fresh guilt.

These last few days had been hectic. With Dorrie in tow she had visited all the importing companies and warehouses that stocked drapery goods, buying up stocks of trimmings and materials as yet unavailable in New Zealand. All purchases were delivered to the *Manu Moa* to be added to their few items of luggage.

Dorrie made only one hesitant protest. Though she dreaded returning to New Zealand, worse was the thought that Auntie Dora was planning to embark on such a binge of hatmaking that she would ruin her health, her eyesight, and her temper.

"Auntie, let me go into service instead," she pleaded as Dora added still more items to a long list of things the aproned young warehouse man was packing at the counter. "You know what a strain it was before when you were working such long hours—"

"I'm perfectly capable of running our lives, thank you, Dorinda," she said, pulling her hand away as if Dorrie's touch were tainted.

The gesture hurt more than a slap. Dorrie withdrew.

Now she said, "I think I'll go up on deck for an hour before luncheon. Is there anything I can do for you first? Bring you a glass of water, perhaps?"

"No, thank you, Dorinda."

"I do hope that you have a comfortable voyage this time."

"Hmph," said Dora.

It was clear that no further conversation was likely. Taking her parasol from the silver-bracketed stand behind the door, Dorrie climbed the one flight of broad stairs to the promenade deck.

From the information sheet in their cabin Dorrie had learned that the *Manu Moa* was a two-thousand-ton steam and sail vessel with two thousand horsepower. It was primarily a cargo ship but could accommodate one hundred and eighty passengers in cabins on the two top decks. She had heard from the stewardess that the ship was almost full and it seemed to Dorrie that most of the passengers at the moment were out crowding the railing on both sides of the ship, admiring the view as the rocks and cliffs of the harbor mouth slid by on either side. Dorrie recognized some of the passengers. A diminutive elderly couple had a small tan and white terrier between them. Further along were three women traveling together, all wearing clothing which would cause a stir when they arrived in Auckland, predicted Dorrie. They wore velvet trousers, soft leather puttees, boots, velvet jackets, and silk shirts with loose knotted ties. All wore gray bowler hats with feathered bands, and the effect was surprisingly feminine. *I hope they come to me,* she thought. *I'll recommend tricorns with single sweeping plumes. They'd look even more stunning with hats of my design.*

After strolling around the deck as far as the penned-off section which contained six racehorses and four pedigreed breeding cows, Dorrie hitched her skirt an inch and trod up the narrow iron gangway to the tiny apron of deck around the bridge. Only two gentlemen were there, young dandies with a nervous look of expectation about them. In response to their curious stares, Dorrie turned her back, snapped her parasol open, and gazed unseeingly at the opposite view of dwindling blue hills.

I'll try to focus my entire attention on work, she resolved. *I'll try not to think about any other aspect of life other than working and striving to make Auntie Dora happy again.* She shivered. Her entire exposed mind was an inflamed sore place that any contact with other people only exacerbated. *I must try not to think,* she told herself. *Try not to think about anything at all.*

She stayed pressed into a narrow corner of railing, feeling inwardly wretched yet at the same time enjoying the physical sensations of being on board ship—the creaking of timber, the crisp tug of the breeze on her skirt, the smell of the ocean, and the vibration of the deck under her feet. *If only the voyage could last forever,* she thought.

But the sun was hot on the water and by the time the lunch gong chimed she was flushed from the glare of reflected light. Realizing that she had a slight sunburn, she hurried downstairs to splash cool water on her face and to see if Dora wanted anything to eat.

She was crossing the downstairs lobby when someone suddenly reached out and plucked her wrist free from where she was holding it close to her waist.

"Dorrie!" cried Nathaniel Rosser, his face alight with pleasure.

"Oh," she replied, dismayed. "You startled me."

"You startled me, too," he said unexpectedly. "Who are you traveling with?"

"Auntie Dora, of course."

"That's all?"

"Of course."

"Of course!" he repeated, laughing. He seemed happier than she had ever known him to be; as he laughed his white teeth flashed at her from below his soft russet moustache. She was pleased for his sake that something was making him so cheerful but dismayed when he began to walk along with her. "I knew it was a ridiculous idea from the beginning. Oh, forgive me, perhaps I'd better explain in detail. A week or more ago I came to your hotel in King's Cross looking for you, and the girl at the desk had the impudence to send me away with the news that you had just been married to that Bob Farrell, of all people."

"It was a mistake—" began Dorrie.

"Of course it was! A few days ago when I went to book passage back to New Zealand I happened to see your name on the passenger list. I guessed then that there had been a simple error."

"You didn't go back to the hotel, did you?"

"To complain? Of course not." He stopped where he was, a few yards from the cabin Dorrie and her aunt shared. "Do you think I might wait and escort you to luncheon?"

"Oh, no!" said Dorrie without thinking. He was as charming and attractive as always—more so if anything, in this exuberant mood—but the innocent references to her wedding were agony to her and she longed to be rid of his company. She realized that she had been rude, so with an effort at a smile she said, "Auntie Dora is a very poor sailor. She may not even want to come down."

"I understand perfectly. Please convey to her my best wishes, and I'll look forward to seeing you later." With a bow of regret he turned and walked back the way they had come.

Dorrie waited until he had gone before she opened the door. Dora was fast asleep and snoring gently with her mouth open. A small blue bottle of *nux vomica* was in the glass shelf beside her shoulder.

"This way, Miss Bennington," said the steward at the saloon door, after he had consulted a plan of the table layout. Following him across the dark blue carpet, between tables skirted in heavy white linen, and past a skylight garden where ferns spread their fronds beneath needle-edged palm leaves, Dorrie kept her head down hoping that wherever he was sitting, Nathaniel did not notice her enter alone. She wanted simply to eat a quiet meal without having to make conversation. She realized how very hungry she was. The saloon was filled with the delicious aromas of roast meats and spicy cooking smells, while a soft chattering muted the clashing of silver cutlery and the chink of stemmed water glasses.

The steward led her towards the far row of portholes where uniform slices of dark blue were just dropping away out of sight. The ship had made good progress and was now well into the open sea, dipping steadily from one side to the other.

"Here you are, Miss Bennington. I hope this is satis-
factory for you," said the steward, pulling out a chair for
her.

As he did so the only other occupant of the four-place
table leaped to his feet. "Dorrie! You were quick. I
hadn't even had a chance to look at the menu." Clearly,
though, he had been waiting for her, just as it was plain
that he had arranged for her and Dora to be placed at this
table, one of the best in the saloon with its view of the
ocean and its slight screening of ferns in polished brass
tubs. He glanced around. "Your aunt—?"

"She's asleep." Dorrie sat down, realizing that there
was no point in protesting. She wondered if there was any
tactful way out of this situation, for if Nathaniel was with
Dorrie and her aunt together for five minutes he would
guess that something very serious had caused a breach
between them.

"Perhaps I should have waited for you, to escort you
in," he was saying, chiding her gently.

She tried to smile at him. Nathaniel Rosser was one of
the dearest people she knew but right now she wished
that he was anywhere but on this ship with her.

The steward was at her elbow, standing silently with
pad and silver-topped pencil waiting for her order. Nathaniel noticed that she was staring blankly at the menu
card. "Are you all right?" he whispered, leaning towards her.

"Oh. I'm sorry—"

"Don't apologize. I'll order something light for you if
you're a little queasy. Nothing fried or too rich; let me
see." Swiftly he dictated his choice: clear beef
consommé, steamed fish with lemon sauce, grilled
chicken with steamed potatoes and beans.

Dorrie permitted the misunderstanding to go uncor-
rected. In a way it was true. She *had* felt queasy since
that nightmarish episode that followed her wedding. The
embarrassment of testifying in a whisper about the intimate details of her wedding night, the shame of facing a

return to Auckland, the disappointment she had caused Auntie Dora, all these things made her feel sick in spirit, emotionally diseased.

When she looked in the mirror these days she saw someone ugly and it seemed incredible now that Nathaniel could be beaming at her with such pleasure as he snapped the wine list shut and turned all his attention to her.

"No dessert for you, but a glass of hock will be the very thing to cure your ills," he told her. "You're not teetotal, are you?"

Her wedding was the only occasion on which she had tasted wine and that recollection made her wince, but she managed to say lightly, "I'm a weekday wowser. Special occasions only."

He laughed, delighted. "I like that."

"Thank you, and thank you for laughing. You must hear all the jokes that have ever been told."

"Most of them. But humor is more than jokes. It's personality, and if you don't mind me saying so, your personality is delightful. I've always thought so."

If he'd said that intently she might have been embarrassed but it was tossed off as casually as a smile. He rested his wrists on the edge of the table where the rough-weather boards made ridges under the cloth. Picking up his fish knife he began drumming it softly on his starched napkin water lily. He was like a little boy enjoying himself, unable to keep still, fidgeting with anything within reach of his fingers. Any minute he will burst into song, she thought.

The soup came and she took a sip, but finding it too hot, she rested her spoon while she waited for it to cool. Nathaniel gulped his down scalding hot, then coaxed her, saying, "There's nothing like consommé to soothe feelings of nausea. Go on, drink it up, Dorrie." He was enormously encouraged when with a little smile she obeyed him, spooning up the delicious mouthfuls of liquid. "There, doesn't that feel better?" he said.

"Indeed it does." The soup had dulled the sharp edge
of her hunger yet left her feeling ready for the fish that
was to follow.

"Good." The steward was at his side now, with wine
bottle, ice bucket, and clamp for the cork. She watched
the little performance with intrigued amusement as the
cork was drawn and examined, the wine sniffed and carefully tasted. When Nathaniel had declared it perfect and
directed that Dorrie's glass be filled, he glanced across
the table and saw the expression on her face. "What's so
funny?" he wanted to know.

"Why, the cautious way you were sniffing and tasting
as if you expected it to splash out and sting you!"

"This hock is our best white wine, ma'am," the steward informed her stiffly.

Dorrie's cheeks puffed and her lips compressed. She
looked at Nathaniel and they burst out laughing.

She felt better at once. *I haven't laughed for weeks,*
she thought. *This is the first time for ages that I've had an
honest-to-goodness laugh about nothing at all.*

His glass rim clicked against hers. "Here's to your
good health."

"Thank you."

"And to a happy voyage. Drink. It will clear your pal-
ate."

The hock was excellent as promised—clear and sharp
with a dry, fruity aftertaste. She nodded in appreciation
and as the miniature platters of fish were set before them
said, "Are all your voyages happy ones?"

"I love the sea, and never mind how rough it gets. An
ideal life for me would be to crisscross oceans constantly
providing I had enough paperwork to occupy my time on
board, of course."

"So you spend your voyages working?" The fish was
excellent too, flakes of moist flesh white as milk with a
fresh taste of the sea coming through the lemon tang and
the dusting of bittersweet chopped herbs.

"Normally I work all day except for mealtimes and

short strolls around the deck, but not this voyage.'' He smiled at her and then turned his attention to his food.

Something in his tone warned her not to ask what was special about this voyage. *He's crowding me,* she thought, then immediately, *No, of course not. Nathaniel is just naturally friendly and considerate, and he wouldn't want me to feel that I was keeping him from something important.*

She watched him in brief glances while they ate. His fidgeting was over and he ate with an economy of movement, like someone who has more pressing things to attend to. His lips were firm and dry and the muscles in his square jaw moved rhythmically. He kept his eyes fixed on his plate, surprisingly thick, curving lashes screening them from her. It's no wonder that Marguerite has always been so attracted to him, she thought, noticing that though he was almost aggressively handsome there were touching little details that made him seem oddly vulnerable—the way his hair sprang up in thick tufts, obviously resisting his efforts to smooth it down, the tiny worry lines around his eyes, a scar along the hairline at one temple, the way he looked up at her when he pushed his plate aside, as if he were eager for her approval. The last thought almost had her bursting out with laughter again. She was getting ideas well above her station if she fancied even for a second that Auckland's most eligible bachelor would be anxious for *her* approval.

''That was splendid,'' he announced with satisfaction, ''but you've scarcely touched yours.''

''I'm just a slow eater.''

''Yes, and I bolt my food. Bad habit, I know. When I was little my nanny made me chew every mouthful twenty times and I think I've been rebelling ever since.'' He twirled his wineglass by the stem, changing the subject abruptly. ''It's a shame I didn't catch up to you in Sydney. I could have taken you and your aunt around, shown you the sights.''

He was looking at her in a speculative manner.

Terrified that he might ask questions about what they did in Sydney, Dorrie rushed in quickly to say, "What new projects are you working on? Have you arranged more Cinematograph displays?"

"I didn't think you were interested."

"What makes you say that?"

"You haven't been to see one, yet."

"I'd love to, I really would, but Auntie Dora—" She bit her lip. "I hear a lot about them, though. My customers were full of chatter about your last show, the funny one about the soldier who wants to marry the farmgirl. They said that it was incredibly lifelike, with the milk tipping into the buckets as if it were real, and steam hissing up when the blacksmith plunged the hot metal into the water trough. Everybody says you are marvelously clever."

"Easy on there. I only presented that show."

"But Marguerite says that you are making your own Cinematographs now."

"In a limited way, so far. I bought a Paul cine camera and a Theatograph projector some time ago, and went into the outback, the never-never land of the Aborigines. A team of us made several Cinematographs depicting native dances, hunting customs, and so on. I showed them in Sydney but the response was disappointing. Crowds there were more interested in my imported show of the Prince of Wales' horse winning the Derby."

"Persimmon? Yes, Marguerite told me about that one. She said the atmosphere was captured perfectly. I'm sorry that your native films didn't do so well, though."

"They're causing something of a sensation in England and New York, so all is not lost." He laughed. "I do wish I'd known that you and Miss Bennington were in Sydney. I'd have insisted on escorting you both to at least one of my own shows. Even if your aunt is against photography as an art form—that's what it is, isn't it?—she'd have enjoyed the railway diorama. Observers sit in open railway carriages and watch painted scenery roll by on either side. It doesn't sound like much to describe, but lighting and sound effects provide sunrises, sunsets, rain, and thunderstorms. It's all very effective. At the moment the show is called 'A Journey into the Past' and the idea of it is to whisk the spectators past the ancient civilizations of Greece, Rome, and Egypt. It's a bit disorienting but a lot of fun.''

"Auntie Dora might have liked that.''

"Then I'm doubly sorry I missed the opportunity. I keep hoping that she will accept one of the invitations that I send her, but so far she has declined them all.''

"Yes—'' Dorrie decided she could trust him with a confidence. "It's just that she won't go anywhere that she might accidently meet—certain people. And knowing that her cousin May was always very interested in photography . . .'' She shrugged unhappily.

"She's right there, of course. Mrs. Teipa-Bennington is a gifted photographer. Exceptionally gifted. It's she who will be giving me advice about lighting and camera angles for the Cinematographs I plan to make in New Zealand this coming summer. She's told me a little about the feud—if it could be called that. It's a shame really. May Teipa-Bennington is a delightful person. You'd like her, I know you would.''

"So is Auntie Dora,'' Dorrie pointed out swiftly. "I'm an orphan, you know, and she's done everything for me. She's made sacrifices and taken an interest in my education, she's helped with everything worthwhile I've ever done. I don't know where I'd be without her.''

"Then you're fortunate,'' he said smoothly. "Many of us with living parents aren't so lucky.''

"Are your parents alive?'' she said after a silence.

"My father is, but he's bedridden. I'm afraid he and I don't see eye to eye. Father thinks that business must be sober and dull to be properly respectable.''

"So you're a black sheep?'' She paused. "I'm sorry, that wasn't a very flattering thing to say.''

"I don't particularly enjoy being flattered, and please,

Dorrie, stop apologizing for yourself. You've nothing to be sorry about.''

Yes I have, she thought. *From now on my life will be one long apology. Making things up to Auntie Dora is going to take everything I have.*

"Besides," he continued, "I've always thought that there was something ruggedly individualistic about black sheep. They don't mind standing out in the mob, do they now? Unfortunately Father doesn't see it that way. He'd like to see me as an anonymous businessman, but I reckon he should have thought of that twenty-nine years ago.''

"Pardon?"

"When he married my mother. She was an entertainer in a traveling troupe of players. They used to go around all the outback stations, goldfields, places like that. Father always hated her to talk about her life before she married him, but she was proud of it—I think she missed it a lot, too. Some of my happiest memories are of the stories she used to tell me about the 'rampage days' as she called them.''

"She sounds marvelous.''

"Father's a great fellow, too. He's a dry old stick, but a lot of his grumpiness is frustration. He doesn't approve of the way I run things—especially as the business is moving along very nicely without him—and he's too ill now to come back in control. His doctor forbids him to do more than scan the annual reports. Heart attack a year ago, it was. I tell you what, though—I reckon he'd have rallied no end if I'd taken you and Miss Bennington to the house to meet him. He'd have liked you, that's for sure. He's always asking me why I never think about marrying again.''

"Marrying *again?*'' She was so astonished that the juxtaposition of her name went unnoticed.

His eyes clouded and she could tell that the subject caused him pain. "I'm sorry,'' she said at once. "This isn't really any of my—''

"No. I've been wanting to tell you about it, but I'm not quite sure how, that's all. Some things never quite lose their sting, and this particular subject is still tender. I've never even mentioned it to the Duptons."

But he wanted to tell *her*. Dorrie was suddenly afraid to listen. The weight of a significant, private disclosure was something she was unwilling to bear. "Nathaniel, I really don't think that I'm the right person—I mean to say, if you've been married before, that's none of my business, is it?"

"I want to tell you about it." He picked up her hand where it lay on the table like a forgotten glove. She watched and listened with a kind of helplessness.

"I wasn't married—it didn't come to that, quite—but since I was a child it was assumed that she was the girl for me. She was my cousin—Mother's niece, and very like her, too. Vivacious and elegant. Rather like May Teipa-Bennington, actually." He paused so long that Dorrie began to wonder if he had an unrequited crush on that particular lady, then he gathered his thoughts together and said, "She died just a few days before we were due to be married."

Dorrie said nothing. Her hand was still in his but he seemed almost to have forgotten her existence.

"It was such a silly, little thing. One expects the great moments of one's life to be filled with drama, but so often the tragedies hinge on tiny details that one would never suspect of harboring evil. I'd gone over to her house and we were sitting at the dining table opening wedding gifts together. I'd bought a basket of cherries on the way and we were munching those, discussing the gifts and who had sent them. Well, one of our other cousins had sent us a joke gift, a brass bootscraper in the shape of a crocodile with its mouth open. It had such a wicked expression on its face that both of us began to laugh the minute we saw it. It really was extremely funny. I was laughing so hard that I didn't notice she suddenly went very still. When I looked at her I saw that she'd gone white and her eyes were terrified. She tried to speak, half got up out of her chair, and pitched over on the floor, dead.'' He shrugged. "She'd choked on a cherry-stone. It had blocked her windpipe, apparently.''

"How terrible for you.''

"Worse for her, but it took me ages to stop thinking about it. It was shortly after that I began traveling. They say that life goes on, but it goes very slowly and in never quite the same rhythm. Until that day I thought the whole world was beautiful and nothing bad would ever happen to me. Perhaps I grew up when the sun went out and I realized that rain could fall on me, too.''

I had a day like that, thought Dorrie. *On the day of the Regatta my life changed in exactly the same way.*

Her heart went out to him.

By the time Dorrie returned to the cabin the ocean swells had deepened into great curving troughs. The *Manu Moa* ploughed them like a rocky field, determinedly nosing into the depressions and forging up over the crests with shudderings and grindings whenever the huge propellors lifted free of the water.

"Your aunt's in a bad way, I'm afraid," said the starched stewardess emerging from the doorway. "She's been ill twice already, and unfortunately the weather looks unlikely to improve. I'm afraid we're in for a rough passage.''

Dora struggled up onto her elbows when Dorrie came in.

"What's this I hear?" she said in a dry voice. "I've just been informed that you've been sitting at a table alone with a man and you've been holding hands with him.''

"Who told you that?" though she knew it must have been the stewardess.

"Never mind who told me. The point is, is it true? Dorinda, answer me.''

Dorrie sat down on one of the little gilt chairs. It tilted

one way, then the other. "There was nothing . . . romantic about it, Auntie. Honestly." She could see that
she had no recourse but to admit everything. "It was Mr.
Rosser. You know that we're friends anyway. I saw no
harm in having luncheon with him. There really wasn't
any way I could politely—"

"No harm in it! Dorinda, have you gone mad?" She
groaned and groped for the bowl, retching, then fell back
and wiped her mouth with a handkerchief. When she had
recovered she said, "I can see that you're hell-bent on
rushing from one disaster to another."

"Auntie, please. There was no harm in it. He was telling me about something tragic that had once happened to
him and when he picked up my hand I don't think he even
realized what he was doing."

Dora dabbed at her lips again. "Don't argue, Dorinda," she said wearily. "Holding hands in a public
place is harmful no matter what the motive, and frankly,
I don't trust that Mr. Rosser. He'd be just as likely to
make use of you and cast you aside as that other fellow
did, but anyway you have to realize once and for all that
you can't have anything more to do with young men.
You *do* see that, don't you?" She paused, then added,
"It would be drastic if you ever encouraged a young
man—even without meaning to—to the point where he
became seriously interested in you. You couldn't be honest with him, and that wouldn't be fair. If you *did* encourage him, it would only be like this fiasco all over again."

"I suppose it would."

"Of course it would! Never mind, we'll make ourselves a good life, you and me together. It won't be what
we'd hoped for, but life seldom is, anyway."

"I suppose you're right."

"Good. Now, young lady, the matter is settled. No
more Mr. Rosser, and you shall take your meals in here,
with me."

"Oh, but Auntie—"

"No arguments." She gasped as the ship dropped away beneath them.

Next morning Dorrie woke to a dash of foam that spattered noisily against the porthole. Despite the high green waves, Dora was solidly asleep, breathing with long, shallow tremors. The cabin stank of vomit. The acrid smell stung the back of Dorrie's throat. She needed fresh air.

After dressing quietly, she rinsed and replaced her aunt's bowl. Dora did not stir. Her eyelids were the only patches of color in her face, small and pale as fading bruises. The lashes and the whiskers on her moles looked like ragged scraps of white cotton thread left by an untidy embroiderer.

At the mirror Dorrie put on a powder blue cape and bonnet, more of Roseanne's cast-offs she had deftly refurbished. She tried not to look at her face as she tied the chin ribbons.

The deck was leaning this way and that as if it could not make up its mind which way looked best. Gobbets of wind-borne spray dashed like popcorn into the open mouth of the gangway as Dorrie forced her way out into the wild weather. Gusts of wind scoured the deck and punched into the hoop of her bonnet, snatching her breath away. She struggled to keep her balance as she made her precarious way along to the "hurricane deck" where in comparative shelter deck chairs had been set out under a billowing awning.

Most of the chairs were already occupied by stoically silent sufferers with faces the color of soured milk. She saw the three feminist ladies in yesterday's clothes, their spread, mannish overcoats indicating that they had spent the night here.

Dorrie sank into a chair near a corner, where a loose rope was rattling in the wind. At that moment one of the feminist ladies struggled to her feet and tottered to the rail. Nobody watched as she was sick over the side.

"You don't look in the least bit ill," said one of her friends, accusing Dorrie. "Found your sea-legs already, have you? Then tell me where you looked. I could certainly do with mine!"

"I'm just out for a walk," said Dorrie, getting up before they could unburden all the details of their night's ordeal to her.

As she rounded onto the aft deck she almost collided with the elderly couple, out with their terrier. The two walked one behind the other, inching along with both hands on the rail, while the dog cowered at the end of his lead, eyes slit against the wind.

"Isn't this *exciting!*" the woman shouted at Dorrie. Her ringlets jerked in the wind. "We had a grand night listening to the storm but Tessie was so sick, poor lamb."

When Dorrie reached the iron gangway she climbed again to the tiny apron of platform by the bridge. This time she had it to herself, a shuddering perch above the spray's drift with the majestic seascape view of sliding slabs of greenstone, beautiful as *Riversong* herself.

Dorrie closed her eyes and turned her face to the wind. Pinpricks of moisture stung against her skin and the wind intoned in her cupped bonnet like a seashell song. It's all so clean, she thought. All so pure and cold.

Refreshed, she was allowing her gaze to rise and fall with the sweep of the waves when a lone figure emerged from the gangway below her and moved across to the railing. Nathaniel stood still for only a moment, breathing deeply of the bracing air, before he strode down the deck, hands thrust into his greatcoat pockets. He exuded vitality and purpose; watching him, Dorrie felt herself to be aimless and adrift.

He turned and suddenly she dreaded that he might see her. Remaining immobile, she watched him in the periphery of her vision as he walked back the way he had come. The wind was tossing his hair like the leaves of a

coppery plant and he looked snug and contented inside
that thick coat.

When he was halfway back he saw her. "Dorrie!" he
called at once with hearty joy. "What happened to you
last night? I waited at dinner—"

Turning abruptly, Dorrie fled, her elastic-sided boots
thumping faster than her heart as she dashed down the
iron stairs and pelted along the deck to the other gangway.

By the time Nathaniel had hurried around to that side
of the ship's deck she had vanished.

The "geyser" water heater hissed like a child learning
how to whistle and piped out a plume of steam. Dorrie
picked up the silver teapot with the *M.V. Manu Moa* crest
and held it under the spout. Boiling water frothed over
the tea leaves.

Nathaniel leaned against the doorjamb, watching.
When she turned around and saw him there, she gasped
in fright.

"You startled me!"

"Then we're quits because you've disappointed me.
Almost three days now and I've not had a chance to speak
to you." He nodded at the tray where a plate was geo-
metrically decorated with thick water biscuits and slices
of cheddar. "That's not your dinner, is it?"

There was no escaping from him this time. He blocked
the only way out of the tiny stewardesses' pantry, and
though she picked up the tray he made no move to let her
pass.

"I've had to stay in the cabin with Auntie Dora, looking after her, you see. She's having a wretched time of
it."

He looked steadily at her, then said, "I can't pretend
that I'm having a particularly marvelous time either."

"That's a pity."

"Is it? Look, you didn't answer my question. Is that
your dinner—cheese and crackers?"

"Well, I'm not very hungry. And the smell of hot food makes Auntie Dora feel nauseous, so—"

"Leave that, then. Come into the saloon with me and I'll order something more substantial for you. It won't take them but a minute. What would you say to a nice omelette or some grilled chops, eh?"

"Bon appetit?" His laughter gave her the chance to form her refusal. "I can't leave Auntie Dora. I'd love to, but it's impossible."

"The stewardess can stay with her."

"But they're so busy, and besides, Auntie Dora—"

"There's more to it than that, isn't there?"

"Well—yes. She was upset when she found we'd had luncheon together that first day."

"Surely not! Dorrie, I *am* your friend. Look at me, go on, and tell me that we're friends."

She did as he asked and met a disturbingly intense look in his eyes. Hurriedly she added, "We're all friends together, aren't we? You and Marguerite and Rupert and I."

"I see." He studied the exquisite curve of her profile, realizing how definitely she had removed herself from him. Without comment he stood back to let her pass.

On the fifth afternoon the *Manu Moa* rounded Cape Reinga at the tip of New Zealand and almost immediately the seas slumped and the wind lapsed into apathy. The improvement in the weather caused a quite dramatic increase in the number of passengers on the decks.

Even Dora emerged, weak and giddy, for her first look at land since the Sydney Heads fell behind them so long ago. Nathaniel strolled over to offer his best wishes for her improving good health, and she was too listless to drive him away.

"That's Spirits Bay," he told them, noting the solicitous care with which Dorrie was tucking a rug around her aunt's knees. "That little bay there, with the creamy cliffs."

"With the dot of an island just offshore?" said Dorrie. "Oh, it is pretty. Can you see it, Auntie Dora?"

"Yes, thank you."

"The Maoris call it Spirits Bay because they believe that is the place their spirits journey to after they die. From those cliffs they take their final leap into the underworld."

"That's a delightful story, isn't it, Auntie?"

Dora said, "Just look at that dog!"

Beside them the elderly couple was holding Tessie up so that she could see over the rail, cooing at her and telling her all the things she would soon be able to do when they were back in their "nice wee housie." Tessie's tongue lolled; she was panting gently with the corners of her mouth pulled back in a grimace.

"Look, she's smiling," cooed the lady. "Oh, dear, we're losing our view. Would you believe such a thick fog?"

"Don't worry about this," said Nathaniel's voice. The mist had enveloped the ship so completely that he was now gray as an old statue. "It's nothing to be alarmed about. We often run into fog here. It has to do with the warm ocean currents on this side meeting the cold water beyond the cape. It usually disperses fairly quickly."

"I think it's beautiful," said Dorrie. "Everything looks mysterious—like half-formed ideas, or half-dissolved ones."

"It's cold and damp," declared Dora. "You may help me downstairs now, Dorinda."

An hour later Dorrie pressed her face to the porthole. "The fog is still as thick as ever," she reported. "I can't see the waves at all. I do hope that the captain knows where he's going. The ship doesn't seem to have slowed down in the least."

"Of course it has," said Dora. "Do come away from that window. There's precious little light in here as it is."

Up on deck Nathaniel had been having similar doubts

about their speed. He wondered why there were no fog-
horns blasting, why there was no slackening of pace.
When he was at dinner that evening he asked the second
officer about it.

He glanced up from his roast beef and Yorkshire pudding. "I'll be making an announcement about it directly,
Mr. Rosser, sir. But the captain isn't using the fog 'orns
because he doesn't fancy disturbing the passengers, and
'e's keeping a fast clip because 'e wants to make up for
lost time."

"I see," said Nathaniel. After dinner he stayed in the
saloon to sip watered whiskey until the lights went out at
eleven-thirty, then he found his way up on deck where he
leaned against the railings and stared out into the impene-
trable gloom.

Sixteen

Nathaniel was dozing on one of the deckchairs when the crash came. The force of the impact tossed him from his canvas sling and dashed him hard against the deck rail. He woke instantly to find himself lying sprawled on his back, stunned, his head shot through with a high, loud noise. All around was such dense dark grayness that for a blank second he had no idea where he was or what had happened.

One outflung hand grasped a metal upright and in the same moment he realized he was flat on the deck and that the ship was not moving. My God, we've run aground! he thought.

From below him human shouts and screams echoed through the ship, but closer to him shrieked a fearful, unearthly sound that pierced him through with terror. All the stories he had ever heard about monsters of the deep flashed through his numbed brain before he realized that the shrieks were coming from beyond the canvas awning and must be the horses. Of course, the horses. The poor beasts must be terrified.

Not only were they in fear. By now Nathaniel's eyes were accustomed to the darkness, and though the fog was still low around them, he could see faint white crests of breaking waves and the dark mass of rocks being smothered then rearing out, streaming water, beyond the bows. All around him people were pouring onto the decks, mostly pale shapes in night attire. "What has happened?" they cried. "Are we wrecked?" Sobs and moans tore from throats as folks clung to each other and to the railing while above them wailed the continuous and chilling screams of the terror-maddened horses.

"Dorrie!" shouted Nathaniel, and, gathering all his strength, cried again, "Dorrie! Are you here?" Receiving no reply he plunged into the crowd of people emerging from the gangway and repeatedly shouted her name. He made his way against the jostling throng down and along toward her cabin, groping for doorways in the dense blackness, counting, calculating, keeping his bearings. Just as he reached her door the deck was jolted from under his feet and he stumbled against a now crazily tilting wall.

The door swung open at his touch. "Dorrie!" he called into the blackness. "Are you in there?"

"Yes," came her voice, firm but plainly frightened. "I'm all right but Auntie Dora is hurt. We were both flung out of bed—oh!" as he reached her and put a hand on the side of her face. She took it and placed it against a large metal object. "Can you move this? It's our cabin trunk. It slid against Auntie Dora and I think it somehow trapped her foot. She was crying in pain a moment ago but I think she may have passed out from the shock. Oh, Nathaniel, I'm so glad you came to rescue us. What has happened?"

"We're wrecked, I'm afraid, and if that grinding noise was what I fear, then we'd best get up on deck as fast as we can." He found the outer edges of the trunk, braced his feet against the ship's bulkhead, and dragged the heavy weight away from Dora.

"That's right—that way. She seems to be free now, but she's very limp." Dorrie's voice was wavering now and he guessed she was hovering on the point of breaking down herself. "What—what in the world is that fearful screaming?"

"It's only the horses." In the inky blackness he groped for Dora's arms and managed to heave her toward the door. As he did so the ship tilted a little more and the

free-swinging door whacked him on the side of the head.
He cursed.

"Are the horses hurt? They sound dreadful."

"I don't think so. They gave me a turn, I don't mind
admitting. Can you follow me? It's steep, but if you
reach out here you'll be able to grasp the edge of the
bunks. That's right, good girl. Up this way."

"Auntie Dora?"

"I have her safe. And she's breathing. Come along
now, up and out into the passage here."

"I—I can't. Nathaniel, Auntie Dora and me, we've
only got our nightgowns on. We can't—"

"You have to. Look, there must be seventy or eighty
people up there with only their nightshirts on. Here, hold
your aunt and I'll try and grab some blankets for you."

"Would you please?"

It was an awkward business with the ship now listing
past a forty-five-degree angle, but Nathaniel managed finally to reach right around past the door and pluck a
swathe of bedding from the lower bunk. He thrust it into
Dorrie's arms, telling her to bundle it up and then follow
close behind him. Slowly, with him half-dragging the
very heavy Dora and Dorrie following behind gabbling
anxiously every step of the way, they stumbled out onto
the deck, now lit by a rinse of moonlight.

Pandemonium greeted them. On all sides people were
shouting conflicting advice to each other: "Climb into
the rigging!" "Jump clear of the ship!" "Find a lifebelt
and cling to that!" Nathaniel reached a hand out to Dorrie and felt her shoulder quiver under his touch. He
leaned toward her and said urgently, "Stay calm whatever happens. Will you promise me that?"

"I—I'll try."

"Come on. I'll get you into a lifeboat."

They could now see the elongated shadow of one of
the boats being winched over the side nearest to them. In
it were several men, their profiles cut out of darkness.

Nathaniel shouted up to them, "I've two women here! Give us a hand, mate!"

People were crushing around them, thrust downward by the gravity of the steeply leaning deck. As the lifeboat drew level with them the fog began to clear and the faces of the men in the boat became recognizable as they reached over to heft Dora in beside them. The ruffled mobcap was knocked from her head, loosening the tangle of gray hair.

"Be careful with her," ordered Nathaniel to their dining steward, and he flung the pile of bedding to him. "Wrap her in that. She'll get a bad fright when she comes to." He turned to Dorrie. "Come on, you're next."

Dorrie was fumbling with a lifejacket that had been thrust at her by one of the stewardesses. Dorrie shouted above the wailing of the horses and the clamor all around them. "I'm not ready. Help this lady first."

"Me!" cried the elderly lady with the terrier. Her husband pressed close, too, holding Tessie. The woman wore a white nightdress with some kind of dark jacket over the top and her face peered from under a snug white bonnet of the type Dorrie had worn as a child.

"Over you go, ma'am," said Nathaniel. As he reached for her she quickly kissed her husband and took the dog he was holding in his arms, hugging it to her chest. In both hands she was already clutching knobbly calico bags. Nathaniel swung her over to the boat but as the men were receiving her the old lady's grip on her pet slipped and the dog thudded to the deck with a yelp of fright.

"Tessie!" screamed the woman. "Where's Tessie!"

Dorrie felt the animal scrabbling by her bare feet. With difficulty, for the lifejacket was hampering her movements, she reached and scooped the dog up, passing her to Nathaniel, who tossed her roughly into the boat. His voice was sharp with urgency. "Now you, Dorrie. Quickly! It's almost out of reach. I'll have to—"

As she moved into the circle of his arms the winches

groaned and the boat suddenly dropped at one end. There was a confused shouting of orders and the shriek of wire rope as the other end plunged, too, and the boat splashed, then bobbed on the ocean swell. As it pulled clear of the ship Dorrie could see Dora's slumped body, her night-gown up around her knees. *It's just as well that she can't see herself now,* thought Dorrie. All the painstaking care with which she dressed to go to dinner last night and now, a few hours later, this. Bare legged, hair straggling and legs exposed above the knee.

"Should we jump in and swim for the boat?" asked Dorrie, dismayed that it was pulling away so fast.

"We'll find another. They can't all be launched yet," he said, though he could see four already, rowing around in circles picking up swimmers. All around them people were jumping into the water, though more elected to stay with the ship. The rigging above their heads was so full of people clinging to ropes and spars that the whole thing had an appearance of a giant spider's web netted full of flies.

"Along here!" He grabbed her arm with one hand and reached for the winch supports with the other. Inwardly he was cursing that damned dog, sure that if time had not been wasted Dorrie would be away safely by now.

Right then, as he seized the winch support to drag them both along, the ship seemed to lift in a kind of sigh as the waves bolstered her up from below. With a grinding sound so loud that it obliterated everything else, she scraped right over on her side.

The confusion was nightmarish. Down the deck flung everything that until now had given some semblance of being securely fastened. Hatch-covers, cases, luggage, the pens that had contained the horses, and the horses themselves all hurtled thumping and shrieking and tumbling into the dashing surf.

Instinctively Nathaniel had clung fast to the winch support and with one arm around Dorrie had managed to hold her there, too. In horror they watched the devasta-

tion taking place around them as they balanced, feet on
the railing and hands gripping the iron support. Below
them the churning sea sucked at the underside of the ship
and the tops of the waves slapped over their feet.

Dorrie had managed, miraculously, to stay calm, but
when something squawked and flapped wetly in her face
she choked on a cry of fear.

"It's only a hen," Nathaniel shouted in her ear.
"Keep your head, Dorrie. Don't panic. You're doing
splendidly so far. Try to keep calm—just a little longer."

It was difficult not to succumb to panic. People were
struggling in the water, waving their arms and crying pit-
eously for help while among them horse hooves were
flailing frantically.

"Grab the railing!" Nathaniel was shouting at the people nearest to them. "Reach up for it! Try not to get
dragged under the ship!"

A girl bobbed close, a hand reaching up, clawed in
desperation. Her face was covered with a streaming curtain of hair, slick ribbons like seaweed. Nathaniel
stooped, offering her one hand to help her up. She
snatched at it with the sudden grip of a rat-trap and kicked
and thrashed her legs until she was kneeling, gasping, on
the railing.

"Try to climb up into the rigging as soon as you re-
cover your strength," he told her.

Seeing her climb to safety, others tried to follow the
example. Many managed to reach and clamber up, too,
but a few wretches were swept right under the side and
were washed out again, faces down, hair swirling like
seaweed.

One of the deckhands swam powerfully toward them
through the jumble of flotsam. He was a burly fellow securely strapped into a lifejacket. "Give us a hand, will
you, mate?" he shouted to Nathaniel, treading water as
the waves lifted and dropped him just within reach.

Nathaniel grabbed the man's hand, but instead of
thrusting himself up onto the rail by kicking his legs in

the water, the man braced his feet on the handrail and let
Nathaniel take his full weight.

''Hey! Not that way you fool!'' roared Nathaniel, trying to free his hand.

It was too late. His grip on the winch support slid away
and he was dragged head first into the pitching mess of
debris.

Dorrie screamed. The deckhand was floundering
about, striking at the water with open palms, but for a
few seconds Nathaniel disappeared completely. Then he
floated to the surface, facedown and a short distance
away from the ship.

Without pausing to consider what she would do next,
Dorrie plunged into the foaming waves. The water was
so cold that it momentarily stunned her, but recovering,
she launched out briskly and in a half a dozen strokes
reached Nathaniel's side. Grasping his shoulders, she
turned him onto his back and held his face clear of the
water while she looked around to assess the situation.

Her hopes froze as she realized that it would be impossible to climb back to where they had been before, and
with the danger of being dashed onto the rocks or sucked
under the side of the ship it was foolhardy to stay here.
Fighting to keep control of herself she swam farther and
farther away from the ship, taking a few strokes at a time
and resting when the massive ocean swells lifted her up
to where she had a partial view of the water around her.
After some time she realized that the lifeboats had all
pulled away from the ship and appeared to be heading
for the shore somewhere beyond it. On this side of the
wreck she could see nothing but waves, white and roaring where they thundered over dark rugged shapes of
rocks.

For a minute or so she almost broke down completely.
Nathaniel was a dead weight in her arms and she did not
know how badly hurt he was. Every few seconds, it
seemed, she was either bumped on the head by some
floating debris or slapped in the face by the ragged edges

of a wave. Already she had swallowed gulp after gulp of water. She was sick, frightened, and hovering dangerously on the edge of total panic. The shore—if there was a safe shore around there—seemed as far beyond her powers of strength as it would be to fly there. The struggle not to cry was exhausting her as much as the fight to keep Nathaniel afloat.

It was then, when despair threatened to swamp her, that she saw the hatch cover. It was three or four hundred yards away, a tiny square in the black and silver ocean, but she could see that it was riding like a raft in the water. Striking out for it, she propelled herself along sideways, one arm and both feet swimming, the other arm supporting Nathaniel under the chin. Though it was a long way away, she now had a definite and achievable goal to aim for and that encouraging fact gave her all the extra strength she needed. It took her almost an hour to reach the raft, for to do so she had to swim against the flow of the tide.

She arrived there to find that others had had the same idea. Three men were already crouching on the wooden platform and more clung around the edges of it. Grasping a piece of rope that dangled in the water at one side, Dorrie called up to the men, "Please, could you help this gentleman? I don't know if he's—" and at that point the terror and fatigue of the past hour at last claimed her and she crumpled into sobbing.

"Here, I'll help yer, miss," said one of the men, reaching out to pluck Dorrie up by the wrists.

"No!" she cried. "Him, help him."

"Leave him be, miss. He's done for."

"No!" she was wallowing in panic now. "I—I swam with h-him all the w-way from the ship. P-p-please help me."

"What? Yer dragged him all that way? All right then. We'll see what we can do." At that point one of the others roused himself and together they hefted the sagging body of Nathaniel up onto the raft.

As soon as she saw him safely taken care of, Dorrie's mind stopped spinning uncontrollably. Somehow she dredged up sufficient strength to pull herself up beside him. The two men were nodding their heads over him while the third still huddled in an apathetic heap. Dorrie shooed them aside.

"Mrs. Weak taught us what to do," she said. "Here now, help me hang his head over the side so any water runs out of his mouth. Good. Now we have to raise his legs just for a moment, that's right. Then put him on his back—*so*—and restore the respiration like this." Kneeling above him, she alternately raised his elbows and pressed down on the lower part of his chest.

The men watched in silence until one said, "That's all very well and fine, miss, but he's not drowneded, yer know. Knew it the minute I heaved him aboard that he's breathing jest fine. He's had a bad knock on the head, that's all."

"That's all?" Dorrie began to shiver violently. She was shaking so much that the strong outlines of Nathaniel's face and his spiky cap of sodden hair blurred in her sight. "He's all right?" she cried. "He's all right?"

The man watched with sympathy. She looked as though she was made of moonlight, he thought, with that white nightgown slicked against her body and that ragged silver cape of hair. Poor lass was completely done in, and no wonder.

"Yer saved his life, yer know," he told her. "He'd a' been done for fer sure if yer hadn't kept his head up all this way. Yer husband, is he?"

Dorrie shook her head. *He'll be someone else's husband,* she thought irrelevantly. As shudders rippled through her she began to sob, her arms clenched about her body, her head lowered, hoarding her weeping entirely to herself.

All night the little raft drifted and eddied in the curve of the bay. Toward dawn when the moon was at its brightest, they could see to their east the wreck pitched on her side and the long ribbed reef of rocks on which she had come to grief. Far to the west was a broad scythe of pale sand on which they could make out the dark ovals of life-boats and the shapes of people and horses moving about. *The horses must have instinctively followed the boats,* thought Dorrie. In the night they had drifted close to only one drowned animal, a cow with its head bobbing above the bloated body like a dinghy riding the waves behind a tug. They had also seen several bodies of drowned peo-ple, securing those they could reach to the ropes around the hatch cover. In addition, half a dozen more people had been rescued alive from the sea.

Nathaniel remained unconscious for what seemed like hours. His breathing was steady and from time to time a gurgling moan bubbled from his throat. Dorrie stayed hunched beside him, her senses utterly dazed. Even being on the raft was a nightmare; there was barely room to squat, a freezing wind beat at them, and the raft tipped precariously whenever another person was rescued. The mood of those aboard varied from hysterical to catatonic.

Only the man who had helped Dorrie was unstintingly cheerful. Because she was the only woman there he took special trouble to encourage her. "He'll come round just fine, yer'll see," he kept saying.

At daylight, when a party of sailors was rowing out to rescue them, Nathaniel stirred, opened his eyes and whispered, "Dorrie? Is she all right?"

"I'm here," she said at once, grasping his hand and holding it on his chest, cupped between both her hands. "Can you see me?"

"Beautiful," he murmured. Below his straggling moustache his lips twitched into a smile. "We're not dead then?"

"No." She was too choked up to say more.

"Thought not. It's too uncomfortable for heaven and far too cold to be hell."

He's all right! she thought, her heart bursting. *He's all right!* "How's your head?" She placed her fingers against the bump, hard as ivory and warm under the wet hair.

"Hurts. What about you?"

The cheerful man said, "You've woken up in a good mood, I must say."

"I like to start every day with a smile. Sure beats a—" Closing his eyes, he slumped back again. In the hard light he looked as pale gray as cigar ash.

Dorrie stopped worrying. Hugging her knees fiercely, she squinted at the approaching lifeboat as it danced clumsily, dipping and bowing over the breaker line. Thin slices of water slid from the oars and shattered like glass between each stroke.

"Are we glad to see you!" yelled the cheerful man, standing up to wave a greeting. "Mind how yer go there. Give us one good bump to broadside and the whole shooting-box will disintegrate, I wouldn't be surprised."

The dining steward was standing in the prow like a figurehead, hands bracing backwards. Unshaven, he had lost all his professional gloss. "We'll be towing you in, but we'll get some of you aboard, at least. Miss Bennington! Your aunt has been out of her mind with worry. She's in a lot of pain, but safe. Have you seen anything of Mr. Rosser?"

"He's here."

"Good." The boat was looming up now. The water hissed as it parted at the bow line. The steward looped a rope in his hands, fat white strands. "We'll have you over in a jiffy," he said.

In the flat daylight Dorrie was aware for the first time how inadequately clothed she was. The thin nightdress was practically translucent, and, plastered as it was against her body, she might almost have been naked.

"I'll stay here," she said when the men in the boat called to her. Hunched in this position, she was at least modestly arranged. "Mr. Rosser shouldn't be jolted around, so I'll stay with him."

"She's right, sir!" called the cheerful man as he helped others make the see-saw leap into the pit of the boat's ribbed stomach. "Less he's moved the better, I'd say."

The steward frowned. As the raft was being secured for towing he stripped off his jacket and tossed it over to Dorrie almost as an afterthought. "Here, Miss Bennington. You might find this useful."

"I might indeed. Thank you." She smiled at him, thinking, *People are wonderful.*

The bay was a perfect semicircle bitten out of the land, edged by a border of sand ridged neatly as a cockle shell by successive outgoing tides. The sea breathed softly in fluttering sighs as it exhaled up the beach. Beyond the low dunes Dorrie could see smoke and a couple of thatched roofs, then a thicket of gray-trunked cabbage trees. Farther back the steep bush-covered hills looked moist in the clear early light.

At first the beach seemed deserted, for the other lifeboats were out at the wreck on rescue missions, but as the craft slapped and pitched its way over the breaker line and ran with a long *aaaah!* up into the shallows, Dorrie heard a shout and looked up to see three or four people on the dunes. As if attracted by a magnet, more and more came to cluster around that dark little center until there were fifty or sixty standing there, hands shading their eyes. Dorrie thought of the sodden, drowned bodies tied behind the raft and her heart contracted with pity for their relatives and loved ones.

They filed down the beach and watched in silence until the first of the rescued stepped ashore, then they rushed forward, clamoring. "Have you seen—?''; "Is there any news of—?''; "John! John!''; "My little sister? Has anybody seen her?''; "My wife, for God's sake, is she among you?''

One big man shouted, above the din, "There's only two people I'm anxious to see alive. One's me brother and the other's the captain, and by heaven the captain won't be alive for long, I'll swear to that!''

This threat brought a round of scraped-up cheers, followed by cries and mutters that Dorrie had heard on the raft: that the captain had been drunk at his post, that he had been smoking opium in his cabin all afternoon, and that if he survived the wreck there'd be a party to string him up to his own rigging.

Dorrie stepped ashore, covered by the jacket which reached almost to her knees. She was immediately claimed by the elderly lady who had Tessie lumped bemused in her arms. She was still wearing her nightgown, jacket, and funny little bonnet, and there were tears in her eyes as she plucked at Dorrie's sleeve and wavered, "Have you seen my husband, dear?"

"No, I'm afraid I haven't."

She gulped. "I see some—some bodies with your raft—"

"No." Dorrie was able to reassure her with confidence. "He's not one of those. They're all women and children, poor things."

Immediately the woman perked up. "I'll take you to your aunt. She's in fearful agonies, but she's being terribly brave." She lowered her voice. "I gave her my valuables to look after for me. I thought a little responsibility might take her mind off things—you know what I mean. After all, I have my Tessie to take my mind off the worst of it."

Dorrie did not think she was mad and could even regard her with sympathy, remembering how poor old Misty used to comfort her when she was feeling sad. She let the woman put an arm about her to help her along; her muscles were painfully cramped from being huddled on the raft all night.

At the dunes she turned and looked back. Nathaniel was sitting up, a shadow against an explosion of sunlight on the water. Two men were assisting him. She waved to him and when he waved back she continued on her way.

"What a terrible, terrible night," the elderly woman said. "The Moo-aris have been so very kind to us but I haven't had a wink of sleep for worrying about my poor Arnold. And Tessie is a nervous wreck, too. They *eat* dogs, you know."

Tessie did look nervous, now pattering along on her little white paws and looking back continuously with white-ringed eyes, while her mistress trotted along on her bare blue feet, nightdress snagging in stuttering jerks on the sand-grass. Her round eyes stared unblinkingly at Dorrie the whole time and her prattle kept coming.

On a sheltered flat behind the dunes were three Maori shacks, made entirely from woven flax in the traditional fashion over pits in the ground. The doors were so low that one had to enter on hands and knees; that way there was less chance of a surprise attack.

In the center of the flat area blazed a bright fire. Two Maori women with scarves over their heads and pipes in their mouths squatted on their haunches tending a quartet of black, three-legged pots. A cluster of naked brown children played nearby and farther away a large number of horses grazed. Two were tethered by long lines to logs of driftwood and the rest, she assumed, were the racehorses from the ship. They appeared not to have suffered from their ordeal. All this she noticed while the elderly lady chattered away to her.

The Maori women looked up. "Ah," they said.

"*Kia ora,*" said Dorrie carefully.

They gaped at her in astonishment, then removed their clay pipes and giggled, hands covering the gap-toothed smiles. One shoveled some food onto a plate. "Here, eh? *Ka pai te kai.* Good food, eh?"

"*Ka pai,*" agreed Dorrie, accepting it. The plate was crazed with dark cracks and bore a steaming sweet potato and a hunk of plain boiled fish stabbed through with floury-looking bones. Still, no chef's creation presented on the best Wedgwood had ever looked so delicious. Blowing on her fingers, Dorrie broke off pieces of food and ate rapidly as they walked together to the far shack. The food warmed her through, and by the time she put down the plate and stooped to enter the door she was feeling almost human.

The elderly woman rushed ahead of her into the light-speckled darkness, exclaiming, "Miss Bennington! We found your niece! She's safe and well. Some kind men rescued her and brought her ashore on a raft!"

There was a strong smell of dried fish in the hut. As Dorrie moved forward she could see a low bed of dried ferns heaped at the far end of the earth pit; on it lay her aunt. It seemed to Dorrie that a hundred years had passed since they last saw each other.

"Oh, Auntie, I'm so glad you're all right," she cried. "There have been so many people lost, so many drowned. What a terrible night this has been."

"I'm not all right. Far from it." Dora heaved herself into a sitting position. Even in this low light Dorrie could see that her aunt was in a shocking state, hair straggling, face puffy, eyes squinty without her spectacles. As she moved to embrace her she caught the odor of sweat and vomit, unpleasantly mingled.

"My heavens, Dorinda, you do look a mess," she declared, looking down her nose. "If only you could see yourself right now. Why are you laughing, pet?"

"Never mind."

"I was worried about you. Very worried. Where on earth did you get to?"

She's acting as she used to when I was a few minutes late home from school, thought Dorrie in disbelief.

"Mr. Rosser saved me, just as he saved you. He came down to the cabin and freed you from under the trunk, then carried you up on deck and saw to it that you were put safely in a lifeboat. I wasn't able to climb aboard in time so he stayed there with me until we managed to swim to a raft. Both of us owe our lives to him, Auntie."

It was clear that Dora knew nothing of this. She gaped

wordlessly at Dorrie for a few seconds, then her face bunched and she began to cry.

"Oh, Auntie, it's all right. We're all safe now, all of us." She embraced Dora again, noticing this time how hot her skin was, feverishly hot.

"Careful of her leg," said Tessie's mistress behind her. "It's given her such a lot of trouble." She moved forward and lifted up one of the cabin blankets to reveal Dora's bare foot where it was propped on a bolster of ferns, grossly swollen and purpling.

"Oh, Auntie—"

Dora's blanket-swathed body undulated with sobs. "It's not my foot. I can bear that. I've lost the brooch, my father's portrait. All night I've been lying here thinking about it, about how he's lying on the bottom of the sea, and now his portrait is lost to me, too. That brooch has been with me ever since he died."

"You've got my trinkets there, Miss Bennington," said Tessie's mistress brightly. "You may have your choice of anything of mine that takes your fancy. Can't have you upset over a silly brooch, can we?"

"Do go away," said Dora. "Go away, both of you. I hated that ship. If only we hadn't had to go to Sydney, none of this would ever have happened."

It's all my fault, thought Dorrie.

Seventeen

At night she sometimes woke suddenly. She had been walking along the beach on that first afternoon ashore, striding as fast as she could across the sand as if by putting distance between herself and the shipwreck scene she could block the nightmare from her mind.

It was when she skirted round a clump of rocks that she saw him. The corpse of a man dressed in ragged pajamas. He was lying on his back with blank eyes staring up at the sky, and before she realized he was dead she had recognized him as Tessie's master and had made that first, involuntary start toward him.

Only in the second glance she saw that his jaw and one cheek were bashed and blackened, and that the receding tide had scooped his mouth full of sand.

All the stuffing's knocked out of him, she thought. She turned away and vomited, clutching the rock for support. *All the stuffing's knocked out of him.*

The sight of his face woke her in the night and she sat up, the same clammy sweat on her face, the same sickening feeling cramping her stomach.

Incredibly, she'd forgotten everything. Forgotten the wedding, Del, their hasty departure; in fact it was with a dull sense of surprise that Dorrie arrived back in Auckland to find that she had nowhere to live. The gatehouse had been bought by Ellen and now housed Fintona's groom with his wife and three children.

Refusing Ellen's hospitality on the pretext that she needed to be close to Dora, she rented a room near the hospital, thankful that when the landlady heard the name

Bennington she did not ask for money in advance. After
negotiating with Mr. Cambridge at the warehouse, Dorrie trudged back to her lodgings with a heavy covered
wicker basket filled with silk samples, thread, wire, and
tape. These she spread out on the bed in her tiny room
and immediately began making artificial flowers.

She worked constantly, breaking only for snacks or for
the short journeys to and from the hospital ward, where
she sat on a low stool beside Dora's bed, her hands never
pausing as she labored over the bright silk blooms.

By the end of the first week she had earned enough for
a month's rent, and by the end of the second she had paid
off the basket and materials. In the third week she bought
Dora an orange and had the first proper meal since the
day she shared luncheon with Nathaniel Rosser on board
the *Manu Moa*. She bought a pork pie with peas and
mashed potatoes and a dollop of gravy and ate it standing
at the high scrubbed counter in the workingman's "bob
for a nob" shop, where every meal cost the same, a
"bob" or a shilling. Though her pie and potato were cold
and the gravy had congealed to grease she forced down
every mouthful.

Afterward she walked home slowly, swallowing to rid
her mouth of the gritty sensation of cold mashed potato
and trying to smother an uneasy biliousness. She had
reached the crest of the hill and was about to turn into
Inkerman Street when Rupert called to her from across
the road and she glanced up to see him waving to her.

"Come for a ride with me," he said, pushing the
buggy door open. Certain that she was about to refuse he
added, "Please, Dorrie. I haven't seen you for ages."

"Just a few minutes then," she agreed, for Dora expected her at noon, but she settled into the buggy and
smiled at Rupert with genuine affection. There had always been a casual easiness in their relationship, partly
because they felt a certain sympathy for each other and
partly because neither expected anything of the other.
She said, "I hope you don't want to talk about Margue-

rite, because I've seen almost nothing of her these past weeks.''

"Marguerite.'' He shrugged unhappily and Dorrie felt a pang of pity for him. "She's spending all her time at Fintona helping Roz get ready for the big day. You should come 'round, too, sometimes. Why don't you? Mama thinks it very odd that you won't come to dinner. She's dying to show you off, you know. Roseanne pasted those newspaper stories about you being the heroine of the shipwreck into her scrapbook and Mother never stops basking in the glory of *her* famous, brave niece. She keeps telling everyone you'll be awarded a medal. You deserve one, mind. That rescue was a sensation.''

Too much of a sensation, thought Dorrie, recalling Marguerite's controlled reaction to the fuss. She was *overwhelmed* that Mr. Rosser had been saved and was *thrilled* that Dorrie was acclaimed as a heroine, but an underlying coolness was apparent. How much more pleased she would have been had Mr. Rosser survived without Dorrie's help.

"Do apologize to Aunt Ellen for me, will you, but tell her that Auntie Dora needs me. I stay to help feed her in the evenings. She still isn't eating properly and I'm worried about her state of—'' She reached behind her and pulled out a book that was wedged into a fold of upholstery. *"A Fool and Her Folly,''* she read. "Is this yours? Yes, silly question. If you've finished with it, do you think I might please borrow it? If Auntie Dora could read to me while I'm sewing, it might help take her mind off the pain.''

"While you're sewing?'' He sounded incredulous.

"Yes. She has her spectacles now. Some of our things were recovered from the cabin—not Auntie's mourning brooch unfortunately—but I suppose it's something for her to have her sight back.''

"Are you *sewing* at the hospital?''

She realized why he had sounded surprised and tried to cover by saying, "Just a little mending, odd things. I'm not making hats—well, you heard me say that when Roseanne—''

''Asked you to make her another dozen, as if you didn't have enough to worry about.''

She flushed when she heard the indignation in his voice. To change the subject she asked, ''How is Mr. Rosser? I haven't seen him, either, but he wrote me a delightful note and sent Auntie Dora a beautiful bouquet of pink carnations wrapped in a cornet of silver paper.'' She did not add that Dora, suspecting the flowers had come from Captain Yardley's hothouse, had promptly given them to the woman in the next room.

They were trundling along the Domain Drive now, whipping at a smart pace between the double row of trees toward the lake that lay flat as a blade in the distance. Rupert said, ''I'll leave it to Nathaniel to tell you how he is. He complained to me that he was unable to reach you, to talk to you, so I brought you here to meet him.''

He was out of his carriage, smoking a thin cigar which he tossed into the water, when he saw her, and strode towards her holding out both hands in greeting.

Her appearance shocked him. Dark rings like hoofprints were stamped under her eyes and a pinched starved look around her mouth accentuated that pointed chin. In her faded black dress and bonnet she reminded him of a beggar girl he had bought food for in London long ago, a waif with arms thin as matchsticks and her hair dragged back off her face as though to declare she no longer cared what image she presented to the world.

''I wouldn't have come willingly,'' she said. ''But I'm glad to see you looking so well.''

Nathaniel told the driver to keep driving around the lake, and he unrolled the blinds on the land side of the carriage so that nobody would see Dorrie alone with him. A fine rain was sifting through the sunshine. As it fell on the lake's surface each droplet exploded into a burst of light and the water seemed alive with thousands of tiny gold butterflies.

"I wanted to ask a favor of you," Nathaniel said. He was sitting very solemn, very upright opposite her. His tie was navy silk, immaculately folded, and his shoes wore a high gloss. He seemed a little nervous, and he rubbed the side of his jaw as if his collar were too tight. She said nothing, just watched him expectantly, so he continued, "You saved my life, Dorrie. I know it isn't enough merely to say thank you."

"You mustn't go on about that! You shouldn't have told the newspapers and you certainly don't need—"

"Please. How does one repay a saved life? If you'd rescued a favorite dog, or a prize horse, I'd be pressing a hundred pounds' reward into your hands, but this isn't a dog or a horse we're talking about. It's me. *My* life."

"Mr. Rosser, *please*, I–"

"Nathaniel."

"Nathaniel, then." She bit her lip. "I must ask you not to go any further. It wasn't a simple matter of my saving your life. I'd have drowned if you hadn't been there. Having you to think about saved my life, too, because I'd have gone into a complete panic if I'd been alone. I know I would. So please—we saved each other, and that's the end of it."

"It's not, you know. I won't rest until I've done something to repay you. What about the hospital bills?"

Dorrie's heart shrank. The hospital bills were something she'd rather not face. "I'll manage," she said lamely. "Aunt Ellen said that if she could do anything to help—" The lie faltered and died, as she recalled Rupert's blunt words: *I'd ask Mama to spring for the expenses, but she's throwing a fit about the cost of Roz's wedding breakfast. Mama's tighter than a tomtit's tail at the best of times, but now*— and he'd rolled his eyes.

Nathaniel was watching her face carefully. She turned her eyes toward the window and gazed at the slow parade of willow trees, but she could still feel him staring at her.

He was saying, "We'll drive around here all day if necessary until you tell me how I can repay you. I've already made up my mind that I'm going to, you see, so now you have to tell me what it is that you want out of life and I'll decide how I can help you achieve it. I have more money than one human being could ever possibly need and from what I understand you are in need of some. So let's reach an agreement, shall we? What about the hospital bills?"

Dorrie shook her head. "Auntie Dora would think that Captain Yardley or her cousin May had paid for them. They have offered, you know."

"I know." He laughed, recalling the Captain's comment: *She looked as though she was at Hell's gate but she had enough strength to hurl some very salty remarks at me. Any of my sailors would have been proud of her.*

Dorrie said, "I hate to bring myself to do it, but Auntie and I are going to face the fact that we have to sell *Riversong.*" She turned and looked into his face, and he thought that she looked like a beaten, middle-aged woman. "Auntie Dora and I have been through some very tough times together but we've always managed to hold out—without charity—because it means such a lot to us to keep *Riversong,* just to know that she's there and she's ours, and—"

Gently he said, "By *Riversong* I take it that you mean that beautiful pendant at the museum?"

Dorrie nodded. She was twisting a handkerchief between her fingers, nervously plucking at the fine rolled hem.

"But you couldn't possibly sell it."

"*Her.*"

"Her, then. You couldn't consider that. It would be a crime to—"

Quite suddenly Dorrie burst into tears.

He was beside her at once, putting his arm around her while she wept into her handkerchief, her shoulders shuddering. In bursts and snatches she told him her story, how Dora had long ago flouted Grandmaire's wishes by adopting Dorrie in the first place and how this had caused Dora to lose much of her promised inheritance.

"She always used to say that I was more important to her than money ever could be, but right since I was old enough to make plans, I decided that one day I would make it all up to her and reward her for all the sacrifices she's made for me. I've always had this dream that one day I would set her up in a grand home of her own, beautifully furnished with the walnut tables and chairs upholstered in brocade, with velvet curtains and soft carpets, servants with uniforms, the finest food to eat, and the most exquisite clothes to wear when she drove out in her own carriage."

"That's quite a dream."

"I know, and I never really had any clear idea of how I was going to bring it about. It's no more than she deserves, you know—but l-look at what I've done for her instead!" Dorrie choked. "She's crippled and she's in terrible pain and we're going to be spending the rest of our lives in miserable poverty and it's *all my fault!*"

He was shocked by the outburst. Resting his cheek against the black bonnet, with one hand cradling a thin, quaking shoulder, he tried to assure her that it wasn't so.

"It is, it is! But the worst of it is that I've tried so very hard to succeed. I worked and worked at home, but Auntie Dora had to help me. There just wasn't room for a servant to tidy up and cook around us there, with all the millinery things spread all through the cottage. So we ended up wearing ourselves out and eating scratched-together meals late at night. I don't think Auntie Dora has properly recovered from that. She's still overtired and run-down, and that's why the injuries were much more serious than they might have been otherwise."

"You're overtired, too," he said gently. "Yes, of course you are. That's why you're so harsh with yourself." Nathaniel realized that he had never felt so protective and warm toward anyone in his life before. It was no longer merely a matter of wanting to help her; now it was of supreme importance that he did whatever was necessary toward helping her make that dream a reality.

"I wanted it so much," she confessed in an exhausted whisper. "When our hatmaking venture didn't work out as well as I'd hoped, I even thought that the answer might be to marry someone wealthy, but that didn't work out either."

"Farrell?"

She nodded. "But marriage isn't the right thing for me. I have to work, but the trick is to make the business successful, and now that I won't have Auntie Dora to help—"

"You have me. And I have a few ideas that may be just what you need." He looked at her speculatively. "Only, what you said about marriage not being right for you—"

"It isn't," she said quickly. "I enjoy work, really. And I've made up my mind that I'll never get married now."

Never? What did happen in Sydney? he wondered. "All in good time and you'll change your mind," he smiled.

"Never." She sounded as if she meant it.

"Five hundred pounds?" said Dorrie next day. "But that's an enormous amount. Unthinkable."

"Don't argue with Mr. Rosser, *chérie*," cooed Marguerite from where she stood behind his chair, almost hanging over his shoulder.

They were in the Duptons' garden room, a spacious area originally added to their riverside home so that Aimee could come and go freely without having to negotiate the half-dozen steps to the verandah. The piano was here, and easy chairs, and a great many thick-leaved and dusty plants all grouped at one end under the skylight. Rupert, Dorrie, Nathaniel, and Marguerite sat at a scratched oak table near the french doors. Beyond, on an apron of lawn above the river Aimee was firing arrows into a straw target and shrieking orders at the garden boy whose job it was to retrieve them for her.

"But five hundred pounds is a *frightening* amount," Dorrie said, glancing at the page where Nathaniel was making swift calculations.

"Not if you do everything properly. It's bad business to keep running out of basic materials and wasting valuable time on frequent shopping trips. No, that's what we need to begin with."

"There's one more thing," Rupert reminded them. "Where is this venture going to be set up? Dorrie can hardly start a millinery shop in lodgings, can she?"

"What about here?" offered Marguerite.

Nathaniel glanced out to where Aimee was whacking an arrow over the arm of the wheelchair. "I think not," he said. "She needs somewhere quiet yet easily accessible to customers. Rupert, do you know of any houses for sale near here?"

"*I* know the perfect place," said Marguerite. "The Wrightsman's place. They are going back to England, and they haven't been able to find a buyer. Their price is too high, *Maman* says."

Nathaniel was instantly alert. He turned to pat her cheek in approval and she flushed with pleasure. "You are a genius, Marguerite! That house is the answer, of course. It has entrances from two streets, ample parking space for carriages, and it's close to the jetty for the ferry from town. As you say, Marguerite, perfect."

"It's out of the question," said Dorrie.

"Why?" they asked.

She turned her palms up in a gesture of hopelessness. "Because five hundred pounds alone is too much, but that house, why, it's palatial! It's grander than Fintona. Even visiting there was like something out of a dream, and as for the thought of living there—I'm sorry, all of you. I know you're all excited by the thought of being involved in this project, but it wouldn't be proper."

"Dorrie, *chérie*, don't argue with Mr. Rosser. He said

it will be all drawn up properly, a proper loan, and you will pay him rent, *non?*''

"A proper business arrangement, then," said Dorrie. "But only if your investment is properly protected. If I fail, then *Riversong* will be sold to pay you back. You can write that into all the documents."

"Done. That practically guarantees you success."

"What do you mean?" asked Marguerite, leaning over his shoulder again.

He turned to explain to her that Dorrie would do anything rather than have to sell *Riversong*. As he was talking Aimee came in panting, thrusting at the wheels of her chair, heaving herself along until she was at the piano keyboard where, in a cascade of flawless notes, she began to play, very loudly. Nathaniel stopped talking to Marguerite and turned to listen.

"She's brilliant," he said.

"Do you share lots of secrets with Mr. Rosser?" asked Marguerite. When Dorrie looked startled, she said, "That *petit peu* about you never wanting to sell *Riversong, non?* When did you tell him that?"

"On—on the ship, I suppose." Dorrie was alarmed by the violence in Marguerite's tone.

"Were you friendly with him on the ship? You know, I often wonder why you and your *tante* went off so suddenly to Australia. Did you see Mr. Rosser by any chance when you were there, too?"

"Marguerite, I've *told* you. I went to see Mr. Farrell again, to reconsider his proposal. It didn't work out, so we came home."

"Now you're cross with me, *non?*''

"No, I'm not."

In truth she was weary of these sudden sharp interrogations, yet despite her almost paranoid jealousy over Nathaniel, Marguerite was proving to be a valuable help as Dorrie made the preparations to begin her business. At first Dorrie suspected that Marguerite was only pre-

tending an interest in order to make sure that Dorrie and
Nathaniel never spent any time alone together, but now
that she realized that her friend was genuinely enthusiastic about the project, too, she felt ashamed of her suspi-
cions. Marguerite was hopelessly infatuated with Mr.
Rosser and, knowing how painful unrequited adoration
could be, Dorrie tried to be patient.

Now, as they trundled towards the new house, jammed
into the Duptons' coach with a load of millinery materials, Marguerite sighed, "If only he would notice me,
really *notice* me. Perhaps the wedding might be the perfect occasion to do it, *non?* A wedding often puts romantic ideas into a gentleman's head."

"And you look very bridal in your attendant's gown,"
said Dorrie. She felt old and a little sad. It seemed years
and years since she had been foolish enough to think of
romance.

"Are you really not coming to the wedding?" asked
Marguerite. "Your Aunt Ellen expects you there."

"No," said Dorrie. It seemed years and years since
she had felt any pain, either. "I won't be there. You'll
have Mr. Rosser all to yourself."

"Don't sound so miserable about it," said Marguerite,
unable to keep from sounding pleased. She rapped on the
roof and the driver opened the hatch. "Stop just inside
the gates, will you? *Merci.*"

"Why?" asked Dorrie.

"So you can admire the house. It's what you like to
do, *non?*" replied Marguerite with a mysterious smile.

"I do," admitted Dorrie. "I just can't believe that I'll
soon be living there." She leaned forward as the sweep
of drive came into view. There were the bushes, clipped
into poodle shapes, the flower beds like strips of floral
cloth flung across the lawns, the gracious house with its
arching, tiled roof, the generous verandahs supported by
tall carved pillars, the silver-and-blue-striped awnings on
either side of the door, the swinging sign in silver and

blue—*Le Chapeau*—surrounded by silver scrollwork and tiny bluebirds.

Dorrie said, "Where did they come from? The sign and those pretty awnings? They're *beautiful*—"

"It was my idea," said Marguerite. "I chose the name, and you said you wanted blue and silver for your hatboxes, so *violà!*"

"*Le Chapeau!*" read Dorrie. "That's perfect."

Nurse Canterbury was tall and stern. She wore her uniform like a suit of armor—to intimidate, thought Dorrie when she first saw the black serge gown, the ankle-length white apron, high white collar, and wide starched cuffs. Nurse Canterbury's jet black hair was coiffed into an onion knob like Dora's and was topped with a high frilled cap like a cutlet ruff.

"There's no change," she told Dorrie in her diluted-vinegar voice. She always said the same thing and she always walked on ahead as if Dorrie were a servant. Her boots snip-clipped on the polished floor and she trailed, unexpectedly, an aura of lavender perfume, sweet and musty.

Dora was lying with eyes closed, looking wasted and so ill that Dorrie's insides contracted with a spasm when she first looked at her. "You're late," she accused when Dorrie bent to kiss her.

The nurse whisked around pulling curtains back and checking the water. The beaded cover rattled on the sides of the china jug. When Dorrie had hung up her coat and bonnet she helped the nurse raise Dora to a sitting position. Dora was so thin that Dorrie hesitated to touch her. "Come on, we haven't got all day," Nurse Canterbury said.

"Be careful," snapped Dora.

"I'm sorry," said Dorrie, unraveling Dora's braids so that she could brush and dress her hair. While she worked she reintroduced the subject of the millinery business. She had decided against springing the whole plan on

Dora full blown, as it were, but instead to tell her a little at a time, to enable her to get used to the idea.

This was not successful. The pain in Dora's leg had her swinging between irritability and dull acceptance, which meant that she either displayed no interest or asked awkward questions about where the money was coming from.

"Le Chapeau?" she sniffed today. "What manner of a silly name is that, eh? Something thought up by that fancy little friend of yours, no doubt. What's the matter with a good plain English name?"

Dorrie ignored that. "Marguerite wanted to call it *Le Joli Chapeau,* which means 'the pretty hat' but she decided that would be overdoing it, so she had the sign written *Le Chapeau* instead."

"Something to be thankful for, I suppose. Who is paying for all of this? Marguerite has no money of her own to be frittering on expensive signs and awnings."

"I suppose Mr. Dupton paid for it," Dorrie said, knowing full well that Nathaniel's money had been spent there, too. "Our friends have been very supportive."

"All the more reason not to go borrowing money off them," harped Dora. "I don't like this plan of yours, Dorrie. You're encouraging Mr. Rosser, and that's not being fair to him."

"Auntie, *please!*" Dorrie glanced anxiously toward the door, afraid Dora's voice might carry. "The solicitors are advancing me the money in a businesslike way, and all the dealings will be made through them. There, that's done. Would you like to read to me now?"

"No. I shan't bother, thank you. It always reminds me of all those years I spent reading aloud to Grandmaire. And this stuff of Rupert's is such awful rubbish." She prodded *Good-bye Sweetheart* and toppled the book to the floor.

Dorrie sighed. Every day it was the same. Nothing suited, nothing seemed agreeable.

* * *

At midafternoon Nurse Canterbury poked her head in at the door and looked around. "More visitors, Miss Bennington," she said, then swung the door wide to admit Ellen, a regal figure in navy blue, then the bridal couple, Rupert, Marguerite, and Nathaniel.

"Surprise, surprise, Auntie," giggled Roseanne, her face scarlet with pleasure. "You may wish me well! I've just become Mrs. Arundel Blackett."

"Congratulations," said Dora. She looked surprised, but not pleased.

"How gratifying to find you looking so very well," remarked Ellen, squeezing her tiny mouth into a goldfish pout which she dabbed at Dora's cheek.

"I'll be dancing soon," said Dora.

Roseanne giggled. "Don't we make a handsome pair? Del bought a new suit especially. The tailor had to import the cloth from Australia."

"All the best things come from Australia," chirped Marguerite. "Don't they, Nathaniel?"

"The happy couple insisted on coming to see you," said Ellen.

Dorrie backed around the end of the bed and grasped the foot-rail with hands that suddenly would not keep still. *I won't look at him,* she vowed, but in the periphery of her vision she could see the space he occupied, a dark shape motionless beside the slender sateen tube of Roseanne's gown, partly obscured by the fountain of lace veiling. He was looking at her, she could tell, and she felt her face grow warm under the pressure of his stare.

At Dorrie's elbow Marguerite whispered, "This was my idea! I guessed you might be here visiting so I suggested that the whole party roll around here. Isn't it fun?"

Dorrie nodded mutely.

"We brought the wedding bouquet to show you, Auntie! See, it's stephanotis and white carnations. The florist made it to match the floral bell that's hanging in the ballroom under an archway. We'll be standing under it to greet everybody. Our first official duty together, as Del says, don't you, Del?''

Del didn't seem to be saying much of anything. Dorrie heard him mumbling something indistinct but then Ellen cut in.

"The nurse said we could only stay a minute, mustn't tire you, you know. You'll have to take my word for it that everything is absolutely perfect—despite this weather that's only sent to vex us, I'm sure. There's a king's ransom of wedding gifts, dear. An absolute ransom. What a pity you can't be there to see them.''

"It's quite a disappointment.''

"Before we go, Dorrie must kiss the groom,'' said Roseanne. It was a frivolous remark, gaily spoken, but her eyes were fixed on Dorrie as she uttered it.

Back in the doorway Rupert and Nathaniel were watching Dorrie, too. They saw her raise her chin, fix a smile in place, and say lightly, "No, thank you.''

"But of course you must. Del's kissing absolutely *everybody,* aren't you, Del?'' She giggled, a sound frothy with malice.

"For heaven's sake,'' snapped Dora. "Leave the poor man alone. He has quite enough to put up with as it is.''

Which quieted Roseanne.

Against her will Dorrie felt her attention being tugged towards Del. He was regarding her soberly, his face and eyes seemingly rinsed of color. There was a tight, anguished set to his mouth.

Dorrie waited for the pain, for an answering spasm of anguish of her own. There was nothing, no pain, no sensation at all.

I'm free! she thought, dazed. *I was terrified of what I might find, but when I looked there was nothing there. I'm free!*

She smiled. "Good-bye, Del,'' she said.

Observing that brief exchange, Nathaniel was puzzled. He stood back while the others in the party filed through the door, then asked Dorrie if he could have a private word with her.

She stepped out into the corridor, drawing the door shut behind her. The others were clattering into the shadowed hollow at the far end of the building. Marguerite glanced back, hesitating.

"I mustn't leave her alone," lied Dorrie. "And you mustn't make the others wait for you."

"Only a second." He drew a flat package of tissue paper from his waistcoat pocket and unwrapped it to reveal Dora's mourning brooch, tarnished and ruined by sea water, the hair border fraying, the picture blotched but recognizable just the same.

"Nathaniel! How did you find it? Oh, she'll be overjoyed—"

"When you told me how upset she was about losing it I asked the Shipping Company divers to keep a special look out, but nobody found it, so eventually I posted a reward with the tribe up there and one of the young Maori fellows decided to take the risk and dive for it. Here we are, then."

"Why didn't you give it to Auntie Dora?"

"I thought I should consult with you, first. It could be fixed, the hair rewound, the silver polished, new glass fitted, and the photograph itself retouched. Should I have that done first, or do you think she'd prefer it like this?"

"Would fixing it be expensive?"

"Threepence at the most." He was twinkling at her, mocking her earnest expression.

She relaxed. "Thank you, oh, thank you. Nathaniel, you are the sweetest, most wonderful man—"

He was tempted to kiss her then. Never mind Marguerite watching from the shadowy end of the corridor and the old woman lying there, ears straining, no doubt, to catch every word. Not that she could hear or see anything. He touched her cheek with a fingertip.

"You're beginning to look better," he said. "I was so worried about you—"

Marguerite's voice encircled them like a rope. "What's keeping you back there?" she cried.

"Go," whispered Dorrie as Uncle Samuel came stamping along the corridor looking cross.

"You might have told me you were coming up here," he huffed to Nathaniel. "Left me at the reception—"

"Sir, I apologize. I didn't realize—"

"All right. Not your fault." He thrust out a hand and shook Nathaniel's hand warmly. "Forgot to mention it. I appreciate everything you're doing for these two. Fine thing it is, setting them up after they lost everything in that shipwreck."

"I'd have lost everything, too, if it wasn't for Dorrie," said Nathaniel with such warmth in his tone that Uncle Samuel glanced at him shrewdly and was still watching as he walked away to join Marguerite.

"The fellow's in love with you, I shouldn't wonder," he mused.

"Don't be *silly*, Uncle Samuel," said Dorrie. "And for pity's sake don't talk like that in front of Auntie Dora. She'd have fifty fits."

"Don't see why," he said, surprised.

"It's a long story," Dorrie told him.

Eighteen

Rubbing her hands on her work apron, Dorrie walked along the verandah and down the steps onto the tarred yard.

"Over 'ere, miss!" called Mr. Timmins from the shrubbery beyond the flagpole. "Could yer come an' tell us what yer want doin' with these 'ere azaleas?"

Dorrie sighed. The gardener was not her idea; Nathaniel had hired him and was paying his wages as "upkeep on the property," which sounded reasonable when he explained it to her but was yet another way he could dip into his pocket to help her.

"They're crowdin' each other out," Mr. Timmins said, nodding his head like a bird pecking wheat.

Dorrie knew nothing about azaleas. "Whatever you think best," she said vaguely.

"Very good, miss," he replied smartly, as if she had given him precise orders. She smiled; their interviews were always the same.

Turning to go, she automatically glanced out through the red brick archway beyond the stables to catch a glimpse of the white sentry box outside Government House where the black-and-red-uniformed soldier was on duty. On rainy days he stood at attention in the box while the water hung a bead curtain in front of him, but today he was marching back and forth while the inevitable cluster of children stood nearby, watching and mocking him. She was admiring his tall fur busby, shiny as a metal knob in the sunshine, when a hansom cab trotted in at the driveway and Marguerite alighted.

"I couldn't possibly walk into town dressed like this,

not with the road so dusty,'' she said, pirouetting so that
Dorrie could admire her peacock silk dress.

"You're going shopping, dressed up like that?"

"You're a fine one to talk," retorted Marguerite.
"Look at you, still in that drab black. I do wish you'd let
me give you some of my cast-off things. Yes, I know, no
cast-offs! But they'd be better than that scraggy old
thing."

"Where are you off to?" asked Dorrie, declining to
enter that worn argument.

"Have you forgotten? The steam packet is in from
Sydney with a certain passenger aboard. He always at-
tends to business with *Papa* right away, and if I contrive
to bump into him he sometimes buys me tea at the park
refreshment gallery."

Dorrie sighed. *Is this what it feels like to be very old?*
she wondered. *No more false hopes, no more sentiment,
no more anticipation?*

Marguerite hurried up the steps beside Dorrie, the blue
flowers on her gray boater ruffling with each bob of her
head. The hansom driver strolled over to chat to the gardener. Marguerite followed Dorrie inside, still chatting.
"Oh, you still haven't got any furniture for the hall," she
said. "That display of flowers is lovely, but you need
chairs, and a carpet of some sort."

"All in good time. You know the customers' *salon*
had to come first and then I want to make Auntie Dora's
room as pretty as I can. Will you help me choose the furniture for that later on? I want to make a proper welcome
for her when she eventually comes out of hospital."

"Does she know about the house yet?"

"Not that we're in the Wrightsmans' old house." She
glanced in at the salon where mirrors and soft drapes
highlighted a display of *Le Chapeau* hats, then walked on
to the next room and swung the door open. "Welcome to
our little beehive," she said. "There's always a busy
hum in here, isn't there, Iris?"

"Oh there you are, Miss Bennington!" and Iris Pine

came hurrying over while Marguerite gazed around with interest. The workroom had once been a nursery. Tall windows permitted light to flood in, but gaslights illuminated the shadowy corners so that the room was filled with a white sheet of light. Two long tables were heaped with bright materials and around them sat seven young women, stitching and snipping as they talked in low voices.

"Miss Bennington!" repeated Iris. "Mrs. Lambert is calling for her turban this afternoon but she changed her mind and wants a dark blue forget-me-not trim, only we've no darks here, only ice blue. I sent the stable-boy along to Ruby's house to see if she's got any, only her mother's sick so she's out, and none of us here know how to make them proper—and you know how particular Mrs. Lambert is."

"Quite, but we must be particular for all our customers, mustn't we, girls?" Dorrie raised her voice as she spoke. "I'll fix some dark ones for you," she said, then glanced at Marguerite. "Do you want to be on your way then?"

"I'll stay and watch." She slid the cover from her wristwatch, then said, "The steam-packet's not due in for another hour or so."

First, the fabric punch stamped petals tiny as particles of confetti from the sheet of stiffened velvet, then Dorrie's fingers twisted and nipped them into minute petals, binding them with fine wire and tiny bunches of yellow thread that had been knotted to make stamens. She worked so fast that it made Marguerite feel dizzy.

"Don't forget that I've made literally thousands of these," said Dorrie when she commented. "I could probably make them in my—" She glanced up and stopped in midsentence.

Nathaniel was leaning on the door frame, smiling at her. She felt a rush of warmth, of pleasure, to see him.

"Well!" said Marguerite, pleased too, but clearly piqued that he had come here first. "Look what the tide's washed in!'' And she threaded her hand through his arm in a gesture of ownership.

"The pilot boat dropped me at your jetty,'' he said to Dorrie. "I came right here to tell you the news. That high-fashion store in Sydney wants a special consignment of two hundred hats, and at the right price, too.''

"Did you hear that, girls?'' called Dorrie, and though they were all listening openly, she repeated the news. "Two hundred hats and a bonus for each of you when the order is ready. But they have to be absolutely faultless, mind.''

"*Magnifique,*'' said Marguerite too pertly. "You'll really have something to celebrate on Saturday, *non?*''

"Saturday?''

"Hasn't Marguerite asked you about the cruise?'' said Nathaniel. "I told her she was to invite you and not take your usual polite refusal as an answer. There will be music and dancing and I'm putting on a special open-air Cinematograph show on the top deck. You must come, Dorrie.''

She didn't dare look at Marguerite. "I'm sorry, but I can't. Truly I can't. I'm much too busy here. In fact I can't even talk now.'' She managed a light-hearted laugh. "Marguerite will give you a lift downtown in her cab. Wasn't it lucky she stopped by?''

"Very fortunate.'' Disappointment was plain on his face.

Iris Pine came and sat beside her as she finished the spray of forget-me-nots. She kept her voice low, below the level of the others' conversations.

"I don't know why you always push Mr. Rosser at Miss Dupton,'' she said. "It's you that he's hankering to court, Miss Bennington. Plain as the nose on my face, it is.''

"Really, Iris, you're worse than Uncle Samuel with your gossiping.''

"But it's true, miss. You are the one he wants. The girls and me were saying—''

"Never mind. You were mistaken, and I'll have no more of it, do you understand?"

Iris looked at the pink face, at the clear gray eyes snapping with—with what? Not anger. Unhappiness.

"Yes, miss. But we ain't mistaken."

Dorrie ignored that remark.

Dorrie hurried down the tarred path between the beds of sprawling granny-bonnets, stocks and wallflowers, all English flowers so beloved by Colonial ladies. Mrs. Wrightsman had nourished herself on their sight and scent until the longing had become too keen, but now it was the customers who admired them as they came and went. Dorrie was always too busy to do more than trot briskly past.

She was panting as she emerged from the thicket of ferns and flax and *toe toe* bushes and quickened her step as she approached the Patenes' cottage.

Three *kuris* accompanied Mrs. Patene out to meet her. Like their owner the dogs had become hunched and gray with age, but unlike her they had developed a kind of cringing servitude. Mrs. Patene's dignity had strengthened with the years; as she greeted her Dorrie thought that this was a face that offered reassurances about old age.

The cottage was faded and peeling, splintering like ancient bones. It smelled of smoke and of the breeze that blew fishy smells off the harbor.

Dorrie sat on a straight-backed chair while Mrs. Patene settled on the sofa between two cats that were curled up like cushions. One reminded Dorrie of Misty. Behind Mrs. Patene the wall was covered with framed pictures, a Coronation print of Queen Victoria in the center, then rows of photographs of Albert, many of them engravings cut from the daily newspaper when he had won some sporting or scholarly prize. The pictures made Dorrie feel uneasy; she felt for some reason that they

were unlucky, but she commented on them with genuine
interest.

"Is that taken at the horseraces?" she said.

"Ah, yes. My boy Albert, he takes me every now and
again, just for a little flutter, eh. He knows his horses
too. He's a smart boy, is my boy Albert. Picked *Grafter*
for the Melbourne cup, eh, and we bet a bob each way.
Boy, but it was a good feeling to hear it won."

"I wouldn't know. We've never been to a race meeting."

Mrs. Patene's surprise was justified. Almost everybody in New Zealand attended race meetings. She said,
"Your grandfather, the one Miss Dora wears the picture
of, he was a great man for the horses. Flash Jack Bennington, they called him."

Dorrie said, "I came to see you about Auntie Dora."

"How is she? Bad news about her leg, eh?" She
clicked her tongue, expressing sympathy.

"She's still sick, but the hospital is letting her come
home as soon as they think she can sit up in a wheelchair.
The thing is, she's going to need constant attention. A
companion, perhaps. I was wondering if Emere could
come back to work for us."

"My Emily has a job." She paused. "Wednesday is
looking for work, though, eh. She might be just the
story."

"I don't know." She had seen Wenerei around town
on her trips to replenish supplies. Emere's older sister
was a scraggy, slatternly looking creature with a screech-
ing laugh and a boisterous manner. "I was hoping to persuade Emere to come back. You see, it's the position of
companion rather than servant. I thought that Emere
would be ideal because she and Auntie Dora get on so
well."

"Not so well, Miss Bennington. Your aunt did dismiss
her."

"Mrs. Patene, no! Auntie Dora was so upset when she
left. It wasn't her fault. Please don't hold it against her,

not now that she's so ill. Look, I hoped you'd understand, and I did hope Emere would be interested. The
work is good and it will pay better than her present job,
and it's so handy for her to pop home and see you.''

"Ah, but Wednesday is the one without employ-
ment.''

"I see . . . Can she do laundry?''

"Yes, she can. And she can sweep, and dust without
too much breaking things, eh.''

"Then I'll take them both.'' She knew she was being
manipulated but there was no choice. "Give my best
wishes to Albert, won't you? I saw him on his way to law
studies at the university once, and he looks a proper
Johnny with that gray top hat and that cane with the silver
bands.''

"Ah, that day he was going to court. I went to watch,
eh, and I can tell you I was so proud. He's a clever boy,
is my boy Albert.''

"That's wonderful,'' said Dorrie.

"We decorated your room in the latest style,'' said Dorrie, hurrying ahead to open the door as Uncle Samuel
pushed the wheelchair up the hall. She stood back just inside a sunny room with a floor like amber glass and a
lofty ceiling of molded plaster. Different wallpapers had
been used above and below the high picture rail from
which hung the dark oil paintings from Fintona's formal
parlor, the old "blue room.'' The bedroom looked like a
picture itself, with a set of matching maple furniture—
bed, washstand, wardrobe, writing desk, chaise lounge,
and commode, all with fancy gold paneling and ugly,
clawed feet. Blue velvet had been used for the bedspread
and chaise lounge, and a vase of dark irises, dainty as spiders, stood on the bedside table.

"It looks so pretty at night with the gas lamps lit,''
said Dorrie. "Just imagine, Auntie! No more smelly oil
lamps.''

"Gas lamps will always remind me of hospitals,'' announced Dora. "Where in the world did those paintings come from?"

"Aunt Ellen donated them. She said they'd bring back memories of the old days."

"That's the last thing I want. And I'm not a charity receiving donations."

Dorrie and Samuel exchanged glances. "Shall I take them down then?"

"If it's not too much trouble."

"Of course not. I only want to please you."

"Do you, Dorinda?"

Oh, Auntie, thought Dorrie, her heart aching. *Here is everything I've longed to give you. Can't you see that? Can't you care?*

Dorrie pushed the chair over to the dressing table near the bay window where the lace curtains bulged in a gentle draught. Wenerei's shrill laugh rattled in as she exchanged sallies with the groom. Dorrie was too upset to be irritated by it, but she smiled, hiding her feelings as she watched to see what Dora would do.

On the dressing table Dorrie had lovingly arranged those meager few personal things of her aunt's that had been left behind when they went on their ill-fated journey to Sydney. On a crescent of Dora's finest crocheted doilies were a pin-box, a small framed picture of Queen Victoria and Prince Albert, a hairbrush and tray encrusted with tiny shells, and a camphor-wood music box, a gift brought by Hal for Miss Abby shortly before her death.

"My mother's music box." She held it tenderly between cupped hands, then gently raised the lid. Oriental chimes trembled out the tune "The Bonny Bells of Scotland." Dorrie held her breath as Dora lifted a wafer of tissue paper from the jewelry tray.

"What in the world?" Her head snapped around, then back again. Her hands were shaking as she picked up the mourning brooch of her father, now painstakingly restored and almost new again. She turned it in her fingers; the silver glowed richly in the light. "Where— How—?"

"Mr. Rosser recovered it for you. He knew how much it meant and how distressed you'd been when it was lost. It came back from the jeweler's only yesterday."

"It should have stayed where it was," said Dora harshly and unexpectedly. "It should have stayed in the wreckage and I should have stayed there with it. Like my father—like—" She thrust Dorrie's comforting hand away.

The brooch slipped from her fingers. It snagged in her pathetic, abbreviated lap. She stared at it for a few seconds and Dorrie could not guess what she was thinking, but she stepped back, aghast, when Dora covered her face with both hands and began to cry in ugly, tearing sobs.

In the 1890s the most popular recreation ground in the center of the city was the old Albert Barracks. Most of the military buildings had long been torn down but much of the brick encircling wall remained. The ground on which once the cavalry drilled and soldiers marched with bayonets had now been sowed with springy lawns, ringed with overflowing flower beds, and groups of shade trees.

Here, on a drowsy, simmering afternoon late in the summer of 1899 Marguerite and Dorrie arranged themselves on rugs spread near the heavy-scented rose garden. Within sound of the tossing fountain they watched Nathaniel and May Teipa-Bennington film with their Cinematograph cameras.

"I don't know how to cope with her moods," Dorrie complained. "No matter how hard I try, she refuses to be pleased. It's eight months now since she came home from the hospital and I'm at the end of my rope. All she does is politely refuse everything I buy her or offer her and say her life is over."

"Perhaps she feels unwanted," suggested Marguerite, not really interested. This conversation was not new.

"Unwanted! But she has everything she needs now, and with nine girls working for us—plus outworkers—

and Iris being such a marvelous manager, the place is practically running itself.''

"That's not true. You're working longer hours than you ever did before.''

"But I enjoy it. It doesn't *seem* like work—besides, I do only the frilly stuff, talk to the customers, make special trimmings, design new models, all that kind of thing. Iris runs all the practical aspects. She even hires the girls. Well, they do have to work with her. What I mean is, *I'm* happy now, but I do wish that Auntie Dora could be.''

"Mmmm,'' said Marguerite. She lay daintily on one elbow, smiling at Rupert's efforts to organize the young Maori girls into rows for the next item. Today Marguerite was all in white with a single red rose near the crown of her hat, nestling in a froth of snowy tulle. Nathaniel had said that she looked like a dish of ice cream with a cherry on top. She would live on that remark for days.

"I do wish he wasn't going away so soon,'' she said, with a dramatic heave of her bosom. "It's bad enough when he goes back to Australia, but to *England!* It will mean months and months of waiting. And then when he returns he still probably won't notice me. I wonder, if I had my hair dyed purple, or pink?''

"He'd probably offer you a job in one of his vaudeville troupes. I'm sorry I'm being so tedious about Auntie Dora—''

"You are, rather.''

"It's just that she worries me so much that the slightest little thing starts me fretting. Like her cousin May being here today, I'd not have come if I'd known in advance. I'd have left Auntie Dora at Fintona and returned home. I mean to say, she'd have fifty fits.''

"I know, that's why I didn't tell you. Actually, I think *Maman* would have the vapors, too, if she could see Mrs. Teipa-Bennington's condition. She thinks a lady should stay in her room until the entire distasteful business is over. Still, what is poor May to do if her state is perpetual? This is her tenth, *n'est-ce pas?*''

Her condition? Dorrie studied May thoughtfully. As usual she was wearing a voluminous garment, in this case an artist's smock over her gown.

"I tried to count them once," said Marguerite.

Dorrie watched the filming. May and Nathaniel had identical Cinematograph cameras, great boxy things on splayed tripods. They looked into viewfinders at the top and wound the film along with waist-high wheels like sewing machine handles.

The action was being filmed from different angles. Six teenaged Maori girls swung long *pois,* flax balls on strings. Out of camera range a very fat Maori man played a guitar and a dozen or more people sang in exquisite harmony. They seemed to be enjoying themselves most, chuckling and gabbling away in Maori between songs, while the performers were tense, nervous as young horses. Rupert tried to joke with them, make them relax, but they skittered away from him. Finally it seemed to be right; flax balls thwacked against palms and thighs and the *piu-pius,* the skirts of rolled flax parted and bunched, parted and slithered as the girls stamped their feet in unison.

"Excellent!" called Nathaniel, winding carefully. His elbow pumped smoothly as a train piston. Dorrie was fascinated.

Marguerite had seen it all so many times before. She picked a daisy and slit its stem with her thumbnail. Did Dorrie know what had happened when Del went to Wellington for the Poultry Judges' Seminar recently? Roseanne called the Auction Mart and had them come and clean the entire house out. When Del came home there were painters' things all around the house and no furniture, nothing. "It was spite, I think," whispered Marguerite. "Del wouldn't let Roseanne so much as touch any of his mother's things, or so Sylvia Prescott says."

I brushed my hair with his mother's silver hairbrush,

Dorrie thought. "You know how Sylvia exaggerates," she said.

"Perhaps. But Del spent weeks trying to track everything down. He only recovered a few items and had to pay ten times what Roseanne had accepted for them. Sylvia says he beat her and she went back to Fintona for a few days. Her mother threatened to call the Constabulary. Just think of it! Del a wife-beater!"

"What's the joke, then?" Rupert plonked himself down between them.

Marguerite pulled his cap forward over his eyes.

"Hey, May wants you both to come and pose with the Maori girls. So Nathaniel can show the Queen that her New Zealand subjects aren't all brown-skinned natives, or some such rot. Take your hats off and come and look pretty."

"But our eyes will go all squinty in the sun!"

They posed hatless. Giggling, the Maori girls closed around them, enclosing them with a scent of warm jasmine oil. The sunshine was so hurtfully dazzling that when Nathaniel said, "Look up now, and say, 'Honey!' " Dorrie only wanted to cry.

"Perfect, just perfect," approved May, flailing her handle. Her face was sliced diagonally by the brim of a hat Dorrie recognized and her eyes were enormous and clear, not in the least squinty. "Here comes my darling Patrick!" she cried as a large coach squeaked to a halt nearby and disgorged four nurses, two servants carrying a hamper, and a flock of children all dressed in white, snowy as geese with faces like discs of pale toffee.

The children had their own hamper and rugs nearby. The housemaids supervised unobtrusively as the older children helped the younger ones with their plates of food. Dorrie counted six children, two toddlers and a baby in a basket.

May said, "I like to have the children near me as much as possible, but we try not to let them *intrude*, don't we, dearest?"

Patrick smiled into his wife's eyes. May twittered around him, cutting up morsels of cheese for him, choosing pickles and peeling segments of apple for his plate as if he were a child himself.

They radiated such happiness that, watching them, Dorrie was gripped by a wistful longing. The sense of standing on the sidelines while life passed by before her eyes was so painful that she felt that if she touched herself anywhere blood would seep through her skin. She ached all over. *My life will never be like this,* she thought.

Nathaniel leaned towards her. "Are you enjoying yourself?" he asked in his intimate, one-to-one manner.

It took her every ounce of effort she had to smile at him.

"It would be lovely to be as happy as they are, *non?*" said Marguerite in the salon of *Le Chapeau* while Dorrie matched samples of fabric for a hat to complement her friend's new crushed strawberry silk gown.

"Hush," warned Dorrie, for there were two other ladies in the room. Both were browsing through books that displayed the latest Parisian styles.

Marguerite was unrepentant. "I do like her, she has such style, such *chic,*" she continued in the same loud voice. "She wears your hats, did you know that? I saw her coming out of Caugheys' with a *Le Chapeau* hatbox just the other day. And she photographs so beautifully, too. Mr. Rosser included—"

"Wait," said Dorrie. Both the customers were openly listening, and as Marguerite had already ignored her request to "hush," Dorrie beckoned her out into the hall. It didn't do for the proprietress of *Le Chapeau* to gossip in front of the customers.

"Mr. Rosser included her in his film, and she looks simply elegant, *très chic,* which is more than we do, alas!"

"You've seen it?"

"Yes, after dinner on Friday. You *were* invited, you

know, but you said that your *tante* had a chill so you wouldn't leave her alone. Excuse number twelve, *non?* Mr. Rosser projected the film onto a sheet pinned across the parlor curtains. Oh, but it was funny! *Maman* laughed so much that she had to go upstairs and loosen her corsets. Can you picture that? *Maman!''*

"I'd love to have seen it.'' She could hear the squeak of rubber as the wheelchair rolled along the verandah.

Marguerite was choking with laughter. "You and I looked truly terrible! My eyes were all screwed up, la! And you looked as if there were something sour stuck in your throat. Mr. Rosser says he'll cut us out of the film, but I know he really won't. Just imagine, we will be pulling faces at Queen Victoria herself!''

"What in heaven's name is going on in there?'' called Dora peevishly.

The girls leaned together, laughing.

The cliff-side garden was wearing its bright autumn jacket when Dorrie strolled there with Nathaniel on the morning of his departure for England. Berries mingled with flowers and scarlet foliage splashed over the green.

Dorrie gazed along the harbor, past Fintona's roof to the clutter of the city. "I can see your ship, I think,'' she said. "I suppose you're eager to be aboard and on your way.''

"I'm never eager to leave here,'' he said with a particular significance that made her hurry on quickly.

"It is pretty in Auckland now,'' she agreed, knowing that was not what he meant. *I'm going to miss him so much,* she thought, but instead she said, "I hope the Queen likes your film. And I do hope you abridged it, as you promised Marguerite.''

"I didn't promise, just muttered something vague. The Queen enjoys being amused, anyway, and I rather suspect that she has a soft spot for us rough-and-ready Antipodean Colonialists.''

"She couldn't fault our loyalty or affection." Dorrie bent to pluck off a dead flower head.

"We're the most fervent supporters of Queen and Empire, or so they say. I suppose it's because we're so far away from the fire that we have to generate our own heat."

He stared out to sea. Glancing at him, she wondered if he was thinking about what she called his "Other Life," those broad spans of time he spent away from Auckland. She wanted to urge him to take care. To come back speedily and swiftly.

He turned his head and caught her looking at him. "Dorrie," he said at once, grasping both her hands and gazing into her eyes in a way that thrilled and terrified her. "Before I go there's something I must—"

Her hands jerked back and she sketched a hasty smile, saying, "We do have a few pieces of unfinished business to attend to, don't we? Look, let's go back up to the house. I'll have Ivy put the box of samples in your carriage while Wenerei makes us a cup of tea, and I show you that book of designs I've prepared for you. It's so good of you to go to all this trouble for me. And it was so brilliant of you to suggest that we make the samples up in miniature. Ivy and I had such a lot of fun with them, and we managed to fit twenty different styles into that one hatbox."

"Dorrie—"

"And perhaps we could discuss the house before you go, if there's time. Last week I asked the bank manager about the prospect of raising a mortgage. He was very discouraging until the clerk brought him the ledger with the details of our accounts, and then you should have seen his face! Talk about impressed—he says that when I've saved—"

"Dorrie!"

This time she turned to face him, sure that the dangerous moment had slipped past.

"Don't rush at this. You're doing extremely well but it

does indicate that you're working too hard. You've spent all that money on your aunt, but when are you going to buy yourself some pretty clothes and things? When are you going to take time out for some fun? How long is it since you've been to a dinner party, or a ball? And you've yet to grace me with your presence at one of my shows.''

"Marguerite tells me all about them.''

"And that's enough to put you off, is it?''

"Of course not! But seriously, Nathaniel, I feel as if I'm being driven. That I *have* to take advantage of every opportunity that comes my way, that I have to strive to make this business successful. I love it! I can spend ten hours trimming and sewing, making flowers and so on with the girls, and then after dinner take a real delight in sketching new designs. I can't imagine having as much pleasure indulging myself at a party.''

She was thriving on her work, he had to admit that. Over the past months she had regained her lost bloom and was again fashionably plump with a soft apricot glow on her cheeks and a clear radiance in her eyes. That swirl of pale gold hair was pinned into the shape of a cresting wave under a jaunty blue raft of a hat. It did not matter that she'd worn the same hat and the blue-and-white-striped dress each time he'd seen her. She was beautiful.

He said, "My father thrived on work, too. Immersed himself in business until he no longer knew how to enjoy life. Then, too late, he didn't know how to stop.''

"Well, I shall stop when the house is ours and there is enough money put away to make our futures secure. Oh, please don't be cross with me. I owe all my success to you and I do appreciate it. You've been so kind and dear and helpful that I could never properly thank you.'' Aware that her voice was shaking, she began to walk toward the house and, when she had recovered, said, "You will sell me the house?''

"Not yet. I'd rather go on the way things are now. I like the excuse to come and see you.''

"Auntie Dora doesn't. Right now she'll be squeaking up and down the verandah complaining to Emere that we've been out of sight for far too long."

In another dozen yards they would be back beside the flagpole. Nathaniel caught her arm and held her back. "Dorrie, before I go there's something I must say to you. I've been putting it off, hoping for the right moment but frankly I doubt there's ever going to be one."

"No, please."

"What do you mean *no?*"

"I have a feeling it's going to be personal, so please, Nathaniel, don't say it. Please, for both of us."

The sun burned hot on the back of her neck, soaking through the embroidered muslin yoke of the dress. Dorrie had a sudden giddy notion that she might be mistaken. Perhaps he had some wonderful news about himself and *Marguerite* that he wanted to share with her. Only, would news like that be so wonderful? *I couldn't bear that,* she thought, then, almost immediately, *Yes I could. I could even persuade myself that it's what I really want.*

She jutted her chin at him, saying, "Is it about Marguerite?"

"What?" He looked so puzzled that she knew she was right after all, and for a second she fought an impulse to place her hand against the side of that strong, fine face. *Treachery,* she thought, smothering a rush of warmth.

"There's something I must say."

"About Marguerite?" she said, trying to free her arm. When he grabbed the other one, making escape impossible, she repeated Marguerite's name, holding it like a shield in front of her. "She's in love with you," she told him. "You know that, don't you?"

"For heaven's sake." He dropped her arms. "Of course she's not. Years ago she had one of those schoolgirl fantasies about me. Her father used to make jokes about it, but that was years ago."

"In all the time she's known you she's never so much as glanced at anybody else."

"Then she should. Rupert adores her, and he's starving for some encouragement from her."

"But you're the one—"

"Why are you doing this?" He grabbed her shoulders and gave her a brief shake. Anger flared in his eyes, but she could see he was more puzzled than enraged. "I like Marguerite. I always have, but as for anything else— I don't understand why you're flinging all this at me now of all times. It's as if you're using her to hide behind."

Dorrie flushed and said quickly, "I want Marguerite to be happy. She's been marvelous to me, kind, generous and loyal—"

"And I'm not?"

"Of course you are." The stupidity of her argument hit her and she ducked her head, ashamed at the way she was managing this.

"All right," he said in a tightly controlled voice. "So what you're saying is that I should marry Marguerite so we can spend the rest of our lives making each other miserable just because she's never recovered from some childish crush and because she's your best friend. Is that it?"

She couldn't meet his eyes. Slowly she said, "All I want is for nobody to be hurt. Surely you can understand that. There are people I care very much about, and I'd hate to be responsible for causing any pain."

He laughed. A short, hard sound that bounced away down the cliff ridges. "What you ask, my dear, is impossible. Totally, utterly impossible. When you try above all not to hurt people you often end up doing far more damage."

"I'm sorry. I—"

"For heaven's sake don't apologize. On top of this ruined morning I couldn't stand that."

Dora could see them from where she sat on the south corner of the verandah, two figures walking stiffly side by side. They appeared to have been quarreling.

Dora exhaled as she leaned back against the ornate wicker arch of her chair. She was dressed in one of the new gowns Dorrie had insisted she order, a gray and emerald figured velvet with tailored bodice detail and wide, comfortable sleeves, the perfect colors to display the collection of greenstone and diamond jewelry she wore, wide rows of jeweled rings, dangling earbobs that flashed emerald fire in the slanting sunlight, and on her much reduced bosom, *Riversong,* resting beside the mourning picture of her father.

Dorrie had insisted that the pendant be brought home for her aunt to wear, and Samuel had added his assent to the idea, so, too weary to argue, Dora permitted Emere to clasp the fine gold chain around her neck each morning when she dressed her.

In use the pendant seemed to have taken on a life of its own. Perhaps it was the warmth of Dora's body, perhaps the constant stroking it received as her fingers sought and rubbed it for comfort. She was stroking it now as she sat there, a regal figure with her hair fastidiously groomed but her expression sour with discontent.

That burning between her legs was irritating her again. She had begun to be convinced that her blood was brewing some acid substance that scalded her everywhere her skin was thinnest. Her nose membranes stung, her mouth was a mass of ulcers, her throat was raw, and her lungs hurt, but this burning was most difficult to tolerate.

"I need to use the irrigator again," she told Emere. "Will you go and set the things out please?"

Emere stopped picking her teeth and darned the pin into the bodice of her uniform as she glided away indoors. Resting her weight on her elbows, Dora stared moodily across at North Head.

"Miss Bennington?"

She'd thought he'd gone when she saw him walk toward his carriage, but there he was again, large as life and twice as handsome with a gold-wrapped package in his hands.

"A good-bye gift," he said.

"So you're away for a year this time?" said Dora. Her tone was flat and unencouraging. "Unwrap the gift for me, Dorinda."

Nathaniel said, "So you've brought *Riversong* home for good? I must say that it suits you. And I suppose that more people would see it here on you than would ever bother to pay a visit to the museum."

"I never see anybody."

Dorrie was embarrassed. It wouldn't hurt her to be pleasant. "Auntie Dora says that the girl seems to almost talk to her at times."

"It's just as well that somebody does," retorted Dora.

Dorrie flustered as she untied the strings. "Mr. Rosser is going to look at those motorized wagons while he is in Europe. You know, Auntie, the ones I showed you a picture of, the ones that trundle along without horses to pull them!"

"And I hope to be seeing the Queen again," added Nathaniel when Dora received that news without comment. "I'm taking another film to show her because she enjoyed the first Cinematograph film so much. Dorrie is in it, and Marguerite, and Rupert, and of course Mrs. Teipa-Bennington, but she helped me make it—"

"Oh, do look at this," interrupted Dorrie with a panic that could have passed as gaiety. "Look at what Nathaniel has brought you!"

"It's a zoetrope," said Nathaniel, wishing he could bite back those careless words. How could he have been so careless as to drop May's name into the conversation. He said, desperately, "Let me show you how it works. You look through the slots here, then spin the bowl, and—"

"Later," said Dora coldly. "Emere! You may take me inside now." And without looking at either of them she turned the wheelchair to the other direction.

"If you'd stabbed me with a knife I couldn't be more

wounded! Socializing with *those people* after all I've told you.''

Dorrie was relieved. At luncheon and again at dinner the matter had remained like a barred gate between them. Now they sat alone in the still skimpily furnished parlor, Dorrie with her sketchpad on one side of a token fire, Dora with her untouched crochet work on the other.

Dorrie laid the sketches down readily. All day the matter had been shifting and changing in her mind. Had Dora insisted on discussing it at once, Dorrie would have apologized, capitulated, and promised never to see those detested relatives again, but now her attitude had toughened.

She said, calmly, "I've never socialized with them, but I think they're very nice. May is lovely, and she speaks very kindly about you. She seems sorry that our families have this misunderstanding.''

"Misunderstanding! Let me tell you, young lady, that May Teipa-Bennington has plenty to be sorry about and no reason to speak harshly about me—not truthfully, at any rate. But as for them seeming nice—Dorrie, you astound me! Have you forgotten what they did to Jon? You saw him beaten up and you saw him die! They're murderers, Dorrie, and you have the gall to sit there brass faced and say you think they're lovely.''

"I don't think they killed Uncle Jon.''

Dora sniffed. "Who then? Answer me that.''

Dorrie hesitated. She recalled what Uncle Samuel had hinted, and she remembered that once Rupert had made some comment about his mother to the effect that she had "no conscience whatsoever.'' Ellen, of course, had good reason for wanting her unloved and unwanted husband out of the way. If she'd come back to New Zealand while he was alive, he could have moved in with her. Would have too, no doubt.

"Well?'' demanded Dora.

"There were lots of others who could have paid those men. The opposing political candidates, for two. And some of the hotelkeepers. There were lots of others, Auntie.'' She hesitated again but could not bring Ellen's name into it. Dora would dismiss that as ludicrous and ungrateful.

''And while we're picking over bones, there's another big one to be cleaned,'' said Dora. ''You vowed you wouldn't encourage Mr. Rosser, yet what is this I see? Walks to admire the gardens, tea alone together in the morning room—''

''We have business arrangements.''

''My eye! You're not being honest with him, Dorinda. You're not free to encourage anyone, not after what happened with that worthless Blackett fellow. You're damaged goods and you should remember that.''

Damaged goods! Sickened, Dorrie got up and walked to the window. *What's happening to us?* she wondered. *We're turning on each other like animals in a cage.*

She lifted a corner of the curtain and stared out into the velvet twilight. One window of the stables was a pale square of yellow. She could hear a plunkety-plunk as someone thumped a tambourine and sang a wavery tune. A cat glided across the driveway and melted into the black hedge. There was the cold, sweet smell of mint.

Dorrie let the curtain fall. She could feel the house around her, this beautiful, palatial house that she would soon be able to buy. In the stables was a white carriage and two white horses. The kitchen contained the best food available in the city at the moment. Dora's room was furnished in luxury. Only Dora did not like the house; she used the carriage only on those rare occasions she was invited to Fintona; she would not eat; and when she was alone in her room she cried.

Dorrie turned on her aunt. ''This is so ironical!'' she cried. ''I have everything I ever dreamed of attaining in life. All I wanted was to give you all these things so that you could be happy.''

''I'm happy when I'm working.''

Dorrie was exasperated. ''You *can't* work. You're

still sick. And besides, the whole idea of all this was so that you didn't need to work anymore. Before, when you were in the gatehouse and we were sewing hats for all hours, you ran yourself absolutely ragged, and—''

''Please, Dorrie, I'm tired.'' She looked withered and deflated, as if all the air had been squeezed from her lungs. ''Call Emere, will you, and have her put me to bed.''

''I'll do it. I'll brush your hair for you and—''

''Call Emere.''

She hates me, thought Dorrie as she sat alone with her sketchpad and pencil. *It's because of her leg. She still blames me for that. It's all my fault.*

Glancing at her pad, she saw that in her exasperation she had slashed a black line right through the center of her half-finished sketch. Crumpling it up, she threw it into the fire and watched it burn.

Part Five

DORRIE

1899-1901

Nineteen

Though it was undeniably true that the sun never set on the British Empire, it was also true that people in many parts of that empire failed to appreciate that good fortune and struggled to free their countries from England's grip. Determined never to let go, England dispatched shipload after shipload of soldiers to quash uprisings, skirmishes, and rebellions from Afghanistan to Zululand.

From the first days of the young colony New Zealanders took part in these battles and followed them with interest. Alma, Kartoum, and Lucknow could be found on the globe by any school pupil. Kitchener was a hero, Gordon a martyr, a military uniform was something of splendor to be revered, and war was, without doubt, the most glorious of occupations.

In 1899 with trouble—real trouble—brewing with the Boers in South Africa, the talk of war crossed every table in Auckland. Uncle Samuel brought it to *Le Chapeau.*

"It's scarcely decent," he scowled, knocking out his pipe on the marble fire as casually as if it were an old coal range. "War hasn't even been declared yet and him that calls himself the leader of this country has volunteered to have our young men slaughtered. The man's war mad! It's only a few weeks since he was breaking his neck to send a thousand of our finest off to be butchered by those cannibals in Samoa."

"Don't let Aunt Ellen hear you talk about butchering and slaughtering," said Dorrie. "Rupert's thinking of joining up."

"He never is!" said Dora.

Dorrie shrugged. "He thinks it's all a bit of a lark. A milestone, too, in a way. This is the first time our country has sent an official contingent to any fight, isn't it? Up until now our men have had to march under the flags of other countries. Rupert says it'll be fun. He's teaching Sateen to lie down on command, and he's put up twenty-five pounds for his uniform, so it looks as if he has a fair chance of going."

"Ellen will be beside herself," worried Dora, stabbing with her crochet hook at the soft pink web she was weaving.

Dorrie smiled at her aunt, thinking how much better things were since the doctor had discovered the root of her affliction. All through the winter Dora had grown steadily more miserable with sores and ulcers until finally the doctor had insisted on a complete examination. The cause of her torment surprised them all. Four of her lower teeth had abscessed, causing poisons to spread through her body. Once the teeth had been pulled, Dora began to recover.

Dorrie said, "I think Aunt Ellen looks on it as an adventure." When Dora cast her a disbelieving look she added, "Or that's what Rupert would have us think. He's getting up a party to go to the Empire Theater on Friday evening. There'll be a gramophone concert to raise money for the War Support Fund. It's only a shilling each and they say it'll be a very amusing show."

"Gramophones?" said Samuel. "Nasty scratchy things. Make me want to fidget. Captain Yardley's got one and he—"

"Let's you and I go, Auntie. You could wear that new heliotrope silk with the cream lace jacket."

"I'll think about it."

"Gramophones!" continued Samuel, snatching the conversation back again. "If you want music, you should go into the bush. All that rich silence, then dollops of bird song laid over like jam on bread. Delightful. You can't beat nature for beauty."

A high screech of laughter reverberated out from the corridor leading to the kitchen.

"That Wenerei," sighed Dora. "There's nature for you."

"She's hopeless," said Dorrie. "But her heart's in the right place. Did you tell Uncle Samuel that she's taken up the Sallie Army, too? She thinks Auntie Dora is an expert on the Bible, and she keeps ducking in here when she should be working to ask her questions."

"I'm glad of the company," said Dora tartly. "The other day she asked me what a concubine was. I didn't know what to say, of course, so I asked what the context was, and she said that King Solomon had hundreds of them, so I told her it was some kind of a musical instrument, like a strumpet."

"A strumpet!" Samuel laughed so hard that his tobacco pouch fell from his knee and scattered shreds over the Persian carpet. "A strumpet! Very good, Dora! There always was a droll side to you."

Only we hardly ever see it these days, thought Dorrie. She was glad of Samuel's visits, they gave her something to cheer herself up for. He was a funny old thing with his endless talk of how the world was going all to pot, with votes for women and taxpayers being held to ransom over the Old Age Pension thing that only decent people were going to be given, not anybody who'd been in jail and probably needed it more. He was rambling on about that now, his favorite topic, though he'd never been in jail himself, and Dorrie didn't know why he should get all excited about it. But he kept Dora entertained and stopped her from complaining, and for that she was grateful.

The afternoon slowly ripened, clear golden as a lemon. Dorrie and Marguerite sat in a buggy in a row of other buggies, all with the tops down so that the occupants could see and be seen.

On the field in front of them soldiers in red-and-black

uniforms strutted and wheeled, heads jerked high while a
brass band throbbed out pulsing music rich as blood. At
the far side of the field Rupert and the other Mounted Rifles watched and waited, stiff backed on their horses. Excited by the noise, the horses arched their necks and
rolled their eyes at each other.

"Poor things," said Dorrie. "I think it's cruel, load-
ing all those beautiful creatures onto a ship."

"I don't know," said Marguerite. "They think it's all
a great adventure."

"Not them, silly. The horses." She shivered, remembering the hideous shrieks those horses had uttered on the
night of the shipwreck.

"Smile, will you?" Marguerite poked her. "You've
been so miserable lately. I'm the one who should be
pining away now that Nathaniel isn't coming home until
after Christmas on account of this beastly war. I should
be downcast, not you. Oh, Dorrie! Look who's arriving!
I haven't seen Roseanne for simply ages." She lowered
her voice, though there was no danger of anybody hearing her. "She was pregnant but the baby died."

"Rupert told me," said Dorrie. "They've had some
bad luck, haven't they?"

"The doctor says she must never have another, but as
Maman says, that's all very well for him, *non?* She's still
very weak, I'm surprised to see her. Let's go and talk to
her."

"You go," said Dorrie. Del was with her, maneu-
vering their new buggy into place at the end of the row.
She was thankful that two other vehicles stood between
them.

"Come on!" insisted Marguerite.

Dorrie ignored her. She kept her eyes fixed on the parade ground where the front row of men were now
kneeling, their rifles stabbing the air in front of them,
bayonets bright as slices of sunlight. Beyond them was a
row of tents like upturned canvas cornets and beyond that
the horses still restlessly tossed their heads.

The crowd was thickening now. People were arriving on foot and on bicycles. All wore hats, of course, the men boaters and bowlers, most of the women boaters with elaborate decorations perched on top like sitting roosters. Someone carried a placard that said, GOOD LUCK TO OUR BRAVE BOYS. People cheered.

Marguerite climbed out of the buggy and went to talk to Roseanne. The soldiers marched off the field and the mounted rifles came on, the horses loping easily as they circled the parade area. These soldiers had a different uniform, fawn trousers as sleek as their horses' coats, scarlet jackets with black braid and elaborate frogging on the sleeves, and little round hats with a pattern of braiding like one of Dora's crocheted doilies.

Rupert looked so *manly* as he sat proudly on Sateen that the sight of him took Dorrie's breath away. He had shaved off those horrid scraggy whiskers of his, keeping only a brush of moustache, and the wide band of his hat slung under his chin gave him an air of authority. Dorrie longed to glance along at Blacketts' buggy to see if Marguerite was watching Rupert, too.

He trotted Sateen forward, swung out of the saddle, stood at attention beside the horse, then tugged at the reins. With an awkward craning of his neck and a flailing of hoofs the horse lay down. There was a burst of applause.

"Do you have any idea how difficult it is to train them to do that?" asked a familiar voice, and Dorrie glanced down to see Del leaning both arms on the buggy door as he stared up at her with those clear blue eyes.

"I startled you," he said when she looked away. "You're looking well, Dorrie. More beautiful than ever, in fact."

She concentrated on Rupert. He knelt in the partial shelter of his horse's body and raised his rifle, fixing his aim at the apex of one of the conical tents.

"What do you think of all this palaver, Dorrie? Our brave boys, and all that. It's just a stupid, ritualistic

game. Children playing soldiers, dressing up in uniforms. Childish, that's what it is. Glory of the Empire,
what nonsense!''

Anger choked her but she kept her breathing even and
stared straight ahead. The worst of it was that she would
have agreed with him a year or more ago. She'd have
thought his arguments clever. At heart she had doubts
about this Glory of the Empire talk, but hearing Del belit-
tle Rupert and the others roused a fierce spirit of patriot-
ism in her.

''What do you think, Dorrie?'' he asked softly.

She watched Rupert, not daring to reply.

Rupert rocked slightly forward over his point of balance immediately before he fired his rifle, just before the
recoil thrust him back again. A swat of sound reached out
and hit them at the same time as they saw a puff of white
blossoming around the bayonet blade like a lily around a
black stamen. Dorrie wanted to clap. She longed to cry,
''Bravo!''

Roseanne screamed, ''Del! Come quickly! Del!''

Everybody craned their heads to see what was the matter. Marguerite was trying to unwind the buggy reins
while the Blacketts' horse, alarmed by the rifle fire,
pitched its head wildly, making a strange, scraping noise.
Roseanne was sitting bolt upright on the blue leather seat,
her narrow face wrung into an expression of anguish.

She's faking, thought Dorrie, guessing that a competent horsewoman like Roseanne would have no trouble
quieting the frightened animal.

Del obviously thought the same thing. ''She probably
prodded it with her umbrella,'' he said, as with an air of
disinterest he watched a cluster of youths surround the
buggy and calm the horse. Roseanne tossed her husband
a furious glance. Her cheeks were hot patches of red.

Del laughed.

Poor Roseanne, thought Dorrie.

Dora and Uncle Samuel were still on the verandah when

she returned swinging through the morning room to call out a cheery "Sorry I'm late," as she came. She stepped onto the verandah and held her breath when she saw the magnificent vista of crimson clouds and a scarlet sea.

"Aren't the sunsets spectacular at this time of year?" she said. "Sometimes I envy you, Auntie Dora. The whole world parades past here for your inspection. Just look at the gold sails on that clipper and the great fat rope of smoke that steam packet is trailing—it looks like a dog that's snapped its lead. Oh, and look at those Maori canoes! There must be a dozen of them, probably Maoris from the market going home for more produce for tomorrow. They certainly work hard, don't they? Up before dawn—"

"Yes," said Dora. "They all work. Maoris never let any of their old people feel useless and unwanted."

Dorrie's heart shrank as she looked from her aunt's stony face to Uncle Samuel, who shrugged helplessly. She was still shaken by Del's unpleasant intrusion into what should have been a delightful afternoon. Dora's acid bitterness curdled what was left of her happiness.

"Auntie, please—" she said.

"Don't mind me," said Dora in a martyr's tone. "Emere! I'll go inside now if you please." Emere stood up from where she had been dozing and moved drowsily to push the wheelchair inside.

When they were alone Dorrie said, "What am I going to do with her?"

He said nothing for a few moments, just watched as she unfolded her fan and began stirring up the air around her face and neck to keep the mosquitoes away. Then, when he did speak she stopped fanning and stared at him in surprise.

"You could stop being so selfish, lass," he said.

When she recovered her shock she rallied defensively. "Selfish!" she hissed in a low whisper. "How can you say that? Everything I've done has been for Auntie Dora."

"Now don't get on your indignation, for it's an uncomfortable mount that one, and impossible to ride. Here, sit down by me and hear me out, will you?"

She sat so close she was breathing the strong tobacco odor of his tweed jacket. He fixed his milky eyes on her and said, "Every time I come here I find Dora looking a mite more unhappy. She's been through a lot, and losing that leg was a bad blow for someone as independent as she's always been. Cast your mind back to when your Uncle Jon was alive. Dora was never happier than when she was fussing around him."

"But he exploited her, and so did Grandmaire, and Aunt Ellen was making shameless use of her when we lived in the gatehouse. Don't you see, Uncle Samuel, it galled me to see the way they treated her like a dogsbody, ordering her about and—"

He held up a scarred hand to stop her. "But she *likes* to be treated like that. She feels useful when she's working. You may not realize this, but your aunt has never known any other sort of a life. Grandmaire took her to work for her when she was but ten years old. She's been a lackey since Adam was a pup."

"Then all the more reason for her to enjoy some luxury now."

"You still don't understand, do you?" He took her hands and she felt as if they had been wrapped in stiff, dry paper. "I know you mean well. You've worked harder than a dozen lackeys yourself getting this business built up so that you could give your aunt everything, but somehow you've taken away what she most values. She's useless as a pet dog the way you've got her cooped up here. And don't say she hasn't complained, because I've heard her many times."

"She's never sat me down like this and explained," Dorrie said. "I've always assumed that nothing pleases her because of the pain. I even asked the doctor—"

Samuel said, "Do you know why she hasn't discussed the matter? Because she's sure you're ashamed of her."

"Ashamed?"

He nodded. "Because of her wheelchair. Because she's maimed. She thinks you don't want her to be seen in that flossy parlor of yours."

"Oh, Uncle Samuel!" Dorrie's voice thickened. "That simply isn't true."

"True or not, it's what she thinks. Oh, I know she makes excuses not to go out and about, and you've probably taken that to mean that she doesn't want to be seen in public, but cast your mind back, lass. When did Dora *ever* want to go out and about to entertainments and such? This is different. I know she wants to be a part of what you've got here."

"She shall be."

"Mind how you go about it," he warned.

"I'll take sick on Monday and be sick for a week," promised Dorrie. She gave him a wink.

"There's a good lass," he said.

"There's a letter for you," said Dora, propelling herself into the morning room with a bundle of letters and a pink-wrapped *Weekly News.*

Dorrie raised her head from the pillow on the chaise lounge and adjusted the rug that was spread over her fully clothed body. She was bored to distraction by the charade of pretended illness and longed to be back in the workroom. It was difficult remembering to sniff constantly in front of Dora and to keep her voice pitched to a low rasp but almost impossible to feign an indifference to what was going on just along the corridor. All morning she had heard the usual noises—the crunch of carriage wheels, the nickering of horses and muted voices from the garden as the grooms talked to each other while they waited for their mistresses to do their shopping—and they were bearable, but what quickened her blood and drove her to an itch of intolerable longing were the trills of feminine laughter and oohs of appreciation she could hear as Dora displayed sample models.

"I heard Mrs. Loppell's voice," she rasped as she pulled herself to a sitting position. "What did she choose? I had some of that midnight blue velvet put aside to show her."

"It was written in the book so I showed it to her. *And* she ordered a plain turban with black cabouchon trim *and* a white shepherdess. I talked her into that. She was saying she had nothing new for the New Year's Day races, so I assured her that white was the luckiest color I know." She smiled, "But you're not to worry your head about business. If there's something I need to ask, then I'll do so, right?"

"Right," groaned Dorrie, subsiding onto her pillow.

Dora said, "There's a letter here, from Mr. Rosser."

Propping herself up on one elbow, Dorrie turned it over with undisguised delight. It was thick and scuffed, bright with varicolored stamps all bearing the same picture of the Queen, and addressed in his heavy, confident handwriting to her. *Miss Dorinda Bennington,* she read. It was as if he were speaking her name aloud, and she could picture him as he penned it, his handsome head inclined over the writing desk, his thoughts for that moment focused entirely on her. The image was as delicious as chocolate and she held it carefully in her mind, not wanting it to melt.

"Dorinda," said her aunt.

Dorrie glanced up. The image melted. Dora was gazing at her with hardness and pity mingled in her shrewd expression. She held her hand out for the letter.

"If you want to be fair to yourself, and to him, you'll give it to me," she said.

"It will be business," pleaded Dorrie, forgetting to croak. "He took all those samples. There might be orders—"

"Then I'll tell you what they are."

Dorrie's gaze dropped from the outstretched palm to the letter. She knew that Dora was right; that it would be far better for her never to read what was inside that enveloping wrapper. She hesitated. It seemed worse that she should permit Dora to read it for that would mean a betrayal of Nathaniel's trust and of his private thoughts.

"I'll do it this way," she said. Thrusting the rug aside, she walked to the fireplace, removed the petit point firescreen, and touched a match to the heap of crumpled paper and kindling wood that was set ready in the grate. Astonished by how much force she had to employ to make herself do it, she tore the letter open and without permitting herself more than a single glance at each page she crushed the pages one by one and added them to the blaze. There were nine sheets of letter, each covered closely by that firm, dark script, followed by a page in which names and figures were set in rows. That she handed to Dora without comment. Eyes stinging from the smoke, Dorrie poked at the ashes until all the charred remains had been pulverized, then returned to her chaise lounge and pulled the rug back over her legs.

This time she did not have to fake misery.

For an hour after Dora had gone Dorrie lay quite still, staring at the ceiling. *He called me "My Dearest,"* she told herself over and over. Those words had leaped off the page at her, both from the first page where he had used them to begin the letter and from the last page where he had said "Until then, my dearest." *My Dearest!*

He loves me! she thought.

Then reality forced itself into her dreaming mind. Dora was right. In making Dorrie destroy that letter she was showing her that the only course of action was to cut off that relationship. She could never think of marrying Nathaniel, for deceiving him was more insidious than the nightmarish prospect of confession. He was no Bob Farrell to be married for convenience and security; he deserved the finest and loveliest of young women to be his wife, someone honest and pure and open-hearted who could offer him pristine love.

"Something I can never do," she whispered. "How

could I have been so stupid? Now I really love someone
and it's too late.''

On Saturday of that week Dorrie spent the evening alone.
Dora had been collected by Rupert to attend Ellen's forti-
eth birthday party, the celebratory dinner having been put
forward from Friday because of the restrictions the Cath-
olic "meatless day" placed on Fintona's cook. Because
Roseanne and Del would be there Dorrie had elected not
to go.

After luxuriating in a leisurely bath Dorrie wrapped
herself in a pink cotton dressing robe and was drying her
hair when the doorbell shrilled. Dorrie tucked her hair
into a toweling turban and padded to the door. Whoever
was calling would have to come back tomorrow, she
thought, as she opened the door a crack and peeked out
into the darkness.

"It's me—Mrs. Patene," said the figure behind the
wavering candle lamp. She sounded agitated. As soon as
Dorrie widened the gap she came pushing past, panting,
and by the light of the gas lamp in the hall Dorrie could
see that her face was creased with anxiety.

"Emily—I came to find Emily," she said, setting the
lamp down on the table and staring fixedly at Dorrie.
"She said she was working late tonight. Where is she
then, eh? I don't like to disturb her but this is important,
Miss Bennington. Boy, it's important all right."

"She's not here," said Dorrie, hugging the wrapper
around her body though she doubted that Mrs. Patene
had noticed her inadequate state of dress. "She and Auntie Dora have gone to Fintona. I stayed home because"—
she coughed—"because I've been fighting off a cold all
week."

Mrs. Patene glanced about distractedly.

"She's not here. Honestly she's not. But can I do anything to help you?"

She had never seen Mrs. Patene so disturbed.

"Look, sit down, at least. Would you like me to telephone Fintona? If it's something urgent I'm sure that Auntie Dora could manage without her.''

"Tele—?''

"The telephone.'' Dorrie indicated the full-breasted object on the wall nearby. "I can call her on that.''

"Oh, would you? Would you tell her to come home now, eh? Can Miss Bennington manage? Boy, I'm so worried that I don't know what to do.'' She thrust out a folded blue paper for Dorrie to read. "It's my boy Albert.''

Dorrie knew what it was before she unfolded it. Rupert had received one to say that he would be sailing next week on the troop ship. "Albert *Button?*'' she read.

"It's the *pakeha*, the European way to say Patene.'' She clutched the sides of her black headscarf, moaning. "The army won't take Maoris, so he even lied about his name to get in. The Queen don't like blacks to fight blacks, that's what he said. Oh, Miss Bennington, we had a terrible row, eh, and he just ran out.'' She was trembling like a dog that was anticipating a blow. "All this time and he's been lying to me. He said he had to study but all the time he's learning to be a soldier. I have to stop him, to talk some sense into that stupid head of his.''

"We all do stupid things.''

"Eh?'' The woman was utterly distracted now. "All I can think of is, my Emily might know what to do.''

"Then I'll call her. Sit down here, Mrs. Patene. There, don't cry. I'll have her sent home to you right away.''

The doorbell rang again not two minutes after she had farewelled Mrs. Patene with the assurance that Emere would be waiting for her when she arrived home.

Guessing that it was the old woman again with something she'd forgotten, Dorrie swung the door wide but when she saw who it was the smile chilled and she quickly pushed it shut again. She was too late.

"Dorrie!" said Del, leaning on the door and forcing her to step back out of the way. "I'm glad I found you up. Your aunt said you'd be here alone, so I thought I'd pop away from the party for a few minutes and square up one or two things with you."

Dorrie barely heard him. She glanced out at the moonlit night where the stars reflected in a million sequins on the harbor and wondered whether she could catch up to Mrs. Patene if she fled after her. Then the door snipped shut and she and Del were alone with only the faint hiss of the gas lamps.

"Don't be afraid of me, Dorrie," he said in that same soft voice he'd used at the military demonstration.

Dorrie shook her head. *I'll ring Fintona again,* she thought, but at that instant the telephone dribbled out the long jangle which meant another of the five hundred subscribers was trying to attract the solitary operator's attention.

He was looking all around, nodding his head with approval over the cream and floral carpet, the embossed wallpaper, the tranquil landscape paintings, and the Italian marble statue of Cupid and the Three Graces.

"Very nice, but then you always did have good taste," he said. "Ah, *Le Chapeau!*" He read the sign on the wall. "You don't mind if I have a look along there, do you?"

Dorrie couldn't believe this. "Del, I do mind. I only opened the door because I thought it was Mrs. Patene again. I'm not in a fit state to have you barge in, and besides I—"

"Never mind about that. This is me, remember?"

She did indeed, and was silent, following with impotent anger as he strolled into the *Le Chapeau* salon and, by the light slanting in from the hall, found his way to one of the gas sconces.

"Please go away," she said in a small voice, knowing it was useless, knowing he would take no notice of her. His manner was pushy yet breezily friendly as if he were

striving hard to make a good impression with the hope of
ultimate personal gain. Except that he had nothing to gain
from her and no chance of making any kind of an impression.

The gas lamp flared into light, illuminating this elegant room with a soft glow. He gazed around, nodding in
appreciation, admiring the hats perched on slender
mushrooms and the Gainsborough reproductions of
ladies stylishly attired in enormous full-brimmed hats
with curling plumes.

She looked at him in despair, praying he would leave.
Since his marriage he had grown sleek and plump-
jowled, a man well satisfied with himself, she thought.
He was dressed in the latest fashion, pegged trousers and
high-buttoned waistcoat of rusty-colored tweed and a
velvet jacket brown as freshly ploughed earth.

"I recall how you used to talk about your dream of setting your aunt up in a beautiful house with her own carriage and the finest and most expensive of everything.
I'm so glad for you, Dorrie. It must be very fulfilling to
achieve everything you ever wanted."

She did not reply but wondered what he was leading up
to.

"When you look back on your life, I wonder what
you'll think of as the happiest times? Now, when you've
got everything you aimed for, or will you think of me and
of those glorious afternoons we spent together?"

She stared at him, incredulous. His eyes were very
pale in the lamplight and he was watching her face with
an expression of hunger.

"Del, please." She swallowed. "I *never* think of—
that. I never shall. I've made up my mind that since it
was all a terrible mistake I shall pretend that none of it
ever happened."

Except for the paying, she thought bitterly. That mistake is something I'll pay dearly for as long as I feel emotions, as long as I can yearn and care—

"I don't believe you." His voice was very soft now.

"It's true. I never think of you, Del. So please go away."

He looked stunned. "But you're constantly on *my* mind. Don't you know what that mistake—as you call it—cost *me?*"

She said briskly, "Please go back to Fintona—to the party. Everybody will be wondering where you are."

He shook his head. "Not until this is sorted out. Do you know how I feel knowing that you keep away from your own relatives' celebrations because I might be there? That you go out of your way to avoid me? Oh, don't deny it. I know it's true."

She shrugged. Her turban was beginning to itch and she could feel a trickle of cold water down the back of her neck. If only he would go! Couldn't he see that none of this mattered any longer?

"My life is miserable because of you. Does that surprise you?" He waited a few seconds for some reaction, then dropped his gaze to a roll-brimmed shepherdess hat and rubbed some of the bobbinet veiling between his fingers.

"Please don't touch that."

"Sorry." He flinched at the sharpness in her tone, then grimaced unhappily. "You've never spoken to me like that before. Look, Dorrie, I realize that this is an awkward time for you. I mean, the way you're dressed—I don't want to embarrass you. I just thought, what with you being on your own it might be a perfect time—but I can see it's not. Do you think I might perhaps—meet you somewhere one day soon?" And when she gaped at him in disbelief he hastened to add, "Just to talk."

"Del, I have nothing to say to you! I never will have. *Never!*"

"But you must!" He was boyishly eager, anxious to convince her of what? His sincerity? "Don't you know what an empty life I have? It's unendurable, Dorrie. If I'd never met you it might have been different, bearable in fact, but you taught me what real love is, and frankly I was a fool not to recognize it at the time.''

His sincerity was unmistakable, but it failed to move her. She looked into his sky blue eyes, those eyes that had once thrilled her with their intensity, and felt nothing but traces of mild pity.

"I'm sorry," she told him, "but it was your choice. It's all gone now. All dropped into the past."

"I can't accept that." He took two steps toward her, hesitated when he saw the hardness in her face, then took another. "Dorrie, I still love you. What can I do?"

"Nothing. Nothing at all." She stood her ground; he was so close that she was breathing the spicy tang of whatever he had used to dress his hair, yet she felt no warmth, either toward him or from him. Though he had explained himself in the clearest terms, she was still at a loss to know why he was here. How could he be so insensitive?

"Your wife will be wondering where you are," she said, thinking as she spoke that these days she never permitted him into her thoughts in any guise other than that of Roseanne's husband.

"My wife?" He smiled wryly, as if to say what a mockery that was.

"If it's any comfort, I'm sorry for you both."

"Sorry? How can you say such a thing? After all we shared? After all the love—the beautiful times we spent together?" His eyes were fixed hungrily on her face again and he glided toward her so smoothly that she did not notice him take those extra steps. "Oh, Dorrie, I've missed you."

"No, Del. No, I warn you—"

"I've ached for you, Dorrie." His arms slid around her and contracted as he drew her close to him and groped with his mouth to kiss her.

She panicked. "Del, no!" With the heels of her hands she shoved at his chest and then at his neck, but she was unable to break his grip on her, until with one concen-

trated push she found a vulnerable spot on his throat and
drove him backwards. Immediately he tried to grab her
again.

"Dorrie, please— I'm not trying to hurt you—"

But his reassurances were too late. Blind with desperation, she snatched up a hatted mushroom and swung it
above her head, dashing it down with force. It struck him
above one eyebrow, tearing the thin skin that lay across
the bone and freeing an ooze of blood. Del swayed back a
pace, bewildered.

"I wasn't trying to hurt you. I never wanted to hurt
you," he said.

The words echoed in her head after she had shut the
door on him and leaned against it, sobbing with relief. *He
didn't mean to hurt me,* she thought, smarting with the
irony of it and knowing it was true, just as it was true that
he had always loved her but that other things—his own
nature, for one—had somehow pushed between him and
that love.

Not that it mattered. It was over now.

As she brushed and braided her damp hair something
else occurred to her, something grotesque. In coming
here tonight Del had offered her the only kind of love she
could ever hope for now, illicit back-door embraces, furtive encounters. An old maid's consolation.

Oh, Lord, she thought. *Oh, Lord, it's a sin I know, but
sometimes I wish I were dead.*

Twenty

We don't want to fight but by jingo if we do,
We've got the men,
We've got the guns,
We've got the money, too!

So sang Marguerite as she swayed around the grass court in her long white afternoon gown and wide white hat with the single rose—her "ice cream with a cherry on top" outfit. Brandishing her spherical tennis racquet as a music hall entertainer might use a parasol, she postured prettily even though her only audience was Dorrie, who waited with dwindling patience at the other end to be served with the ball.

"It's too hot to play. We should have gone swimming instead," said Dorrie. She sprawled on the grass and stared up at the sky.

"You'll ruin your hat." Marguerite subsided in a puff of white skirts beside her. Her face was beaded with perspiration.

"I'll have to get a milliner to fix it. Do you know a good milliner you could recommend? Oooh, but it feels good to be having a break. No more hats and no more customers until next year."

"Except for the husbands who come creeping round tomorrow looking sheepish and asking you to whip up a little something for the missus for a Christmas surprise. Remember what happened last year, and you had to drag Iris and three of the other girls away from cooking their Christmas puddings."

Dorrie opened one eye. She was so tired that she could

349

have dropped off to sleep in the cool shade. "This year I have two dozen little 'somethings for the Missus' waiting with cards and specially decorated hatboxes. Auntie Dora telephoned the newspaper and had them insert a discreetly phrased message to advertise the fact." She wrinkled her nose. "It's not working out completely having Auntie Dora in running the *salon*. She does tend to *tell* customers what they're going to have instead of helping them choose what they want, and I know she's scared away one or two of my favorite ladies, and when Iris and I concoct something really special for display I have to keep it hidden because if Auntie Dora sees it she's at the telephone before you could say 'Mesopotamia' telling Aunt Ellen to come around quickly, there's something new here that she'd simply *adore!*" She smiled ruefully. "But on the whole I have to admit that Uncle Samuel was right, that funny old stick. It's pleasant having Auntie so happy these days. She's even insisting on baking the Christmas cakes. That's what she's doing in all this heat, would you believe it? I wish she wouldn't—her cakes are terrible, they taste like straw bricks and we'll all have to eat big chunks to be polite—but when I was about to stop her, I remembered what Uncle Samuel said and left her to it."

"Now that she's helping you, perhaps you'll change your mind and join the Auckland Amazons, *non?* Sylvia Prescott will be leaving our ranks when she gets married next week. First Roseanne, then Bertha, Mabel, then Violet and now Sylvia. All matching up! She sighed gustily and Dorrie, fearful that she was about to launch into one of her mournful dirges about Nathaniel, hastened to divert her.

"Tell me about these Amazons. They sound like a scream."

"A scream? It's serious! We wear proper military uniforms with slouch hats and chin straps and those bandoliers that hold bullets around us, you know, like mourning sashes. When we are drilled to perfection we shall march in public, at the race meetings and along

Queen Street on Saturday evenings. Don't laugh!" She tugged at a clump of grass and flung the fine shreds in Dorrie's face. It's all very respectable, and not in the least ridiculous. Even Mr. Richard Seddon's daughter is an Amazon, in the Wellington platoon."

"Ah, well, if it's good enough for the Prime Minister's daughter—"

"Will you then? Will you join us?"

"I can't." She sat up, her attention caught by the sound of horses approaching. "You know I'm too busy to—"

It was May Teipa-Bennington, riding through the domain with her husband, both on splendid black horses. May's had a large, leather saddlebag from which protruded the wooden legs of a folding tripod.

"Just what I want," she called, dismounting. "Two ladies at leisure and both in purest white. How would you like to pose for me? I need something special for the annual Photographic Society Grand Competition, and I'm looking for something different, not the usual landscapes."

"We'll pose, won't we, Dorrie?" twittered Marguerite.

"Of course," said Dorrie, flattered to see that May was wearing a *Le Chapeau* riding bonnet of black trimmed with lemon.

Patrick posed with the girls, *à la Manet,* as he put it. May disappeared under the black cloth, and from there called directions and reprimands to her husband, who was whispering to the girls and making them giggle.

As she was packing the camera back into her saddlebag May interrupted the flow of casual chatter by suddenly saying, "Nathaniel is worried, Dorrie. He tells us that he hasn't had replies to any of the letters he's written you. You have been receiving them, haven't you?"

There was a blank silence. May looked from Dorrie's ashen face to Marguerite and then back again. "Oh, my heavens, I've put my foot in it," she said. "Look, I'm sorry."

"No," said Dorrie swiftly. "No, you haven't."

"What letters?" demanded Marguerite.

"All I've had have been orders from London stores for consignments of hats, that's all. You've seen those, Marguerite."

May opened her mouth to protest but was stopped by the expression in Dorrie's eyes. "I see," she said quietly. "Well, thank you for posing for me, both of you."

Marguerite stood stock-still beside Dorrie as they watched the two gallop away down the dappled path and disappear between the stands of young oaks. Then she turned to Dorrie, her face suffused with anger.

"You've had *letters* from him! He's *written* to you! He's written you *letters* and you never so much as shared one with me!"

"Marguerite, I haven't."

"Don't lie to me! No wonder you're not very interested in talking about him. No wonder you don't want to listen to news of him! You know it all before I do!"

Her rage terrified Dorrie. Her mouth was a slit and she spat out words in sharp hissing sounds as she thumped her fists against her thighs. Though she wanted to back away, Dorrie stayed where she was, forcing herself to keep calm, and when Marguerite raised her fists to strike her, Dorrie quickly seized her wrists.

"Listen to me!" she pleaded. "I'm telling you the truth. Look at me! Listen! I swear to you that I have never read one sentence of personal news written by Mr. Rosser. Not one sentence. *That's the truth.*"

Marguerite stopped struggling. Her eyes searched Dorrie's face and she exhaled a long, shuddering breath.

"You are telling the truth, *non?*"

"*Non.* I mean, yes, I am. You know I am."

To her enormous relief Marguerite accepted that, and by the time they were halfway home Marguerite was chattering away as if nothing had happened to ruin the afternoon, laughing about Del, who had gone home from Ellen's birthday party at Fintona and had been discovered later lying in the roadway. He had gone home to check on his hen-houses, he said, and had been set upon by footpads come to steal his prize fowls.

"He had a nasty blow right above his eye, and some of his hens were missing, though Roseanne says they were found next day roosting in the hedge. A likely story, n'est-ce pas?"

"I don't know," said Dorrie.

"Roseanne says he was probably drunk," continued Marguerite. "She says that's all he does these days. Drinks and shouts at her."

"How very sad," said Dorrie.

"You can't wriggle out of this with some flimsy excuse," declared Marguerite, bursting into the workroom one sweltering afternoon in late February where Dorrie was going over the accounts with Iris Pine and young Mr. Flannery, their new bookkeeper. "It's the first film of the South African campaign and *Maman* says you must come and see it again with us—we've seen it twice already—because she wants to thank you for that beautiful hat you gave her."

"That's nothing." Dorrie had presented Marguerite and her mother with hats as New Year gifts after discovering that Dora had once again weakened and given the best of their model collection to Ellen.

Iris looked up. "That Cinematograph thing? The one about *Our Brave Lads?* Oooh, but you'll have to queue for ages for that, you will. They say in the first day more than three thousand people were linin' up to see it, and at a shillin' a pop—" She broke off, laughing and showing all the gaps in her teeth. "Silly me! Your dad's the boss of the Empire, isn't he? There'll be no queuin' for you!"

"I can't come," said Dorrie automatically. "We're too busy—"

Iris poked her in the ribs with a stubby finger. "Go on, miss, an' have fun. Your Mr. Rosser's in that, large as life up there on the screen."

"He's *not* my— Oh, what's the use."

"We won't miss you. You could be gone for a month an' this place would keep on running along."

"I don't know whether that's a comforting thought or not," said Dorrie.

Nathaniel wasn't in the film at all—Iris had said that just to provoke a reaction, as Marguerite speculated sourly— but Rupert was there and both girls agreed that he looked very handsome falteringly swinging his leg up over Sateen's saddle in the hurtfully bright, flickering gray of the film. Dorrie thought she saw him again in the scene captioned "Foraging for Firewood" but Marguerite said no, Rupert was much taller and thinner. Then the people in front told them to be quiet because they couldn't hear the piano music. There was plenty happening on the screen, no fighting, of course, but lots of horses and mules trotting endlessly through desert wastelands, all spaced out to present a scattered target. The landscape looked as featureless as crumbled bread and Dorrie felt sorrier for the poor horses than she did for the men; *they* hadn't asked to be taken to that forsaken place where there was no grass, no trees for shade, and no cool streams to roll in.

"Such an adventure!" repeated Marguerite on the way home. "Tents and dugouts and sleeping under the stars. I do wish that I could be there, too."

"Women go there as nurses," Dorrie reminded her.

At once she was floundering for excuses. "I can't—I mean, I couldn't—trust you to be practical."

It was only to be expected. Marguerite often said she wished she could do this or that, but unless the idea was one that would prove purely amusing, Marguerite would never expend any energy on it.

Dorrie rescued her. "You have your Amazons group.

That's a worthwhile contribution, isn't it? After all, Mr.
Seddon says that with you ladies to defend us, New
Zealand is safe from even the most savage enemy at-
tack."

"You're laughing at us again."

"I'm not. After seeing that Cinematograph the last
thing I feel like doing is laughing, because I've realized
today that this war isn't the great lark Rupert made it out
to be. He could be hurt—or killed."

"So could Mr. Rosser," whispered Marguerite. "Oh,
I wish he would come back to this part of the world where
he belongs. He's been away an age already and there's no
hint of him coming back."

Mrs. Dupton glared at her daughter and jabbered
something in rapid French.

"Oui, *Maman,*" she responded sulkily.

She doesn't like Marguerite talking about him, either,
thought Dorrie.

Dorrie was arranging a silver vase of apricot-colored
roses in the salon when Dora wheeled in with a large flat
package in her hands. Nodding to dismiss Emere, she
thrust the package at Dorrie and grimly ordered her to
open it.

"It won first prize at the Grand Competition," said
Dora tersely as the wrappings fell away and Dorrie found
that she was holding a crisp, beautifully detailed, yet
softly moody photograph of two girls in white gowns and
a gentleman, all relaxing on the lawn under a tree.

Dora continued. "The photographs were auctioned to
raise money for charity, and Mrs. Loppell bid success-
fully for that. She telephoned to say that she was sending
it around as a gift for you. 'You might like to have it
framed to display in your home,' she said. Those were
her very words!" Dora paused, but Dorrie said nothing.
There was nothing she could say, after all.

"Can you imagine how humiliated I felt when she told

me about it? Everybody in Auckland knows about my father and that *person's* mother, the shame of it—''

"But it's not his fault. He's nice, really he is.''

"Nice! Those people killed Jon. Don't you care about that?''

For a moment Dorrie wondered if her aunt were going to hit her, or else tear the photograph in two to show her contempt, but suddenly the spirit seemed to ooze out of her and she slumped into the chair looking old and pathetic.

"Emere!'' she called.

The two looked at each other and Dorrie looked away first. There was the subtle scent of roses and the sound of the telephone tinkling out in the hall, then Emere's footsteps running to answer it.

Dorrie was ashamed. She wanted to explain but knew that it wasn't the harmless encounter that Dora really objected to; it was the fact that her friendship with the Teipa-Benningtons had been blown up out of all proportion along with the negative, and that she was displayed as one of their close friends for all of Auckland to see.

"Telephone!'' chirped Emere, dashing in to wheel Dora out to the hall. "It's Mrs. Bennington from Fintona and she sounds in a big hurry, eh.''

Dorrie was still staring glumly at the roses when the wheelchair squeaked back to the doorway again.

"That was Ellen,'' said Dora tonelessly. "Rupert has been wounded. She's just heard. Sateen was killed, and Rupert's in a field hospital.''

"Oh, no! Is he—''

"They haven't heard how badly, but Ellen says she needs me. I think it will be best if I go to stay at Fintona for a few days.''

Dorrie nodded. *One disaster after another!* she thought.

This war has touched us all, reflected Dorrie as she

paused during *Le Chapeau*'s Christmas party to study the faces around her.

Resting her fingers on the piano keyboard, she took time to muse that their lives were not as insulated as she sometimes liked to think. It suited her often to pretend that nastiness and violence were far outside their lives, snug as they were here in their pretty cocoon lined with lace and bright silks and velvets. But it was impossible to avoid the fact that the war across the world had touched each one of them in some way. Betty had lost a cousin, Rose's husband had come home wounded, and Iris, poor Iris's husband, had not come home at all. He was buried somewhere near Mafeking. Vinny and Mary and Maude all had young men still away, fighting, and though young Elizabeth, the high-spirited new lass, always leaned out of the workshop window to flirt carelessly with any handsome groom that passed by, Dorrie knew that she was at heart deeply worried about her brother who had not been heard from in almost two months. And the Patene girls . . .

"Come on, miss!" cried Iris, wondering why Dorrie was so quiet and thoughtful all of a sudden. "Let's be having another. *Ta-rara-boom-de-re!* How about that one, miss? Do you know that one?"

"Indeed I do," said Dorrie with a wry smile, for the tune always stirred up unwelcome memories of that ridiculous wedding breakfast she had shared with Mr. Farrell.

"Come on then!" cried Iris, a jolly figure in black.

"Not now," said Dorrie, standing up and turning to face them all. "Now that the food's all eaten, and that most of the songs have been sung, there is something serious that I want to say to you. On that shelf over there you may have noticed a dozen miniature hatboxes, just like the ones we used for our overseas samples. When you take them down, you will notice that each one is labeled with a name—your names—and that they don't contain hats at all, but a gift for each of you from Miss Bennington and me, and also a bonus, some extra money which I've calculated by counting how many days each of you worked this year." She held up both hands, asking for silence. "It's lovely if you want to thank us, but really, we are the ones who should be thanking you. *Le Chapeau* is a great success and has been almost from the first day, partly because Mr. Rosser was able to lend his professional assistance to the venture and prevent us from making a few basic mistakes, such as the ones I made before. But as I'm sure he would acknowledge the real success is due wholly to you ladies. I know that many of you have personal problems, people at home who depend on you, young children prey to ill health, and worries about your menfolk away fighting, but despite all manner of hardships and suffering you girls have constantly given us your loyalty, your industry, and your careful attention. That last quality is the most important of them all, and I do appreciate the way you always give me your best work—it's never shoddy or half-hearted but always meticulous."

"It's got ter be, ain't it!" piped up Elizabeth with a toss of her gingery curls.

The others laughed and Dorrie smiled. "True," she admitted. "I don't suppose any of you would last here long if Iris found real fault with your work, but she hasn't, has she? We appreciate your care, and the fortunate ladies who buy your hats appreciate it, too. And how could we have won those overseas orders if every snip of your scissors wasn't precisely measured and every stitch invisible? You deserve those bonuses, so have fun spending them and a Merry Christmas to you all."

She sat down amid enthusiastic applause as Uncle Samuel entered, pushing Dora's wheelchair. "You missed the speeches," Iris told them.

"Is that what it was? I thought there was a riot," joked Samuel and the girls all laughed in appreciation.

Samuel's gaze lingered on Dorrie as she turned back to the keyboard and struck out the first few chords of "Sons of Zealandia." Who would have picked her as a busi-

nesswoman, he marveled, admiring her poise, her flawless grooming, and that fresh beauty that always reminded him somehow of a newly opened rose. There was
something dewy and untouched about her. Bending low
so that he could whisper in Dora's ear, he commented
that it was a pity Dorrie was wasting herself on business.

The reaction astonished him. "Only a man would say
a fool thing like that," she snapped at him. "Dorrie pre-
fers work to being married so you might as well know
that now." She tapped his knuckles sharply with her folded
fan. "And don't you go trying to turn her head, either. Her
mind's made up and that's the way it's staying."

"You don't say," he replied, thinking that May Yardley had once said much the same thing and now look at
her, ten children and another on the way.

Dora twisted her head and glared at him as if she could
read his thoughts. "I do say, so don't you go stirring in,"
she warned him.

Samuel was silent. He wondered how much truth there
was in May's theory that Dora was intercepting Dorrie's
letters from that nice young Mr. Rosser. May was adamant that he'd written to her many times and said that
Dorrie insisted she'd received none of them. It was all
very odd. Would Dora be capable of interfering like that
to break up a promising relationship for her own selfish
reasons?

Samuel stared down at the top of her head. All he
could see was the frilled black lace cap, a curve of
doughy cheek, and then the flash of greenstone as Dora
caressed *Riversong* with her plump white fingers. Surely
Dora wouldn't . . .

"She's a beautiful lass," he repeated defiantly. "Such
a pity to let her go to waste."

"Fetch me a cup of tea, you old fool," said Dora.

The party was over. Vinny and Mary were helping wash
dishes in the kitchen, Maude was wiping down the tables
while Rose and Iris unpinned decorations from the walls

and Betty and the others swept the floor. Suddenly a
shriek from Elizabeth had them all running to hang,
gaping, out of the workshop windows.

Puffing and snorting in the middle of the driveway was
a contraption like an outsize baby perambulator with four
rubber-tired wheels and a silly little step like a grain
scoop. Sitting up high, looking not only precarious but
uncomfortable, muffled as they were to the eyes in winter
coats, scarves, and hats, were Marguerite, Mrs. Dupton,
and a proudly beaming Rupert.

"He's home!" screamed Iris, for once her voice
louder than Elizabeth's. "Miss Dorrie, come quick, he's
home! An' look what he's ridin' in!"

"It's one o' 'em 'orseless coaches, that," said Elizabeth.

"Nathaniel," whispered Dorrie, suddenly weak. She
hurried to the front door and pushed past Dora and Uncle
Samuel. When she saw who it was, disappointment hit
her so hard that her legs almost gave way and she
clutched at Samuel's arm to stop herself from falling.

"Isn't that a fine sight?" said Samuel. "We know he's
safe now, don't we?" Leaving Emere to push Dora down
the ramp, he strode out toward the carriage, saying,
"Strike me pink! Well, strike me pink!"

"Do you want to take it for a drive, Uncle Samuel?"
offered Rupert.

"Don't!" called Dora. "It looks as if it might bite."

Marguerite was bouncing out of one side while Rupert, leaving the beast snorting gently where it was,
swung his stiff leg out and placed it, with a care that betrayed pain, onto the step.

Marguerite said, "It arrived with him, on the same
ship. *C'est magnifique, non?* What a journey we've had
here! Everybody stares and the dogs run after us,
barking. It's nerve-shattering, I can tell you."

Dorrie's eyes were fixed on Rupert. His jaw quivered
as he stepped down to the ground. His hurt foot came
down with a jarring thud that rocked him sideways but

only momentarily, and he clutched the side of the carriage until he could fix his grin in place again.

That could have been Nathaniel, thought Dorrie. *But for God's grace he could have been injured like that.*

Rupert's little show was worthy of the Empire Theater, she thought as she watched him greet everybody—Timmins the gardener, the girls who were clustering outside the service door—then with only his iron-set jaw revealing the effort it cost him to walk he strolled back and greeted Dora with an embrace and a kiss.

"Emere!" he said and glanced at the brooch pinned to her smock bodice, Albert's portrait and a wisp of his hair, black as a moustache, twisted into an oval silver frame. Dorrie hated it; it made her feel uneasy, like the wall of photographs in the Patenes' cottage.

He had never spoken to Emere before; Dorrie was surprised that he even knew her name. It was all part of his act, she guessed, as he nodded at it and said, "Sergeant Button, isn't it? Don't worry, your Albert's doing fine out there. He visited me once in the field hospital. I asked him how long he thought the hostilities would last and he said a hundred years, at least."

"A hundred years?" Emere's face was blank.

"It's only a joke," he explained. "That the war will last from the nineteenth century to the twentieth. It will do that, all right. Just over two weeks to go, hey?"

Marguerite was squeezing Dorrie's arm. She whispered, "Nathaniel will be here soon. He's stopped to visit his father in Sydney, and Rupert says he'll be on the first steam packet after Christmas. Just think of it! He might be here to help us celebrate seeing out the old century and seeing in the new. *Magnifique, non?*"

"Marvelous," said Dorrie. She watched Rupert's face. He was darkly tanned now, and thin as cured leather. She wondered if Nathaniel would be tanned, too, and if his face would have acquired that same wise yet sad expression that she could see here, deep in Rupert's eyes. She wanted to ask him a thousand questions and every one with Nathaniel's name attached, but because Marguerite was there she only smiled at Rupert and told him how wonderful it was to see him.

Twenty-one

The pilot boat dropped Nathaniel at the jetty closest to Fintona. "Wish me luck!" he called as he leaped onto the scuffed boards.

"Luck, Mr. Rosser?" queried the pilot with a dry laugh. "What would you be wanting more luck for?" he shouted above the grumble of the engine. "If I had half yours I'd count myself the luckiest man alive."

The boat moved away in a beating of froth and Nathaniel stood on the bank, the early morning sun warming his back as he scanned the clifftop. Little seemed to have altered in the twenty months since he had been away, just a tree or two chopped down and others grown taller, a house above the Patenes' cottage where there was only hillside before and, at Dorrie's, a dainty blue and gray gazebo on the hilltop above the glorious paintbox spill of colors. It was just as Marguerite had described it in one of her frequent, politely received but dreaded letters. Dorrie had designed the gazebo herself and it did look like a hatbox, with its striped sides and curl of wrought iron, a delicate, lacy bow on the top. Nobody could fail to see *Le Chapeau* now.

Leaning against a stump near the top of the path, Rupert was licking his fingers as he turned the pages of a book.

"How's your leg, old buddy?" asked Nathaniel, startling him. He picked the book up and read, *"Red as a Rose is She."*

Rupert snatched it off him. "My leg is healing, and it gives me all the attention I'd hoped for—well, almost. And as for this," he tapped the book, "what you have

363

planned for today is far soppier, if you don't mind my saying so."

"You may say what you please."

"I will then. I honestly don't know if it will work. Dorrie hasn't mentioned you once, not once." He saw Nathaniel's face tighten and added, "I rather suspect that it might be because of Marguerite. She's there all the time and I mean *all* the time. Whenever I've mentioned your name I've watched Dorrie to see what her reaction is, but Marguerite watches her, too." He shrugged. "It's pretty discouraging, really. I had visions of coming home a hero and having Marguerite fuss around me—she does, but it's not the way I'd hoped."

"Things might change after today. I thought I'd go out to Duptons' first and have a quiet word with Marguerite. Tell her frankly what the situation is. What about the picnic? Is that all arranged?"

"To the letter of your instructions. The kitchen staff is buzzing with speculation, wondering which fortunate young lady I'm favoring today." He began to walk very carefully towards the stables. "You've got a full day in front of you, so you'd better be on your way. I'd offer you a cup of tea but I don't want to disillusion the kitchen staff. They think I'm turning into a proper devil."

"I'll get something at the Duptons'. I mayn't be welcome there after today so might as well make the most of it. Wish me luck, will you?"

"I certainly will," said Rupert. "If anybody needs it, you do."

A long trestle table had been set up near the fig trees on the lawn behind *Le Chapeau*. Dorrie was there, helping spread the starched tablecloths and arrange the punchbowl and glass cups and the silver dishes of wrapped toffees, nuts, and boiled sweets.

Nathaniel left the gig in the care of the stable-boy, and following the lad's directions, he strolled through the rose garden until he heard her voice.

"Isn't it exciting, Mr. Timmins?" she said. "The last day of the century. What a wonderful landmark to be celebrating! No, Mr. Timmins, we'll have those chairs over here, if you would."

Nathaniel slowed his steps, listening, absorbed by the sound of her, all other senses muted as he strained to catch each lilt and inflection. Her voice had altered, he noticed. Some of the shy deference had melted away and there was now a new, firmer note of authority there.

It was not until he reached the splashy shade of the grape arbor that he saw her and stopped, catching his breath, surprised anew by her beauty. She looked so poised and sure of herself that he wondered again whether his rash plan would succeed. A sweet, biddable Dorrie might be swayed by powerful persuasion but this self-possessed young woman looked as if she could not be coerced.

She was discussing luncheon arrangements with Mr. Timmins, one hand raised to shade her eyes in a gesture of unselfconscious grace. She wore a butter-colored silk blouse; its long sleeves were styled in the latest fashion with extravagant bunched gathers from shoulder to elbow. A long skirt of brown velveteen fit her slimly, and in an odd and appealing contrast her hair was pulled back softly and tied high at the back of her head with a narrow brown ribbon.

Sensing that she was being observed, Dorrie glanced up across the grassy court and saw him.

One hand fluttered to her throat and even at that distance he could see that she gasped, both thrilled and terrified to see him. *Terrified of what?* he thought as he strove to close that distance between them. *Of me? Surely not!*

She swallowed. There were no words of greeting, only a dry whisper, "You're not expected until tomorrow."

"That's the general idea. I came to see you alone."

Mr. Timmins was beaming and twisting his cap between his hands. He waited for Nathaniel to nod to him, then said, "How very nice ter see you, sir."

Uncle Samuel's voice rang out, too. "Rosser! Well, strike me pink!" He was leaning heavily on his stick as he picked his way across the croquet lawn toward them. In the background Dora was sitting in her favorite place on the verandah, the vantage point from which she could watch the world's comings and goings. Her face was turned toward them, her hands folded in her lap, and Nathaniel could see the dark sheen of *Riversong* pillowed against the slate gray fabric of her gown.

Nathaniel bowed slightly to Dora as Samuel called, "This is my lucky day indeed, young man! I thought I was going to have to sit up at luncheon with no moral support whatsoever, a lone rooster amongst clacking hens, but now you can join me, and welcome."

"No, Uncle Samuel," said Dorrie quickly, then she recovered her manners and added, "Of course you *are* very welcome, and we've enough food for a proverbial army . . ."

He was watching her steadily, but she was unable to meet his eye. Instead she glanced about distractedly, from the trestle table set and decorated with pretty touches he recognized as hers, to his boots, to the balloon-and-ribbon-festooned awning.

"Sorry to have to break up the party, but I'm taking you out for lunch."

"Out?" she asked his boots.

"A picnic. Just the two of us, Dorrie. You and me. Alone."

"Alone?" She did look at him then, a clear-eyed, startled look that would have suited a woodland deer.

Uncle Samuel heard this exchange, too. Though Mr. Timmins had quickly retreated a tactful distance beyond earshot, Samuel hobbled closer, his eyes alert and interested.

"You and I have unfinished business to settle, Dorrie, and we're going to settle it today. So get your bonnet on and let's go. Oh, and a wrap might not be a bad idea, either. It could be cold again by the time we come back.''

"Cold?'' She was still gaping at him, uncomprehending.

"Yes, we could be gone all day.''

The enormity of what he was suggesting penetrated at last. He was going to propose marriage to her; he was virtually proposing to her *now* for that matter, and by the look of grinning delight on Uncle Samuel's face *he* thought it a splendid idea. Well, little did he know how impossible such a notion was. Not that it was any of his business.

Her chin lifted a fraction. "It's very kind of you to invite me, Nathaniel, but I'm afraid it's impossible. What you see here— We've having an 'End of the Century' party and all the girls who work here, and—and *Marguerite* will be—''

"I've just come from Marguerite,'' he said quietly. "I've already told her. I don't think she'll be here.''

Dorrie could feel the jaws closing on her. What defense did she have when every protest she raised would be immediately answered, every objection swiftly overruled? She glanced helplessly at Uncle Samuel for He winked at her. *Winked!*

"Nathaniel, I can't come. I truly can't.''

He was laughing; that sidelight with old Mr was amusing and it told him that he had one fi least. "Of course you can. And you will. They without you here, isn't that so, Mr. Peridot?'

Before he could reply Dorrie said, "I'm thaniel, but this really is ridiculous—''

He hadn't expected it to be easy. "Are y get your hat?''

"You don't understand!''

"Then you have all day to help me und said, and with a brief "excuse me'' to Un whipped the boater from his head and in on

scooped Dorrie up in his arms and began marching back
the way he had come.

"Well, I'll be—" mused Samuel, scratching his hatless head.

"Uncle Samuel?" called Dora querulously. "What in
heaven's name is going on over there?"

"Great news, I'd say! Young Dorrie's getting married."

"Of course she's not, you silly old fool!" Dora's fist
beat on the balustrade. "Get after them and stop him."

"Not on your life," said Samuel. "I've never seen a
fellow more determined about anything in my entire life,
and let me tell you, lass, I've seen a lot. Yep, that's determination all right."

She tried to kick herself free but he scooped her tighter to
him; she tried to plead with him but he refused to listen.
When he seated her in the gig she promptly scrambled
down the other way, so he was forced to keep a hard grip
on her wrist while he unwound the reins with single-
handed awkwardness and maneuvered the horse out of
the driveway.

A mail coach was trundling toward town, dragging a
long boa of dust behind it. While he waited for the air to
clear, Nathaniel said quietly, "You know I'd not have
disrupted your plans if I had any other choice, but the fact
that I've only one day here in Auckland. By rights I
wouldn't be here at all because my father is seriously ill
I'll have to be on my way back to Sydney tomor-
— Are you listening to me, Dorrie?"

She nodded, face downturned, hands sulky in her lap,
n smarting where it was still clamped in his hand.
filled her like black oil, suffocating her and clog-
thoughts. What was the possible use of this rash
the d given him his reply. On her knees in front of
read, e, crumpling and burning pages she ached to
voured yes stinging as the flames mercilessly de-
her soul was starving for. Oh, she'd an-

swered him, all right, in an agony of deprivation—
pretending to Marguerite that she wasn't really interested, trying not to think about him, never encouraging a
daydream that could never be. Why hadn't he accepted
her reply? Why was he dragging her away like this?

"I was determined not to let the old century end
without resolving this business between us," he told
her. "So we're going to spend today together. All
day. You may be congenial or not, enjoy yourself or
not, but you'll make your mind up—else I won't let
you go." He smiled at her bent head, indulgent as a
parent, then flipped Uncle Samuel's boater into her
lap. "Here. Put this on. We can't have you of all people riding about hatless, can we? Think what damage
that would do to your reputation!"

She said, as a last resort, "Please, Nathaniel, *please!*
This won't do either of us any good."

"Won't it?" He glanced at her quizzically, raising one
eyebrow. "What more appropriate thing to do on the last
day than to clear out the ghosts and re-evaluate our lives?
Today we'll have answers, Dorrie. I don't like unanswered questions, or unanswered letters for that matter.
Or evasions."

I have nothing but evasions to offer you, thought Dorrie hopelessly.

He turned the gig to the left and soon they were spinning along the coast road away from town, past the
Edelburts' and past the old primary school she had attended with the Patene children. It was deserted today;
the rooms hollow-eyed, the flagpole bare. Farther on, at
the intersection with the Panmure Highway a group of
people stood in the shade of a dusty marcoracarpa hedge
waiting for the horse-drawn bus. There, with them were
Iris Pine and two of the other girls, bonneted, shawled,
and open-mouthed with astonishment as the gig swung
by.

"Nathaniel, please stop! There's Iris. I must—"

She beckoned as they rolled to a halt. Iris came pound-

ing after them, one hand flung over her black hat, the
other clutching her black skirts untidily sideways.

"Miss! Where are you going? Whatever is the matter?"

Dorrie ignored the gasped question. "Iris, this is very
important. Emere has the day off and Miss Bennington
has nobody to look after her." She glanced at Nathaniel
and, understanding, he released her arm so that she could
lean right out to whisper, "She will need to be *helped* in
certain ways—do you know what I mean? Will you mind
her for me, please?"

Iris nodded, saucer-eyed.

"And will you please stay with her until I get back this
afternoon?"

Nathaniel turned to interrupt. "It won't be until this
evening, and it could be late. And could you please tell
Miss Bennington that her niece is in no danger?"

"Danger, sir?"

"Yes, Iris. I whisked Miss Dorrie out of there so fast
that I'm wondering if her aunt will have the constabulary
on me."

"Oh." The beginnings of understanding dawned.
"Congratulations, sir!" Iris looked from one to the other
and began to giggle.

Dorrie said crossly, "Iris, it's not—" but by then Nathaniel had already snapped the whip over the horse's
back again and they were rolling away down the gravelly
road.

"It's going to be a scorcher of a day," said Nathaniel
when they had jolted along for some time in silence.
"I'm going to miss the New Zealand weather. These
clear, bright days have an intensity that no other place
can quite duplicate."

So he was going away forever, is that what he was telling her? Well, it was all for the best, but why did he have
to come back now and stir everything up?

She dreaded the answer to that.

Despite her discomfort at being seized against her will,

the practical side of Dorrie's nature swiftly came to the surface. It would be impossible to shut Nathaniel out of her mind, so she might as well enjoy his company and treat him as the dear and valued friend he had been for so many years. She owed him courtesy and consideration, and besides, she thought with a quick rush of remorse, she owed him an apology for her rudeness. The least she could have done was penned a few brief lines expressing regret for the unfortunate way things had developed between them. Had she been given the foresight to do that, then he would not have come barging into her life and swept her away like this.

Looking at him from under her lashes, she decided that well intentioned or not, today's gesture was certainly a romantic one. What a dramatic fellow he was. The tussles of business were so easily won for him that he filled even the edges of his life with excitement. *Oh, if only*, she thought. *If only I hadn't been so stupid.*

He was right; it did promise to be a glorious day. Already the sun was climbing to its dazzling heights. To their left the ocean basked, a peaceful dark blue edged with frilly petticoat lace. When the road dipped to cross a flax-fringed marsh, they caught a glimpse of hot-baked beaches. The sound of the gig disturbed scatterings of sea birds that rose and wheeled above piles of driftwood.

"I've never been beyond here," said Dorrie when they passed a bleached-gray shack where tousle-headed Maori children interrupted their game of marbles to stare as they trundled by.

"I don't believe you."

"It's true. We had a school picnic once, on that last beach near the cabbage trees, where those scraggy-looking horses were grazing. But that was years ago."

"That's incredible. No, on second thought it's not. The family feud, of course."

"What do you mean?" The road wound up onto a ridge and a breeze was blowing off the sea. Dorrie clutched the boater with one hand, then gave up and held it in her lap.

"All this land from here on belongs to the Yardley and Peridot families. Some of it's probably yours, by rights. May was saying once that it's all tied up so that it can't be divided or sold, but originally the Maoris who live here gave it jointly to Captain Yardley's wife, Juliette, to your Uncle Samuel, and to your grandmother, Miss Abby. It was to avoid having the land confiscated by the government after the Maori wars apparently."

"But nobody ever mentions it."

"I rather think that the Yardleys spoiled it for your branch of the family by building their home out here and setting up as if it was theirs exclusively. Look, there's the house now."

Against a backdrop of sun-soaked hills stood a gracious colonial mansion, turreted and ornate with a double-storied span of wide shady verandahs. Gaudy azalea bushes crammed the spaces between velvet lawns and flagged pathways, pergolas dripped with flowering vines, and a copper weathervane swung lazily in the breeze. On the side lawn beside an orangerie a cluster of children were playing with a sherry-and-cream-colored pony.

"Do the Teipa-Benningtons live here, too?"

"Most of the time. May has her own photographic studio around the back. It's glass-roofed to the south to catch the best light—all very interesting. The house suits them well."

"You sound as if you think a lot of them."

"They're the finest people I know." He drew up outside the gatehouse as a familiar figure stepped down from the verandah and hurried down the drive toward them. Sunlight burnished her mahogany-colored hair.

"She seems to be expecting us."

"You don't mind, do you?" He leaned towards her and whispered, "If you don't put your hat on, you'll come out in freckles. Not that it matters. I adore freckles.''

She put the hat on, tossing him a glance of reproach as she did so, only to be met by a gaze of such warmth that her heart melted. *He knows I love him*, she thought. *Oh, dear Lord, please help me get out of this mess.*

"You look radiant," called Nathaniel as May approached. "How's young Christabel?"

"Christianne," May corrected him with a flash of smile. "She's flourishing, as they all do. Fifteen months old and she's organizing us already. Dorrie! How delightful to see you. It's been far too long. Would you like to come in and freshen up or could I offer you a cup of tea before you embark on the picnic?"

"That's very thoughtful." Dorrie was touched. "But I'm fine, thanks."

"Nathaniel is the thoughtful one. He's planned this down to the last detail." Her eyes crinkled as she turned an affectionate smile in his direction. "Now then, Dorrie. My role in this is to offer to be your chaperone. Nathaniel worried that you might feel uncomfortable off in the woods alone with him. I won't intrude; I've my cameras all ready and I can have a go at a landscape near the waterfall that I've been dying to photograph for ages, but if you don't want me I'm just as happy to stay here. Happier, in fact." She paused, but before Dorrie could answer her she burst out again, "Forgive me for being personal, but why in the world are you wearing Uncle Samuel's old hat?"

Dorrie looked flustered and Nathaniel roared. "That's a long story. Perhaps she'll tell you all about it some other day."

"I'll hold you to that. Well, Dorrie? Do you feel safe with this great brute or do you need me along?"

"We'll be fine, thanks. Thank you very much."

"You're more welcome than you know. Have a very special day, won't you?" She stepped back but not be-

fore Dorrie noticed tears in her eyes. In a choked little
voice she said, "God bless you, my children."

She loves him and wishes him well, Dorrie realized
with a nasty stab of guilt. *They all love him, Uncle Samuel, May, even Iris and the girls; all of them want me to
marry him so that we can be happy together, and not one
of them has the faintest idea how insane this is, how
wrong and unsuitable I am. Oh, dear Lord, please help
me get out of this without hurting him.*

"You can tell me now why you didn't answer my letters," said Nathaniel as he lay back on the tartan rug, his
head pillowed on his folded jacket.

It was late afternoon, and between them existed a state
of ripening, if blighted happiness. Together they had
climbed the precarious path beside the misty waterfall
that hung like gauze over the cliff face. Quietly they had
paused in the deep shade and listened to bird song in the
native bush, and holding their breaths they had stooped in
the ferns at the meadow's edge and watched rabbits lol-
loping and playing in the sunshine. Only when Dorrie
confessed she was famished did Nathaniel move to open
the hamper, and then on Fintona bone china he served her
helpings of cold roast chicken and pink, thinly sliced beef,
delicate sandwiches, and a pie with juicy peach filling.

"I hope you appreciate that what we're eating is a feast
designed to promote Rupert's romantic life. They think
he's quite a devil with the ladies, now."

"I can't quite imagine that," said Dorrie, laughing.

"Neither can he," replied Nathaniel.

They ate slowly, sipping champagne from Fintona
crystal, and, as they had been doing intermittently all
day, they talked. Nathaniel was carefully casual,
nudging the conversation along in one direction and then
another so that in a space of a few hours they had
skimmed the surfaces of both their lives, roaming over
everything from her minor problems in the millinery
business to his grave concern about his father. His reason

for whisking her away with him was shelved, but from time to time he tossed in reminiscences. Did she remember that day at the hot-air ballooning when her ice cream fell in the mud? Did she recall that other picnic when they'd had such fun posing for the Cinematograph camera? And the horror of the shipwreck, did she still think about that or was it consigned forever to the realm of nightmares?

Yes, he'd planned even this down to the last detail, mused Dorrie. It didn't really surprise her that after that awkward beginning she had relaxed and was enjoying herself immensely. *I feel like a room all musty and closed up that is suddenly flung open to the sunlight,* she thought. *Being with Nathaniel is such a delight, such fun.*

Yet underneath the shadow remained. Several times in the past half-hour she had glanced up and found him watching her intently with an expression she could not fathom. And now, she accepted with a withering of pleasure, now had come the reckoning.

He was tilting the tulip-bowled glass between his strong fingers, watching the way the bubbles clung first to one side of the glass and then to the other. His voice was almost toneless as he said, "I've thought of many possible explanations behind your failure to answer my letters. I even made a list once, covering everything from paralysis that prevented you from holding a pen, to an elopement with a dashing stranger. That list was torn up the moment I decided to obtain the true story from you. Well, Dorrie? Are you going to tell me why you didn't answer any of them?"

Miserably she stared at the tangled patch of grass between the hem of her skirt and the edge of the rug. A ladybird with a perky red-and-white-dotted coat was making its way up and over some of the long grass blades. Dorrie wished she could change places with it.

"Well?"

She fixed her eyes on the tiny insect. "I didn't even read your letters," she whispered.

"What?" He reared forward, propping himself on one elbow, profound in disbelief. "All those hours spent finding just the right word, racking my brains for witty phrases—*really* racking them, I might add, for the very thought of you is enough to turn me into a tepid fool with a stunned brain. And you sit there and blithely tell me all that work was wasted! You didn't even *read* them? Why not?"

"Auntie Dora and I—"

"Auntie Dora!"

"No—please ignore that. Please. It was my decision alone. I thought it best, after our last interview, you know, when we walked in the garden, do you remember?"

"Of course."

She shot him a frightened look and hurried on. "You seemed to be developing a certain . . . interest in me that was impossible to be fulfilled, and I considered it best to let the matter die there. It was best for both of us."

She glanced up at him. He was stroking his moustache, his dark eyes shadowed by his hat brim. She was silently congratulating herself that she had tidied the matter away to everyone's satisfaction when he said abruptly, "That's a neat little speech, Dorrie, but now will you please answer the question?"

"But I—"

"The truth, Dorrie. Don't be afraid."

But she was, of course. Afraid to really look at him, afraid of her own weakening resolve, afraid above everything of hurting him.

"You're an inquisitive young woman with a healthy curiosity so I don't understand how so many bulky letters could pass through your hands unread. Unless the truth is that you never received them. That your aunt intercepted them."

"No! Absolutely not."

"Then it must have been hard to resist."

"It was," she said, and added unguardedly, "Burning

them was one of the most difficult things I've ever done.''

Had she been watching him then she would have seen a glint come into his eyes. "Then tell me why you did it," he said gently.

"You know why!"

"Marguerite?"

She nodded. The ladybird was clinging to a seed-stalk. It had folded its coat and was fanning itself with wings clear as water.

"Good," he said unexpectedly. "If Marguerite is the reason behind your concern, then you may, with a clear conscience, put that reason aside. As I told you earlier, I visited her at home before I came to collect you. I told her exactly how I feel about you, I told her that I'd always regarded her as a very dear sister and I hoped she'd wish me luck for today.''

"What did she say to that?"

He shrugged. "I'd say I botched it. She jumped right on her high horse, said she didn't know why I bothered to come to *her* first. I said I wanted her blessing because of the high regard in which we both hold her, but she went very white around the mouth, and I thought she was going to slap me. Instead she slammed out of the room. Damn it all, Dorrie, don't look so shocked. Every letter I wrote to the family—and they were all to the *family* and not just to her—I mentioned you so many times that if Marguerite had any sensitivity at all she'd have guessed. But no, when I arrived and asked to see her she came gliding in all husky voiced and reached up to kiss me in a way that—"

"She's my friend, Nathaniel. She's been my friend for a very long time."

"Has she? I don't recall her sticking by you when you needed her friendship."

"That was because of you—and later when we made things up again she said that she'd missed me. She *is* my friend and she's been good to me. When I first began making hats on my own account, she helped by having that luncheon.''

''She's told me many times how you owe all your success to her.''

''It isn't like you to be so hard!'' As she stared up at him the ladybird flew across her line of vision, blurring the image of him momentarily as it passed between their faces.

''All right. I am being hard. But she's received benefits by the dozen from that first favor she did you. Look at it this way. You owe her loyalty and consideration, just as I owe Rupert loyalty and consideration. I'd probably risk my life for him if necessary, but there is no way whatsoever that I'd sacrifice my life or my happiness merely to *please* him. That's a different matter altogether.''

Dorrie was silent for a long time. Then, hopelessly, she said, ''You don't understand.''

''I think I do. Rejecting me isn't going to drive me into Marguerite's arms no matter how fervently you might wish her happiness. *You're* the one I'm going to marry, not her. I've told her so.''

He said it lightly, and he was smiling as he spoke, but he watched her face carefully and saw the jolt his words gave her. Her face crumpled.

''Nathaniel, please don't propose to me. I can't accept you.'' She struggled for calm and felt her grip slide away. ''I—I—''

''Darling Dorrie!'' He was on his knees beside her, an arm about her shoulders, touching her for the first time since he had helped her down out of the gig.

Oblivious to him, she was weeping mutely, the tears flowing down impassive cheeks. It was as if she had shuttered herself up on the outside while inside the grief gushed unchecked. He tried to comfort her but she seemed unable to hear him, incapable of sensing his caresses as he stroked her face and her shoulders in an attempt to soothe her. The intensity of her misery alarmed him.

Instinct told him that this outpouring was not his fault, that the wellsprings of this distress had been shaped by forces quite separate from him. It's not Marguerite either, he decided. She flew to her defense like a ruffled hen, but even through her indignation she must have known that I had a valid point there. No, this is something far deeper.

"Dorrie, love," he murmured against the warm skin of her brow as he tucked her against his chest. "Don't cry, darling. I love you, Dorrie. Nothing else matters but you."

Nothing matters, especially me, she thought wearily. Nothing but to indulge in the luxury of a total release, to let free all the tears, the useless anguish, the purposeless remorse and self-hatred, wash them all away, send them down the watershed until they are marooned far beyond my recall to never haunt me again. For this is my bitterest moment, to acknowledge that our true feelings, finally revealed, are doomed as blossoms in a storm.

But she allowed him to cradle her in his arms, treacherously permitting it while she struggled to rebuild her defenses and remarshal the pathetic arguments which she hoped would drive him away from her.

At length the tears dried.

"There," he said, pleased as if he had stanched the flow himself. And, in tones of great tenderness, "Whatever made you cry like that must have been a mighty big night horse. Probably the biggest ever, I'd reckon."

"Night horse?"

"That's what my father used to call them, when bad dreams woke me and sent me staggering into his bed, sobbing—dare I admit it?—sobbing. He used to murmur, 'Are those wretched night horses chasing you again?' but he'd lift up a corner of the sheets and let me slide in and snuggle up to him. His bed was always feverishly hot—I used to wake up in a sweat, always, but he smelled of peppermint oil that he used for toothache. I still find that smell comforting, for some reason.''

''Your father sounds like a dear.''

''He's a gruff old thing, but soft as a brush underneath, of course. Like me.''

''You're not gruff.'' Dorrie dabbed at her eyes. Her face and hands were sticky with tears and the skin around her eyes was hot and sore. She felt utterly dreadful, as if she was halfway through some wretched illness.

''I will be gruff if I have to spend my life alone,'' he said lightly. ''Come on, Dorrie. Tell me about your 'night horse.' ''

''I can't. I would if I could, but I can't.''

''I see. Or, to be precise, I don't see.'' He gazed up at the curdling sky. It would be dark in half an hour. Giving her shoulder a squeeze, he said, ''Are you sure it's not your aunt, pressuring you to discourage me? I can quite see why she'd want the status quo to continue as is, but—''

''No, truly.'' Dorrie crumpled her handkerchief into a spongy ball. ''You mustn't blame Auntie Dora for any of the things I say. She only wants my happiness, and, though you may not believe it, she wants what's best for you.''

''I may not believe it.'' With one fingertip he lifted a loose tendril of hair from her brow and smoothed it back. Elaborately casual, he said, ''So it's not Auntie Dora, and it's not because you don't love me.'' He expected no denial and received none. ''I've known that you loved me since before that day in the garden, when you more or less told me to go away. I knew it again when I carried you off. You could have jumped out at the bus stop, and May certainly would have given you refuge if you'd wanted it, but you elected to come with me—''

''I shouldn't have.''

''But you did. And all day you've been happy as a singing dove, haven't you? It's been as if today is the first day of a marvelous life for us . . .''

As he spoke he gathered his own resolve. Though he had been with enough women to learn all the signs of acquiescence, Dorrie still mystified him. He knew she loved him—or at least hoped it to be true strongly enough to call it knowing—yet there was a restraint about her that puzzled him. Never had she given him the slightest intimation that she might welcome a kiss or an embrace from him other than those brotherly "hello and good-bye" kisses she dispensed with no more thought than if she was distributing visiting cards. Now he knew that he had to breach this strange reserve of hers and, looking at her bent head he now understood Joshua's baffled frustration when he circled the walls of Jericho searching for some flaw in those unbreachable ramparts.

"Dorrie, look at me," he said harshly.

She raised her ruined, tear-swollen eyes and gazed obediently into that handsome, tender face, reading in it all the warmth of love and concern that she ached to accept. He was so dear to her that his obvious physical attractions had long gone unnoticed. She had always left it to Marguerite to rhapsodize over the depths of his glowing brown eyes, the broad smoothness of his brow, the classically perfect proportions of nose and chin, and the warmth of his smile. To her he was simply a treasured friend, an *especially* treasured and dear friend, someone to be protected from hurt at all costs.

"Please, Nathaniel. Please listen to me," she begged too late.

He had stopped listening. She saw the expression of blind, helpless hunger on his face and then he bent his head and covered her mouth with his.

Her resolution shattered. She could almost hear her fragile defenses splinter and rain in a tinkling of useless shards around her. Exposed and vulnerable, she was crushed to a boneless pulp, unable to move to free herself, forced to watch and participate against her will as her mind crumpled and broke, releasing the bitter, seething emotions that had been walled up there for so long.

His mouth was the most heavenly thing she had ever tasted, moist and warm and starving for her. The scent of his skin blocked her head with the faint minglings of bay rum, tobacco, and dear warm person. She flung her arms up around his neck, twisted her fingers in the thick strands of hair as if they, too, ached and could only be soothed by the touch of him; she was dying and only he could save her, in a torment of pain and he alone could quiet the agony, she was screaming for him, and he was rushing toward her so fast that they were spinning through space and there was a dull roaring in her ears.

His mouth tore away from hers and he pressed his cheek hard against hers. "Dorrie, I love you—I've loved you for so many years I've lost count. I've dreamed of you for so long that at times I wondered whether I was going to go mad from wanting—"

"Nathaniel, no!"

She had twisted herself away from him with a sudden thrust he instinctively responded to by letting her go at once. Now she faced him, her eyes reddened, her face blotched but with a ferocious determination about her that astonished him. He could see that she was shaking as she stood up and moved back a step. One hand trembled against her throat in a gesture of vulnerability.

"I don't—I don't want to hurt you," she managed to say. Her face was distorted with pain and fright; in this shadowy dusk she looked almost ugly.

"Dorrie!" he called in alarm, then scrambled to his feet as she turned and began to lurch away toward the road.

He caught her before she reached the stile and they leaned against it, panting, he half-smiling for he was sure this was a game until he tipped her tight chin up and saw that she was crying again, worse than before.

"You're going to have to tell me, you know," he said.

She was exhausted, defeated, and drawn to the limits

of her endurance. Like a fighter who knows he is beaten, she said, "All right. I'll tell you why I can't marry you."

He waited, respecting the effort it must be costing her, but when she remained silent, gripping the fence-wire with whitened knuckles, he tried to give her confidence by jollying her along.

"Don't tell me. Let me guess. You're already secretly married to Mr. Timmins, the gardener."

A moment later he was cursing his flippancy, but later still he forgave himself. He'd been positive that her reasons for rejecting him were trivial ones—important to her perhaps, but trivial in the great scheme of things—and he was stunned, therefore, when she planted herself before him and in a voice like fury said, "For a first guess that was excellent," and went on to tell him all about it.

He couldn't look at her while she told it. He could hardly endure the listening. Once he asked her to stop but she countered angrily that he'd browbeaten and badgered her and now he could hear the whole sordid, shameful mess. She made no excuses for herself, offered no apologies. When it was over she said curtly that she'd wait for him in the gig and with that turned to go.

He seized her arm as she was setting foot on the stile. "Why, Dorrie? Why?"

The pain in his voice would hang like a curtain in the windows of her brain forever, she thought. Everything she looked at from now on and for the rest of her life would be sieved through that dreadful reality.

"I don't know," she said flatly. "I was terribly sorry later, but it was too late then. And for what it's worth, I'm already sorry I told you. I just wanted you to go away. I never wanted to hurt you."

The irony of that smashed her even before his grip on her loosened. *I never wanted to hurt you.* That was Del's feeble protest after he'd used and abandoned and cheated and deceived her.

Sobbing, she stumbled along the path that wound down the darkened hillside. Only the sea was clearly visible, glittering and ghostly beyond the tufted blackness of the shore hills.

Somewhere close by a *more-pork* hooted as she hurried by. It was a hollow, mournful sound.

Back in the clearing Nathaniel moved slowly to gather the remnants of the picnic together. At first he felt nothing either, but when the shock released its grip enough to permit him to think, he reflected only that he was living out this action on two levels, groping in the gathering darkness as he scooped up the crushed pieces of his dismembered hopes.

Twenty-two

By the time they reached the outskirts of town darkness had dropped completely and the chilled night air was settling the dampened odors of dust and cut grass. A halo of yellow light hung over the central city and already the first rockets of the evening were fizzing through the sky, threading the stars onto tinsel necklaces. From backyard kennels dogs barked applause. Firecrackers snapped and popped everywhere.

Few houses were lit. As they progressed Nathaniel had to slow the gig more and then reduce speed to a walk as the road thickened with horses, carts, and dozens of lamp-carrying pedestrians all moving into town for the celebrations. "Happy new century!" was the cry they exchanged.

Dorrie was shivering under the rug. Since the outburst at the stile she had uttered nothing but a tired "thank you" when Nathaniel tucked the rug around her shoulders. He had treated her solicitously, as if she were old and ill, and that was exactly how she felt, too exhausted and apathetic to go on.

They were almost at the corner of Cardigan Street with only half a mile to go when Nathaniel finally dented the silence that seemed fixed between them. "You'll have to forgive me if I took that news rather hard, Dorrie. I imagine you don't feel like talking right now, but I must know one or two more things."

Why not? She closed her eyes wearily. He might as well snatch away her last pitiful vestiges of privacy.

"Miss Bennington—didn't she ever give you any advice or instruction about how to act with young men?"

385

Dorrie thought. "Not about—*that*. She gave me a great big book on etiquette and made me read that right through. It was all about when to wear gloves and the proper time of day to call on people."

"Etiquette!" He snorted. After an enforced pause, during which time a family group was walking too close to them to permit intimate conversation, Nathaniel said, "What I really want to know, Dorrie, is *why* do you think it happened?"

She shrugged unhappily. "I've wondered that lots of times myself. I was very lonely; I didn't have a single friend at the time. Auntie Dora was all wrapped up in what Uncle Jon was doing—he absolutely dominated her life, you know—so I didn't even have her. And Del was very persuasive. He said he loved me and because I was naive I suppose I never once doubted his word."

"And now?"

"I don't know."

"I mean, how do *you* feel about him now?"

The last strip tore away. "I don't feel anything for him."

"Are you sure?"

"Positive. He came around to the house one night when Auntie Dora was at Fintona, and he told me he still loved me and he'd made a dreadful mistake in marrying Roseanne. While he was telling me all that, I was thinking that even if he *was* free I wouldn't want to marry him. I was looking at him then and trying to work out why that love affair between us had ever happened. He was using the same tone of voice, saying the same things in the same way, but this time it was impossible to be persuaded by him. I couldn't understand how I'd been stupid enough to listen to him in the first place."

"And what happened then?"

"Oh—he tried to kiss me and I hit him with a wooden hat-stand. He went away then."

"I'll bet he did."

Dorrie said, "Nathaniel, all this sounds like excuses

and I'm not making any. It's my fault, too, and I recognize that. I'm really sorry about spoiling your day, but I was silly enough to hope that if you did ask me to marry you I could simply say no, and you'd accept that without a fuss. I didn't want to tell you all this.''

"Does your aunt know about Del Blackett?"

"Yes, I'm afraid so. It was she who pointed out that I had to give up all ideas of ever getting married. She was right, too. No, really she was,'' she cut in as he began to speak. "You only gave me two choices today, either to confess everything or to marry you and try to live out a despicable lie. I couldn't deceive you no matter how much I might want to be with you. You deserve much better than that.''

They were drawing close to the gates now. Dorrie could see the outline of the roof illuminated by the garden lamps and suddenly she could bear this tense, strained interview no longer. Without a word of good-bye she slid from the seat and propelled herself away from the side of the gig, landing safely in the long grass at the roadside. When Nathaniel glanced around she had gone.

Dora and Samuel were on the verandah watching the fireworks display. The harbor was dotted with dozens of tiny lanterned boats sitting on reflections that made them look like clusters of fireflies. The air was rich with the musty scent of flowers closed for the night. Dorrie walked around quietly and climbed the verandah steps.

Uncle Samuel saw her first. "Well, well, our lassie returns at last.'' The false heartiness in his voice warned her that Dora had been giving him a hard time about her all day.

Dora maneuvered her wheelchair around slowly. Iris Pine moved from the shadows to help her but was impatiently flapped away. "Well, Dorinda? What have you to say for yourself? You look terrible.''

Her face was obscured by the darkness and her voice was tight but whether with anger or fear Dorrie could not tell. She said, "There's nothing to say, Auntie. Mr. Rosser behaved like a gentleman all—"

"Yes. So I noticed as he bodily carried you off."

"He had no option, Auntie. He only wanted to talk to me."

"To ask you to marry him."

He never did do that, thought Dorrie. *He didn't ask, and I didn't need to refuse him. At least I spared him that.*

Iris broke into her long silence. "I were instructed to tell you as soon as you got 'ome, miss. Miss Dupton's waiting for you in the *Le Chapeau* salon."

"How long has she been there?"

"All afternoon. Since about three o'clock. I asked 'er if she wanted a cup of tea an' somethin' to eat, but she won't open the door. She's been banging about in there. Cryin' an' such."

"Then I'd better see what she wants." *I know what she wants*, thought Dorrie. *She'll need reassuring, too.*

"I haven't finished yet, Dorinda."

"We've all the time in the world, Auntie," said Dorrie as she leaned over to kiss her. "The rest of our lives together." Under the soft pressure of her lips she felt Dora relax.

"Marguerite?" She tapped again. "It's me, Dorrie."

After a scuffling sound the door opened a slice. Marguerite looked calm and tearless. Dorrie was relieved; she'd dreaded a hysterical outburst.

"Come in," Marguerite invited her, swinging the door wide and stepping back so that Dorrie could get a clear view of the fully lit room. The scene of destruction that met her gaze made Dorrie's breath snag in her chest.

Everything in the salon had been reduced to scraps. It was impossible to guess what had been what. The ornate Italian light fittings were heaps of broken glass, all the hats were mere rags, the mirrors were broken, the expensive silk wall coverings had been shredded, and the car-

pet had been slashed. Dorrie looked from the chaos to
Marguerite's perfectly serene face and a tiny trickle of
fear itched between her shoulder blades.

"Come in," said Marguerite, as pleasantly as if she
were inviting a guest into her home. "Nobody heard a
thing— It was the fireworks, you see."

Dorrie stayed outside the door. "Marguerite, I do understand if you're upset, but I assure you that I've never
wanted to harm you in any way—"

"Of course you haven't," she replied in reasonable
tones. "You've been a dear and trusted friend. From the
first day you met Nathaniel you've been scheming to take
him away from me, haven't you? Remember that little
exhibition you put on that day so that all his attention
would focus on you? I saw then what you were like, and
I'm to blame, I suppose, for underestimating you. You
see, I was always confident that Nathaniel would come to
realize how shallow and selfish you are—"

"You're wrong. Please don't say these things. Look, I
don't care about the room. You can wreck the whole
house if you want, only please don't make yourself unhappy like this. There's no need to. Nathaniel and I—"

"No, Dorrie, I do need to say them." She was standing a pace inside the room with both hands behind her
back. Dorrie was uneasy about that; she wondered what
implement Marguerite had used to wreak such havoc inside the room. She guessed the scissors from the needle-
work kit she kept handy in a drawer in case customers'
hats needed any last-minute adjustments.

"You see, Dorrie, I always believed that Nathaniel
would see you for what you are and would recognize my
devotion for the true love that it is. That's why I've kept
calm all this time, through your lying and deceit, your
cheating and conniving."

"Marguerite, you're *wrong!*"

"And here you are, bloated with triumph, wanting me
to help you celebrate your engagement, no doubt. Very
well, congratulations. I've even got an engagement gift

here all ready for you.'' In a steady movement, watching Dorrie's face, she brought around a large pair of dressmaking shears and held them out in front of her.

Dorrie looked at the wicked points and the bright red bow Marguerite had used to decorate the handles. Strangely, now that she was aware of what Marguerite planned to do, her fear evaporated.

''There is no engagement, Marguerite. Nathaniel changed his mind after I had a talk with him. We are not getting married, so there's no need—''

For a moment she thought she might be getting through to Marguerite, for she hesitated, visibly wanting to believe, then her eyes took on that set, almost animal look and she lunged at Dorrie with the scissors, using both hands and holding them open as if she were attacking a hedge with shears.

Dorrie was ready for her. Stepping swiftly to one side, she turned and shoved Marguerite as hard as she could between the shoulders, propelling her across the hall where she collapsed over a yellow velvet wing chair. The scissors spun from her hands and rattled along the corridor where Uncle Samuel picked them up as he and Iris Pine came hurrying to see what was the matter. At that moment the door chimes rang.

''That'll be Mr. Bennington, miss. He called before lookin' for Miss Dupton an' I told him what were goin' on, so he said he'd call back later.''

Dorrie answered the door herself. Her hands were shaking so hard that she fumbled the lock and needed three attempts to snig it open.

''Rupert!'' she said. Then, glancing at the rocket-streaked sky, added, ''Happy new century.''

''Are you all right?''

''Yes.'' She nodded, pressing her hands against her face.

''I say, Dorrie!''

She shook her head. ''I'm all right.''

He stepped into the hall. ''Iris said she wouldn't be

surprised if there was trouble when you got home, so I
thought I'd better come by and see if there was anything I
could do." He saw Marguerite huddled in a chair with
her face in her hands and jerked his head meaningfully
toward her.

"She's all right, too, but she's had a long day and
she's ready to go home now." While he was staring at
Marguerite, Dorrie slipped past him and closed the door
on the wreckage. Dorrie said, "If there's been any sort of
an upset then it's my fault. I realize that, and—"

"How very noble of you," said Marguerite bitterly.
"Rupert, will you take me home, please?"

Dorrie stood on the steps, the sound of rockets fizzing
in her ears, as she watched Marguerite walk away, head
up, without so much as a backward glance.

Iris had opened the salon door and she and Dora were
staring in at the destruction. "Wow!" said Iris. "Oh,
wow! What are you going to do?"

"I'm going to clean it up. But I'm not worried about it.
Marguerite is what I'm worried about," Dorrie told her.

Dora sniffed. "I told you she was mad. That mad sister of hers, and the way she put on airs all the time, tossing those silly French words about all the time when
she's never once set foot in France. I always thought
there was something very odd about that family."

Dorrie was too sick at heart to argue. Not that it would
have mattered.

Dorrie spent the first day of the new century wearing herself out with grueling physical work, toiling alone in the
salon to clear away all the mess before anybody saw it.
Marguerite would be sorry she had done this, she reasoned, and therefore the sooner it was all cleaned up and
mended the less lasting harm there could be. She tried not
to think about Nathaniel.

"I was tired of white and gold anyway," she told Uncle Samuel as ribbons of thick smoke wove through the
heaps of tattered carpet and ribbons of wall covering. "I

think we'll go for *Le Chapeau*'s own colors next time, silver and blue. What do you think?''

''I think you're taking this remarkably well,'' said Samuel. ''That's what I think. In fact, if I didn't know better, I'd think you were a cold-hearted little machine of a woman with no feelings whatever.''

''What do you mean?''

''I mean, lass, what on earth possessed you to send that fine young man packing? If I've ever seen two people that should be wed to one another, it's you and that Mr. Rosser. Strike me pink, lass. What's wrong with you?''

He meant well, she knew he did, but it was more than she could do to answer him. Snatching up the basket in which she was hefting the rubble, she stalked back inside for another load.

''Wake up, miss.'' Emere shook Dorrie's shoulder, jogging her into consciousness. Dorrie rolled over and stared into the shiny, lamplit face.

''What time—'' Dorrie rolled over and squinted at the clock. ''Good heavens! Quarter past nine!''

''Shush, miss. It's still night time, eh. I come to fetch you because Mrs. Teipa-Bennington, she's waiting outside to talk to you, and she won't come in.''

Dorrie struggled to sit up. ''I don't suppose she will. Where is Auntie Dora?''

''In the parlor, eh, with Matua-keke, your uncle.''

''I'll go out quietly, then.''

May was dressed in a long hooded cloak so dark in color that it blended completely with the shade of the hedge. Not until she stepped forward onto the moonlight-silvered courtyard did Dorrie see her.

''Excuse the mystery,'' she said, breathing a violet-scented kiss on Dorrie's cheek. ''Oh, are you all right, dear?''

''Tired, that's all.'' She vaguely recalled collapsing at dusk, drooping and letting go like a curtain slipping from a clothesline, swooning onto the ground. "Emere woke me a few minutes ago."

"I'm sorry, but it is important. Nathaniel asked me to give you something, and he insisted that I place it right into your hands, not trust it to any intermediary."

"Oh."

"Dorrie, dear. I must say that Patrick and I, we're both so terribly disappointed about what didn't happen yesterday. Of course, I told Nathaniel that he couldn't just come breezing in after almost two years and expect to sweep you away in one grand gesture. Still, something must have gone terribly wrong and we're disappointed, both of us."

Yes, thought Dorrie. *Everybody is disappointed.*

"Anyway, Nathaniel asked me to give you this. He spent quite a portion of the morning writing it, we were fretting that he might miss his sailing, and it's important to him to be with his father now—he might have mentioned that he's critically ill." As she spoke she reached into the basket she was carrying and drew out a thin letter. "Needless to say, I've got my fingers crossed that this note mends whatever caused the breach between you. You know," she glanced across at the lighted windows with an expression of regret, "I always hoped that some miracle might occur to permit us to be friends. Even when you were a tiny tot you had a special enchantment of your own, and I think that we're all the poorer in our branch of the family for not being able to enjoy your company in the way we should." She sounded tired herself, and sad. "We hoped that Nathaniel would be that miracle. Still, who knows?" And with another brief kiss she melted into the shadow before Dorrie could even thank her.

Back in her room Dorrie turned up the bedside gas lamp and kicked off her slippers. Tucking her feet up under her, she leaned back on the pillows and looked at the envelope. "Dorrie," it said simply, with one flourish of underlining.

As her fingers plucked it open she felt as if her life hung in the balance.

Dear Dorrie,

You leaped out of the gig so abruptly last night that I was caught unprepared, with so much still unsaid. Though at the time I was annoyed, I soon came to appreciate that the entire day must have been such an ordeal for you that you could tolerate no more of it.

I also understand what it cost you to tell me all you did. I wonder whether it might have been better to leave it unsaid, but again on reflection your honesty moves me and I completely respect your integrity and your motives.

My dear, what happened was regrettable, but it was a very long time ago and by your own admission you feel nothing for the fellow now. If I had led a blameless life myself, I might be inclined to judge you, but searching my heart I discover no blame or recriminations. I would be a hypocrite if I did.

As I have come to learn, the magical part of love is what transpires in the mind and heart. If your revelation had crushed that emotion in me, then this would be a note of regret. As it is, my feelings for you are, if anything, stronger than before, and this letter, therefore, is humbly penned to you in hope.

Marry me, Dorrie! Our poor lives are so brief. Let us spend ours wisely—in happiness, together.

I acknowledge that this is not an ideally romantic proposal. If you can arrange to come with Patrick and May when they leave for their tour of Europe next month, I shall meet you in Sydney and remedy the matter.

My love is with you always,
Nathaniel.

Folding the letter carefully, Dorrie remained still for a long time, deep in thought. Then she stood up, put on her slippers and, carrying the letter, padded along the corridor and into the parlor.

Emere was pouring tea at the sideboard, and Dora and Samuel were seated at an octagonal marble table playing Royal Parcheesi. Dora glanced up at her, the dice cup rattling in her hand.

"Dorrie, pet, you should be in bed," she said, shaking out the dice. When Dorrie walked over and placed the letter beside the heap of tiny mother-of-pearl fish that were used as wagers, Dora said, "What's this? An apology from that wretched girl's family, I suppose. That father of hers should be taken to task—totally irresponsible, he is."

"Easy on there, lass," protested Samuel. "He's a decent enough fellow. Awfully fond of trout fishing."

"It's not from them," Dorrie put in quickly. "Auntie, I'd like you to look after *Le Chapeau* for some time. A long time perhaps. I'm going to Sydney."

"What for, lass?" Samuel looked up, his face alert.

"Be quiet, will you? Of course she's not going anywhere."

Dorrie flapped open the letter and handed it to her to read.

"It's that Rosser fellow, isn't it? I told you he was determined, didn't I, Dora? I said—"

"Oh, do be quiet, you old fool," snapped Dora. She finished reading and raised her face to Dorrie, pushing her wheelchair back a few inches as she did so. Behind the thick lenses her eyes were inscrutable. She said, "So that's what you've set your mind on, have you? Gallivanting off with *them.*"

"It's not like that at all." In her excitement she'd completely forgotten the mention of the Teipa-Benningtons. "Nathaniel only suggested I contact them, I suppose, because he can't come over here for me. He needs to be with his father—he's seriously ill, you see, and—"

"I don't see at all." When Dora shook her head her spectacles flashed with opaque light. The whiskers on her cheeks trembled. "All I can see is that you propose to go off with *those people!* They killed Jon, Dorrie! They're murderers, plain and simple."

"Hey, easy on," began Samuel.

"You keep out of this," warned Dora. "I know that you're not in the least fussy about who you associate with, but this is different. Dorrie is *my* responsibility and what she does—"

"Dora," insisted Samuel. "If you're talking about Patrick and May, they had nothing to do with what happened to Jon."

"Of course they—"

"Ask Rupert what really happened." He had stopped her; she could recognize the authority in his tone. He said, "Jon's death was ultimately a tragic accident, and it would be best all round if we choose to regard it as such."

"Those are lofty words from you." Dora's voice was tight as wire.

"It's the simple truth. That's what Rupert said to me and I believe him."

There was silence in the room, each person privately wrestling with what Samuel had said. Both he and Dora were trying to accept that it *was,* indeed, an accident, and Emere was silently trying, then not trying, to make some sense out of what she had heard. Only Dorrie latched straight onto the truth of it, that Ellen wanted Jon out of the way so that she could at last come home without fear that he would pester her, and Dorrie couldn't blame her for that. But Samuel was right, as he so often was. It was best to leave the whole subject as a gray unshaped mass of maybes and might-have-beens. It was gone, over and forgotten long ago.

Samuel rattled the dice in the cup. "It is my turn, isn't it?" he said. Nobody replied.

Dorrie left Auckland on the day Queen Victoria died. Bells were tolling, people in the roadways shouted the news to each other, and the morning newspaper wore a black border an inch wide.

Uncle Samuel sat on the verandah steps in the sunshine. Old as he was, he could not remember what life was like before that day long ago when he had stared at the new Queen's picture outside the Governor's house in the Bay of Islands. "Sixty-four years," he muttered, shaking his head. "Sixty-four years."

Dora wore black and cried all through breakfast. Her tears may have all been for the Queen, staunch Royalist that she was, but Dorrie wondered whether she had caused some of her aunt's grief and guiltily kept a distance from her. Relations between the two had been as tight and hard as stretched rope since the night the letter came. Dorrie kept up a pleasant demeanor, hoping that if she refused to change her plans or even quarrel about it, her aunt might come round. Now, uncomfortably, she wondered if she should postpone her departure.

"Nay, lass," said Samuel when she whispered her doubts to him. "Go and God speed. If you look back now you may never go."

"But I'm worried about the depth of her unhappiness," fretted Dorrie. "Look at her in there—she looks like Death herself. She's not even wearing *Riversong* or her father's picture. And she didn't eat a thing—"

"Hey, don't you go crumbling away on us." He squeezed her fingers in his papery grip. "I'm staying with her. We'll be all right. After you've gone I'll mosey on down to see Captain Yardley to have a drink or two for the Queen and talk over old times, then I'll bring my bits and bobs back here. This place needs a man around it, you know."

"You talk as if I'm not coming back."

He ignored that. "Not good for a house to have just women in it, you know. Dora likes to have someone to fuss over."

Dorrie blinked back tears, then, when she felt him joggle her hand, she looked into his withered old, babyish face. He was grinning his gummy grin at her.

"Life's to be enjoyed, lass."

She had to laugh. "Don't you go annoying the girls in the workroom," she said. "I know how you love to tease them, but they're being paid to make hats, not to be entertained by your jokes."

"Lunchtimes only, I promise."

"Good." She bent to kiss his scarred cheek. "I don't think I'd have had the courage to go if it wasn't for you."

"Why do you think I've stayed on so long this time?" he asked her. "Now settle yourself down here, lass, and read the newspaper's editorial out to me. I can't see a thing in this bright sunlight. Dazzles me properly, it does."

Dorrie laughed. Uncle Samuel had never used the same excuse twice in all the time he had asked her to read something out to him. Obediently she settled beside him and flapped the newspaper open to the center pages.

Samuel poked his pipe stem at a faintly printed photograph in the top right-hand corner of the page. "That's young Patene, isn't it?"

"Yes . . ." said Dorrie, reading. "Oh, my goodness—"

"Not killed, is he?"

Dorrie glanced up, her eyes alight. "He's been awarded the Victoria Cross! It says here that he is only the third New Zealander ever to receive one." She bit her lip as her eyes scanned the column. "It says, 'On December 2nd, 1899, near Bothasberg this noncommissioned officer was one of a party which was attacked and hotly engaged with a party of some thirty or forty enemy soldiers. Twice when men in his company were wounded and in serious danger of being killed, Sergeant Button risked his own life under heavy fire to crawl out, without cover, and drag his comrades to safety. He sustained an arm wound himself in the skirmish and is at present on the high seas, on his way home to recuperate from the injury he so gallantly incurred.' '' She stood up, clutching the paper. "All this has happened and Emere hasn't said one word. I wonder if she even knows?"

"She will in a minute," said Samuel.

"I'll go and tell Mrs. Patene right away," decided Dorrie. "I can't wait to see her face. 'My boy Albert, he's a fine boy,' she always says. Well, now she'll be able to say, 'My boy Albert, he's a brave boy, too.' ''

"One of the bravest," said Samuel seriously. "They don't give those medals away for nothing, you know. Hey!" he called, for she was up and off down the path with the newspaper. "Take young Emere with you. I'll keep an eye on Dora while you're gone."

"Oh, Uncle Samuel," cried Dorrie, returning to pat him on the top of his old boater hat. "Isn't everything wonderful?"

Rupert came in his little motor buggy to take her down to the *Monowai*. He loaded her two small cases and one large hatbox into the vehicle while Dorrie fluttered around saying good-byes to the girls, the grooms, the servants, and to Mr. Timmins.

Dora's wheelchair was at the foot of the ramp. Dorrie paused as she kissed her. "I wish we could have had a talk," she said finally.

Dora jerked her head up to return Dorrie's kiss. Her face was swollen and pink, for she had been crying ever since the newspaper was brought in to her with her early morning tea tray and it was now one o'clock in the afternoon. She smelled like a sick person.

"Auntie—" began Dorrie, feeling helpless and full of dread.

"Go if you must," said Dora, inflexible to the end. "Iris, where's that parcel for Dorrie?" Iris ran inside and returned with what felt like a tin wrapped in pink-and-white-striped paper. "It's sweet wafer biscuits, the ones you like," explained Dora in a worn voice. "Those ones they serve on the ship are inedible."

"Oh, Auntie—" Dorrie moved to kiss her again but Dora stopped her with a raised hand.

"Off you go," she said.

They drove out the gate, the girls dashing behind, throwing handfuls of rice, squealing and shouting good wishes. Dorrie could still hear Elizabeth when they were far down the road. "Be 'appy, miss!" she called. "You be 'appy, mind!"

Rupert chuckled as he brushed the rice grains from his jacket and removed his hat to shake them from the brim. "Who'd have thought it, you and I driving off in a shower of rice? Not a bad idea, come to think of it. Sure you won't change your mind and run off with me instead?"

"You'd hate that," she said.

Frank as cousins are, he said, "I suppose I would. You've got far too much energy for me. Mind you, you're the pick of the family, you know that? You're the only one among us all who genuinely puts others first. You deserve some happiness."

"Have you heard how Marguerite is?"

"I've called in at the Empire a few times. Her father didn't say much." He paused. "I took him some flowers the other day. Said they were from you. I hope you don't mind."

"Of course not. That was a lovely thought. I wrote her a long letter telling her some of what's happening. Poor Marguerite. She hates me so much, and I don't blame her at all. A lot of it was my fault, you know."

They rattled over the railway bridge. A train had just passed below and the smell of soot was so strong that they could taste it as they talked.

Rupert said, "I'm sorry for Marguerite, but now that I've stepped back a pace from her, as it were, I can see that she's self-destructive. The thing is, I hope she doesn't let hatred poison her as well. It does that, you know—" He glanced at her, hugging the biscuit tin, and wondered if she was still a little nervous of the motorcar.

"Hatred can cripple a person," he continued. "Look at what it did to Mama. She hated our father so much that when we were little all Roz and I ever heard were vicious invectives against him. It got to such a pitch that I think if she'd ever had to meet him face to face the shock of it would have killed her."

Dorrie didn't want to talk about that. She said, "Did you see the picture of Albert Patene in the newspaper?"

"Our Sergeant Button? Great news, isn't it? I was hoping to see Emere when I came to collect you, so that I could tell her how delighted I was to read about his bravery." He paused and glanced at her again. "I've been meaning to ask you, Dorrie. If I asked Emere out to a show with me, do you think she'd accept? I've got to know her quite well. Whenever Aunt Dora and Mama are gabbing inside at Fintona, Emere and I seem to drift out to the verandah together, and—"

"Then you'd know if she's likely to accept or not." Dorrie tried not to laugh. She had been wishing she could have seen Aunt Ellen's face when she heard that the young man she had insulted had been acclaimed as a hero, but this, Rupert and Emere, would really send her into a swoon.

"I wish you all the best, dear," she told him sincerely. "And if you're going to be spending a lot of time at *Le Chapeau* from now on, you will look after Auntie Dora for me, won't you?"

"I think that everybody will," he assured her.

"All unpacked?" said May, settling herself on Dorrie's low bunk. An hour ago they had all been up on deck together, May and Dorrie and Patrick and the nurses with the flock of children all watching the gulf islands pass by in their blue haze.

Dorrie said, "The sun was giving me a headache," though in truth she had come below to avoid seeing the rocks and the little headland where the *Manu Moa* had been wrecked. Nathaniel said he had seen it on every voyage when they had passed that way in daylight. Just beyond the islands, he had said, and if you looked carefully you could still see the masts piercing the waves, with rigging still attached like ropey old cobwebs.

"That's no good." May's face ridged up around the edges into fine creases as she smiled. "Nathaniel says we have to take particular care of you. You're someone *very* special."

Dorrie felt a little embarrassed, wondering how much Nathaniel had told them. May always looked deep into her eyes with such a serious concern that Dorrie felt as if she had no secrets that would surprise her.

"Here, have a biscuit," she offered, tearing the paper from the tin. It was one of Dora's newest tins, embossed with the latest portraits of the Prince and Princess of Wales—now the King and Queen—set in ovals with the Prince's ensignia of feathers between. "They're those sweet, wafery ones," she said, then stopped, blinking uncomprehendingly at the shredded paper that filled the tin. On top was a note, unfolded.

Dear Dorrie,
   It is only fitting that the most valuable thing I own should be with the most precious thing in my life.
             Good luck, pet, and every happiness,
                      Your aunt, Dora.

"No," whispered Dorrie. "No, it can't be."

Her fingers scrabbled among the paper fragments and touched the smooth greenstone. In wonder she lifted the pendant out and held her in both hands, gazing down at her. The rich emerald stone glowed in the subdued cabin light as if it had a life of its own, and though Dorrie knew that *Riversong* was a cold, hard object at that moment it seemed she had an intrinsic softness, a warmth, as she lay there on the palms of Dorrie's hands.

"But that's *Riversong!*" said May. "Oh, my dear, isn't it beautiful?"

She, Dorrie wanted to say. *We call her "she."*

But she was too moved to speak. Tears threatened her vision and there was a hurtful clogging in her chest but she was too awed to cry. Now Auntie Dora had given her everything. Despite that bitter opposition long ago, she had made countless sacrifices to give Dorrie a home, she had always given love even though any expression of emotion went right against her reserved nature, and now, though her better judgment abhorred the idea she was letting her go. Not grudgingly either, as Dorrie had suspected. In the face of her own unanswerable fears Dora was sending her off with such a courageous gesture of love and generosity that Dorrie was humbled.

May looked at the bowed head and said, "It certainly is the most beautiful thing. We used to see it at the museum when we took the children there. Uncle Samuel told me it belonged to Dora."

Dorrie whispered:

> In the stillness of eternity
> I hear the river song.
> The spirit of my ancestors
> Sings a lament for me.

There was a long, tender silence in which the slow throbbing of the engines continued like a gentle chant far in the distance. The *Monowai* had reached open sea and was beginning to list perceptibly, first to one side and then to the other.

"That's really lovely," said May. She sensed the presence of unshed tears. "And now Dora has given *Riversong* to you."

"No," said Dorrie. "I couldn't accept her. She's part of Auntie Dora's life, you see. But I'll wear her with pride on my wedding day, with such love and pride . . ."

After a moment, May stood up and brushed the folds from her skirts. ''Come,'' she said, holding out both hands to Dorrie. ''Let's go and show *Riversong* to Patrick. He was so put out, poor dear, when we visited the museum last time and he discovered it was gone.''

Laughing together, they left the cabin and went up on deck, back into the sunshine again.